FATAL
Conspiracies

R. F. Mineo

ISBN: 979-8-9870826-3-8

PUBLISHER INFORMATION:
This book is published by Conspiracy Theories, LLC.

Conspiracy Theories, LLC
Woodstock, CT

Acknowledgments

I have long dreamed of writing a novel, and now, in my mid 70s, it is a reality. I could not have done it without the many hours of effort and the exceptional contributions of my friends and family.

Wanda, my beautiful wife. Wanda, without your patience, understanding, and input, I would not have ever completed the novel.

Geri Salerno, I have known you since middle school. Geri, you invested a great deal of your time in finding errors and inconsistencies, which significantly improved the novel. Your comments and analysis were spot on. As a result, I started believing.

Nicole Audet, I had known you for less than a month when I agreed to your request to read *Fatal Conspiracies*. You love reading mysteries; you read the novel in record time and understood the storyline's intricacies. Our discussions helped improve the story.

Vanessa Mineo Bonevich, you read this book and understood the nuances of the mystery and characters. Your feedback was important in improving the story.

Laura Steinke, it's been 26 years since we worked together. I can't tell you how much I appreciate your input and analysis. The novel is better, and I sleep better because you contributed your pharmaceutical expertise.

Dr. Debra Campbell, you ensured the medical information contained in the novel was accurate. You also pointed out several conflicts in the storyline.

Vinny Bourgeois, my grandson, you created an excellent book cover and endured my many changes. Your graphic design skills are excellent, and you are a true diplomat. I was motivated by your genuine interest in this project.

Michael Raheb, you proofread this novel's more than one hundred thousand words. Thank you for your critical eye, humor, and love for grammar.

Rick Sellano, my newly found cousin. You took the time to explain the steps on the road to publishing… and gave me the confidence to start the journey.

Fatal Conspiracies

Management of the Purity Pharmaceutical Company is dealing with several complex issues. As a result of a significant downsizing earlier in the year, the production organization has had difficulty making enough products to meet the marketing forecast. Also, a sizable percentage of the pharmaceuticals produced do not meet quality standards. Despite these problems, the CEO wants another downsizing and more women and minorities in management positions. Many employees believe he has already promoted unqualified people into critical jobs.

When two executives, working alone after-hours in the executive suite in a building protected by guards and a high-tech security system, are murdered, a large-scale investigation commences. The murders send shock waves through the company, and production falls as employees are distracted and afraid to be at work.

When the investigation stalls, an unlikely duo – a white executive and a black homicide detective – decide to work together. Despite their intense dislike for each other, they move the investigation forward and expose several conspiracies. Eventually, they identify all the conspirators, which leads to a near-death confrontation within the Purity corporate headquarters.

While working together, the pair realizes they have much in common and become good friends.

Prologue

The pharmaceutical division of the McKenzie Chemical Company, though small compared to most pharmaceutical companies, had several profitable proprietary drugs in its portfolio. Despite having a profitable operation, management understood they had to move new drugs through the development pipeline to secure the future of the business. A recent discovery held great promise for treating most forms of breast cancer. Management believed the new drug could become a blockbuster, with over two billion dollars a year in sales. When the new drug entered clinical trials, the complications overwhelmed the McKenzie medical doctors and scientists involved. McKenzie's senior management decided to solicit pharmaceutical companies for help.

Saga Pharmaceuticals, a well-respected company, was one of many companies that expressed an interest in working with McKenzie. Management decided Saga was in the best position to assist McKenzie technically and financially. After several months of negotiation, McKenzie and Saga reached an agreement.

The companies would form a new company – Purity Pharmaceuticals – owned equally by McKenzie and Saga. McKenzie's pharmaceutical division – physical assets, products, and people – would become Purity Pharmaceuticals. Saga would write a check for $500 million and assign its best management and technical employees to consult on the clinical trials for the new cancer drug. Both companies agreed that the joint venture would remain in force for a minimum of ten years.

Roger Hanson, McKenzie COO, and John Mooney, Saga COO, were assigned responsibility for the Purity Pharmaceutical business.

The new cancer drug does not yet have FDA approval, and the cost of clinical trials has exceeded $800 Million.

Purity Pharmaceuticals
– Structure –

McKenzie Chemical Company
50% Owner of Purity Pharmaceuticals
Responsible Executive
Roger Hanson
COO of McKenzie Chemical

Saga Pharmaceutical Company
50% Owner of Purity Pharmaceuticals
Responsible Executive
John Mooney
COO of Saga Pharmaceuticals

Purity Pharmaceuticals
Company Headquarters
Centerville Delaware

CEO Purity Pharmaceuticals	*Bob Cohen*
President – Proprietary Products	Pamela Robinson
President – Manufacturing	Gary Hazlitt
Vice President – Materials	Kathleen Connelly
Vice President – HR	Greg Iverson

Purity Pharmaceuticals
Manufacturing and Research Operations
Garden City, NY

Director of Operations	*Diane Armstrong*
Director – Manufacturing	Steve Gagnon
Director – Research	Paul Stanley
Director – Quality	Lorraine Waters
Director – Business Resources	Phil Messina
Manager – HR	Abby Stall
Manager – Materials	Joe Jacobs
Specialist – Information Technology	Cynthia Bernstein

Wednesday 11/26

"Phenomenal, absolutely phenomenal!" Bob Cohen, although alone, said out loud as he reclined in his soft leather chair and gazed out of the large window centered in his office wall. Outside, the late fall day was gray and rainy, and the last leaves, brown and brittle, barely hung on the trees in the courtyard. The weather may have dampened his spirits on any other day, but not today. Bob had just finished reviewing Marketing's sales projections for November and December, which lay scattered on his desk, and his spirits soared. *Year-end sales will exceed my forecast, and after-tax profits should come in over $200 million. Phenomenal! Since I've been at the helm, I've nearly doubled profits,"* he thought. *Running a multi-billion-dollar pharmaceutical company… not bad for a kid from Hackensack.*

Bob, CEO of the Purity Pharmaceutical Company, was born with exceptional intelligence. His greatest gift was the ability to assimilate pieces of information that appear unrelated and draw conclusions that allow him to stay one step ahead of his competition. In his youth, Bob led a street gang; he learned about power, its benefits, and how to hold on to it. He also realized he loved having authority. He loved the way people deferred to him when he was in charge. Inner-city gang members rarely grow up to become CEOs, but Bob's intelligence and desire for power made him the exception to the rule.

Thanks to sticking faithfully to his daily four-mile run, Bob remained fit at age fifty-one. From a distance, at five-foot-seven and weighing 140 pounds, he looked much the same as he did in high school, except that his thick hair had turned gray. Overall, Bob was an average-looking man, but from a certain angle, his facial features seemed to come together at the tip of his nose, in a mousy, rat-like way. His face and lack of height were the only things he would change with his life.

All I have left to do today is meet with Pamela Robinson and tell her about the changes in our budget for next year. I'll celebrate Thanksgiving with Marie and my beautiful six-month-old, Emily. Saturday, I'll head up the Jersey Turnpike to Long Island for a belated Thanksgiving with my two boys. It's hard to believe they're already teenagers. Ah, life is good, he reflected.

Garden City, New York, is located in Nassau County, Long Island, almost equidistant from the Long Island Sound and the Atlantic Ocean and eight miles east of Queens County. Stewart Avenue bisects the village from east to west. On the eastern end of Garden City, Stewart Avenue intersects with Endall Boulevard. Purity Pharmaceuticals' Garden City operation is housed in a large three-story rectangular building on the intersection's southeast corner. Protruding from the middle of the second floor, running along Stewart Avenue, is a large oval structure that houses the reception area. Banked by gardens, two wide, serpentine stairways rise from street level to the reception area. Eight parking spaces and an entrance reserved for executives are hidden from view by a well-landscaped berm. Looking like a medieval castle perched on a hill overlooking the Meadowbrook Parkway, the Purity Pharmaceuticals building has become an area landmark.

Having just returned to work after a pleasant business lunch with the Human Resources Director of Computer Associates, Phil Messina stood motionless in front of the executive entrance. He stared as if it was the gateway to hell, not the access to his workplace. His beloved BMW 635csi sat in the space reserved for the Director of Business Resources. After a minute, he flashed his pass in front of the card reader and punched in his code. Upon entering the building, he faced the choice of taking the elevator to his third-floor office or using the stairs. Since Phil carried over two hundred and thirty pounds on his six-foot frame, the stairs would be the best choice, but he took the express elevator. Once on the third floor, Phil took the long way to his office, hoping to avoid his boss. Along the way, he engaged in some obligatory small talk with employees.

Phil's large mahogany-paneled office was standard for director-level employees in the pharmaceutical industry. The employees sarcastically referred to the executive offices as "Mahogany Row." His work area was furnished with a solid cherry-wood desk and credenza, behind which sat a comfortable high-backed burgundy leather chair. The office also held a conference area, complete with a cherry table surrounded by overstuffed leather chairs.

Phil's first year at Purity was grueling despite the luxurious environment. A month after taking the job, he was responsible for implementing Garden City's first-ever layoff, or 'downsizing' in corporate-speak. Corporate management's plan for the downsizing was ill-conceived and wreaked havoc with both employees and site operations. Since the downsizing, the Production Department had experienced significant quality problems and had struggled to meet delivery schedules. Because of the fear of future layoffs, employees started doing whatever they thought necessary to protect their jobs. They would out-and-out lie about other employees if they believed it would gain them some advantage. Office politics were not merely a nuisance; they were lethal.

And today, two Production employees wanted to meet with Phil to discuss the Production Area problems.

Oh well, only sixteen years until I retire. he thought.

Centerville, Delaware, a suburb of Wilmington, was home to Purity Pharmaceuticals Headquarters. Purity's top management is housed in the northeast corner of the top floor of the two-story building. The well-appointed offices and workstations showcased the money generated by the lucrative pharmaceutical business. The executive offices were adorned with raised cherry paneling and furnished with beautifully carved solid mahogany furniture and chairs covered with the finest leather. The latest computers, loaded with the best software, decorated the tops of desks and credenzas along with pens, paper, and other office paraphernalia, all overseen by the watchful eyes of family photos. The executives' offices were on the outside walls, and each had a large window covered with fine draperies. In the center of the management area, referred to as the "bullpen," were workstations for the administrative assistants. Although not as well-appointed as the offices, they still provided an excellent working environment.

Pamela Robinson was not looking forward to her meeting with Bob Cohen. She pictured him giving her a significant assignment and wanting it done by Monday morning. He had done it many times in the past. *Normally, I don't care because I spend most weekends alone, but tomorrow is Thanksgiving. I was looking forward to spending it with my parents. Oh well, I might as well get it over with*, she mused, trying to hide her frown. She looked straight ahead as she walked across the bullpen toward the CEO's office. As usual, her dark hair was pulled into a tight bun, and she wore what the administrative staff described as hideously oversized, black-framed glasses. Pamela wore an expensive, dark blue business suit large enough to hide her curves, which made her seem masculine enough to go mostly unnoticed. The secretaries, tapping away at their keyboards, shuffling papers, or talking on their phones, did not look up as she passed.

"Pamela, come on in, make yourself comfortable. We have a lot to talk about." Bob motioned Pamela to one of the reclining chairs.

"Thanks," Pamela mumbled as she sat.

"I just heard that earnings should come in at over $200 million this year. Not bad for a company whose major product is forty years old."

"Not bad at all."

"You're a major contributor to our success and will be well taken care of."

"Thanks. I appreciate the opportunity to make a difference." Her discontent showed like venom in her voice.

"Enough small talk. I met with our owners yesterday, and they told me we need to increase next year's profit goal by fifty million dollars." Bob watched Pamela closely, trying to gauge her reaction.

Pamela believed it would be almost impossible to achieve the existing business plan, let alone generate another fifty million in profits. "You must be kidding. You know the state of our business, and you know the myriad problems we're facing."

"Let me tell you what else I know. I know our owners are having business issues and won't make the earnings per share projections unless a healthy business, like ours, contributes more."

"Healthy? We're far from healthy! We're in chaos. Morale is at an all-time low, hurting productivity. There is absolutely no chance a new product will be approved in time to produce extra revenue. Manufacturing, especially at Garden City, has lost a lot of experienced employees recently, employees who knew their jobs and who knew how to make our drugs. Hell, Garden City has come close to shipping a defective product a couple of times, and you know that can kill our business, not to mention our customers. For Christ's sake, Bob, we fired over five hundred employees last year, and the remaining employees are scared to death we will do it again." Pamela used the word "fired" intentionally. Although she knew it was risky, she wanted to see the rage on Bob's little rat-like face.

"Fired! You know as well as I do that if we didn't let those people go and increase our profits, we would have been shut down, and *everyone* would be out of a job." Bob tried to sound calm, but the straining blood vessels in his forehead said otherwise.

"I don't believe that for a moment. We earned a hundred million dollars last year. We could have increased profits more slowly in a planned fashion without devastating the business and the employees. You know that our owners would never walk away from a hundred million dollars. But if it makes you feel better to believe you saved jobs, you can continue to delude yourself." She sat back, crossed her arms, and waited for his next move.

"It's easy for you to assume what our owners would do; you don't have to deal with them. They made it clear we had to deliver this year or else. And the same is true for next year." Bob lied. He had proposed increasing profits because he wanted to show his superiors that he was the right man for the job. "There's nothing we could do except deliver."

"We could simply tell our owners the truth. We can't deliver more profits next year. It's just not possible. They need to look elsewhere for the money. If we make any more changes, we'll lose control of product quality!"

"You know that's not going to happen. In fact, I've already committed to the increase because I honestly believe we can do it. I know you always look at the downside of things, but I know you will deliver. Schedule a meeting with management at Garden City next week, and don't come back until you have a plan to reduce their operating budget by twenty million dollars. That's their share of the increased profits. You're also going to be responsible for making it happen at Garden City." Bob got up and started toward his desk.

Pamela decided to take a parting shot, "After the last downsizing, you told the employees at Garden City that downsizing was over forever, and they had nothing further to worry about. Now I must tell them you lied. You're making me your fucking hatchet-man."

"You'll figure out a way to make it all seem reasonable," Bob said with a slight smile on his lips. "I'll tell Hazlitt he's working with you on Garden City. I'll handle the rest of the company and get the other thirty million."

Pamela's remark was out-of-character. Usually, she would just comment on issues Bob raised. Yet the company was in bad shape, and she was incensed at Bob for agreeing to deliver more profits next year at what she knew would be the employees' expense. He was too quick to try to prove himself by agreeing with requests from upper management. Pamela knew that she did not possess Bob's charisma, finesse, or ability to spin the truth, but she knew the business operations better than him. She was the one who put together the detailed information needed to solve problems. Bob simply took her input on complex issues, massaged it a little, wrapped it in flowery language, and looked like a star when he presented it to management. He rarely gave Pamela any credit. Pamela believed she had the knowledge and ability to be the CEO. And if she were? She certainly would not have given in to such unreasonable demands.

Bob's anger subsided after Pamela left. He knew that she would keep this conversation confidential, and he knew she would do the job.

Abby Stall, HR manager, stood in Phil's doorway with two employees behind her and asked, "Are you ready?" Abby reported to Phil, and over the last year, their relationship had grown into one of mutual respect. Phil respected Abby's approach to the job. She strove to stay out of office politics, and her dealings with employees were always honest and straightforward. Abby felt Phil treated her as an equal and was always open and honest with her. Both thought they could say just about anything to each other. "I'm ready. Let's get on with it," Phil replied.

Phil assumed that the meeting was about the recent firing of two employees. Two weeks ago, in the middle of packaging a batch of 2-milligram Thinadin tablets, a packaging operator had found a tablet embossed with a "5," a critical error. Supervision traced the mistake to the compression area. An operator had installed the wrong tooling, and the QC inspector had failed to catch it. Since people with heart disease and other circulatory problems used Thinadin to prevent the formation of blood clots, getting the proper dosage was vital. Thinadin works by increasing the time it takes for blood to clot. An average person's blood clots in twelve seconds. Thinadin increases clotting time to eighteen seconds. Too small a dose and the chances of a fatal blood clot forming increase, while too large a dose causes internal bleeding. Thinadin tablets are embossed with the dosage so patients will not make mistakes.

Everyone in management but Phil had wanted both employees fired. Thinadin generated a significant portion of Purity's profits, and a quality problem might kill the 'Golden Goose.' Though no longer patent-protected, Thinadin had no generic competition. When doctors prescribed Thinadin, they added the phrase "no substitutes" to the prescription because they were concerned about the dangers of the drug. They had confidence in Purity's quality. If incorrectly embossed tablets reached the marketplace, doctors would lose confidence in Thinadin, opening the door to generic competition and resulting in disaster for Purity. Site Management did not want to acknowledge any failure on their part, so they fired both employees. Phil believed Production Management was at fault. Both employees had been thrown into their jobs after more experienced employees were laid off. Job training was minimal, and the demands to produce were intense. The other staff members also knew the situation. Still, Corporate Management had applied a great deal of pressure to fire the two as a lesson to other employees.

Frank James and Gino Arnone joined Phil and Abby at the conference table. After a brief discussion of the daily traffic backups on the Northern and Southern State Parkways, the four got down to business.

Gino started. "Look, we know you were against firing Chuck and Karen, so we're not going to talk about it except to say you were right. They didn't deserve to be fired, and what we're about to tell you should make it perfectly clear." Gino weighed over 300 pounds; his torso looked as if it had been chiseled from a block of granite. His head, though more diminutive, had the same look. An earring dangled from his left ear, and a mustache and goatee decorated his face. His head was clean-shaven, making Gino downright scary looking. But his looks were deceiving. Phil had first met him six months ago, when Gino had become a father for the first time and wanted to review his benefit status. The meeting was a waste of time because all Gino would talk about was his daughter, and as he did, his eyes kept tearing up.

Frank took over. "We're here to let you know how bad things are in Production. Right now, there are five batches of tablets on Quality Hold because they fail one test or another, and no one can figure out why. The hot shot chemists are stumped, but us lowly Production operators know the reason." Quite unlike Gino, Frank did not have the benefit of muscle, making his black skin appear to hang loosely on his six-foot-two-inch frame.

"Go on," Phil said, curious about why they were talking about technical problems.

Speaking slowly, Frank began. "The batches are failing for a couple of reasons. We have fewer workers and are being told to finish batches faster. Operators are skipping some steps that are not documented in the SOPs and are shortcutting others. Supervisors are pushing us hard. They want everything done faster. And we're missing some things."

"Give me an example."

"Okay, you know it's critical Thinadin tablets have the active ingredient spread evenly throughout the tablet. Normally, we do three times as many in-process split checks as the SOP requires. If we see the amount of active ingredient in half of a tablet change, we immediately make adjustments even though it's still in spec. We don't catch changes as soon because we're checking less often. And we can't check more often because now we're running two Compression Machines at one time to meet production schedules. The chemists don't think it's a problem because it was their idea to reduce the in-process checks. Maybe they don't think it's a problem because they've seen what happens to employees who make mistakes." Frank paused.

"Why come to us with a production problem? Why not talk to your supervision?" Phil said, relieved they weren't pressing the firings.

Gino, the more emotional of the two, jumped in. "Let me spell it out for you. The example Frank gave you is the least serious thing going on. SOPs are not being followed, Batch Records are being forged, and we're shortcutting clean-up procedures. We're being told to do whatever it takes to meet the production schedule."

Abby interrupted. "Wait a minute, you're telling me you're not doing all the required steps and in-process tests? And you're signing the batch records to indicate the steps have been done?"

"That's what I'm telling you. We lost a lot of people, and the production schedule hasn't changed. Our supervisors are telling us to go along or look for another job. So, we go along."

"Okay, okay, I see the seriousness of the situation, but, again, why come to us?" Abby asked for Phil's benefit. She wanted to be sure he understood why they didn't go to their superiors.

Frank looked squarely at Phil. "Word in the plant is you're a straight shooter, plus we've known Abby for a long time and trust her, so we decided to talk to you. Personally, I don't give a shit that you're in Human Resources. We're giving you the problem because we don't trust anyone else on Mahogany Row. Besides, you make more money than both of us put together, so you get to work on the tough problems."

"Look, I don't know what I'll do, but I'll do something. And I'll keep you out of it. At least Cohen assured us there would be no more downsizing." Phil looked overwhelmed.

After Frank and Gino left, Abby and Phil stared at each other for a few seconds before Abby spoke. "They wouldn't tell us all that unless it was true. I could see Steve Gagnon short-cutting SOPs and only worrying about making production schedules. He always followed the 'just do it' school of thought and saw checks and balances as a waste of time. What really grates me is how he talks quality in front of the staff because it's 'politically correct.' The son-of-a-bitch will make life miserable for Frank and Gino if he finds out they talked to you."

"They talked to us," Phil said, still trying to grasp the gravity of what he had just heard.

Abby smiled. "You're the higher level in this room, and you need to find a way to surface this issue and protect Frank and Gino. I'll help as much as I can, but I'm not good at working with the politics on the staff. You have the Thanksgiving weekend to figure something out. Good luck. I'm heading back to my office to clean up a few things, and then I'm going home."

As she got up to leave, Phil started to get his bearings. "You're right. I'll come up with a plan this weekend. We'll talk Monday morning. Now forget this place for four days and be ready to kick ass Monday."

Phil had been solving problems like this for a long time, usually dealing with things honestly and head-on. Despite his track record, he still did not trust his peers at Garden City and would have to be creative to keep Frank and Gino out of trouble. Phil decided to call it a day and head home before the holiday traffic turned his half-hour drive into a three-hour crawl.

After dealing with a minor issue, Phil was ready to leave. As he got up from his desk, Diane Armstrong filled the doorway. Dressed in a designer outfit, Diane was trying to look professional. It did not matter to Phil if she was dressed in a designer outfit or jeans and a bowling shirt. Diane was the last person Phil wanted to see before the holiday, but she was his boss and obviously had something to tell him, so he sat back down and listened.

"Pamela Robinson and Gary Hazlitt will be here Monday around one for a meeting to discuss our business plan for next year. Plan to be with them all afternoon, and then we'll have dinner at Ben's. I have a couple more hours of work before I get out of here. See you Monday." She vanished as quickly as she appeared.

Diane took every opportunity to create the image that she worked harder than everyone else, which irritated Phil. She was all talk and would likely leave for home shortly. Diane always bragged about being the first one in and the last to leave, especially in front of upper management. In reality, the opposite was true. She was one of Bob Cohen's diversity trophies, though, so no one at Garden City would say a word. Everyone knew that a negative comment about one of Cohen's 'chosen' could be career-ending.

With that, Phil headed for home.

Thursday 11/27

Phil awoke Thanksgiving morning, well-rested and looking forward to a four-day weekend of family, food, and football. Best of all, Monday morning seemed an eternity away. Phil loved Thanksgiving, he loved the smell of turkey cooking, he loved being with his family, and he loved watching football. Phil's affinity for Thanksgiving was rooted in his childhood and fond memories of family holidays at his Aunt Eleanor's house. Phil's Nonna, mother, and two aunts spent weeks preparing homemade soups, pasta, bread, and desserts. The food, made from the best ingredients, was delicious, and it was made in such quantity that it would feed the thirty or so family members three times over. Phil's family, his parents, and his aunts, uncles, and cousins would spend hours eating, talking, and laughing. After dinner, the men sat around watching football or playing cards while the women cleaned up. As a teenager, Phil had realized that his family was poor and lacked formal education; neither his parents nor any aunts and uncles had graduated from high school. Phil also knew that he would not trade places with anyone in the world just to have material wealth. Being part of this loving group of first-generation Italian Americans was priceless. He felt that he was rich in life. Phil believed his generation would finish college, do better financially, and be successful. He had no doubt.

Phil and Rose's oldest, Ann, left Delaware early in the morning and headed for Scranton, Pennsylvania, to pick up Phil's parents. Phil went to pick up his son, Tony, at LaGuardia and hoped to get back home, traffic willing, by one o'clock.

Ann worked in Delaware as a Customer Service Representative for a major credit card company. She spent most of her time on the phone dealing with angry customers. It was not a glamorous job, but fine as a temporary fix. At the tender age of twenty-two, Ann had not chosen her life's work yet and was marking time and having fun. Whenever Phil asked her about her plans for the future, she reminded him of what he had always said when she was growing up: "All I want for you is to be happy." She always added, with a warm grin, "I'm happy, Dad." Phil believed she genuinely was.

On the other hand, Tony, three years younger than Ann, had decided that he wanted to be a mechanical engineer – not that he knew what a mechanical engineer did, but he had heard that they earned a lot of money. In high school, he had participated in a program designed to help high school students find out if they would like engineering. Tony was later exposed to engineers at work for three months, and his desire was now embedded in stone. Tony was in his second year of mechanical engineering at Clemson and was doing very well.

The house was quiet as Rose prepared the Thanksgiving Day meal. Phil had left for LaGuardia, and Ann hadn't yet arrived with Phil's parents. Rose stood at a cutting board, working on the vegetables, sniffling, and wiping the occasional tear from her eye. Rose loved that Phil turned into an excited little boy during the holidays. Holidays had a different effect on her: they brought back memories of her family and the years of suffering her parents had endured. Both of her parents had died too young. Rose's father, Joe, was diagnosed with cancer shortly after she and Phil were married and had suffered enormously before dying two years later. After dedicating her life to her family and nursing Joe for two years, her mother had a massive heart attack. She died instantly while out for a walk. It saddened Rose that they didn't have the chance to enjoy life together after she and her younger brother were grown. Rose was twenty-nine, and her brother was just twenty-five when their mother died.

Rose's life with Phil was a happier story; although they had started married life in less than an ideal fashion, so far, their life together had been great. There were the usual rocky times, but they were far outnumbered by the good times. Phil had turned out to be a good husband and a good father, and he was faithful as far as she knew. She was sure that if he did cheat on her, she would know. The only awful times in their marriage came during Phil's last years working at McKenzie. Phil completely withdrew into himself, ignoring Rose and the kids. Rose could only watch as Phil tore himself apart, agonizing over the employees, especially his friends, who lost their jobs in downsizing after downsizing. She had hoped things would be better at Purity, but her hope ended when Purity decided to downsize. Maybe the future would be better.

Ann pulled into the driveway a little before one o'clock with Phil's parents. Phil and Tony arrived half an hour later. Suddenly the home on Florence Avenue in Oyster Bay was alive with the sounds and smells of a Messina family Thanksgiving. The TV was tuned to the NFL game, and family members talked to each other over the sounds of football. The smell of turkey drifted from the oven while Grandma – Phil would have preferred his kids call her Nonna as he had called his grandmother – stirred a large pot of soup on top of the stove. The family sat down to dinner at four, and it was eight o'clock before the day began to take its toll and the energy level started to drop.

Phil and his father drifted downstairs to the den while everyone else lounged around the dining room table. Giacinto Messina, a first-generation Italian American, was born two years after his parents emigrated from Sicily. As the oldest of ten children, he had left school after the sixth grade to help his family financially. Giacinto had never returned to school and, as a result, worked low-paying jobs. A year ago, he had open-heart surgery. His aortic valve was replaced with a mechanical valve. He then started a lifetime prescription for Thinadin.

"How are you doing with the Thinadin? Are you managing okay?" Phil asked, knowing he would get some grief.

"Why? Are you afraid I'll croak, and your company will go bankrupt?"

'Yeah, that's one reason. The other is I'm just curious, so humor me."

"I'm doing all right, but that stuff is a pain in the ass. Not only do I have to remember what strength pill to take, but I also have to get my blood checked every couple of weeks. It's all costing me a goddamned fortune. It's a fucking rip-off. None of it has to happen. It's all because you drug sellers need to live high on the fucking hog and take money from us poor working people. I say the fucking doctors are getting a kickback, and this shit ain't necessary." Giacinto vented for what seemed like the thousandth time since his operation.

Phil wondered what his father would do if he knew how much less it cost to produce one tablet than how much he paid for it. "Look, Pop, you know if you don't take it, you'll have another heart attack, and if you take too much, you'll bleed internally. You have enough money to last quite a while, so stop the bullshit and listen to your doctors."

They both sat back in their chairs, unbuckled their belts so they could breathe, and stared at the ceiling. The conversation eventually came around to the status of the lives of Phil's many relatives in Scranton. Giacinto enjoyed talking about his nine younger brothers and sisters and their families. He spoke of sick brothers, nephews attending college, nieces getting married, nieces with 'big' jobs, and sisters with assholes for husbands. He didn't shut up until he went to bed.

Phil found his mother, wife, and daughter relaxing in the living room. The dishes were done, and the house had been straightened. As he entered, he asked, "What happened to Tony?"

"He went to bed. He said he's been studying a lot lately and not getting enough sleep," Rose responded. "He doesn't look too good, and he's losing weight. I'm worried he's pushing himself too hard."

"I'm glad you're worried, so I won't have to be," Phil said, then changed the topic to his mother's family. "How's Uncle Nello doing?"

After a brief discussion of Uncle Nello's health, the Messina's first Thanksgiving on Long Island ended.

Monday 12/1

The nude woman staring back at Pamela Robinson from the full-length beveled glass mirror pleased her. She placed her hands under her breasts and lifted slightly. *I would be happier if they pointed up a little more,* she thought. She then turned sideways, did the same with her butt, and decided tighter would be better. *I look pretty damn good for a forty-four-year-old. Yeah, losing a few pounds and tightening up some areas would be an improvement, but why bother? Marrying and having a family are pretty much behind me.* She was not seeing anyone at the moment, and even if she wanted to, her history with men usually ended in disaster. Pamela had dated several men over the years. She had even lived with a few for a while, anticipating marriage, but the relationships had soured.

Dating a powerful woman who earned significantly more income had not been a problem for Pamela's previous partners… at least, early in their relationships. As each relationship matured, she realized that her partner wanted to be in control, and she would inevitably refuse. In each case, Pamela ended the relationship. She felt that most men at higher levels on the corporate ladder were usually married and only looking for sex, all the while silently trying to sabotage her career. Besides, she found corporate types to be superficial, awed by power and authority. They tended to treat each other according to their relative levels in the organization. The men she worked with treated her with respect, at least to her face. The possibility of getting honest conversation or a straight answer to a business issue decreased the higher she rose in the corporation. Pamela met mostly corporate types who fit this stereotype, which was unfortunate for her personal life.

Her thoughts drifted to Phil Messina. Phil, unconcerned with politics, spoke his mind. Despite Bob Cohen continually saying he did not want yes-men in his organization, the truth was that he only wanted sycophants around him. Phil's approach had served him well in his career with McKenzie's Medical Diagnostics division, but now he would flounder.

Too bad about Phil. He was beginning to positively impact the culture at Garden City, Pamela thought. *Oh well, time to get my sagging ass in gear. I have a train to catch.*

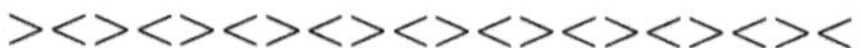

As Pamela Robinson stood in front of her mirror in Hockessin, Delaware, Abby Stall lay awake in her bed in Massapequa, Long Island, thinking about the day ahead. She had slept poorly last night, as she did almost every Sunday night. The man she loved deeply, her husband of six years, slept peacefully beside her. They had a lovely home on a street that ended at the Great South Bay. The 'Freedom,' a 28-foot cabin cruiser, rocked in its mooring in a canal behind the house. They set off in Freedom on summer weekends and most calm evenings to fish and find a sandy beach for a cookout. When not boating, Abby frequented the local gym, went to the city for a play or concert, or relaxed at home with George.

George, like many other employees, had been demoted earlier in the year and had sunk into a deep depression. He had been comfortably ensconced in Research management for over twenty years, and, as with most men, his identity was intertwined with his job. George had opted for demotion and a pay cut instead of retirement. The financial consequences of a previous divorce had impacted his decision. He soon realized, however, that he enjoyed working as a chemist again. His work produced tangible results, and his workdays were predictable, a far cry from the chaotic days spent as a manager. Most of all, George did not miss the long, often-meaningless meetings he had attended or the frustration of being an intermediary between his boss and the people who reported to him.

Abby knew that she would never sleep soundly as long as she remained in her job. She hated conflict, yet she had to deal with disagreements between supervisors and employees every day. She had to investigate sexual harassment complaints and discrimination charges and recommend the solutions to Phil. Abby's aversion to conflict made her a fish out of water, but working for Phil had helped. He talked her through challenging problems, explained his thinking and listened to her thoughts, and even changed stances when he agreed with her. Yet she still found dragging herself out of bed for work, especially on Mondays, difficult.

To lull herself to sleep again, she curled up next to George and closed her eyes. She envisioned herself as an administrative assistant in a cubicle: taking calls, tapping away at a keyboard, and shutting out the rest of the world.

Abby was stumbling through the cafeteria with a large cup of coffee in her right hand when Phil saw her. Abby had dark circles under her eyes, her hair was not quite right, and she looked drowsy. Phil could tell that she had not slept well last night, and he knew why. Abby had told him her feelings about her job and how they affected her on Sunday nights. She also had told him that she wanted to return to administrative work. Phil had assured her that when she felt ready to move to a different job, he would help her land a position. He also assured her he would miss her because her performance was excellent.

"You look like hell," Phil said, smirking sympathetically.

"Well, good morning to you too. You look pretty shitty yourself, and you probably slept last night," Abby replied. She would not have talked to her previous bosses in the same way, but Phil could take a sly jab or two.

"Thanks. I think I have a way to handle the problem we were handed. Let's head to my office so I can bounce it off of you."

"I knew you'd come up with something. I hope it's not too devious." Abby smiled as they headed toward Phil's office.

Abby could not wait a moment longer as they entered Phil's office. She sat down haphazardly in one of his leather chairs. "Okay, Einstein, let's hear your plan."

"I'll get to it, but first, what's your opinion on what Frank and Gino told us? Do you really believe Production is as out of control as they say?"

Abby leaned forward in her chair. "Steve Gagnon has always been a loose cannon. He believes rules and procedures are obstacles, and the only important thing is advancing his career. A year ago, he was named Production Manager and immediately made operational changes designed to increase output. Product quality became less important. When we downsized and the older, experienced operators left, I knew Steve would do whatever it took to meet production schedules. His staff likes the way he runs Production. It saves them work, so they go along with the shortcuts."

"I don't understand why Steve would risk making bad batches."

"The cost of chemicals for a batch of Thinadin, including the active ingredient, is insignificant. Look at it from a total cost standpoint. It's cheaper for an operator to run two compression machines rather than one and assume Quality will catch and reject any bad batches." Abby said.

"That assumes Quality Control is perfect and catches every bad batch. That's a pretty big assumption."

"One last thing. I hope you realize how ruthless Steve is. He will do whatever's necessary to protect himself: he'll lie, forge documents, spread rumors… whatever it takes. So, don't take him lightly. And his staff will do the same." Abby paused, took a swig of her coffee, and spoke again. "All right, let's get to this brilliant plan of yours."

"Okay, but if you assume it's brilliant, I'm afraid you'll be disappointed. Next Monday, the FDA starts an on-site audit of our pain medication, 'Relieve.' Lorraine will be spending every day in the Main Conference room with them." As Phil talked, Abby nodded slowly; she had been involved in several FDA audits and knew the drill. "I've heard the audit will last about six weeks, so Lorraine will need some help running QA. I called her this weekend and volunteered to help by taking care of any problems that might come up. I also volunteered to do the final quality review of Batch Records. Reviewing Batch

Records should allow me to check Frank and Gino's story. Lorraine jumped at the suggestion. Although she was a little surprised, I even offered. Well, what do you think?"

"I think you should be able to verify everything Frank and Gino told us, and then all we'll have to do is figure out how to get it to the staff." Abby's mind whirled, analyzing the possibilities as she spoke. The thought of Steve Gagnon being fired brought a smile to her lips. "Do you think Diane will let you do it?"

"I don't think Diane will care if I take on more work. And why do you look almost happy? It's not that good of a plan, is it?"

"No, it's just that some good should come out of it if it works." She continued to smile.

"I'll need your help going through the Batch Records. I'm afraid I'll miss some things because I haven't worked in pharmaceutical production." Abby had worked at Garden City for her whole career, starting as a Secretary in Production Planning. After getting a degree through night classes, she had been promoted to Packaging Supervisor and had held the position for five years. Her crew had packaged tablets and liquids for shipment. Her next assignment had been to supervise the Compression Area, which was responsible for compressing tablets. Four years ago, she had been promoted to Personnel Supervisor. She knew pharmaceutical production in detail.

"No problem." Abby had always wondered about Phil and Lorraine's relationship and decided that it was time to ask. "Will you answer a personal question for me?"

"Sure. If I can."

Abby spent a moment trying to think of a way to phrase the question to not anger Phil, but she was unsuccessful. "You and Lorraine are close – very close. Is there more going on between you and her than meets the eye?"

Many employees suspected that Phil and Lorraine were more than friends, and Abby was brave enough to ask. Phil was unsurprised by the question. In fact, he wondered why it had taken her so long to ask. "Why, Abigail, your dirty little mind is working overtime."

"Come on, Phil, answer me. Please."

"There is nothing between Lorraine and me except friendship. I love Rose and would never do anything to jeopardize what we have."

Abby believed him. She could tell just by looking at him that he was telling the truth. "Okay, and I won't ask again."

"Good. Anything else while you're here?"

Abby knew that Phil would ask that question, and she had been genuinely hoping that he would. Last night, she had lain awake for hours, drifting in and out of sleep with snippets of conversations and observations swarming through her head like bees around a hive. Although those tidbits of information seemed disconnected, they had caused her to become even more concerned about Phil's job security with Purity. She had sensed that Phil was in deep trouble and felt that she needed to warn him. She struggled to put a finger on exactly why until, halfway between asleep and awake, she had an epiphany. It was an experience almost everyone has had from time to time: when you know something is wrong but cannot quite figure out why, your subconscious decides to give you the answer to the riddle. Abby's thoughts last night had centered on Russ

Cady, Bob Cohen, Diane Armstrong, and Phil. From that jumble, she had concluded that Bob Cohen wanted Phil fired.

Abby sincerely liked Phil and enjoyed working for him; she did not want to see him lose his job. He understood the functions of Human Resources and took the time to teach her. She had learned more about HR in the last year than she did in her first three years in the department. Phil cared about the employees and always tried to solve their problems. Unfortunately, when it came to seeing what directly affected him, Phil was blind. Phil had some behaviors that he needed to correct. Employees generally saw him as a good person, for example, but still believed that he was naïve, always trying to shine a positive light on company issues. When an employee backed him into a corner, Phil tended to hide behind company policy rather than criticize the company or someone in management. Overall, though, he was a good man and the employees knew it.

"Yes, I'm worried about Russ Cady, and I'm also worried about you," Abby said in reply to his "anything else" question.

"What's wrong with Russ?" Phil asked, trying to take the attention away from himself.

"Russ believes we are going to have another downsizing. He's heard some rumors, and he's worried about losing his job. It would sink him financially. I think it could happen." Abby was hoping she could open the door to talk about her concerns for Phil.

"Cohen guaranteed there would be no more downsizing. Besides, Russ works for me, and I think he's doing a great job. He has nothing to worry about. He knows how I feel about him, and now so do you," Phil said.

"Not too long ago, that would have been enough, but your influence with management is not what it used to be. Russ wouldn't be worried if you still had clout. When you first came here, it was obvious that Diane supported everything you did, and she wouldn't do anything on her own until she got your blessing. Now she treats you like an alien, and so do the others on the staff. We think you're in trouble with Bob Cohen because of your position on summer jobs for his kids," Abby said, trying to provoke Phil.

"Oh, this is about me, isn't it? Abby, we've talked about this before. Bob and Diane will get over whatever is bothering them, and I don't give a shit about the rest of the staff. I've been around too long and have too many connections back in McKenzie to be fired, so I'm not worried. And neither should Russ be. I still have faith in the system and the people at McKenzie. My job is to try to do what's right for employees and the business, and as long as I do, I will never get in trouble." Phil believed what he was saying, but Abby had sown a seed of doubt. He had expected the issue with Bob's kids to end right after it happened, but it did not.

Abby paused a minute before responding. She had decided last night to shake Phil out of the past and get him to see today's reality. "You're living in the past. You're not safe and secure at McKenzie anymore; you work for Purity now. And besides, the old McKenzie is gone and will never return. I've known Bob Cohen for a long time and don't trust him as far as I could spit. He says one thing to employees in meetings and something different in private afterwards. He also does it to your face as well as behind your back. The only important thing to him is his personal success and desire to be the modern-day Corporate Savior for Purity's women and minorities. And while I'm at it, remember how poorly Diane treated Cynthia Bernstein before she found out that Cynthia was tight with someone on Cohen's staff? After that, Cynthia could do no wrong. Do you think Diane would try to protect you if Cohen wanted you out? Not a chance."

"Okay, okay, I hear what you're saying, but you're wrong about McKenzie changing. I know Greg Iverson supports me from our days at McKenzie, and I still stay in touch with Roger Hanson back there. I'll be all right. Anyway, I thought this was about Russ."

"Russ feels, and I agree with him, that if there is another downsizing, you won't be able to protect him. In fact, your support might even be a liability." Abby got right to the heart of the matter.

"I appreciate your concern for Russ and me, but things will get better. We can't go on doing things the way we have without completely demoralizing our people and hurting the quality of our products. Right now, the barbarians are in charge. They were put there because our owners wanted better returns on their investment. Some tough decisions had to be made, and they needed people in the top jobs to swing the ax. But they won't last long. The pendulum always swings back. The management at McKenzie won't let this continue. They'll step in and reshuffle the top management, putting a more humane team in place to take us into the future." When Phil finished, he felt uneasy with what he'd just said.

"You sound like you're reading from a book titled 'The Company Line.' In fact, you sound like you wrote it. Get real. This is how companies are going, and things will get worse, not better. If you don't start learning how to play politics, you won't be collecting a pension when you're fifty-eight. Look, as

I said, I'm worried about you because you don't see what's happening. I think you're close to losing your job." Abby said all she had wanted to say, and it was up to Phil to think about it. "I've got some things to do. Think about what I've said. I'm trying to help."

"I know you care, and I promise I'll think about what you said. Still, I find it hard to believe it's gotten this bad." Phil stood as she left his office.

Abby makes a lot of sense. I'd better keep my eyes open, he thought.

Amtrak and the Long Island Railroad were the best means of travel between Wilmington, Delaware, and Garden City, New York. At least, Purity employees who routinely made the trip believed it was best. The route began at the recently renovated Amtrak Station on Front Street in Wilmington. It was clean and fresh and full of yesteryears' charm. The lovingly restored columns, ornamentation, and fretwork adorned the building with a feeling of nineteenth-century elegance and luxury. Gone were the homeless folk who dotted the stairs and main concourse of the Wilmington Station a few years ago. Their begging and stink no longer plagued the ears and noses of corporate travelers. Out of sight, out of mind.

Two hours later, when Purity employees would emerge from the cozy steel cocoons arriving in New York's Penn Station, a teeming mass of humanity would immediately greet them. People of all shapes, sizes, and colors would fill the corridors as Purity travelers would walk to the lower level to buy a Long Island Railroad ticket.

Employees going directly to the Garden City operation detrained at the Westbury station. Pamela Robinson and Gary Hazlitt had followed the standard travel plan this Monday morning after the Thanksgiving weekend. A driver expected to meet them at the Westbury Station with the rental car they would be using for the next few days.

Pamela and Gary were comfortably ensconced in the Parlor Car, with a porter at their beck and call, ready to fetch a little breakfast, some juice, or even a Bloody Mary. Still an hour and a half from New York City, Gary Hazlitt leaned back in his oversized, relaxing chair and pondered how to mince his words with Pamela. She would likely ask for his opinion of Cohen's plan. He would have to be careful with his answer; everything he said would go straight from his mouth to Cohen's ears. Gary had been planning to work for a few more years and felt that being open with Pamela might be a poor idea.

"Gary, do you realize the train we're taking out of Penn Station stops at the Merilon Avenue Station? That's where Colin Ferguson randomly shot people in his car."

"Shot and killed some, wounded others, and ruined many lives. It's hard to imagine what it would be like being captive in a railcar with a maniac moving row by row and emptying an automatic pistol."

"He had sixteen clips in his duffel bag, each holding sixteen rounds. If those two guys didn't wrestle him down while he was reloading, he would've kept shooting. Many more people would have died. What the hell motivates someone to do that?"

"He was only after the Whites and Asians because he believed they got all the breaks in society, and he and other blacks didn't. Too bad New York's new death penalty law isn't retroactive. Or maybe we could just put him in a room with the survivors and relatives." Gary smiled.

"Gary, you know it's hard being black in America. Not that it justifies what he did, but it's hard."

Typical liberal bullshit, Gary thought. "Yeah, you're right," he replied.

"Do you mind if we talk about our mission? I'd like to know how much Bob told you and if you think we can let more people go and still meet production demands." Pamela sounded a little condescending.

"Not at all. I'd also like to hear your take on the plan."

Pamela sat up. "I know you're in charge of Manufacturing, but Manufacturing is my biggest concern. You lost a lot of experienced people this year, and with no let-up in the production schedule, you are stretched pretty thin."

Gary thought for a minute, wanting to be sure he got his answer straight. "The manufacturing organization at Garden City was grossly overstaffed. Also, the Standard Operating Procedures we followed were, at best, inefficient. I admit that the downsizing forced us to make changes faster than we wanted, but we're doing pretty well."

"I hope you're right. What about the cuts for next year?"

"Well, they won't be as deep as last year, but make no mistake, they will be hard to implement. All and all, I think we can do it."

"Do you ever think about the people we let go?"

The question surprised Gary. He wondered where she was going with this and what Cohen had to do with the question. "Once in a while, I do, but not often. Why do you ask?"

"Most of the employees we let go believed that as long as they did a reasonably good job and stayed out of trouble, they would work for us until they retired. We had a long track record of providing a high level of job security. Since we were profitable, the downsizing shocked most of our employees. They were unprepared. Then, to make matters worse, we targeted older long-service employees and, in essence, forced them out. I tell you, I don't think it was necessary, and I don't feel good about it." Pamela was not sure if, or how, Gary would react, but she felt better having said it.

"Pamela, you can't do your job and stay sane unless you stop thinking about the employees that were let go. You have to realize that if we didn't downsize, none of us would have a job."

Pamela wondered if he believed what he was saying or just supporting Cohen's position. She decided to get the conversation back to the meeting.

"Since most of the people at Garden City work for you, will you take the lead in this afternoon's meeting?"

Gary was happy she was off the soft stuff. "Sure. Let's spend some time comparing notes."

"Do you think we'll have any problems with the Garden City Staff?" Pamela asked.

"Only two are outspoken: Waters and Messina. Waters has been pretty reticent lately, so she should be easy to deal with, and I'll gladly handle Messina," Gary responded.

"Phil is in some trouble, right?"

"Yeah, he shouldn't have gone to McKenzie management on Cohen's kids' summer jobs. Big mistake. Let's talk about the presentation," Gary said.

Throughout the morning, Abby's concerns occupied Phil's thoughts. He tried calling Greg Iverson to see if Abby's fears were unfounded, but he was unavailable. Phil decided to talk less and listen more at the one o'clock meeting regardless of the subject or what happened. He hoped that he could keep his mouth shut.

As Phil entered the conference room, everyone ignored him and continued with what appeared to be small talk, adding to his growing paranoia.

After a few minutes, Diane, Pamela, and Gary entered via the connecting door from Diane's office. Gary Hazlitt cleared his throat a few times before everyone gave him their full attention. He congratulated the attendees for the great year the company was having and expressed Wilmington Management's appreciation. Gary then gave a status report on Purity's Research and Development projects and when they might reach manufacturing. Since none of what he was saying justified two Division Presidents making the journey from Wilmington, the staff quietly awaited the reason for the visit. After a half-hour of preliminaries, Gary finally explained, "Pamela and I are here because we have increased next year's Profit Objective for Purity." He told the attendees why it was necessary to reduce costs, that Garden City's share was at least

$20 million, and that he believed they should implement the downsizing. When he finished, he asked for comments.

Diane Armstrong responded as soon as the last word was out of Hazlitt's mouth. "I assure you that the Garden City site will reduce our budget by twenty million dollars or more. Bob Cohen can rest assured production schedules will be maintained, and quality won't suffer. And I'm sure my staff has what it takes to deliver. We are a team, and teams can do the impossible." As usual, Steve Gagnon echoed everything Diane said and then emphasized how maintaining quality was critical to the success of Purity. Besides turning pale and mumbling some incoherent sounds, Paul Stanley sat back in his chair looking shell-shocked. Lorraine Waters moaned about how hard losing more people would be on her organization and griped over all the extra work Quality Control would have to do, but she committed to doing her part.

Typically, Phil Messina would have erupted over the impact on employees, their families, and the products' quality. He would have accused Management of losing sight of the human side of downsizing: that employees were real people with real lives, with children, with mouths to feed, with mortgages to pay. Instead, he simply watched, listened, and evaluated the situation, fuming inside. *Diane will call Bob Cohen as soon as the meeting ends and tell him the twenty million is in the bag. She never challenges a fucking thing her management wants. She just passes it along and tells her people they'd better get it done if they want to keep working here. Diane finds it easier to give orders than to rally support. Christ, she's no more than a pass-through. She doesn't add any value to this operation. While Steve talks about quality, he's probably thinking of ten new ways to cut corners in Production. He could be the poster boy for the ass-kissers of corporate America. And Stanley won't say a word. All he cares about is keeping his job: what a waste. But the biggest waste of all is my buddy, Lorraine. When Diane Armstrong got the site director's job, Lorraine crawled into her shell and hasn't opened her mouth since. Before Diane's arrival, Lorraine stood her ground very effectively in controversial situations. Now she goes with the flow.* When the others were done, Phil asked, "Pamela, Gary, do you believe it's possible to fire more employees and not cause major quality problems?"

Phil's Nonna would have called the look Gary gave him 'the evil eye.' Gary simply said, "Yes."

Pamela, sounding as if she meant it, said, "It's doable with lots of hard work."

Pamela and Gary kept the meeting in session until five o'clock: not because they enjoyed discussions, but because they did not want word of more downsizing to leak just yet. As soon as the meeting ended, the participants headed to dinner.

The business district in the village of Westbury was only a ten-minute drive from Purity's Garden City Site. Further north on Post Road past the train station, the sign for Ben's Italian Restaurant appears on the left. Ben's Restaurant was housed in an innocuous-looking building that slightly hinted at the fabulous food served inside. Legend had it that celebrities, the likes of Frank Sinatra, usually dined at Ben's when playing at the Westbury Music Fair. It was also the favorite spot for visiting Purity executives.

The party from Garden City was seated in the back, far-left corner to discuss business without being overheard. Monday nights were generally slow, and only the front tables were occupied. When the appetizers arrived at six o'clock, the group in the rear corner was already engaged in spirited conversation.

Phil had maneuvered himself into a seat next to Lorraine. The McKenzie Company had hired Lorraine, an attractive, intelligent, educated, and opinionated black woman, because they needed to show the world, chiefly the Equal Employment Opportunity Commission, that they were color and gender blind. Even though employees like Lorraine scared the hell out of the white guys running the Company, she was promoted to supervisor.

Lorraine had seized the opportunity, indifferent to the reasoning behind her promotion, and had aggressively set out to learn all she could about supervision. Her need to understand how to work effectively with employees had led her to Phil. At first, Phil had shared his knowledge and experience because he was surprised and delighted that a supervisor would focus on the 'people side' of her job rather than the technical side. Lorraine was a quick study and had soon progressed from student to colleague. While becoming close friends, kicking ideas back and forth, and working out problems, Phil had watched Lorraine advance rapidly in the McKenzie organization. He believed that her progress was partially race-motivated but knew that it was still well-deserved. He believed she had the talent to one day be an excellent CEO.

They remained both colleagues and friends. When she began working for Diane Armstrong, however, Lorraine had decided to fade into the background. Lorraine refused to stand against nor take on Diane, another black woman, no matter how incompetent she might be. Lorraine believed it would hurt her chances for advancement and make her an outcast from other black employees. Phil disagreed with her approach, believing that Diane was hurting both the business and its employees and needed to be challenged.

"Lorraine, I need your opinion on a couple things. Can we get together tomorrow?" Phil asked.

"Sure." She replied. "Let's do it tomorrow morning around nine. Plan a little extra time because I also have something I want to bounce off of you. But if you get all judgmental, I'll kick your ass out. I'm tired of hearing how you think I should go back to being my old self."

"I liked your old self better, but I promise to keep my mouth shut."

As the evening wore on, Pamela and Gary held center stage, talking about the business's long-term trajectory, and committing to next year's objectives. Lorraine and Phil could not say three words to each other for the rest of the evening.

The dinner meeting broke up shortly before eight. As the group was leaving, Pamela asked Diane to gather some information for tomorrow's morning meeting. Diane replied, "It'll only take an hour or so, and I'm used to the long hours this job requires. I'll be in at seven tomorrow morning if you want to review the information."

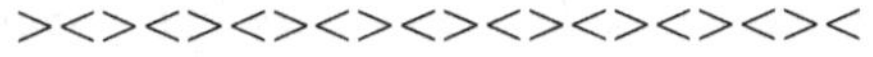

Echo parked a minivan in the public phone area just off the Southern State Parkway Exit 19 and waited for the phone to ring. Echo was waiting for the kill, just like in Russia and East Germany. The exhilaration was the same.

Patience, patience. It's always been a virtue in this type of endeavor. I have to wait for the phone to ring, and then the adventure begins. Funny, the twists and turns life takes. Over three decades ago Echo, the killing machine, was created. Almost a year ago, Diane told me I was losing my job and being downsized. I wonder if she knew I'd asked to be let go: that I wanted a new life, a life away from pharmaceuticals, away from large corporations. I wonder if she knew I was part of Cohen's special team. At the time, I didn't know she was too. I don't think she knows Cohen bought my silence, handed me a check for two hundred grand. I'm sure he'd keep something like that to himself. She, the powerful site director, treated me like shit, the loser told me to leave. Now she's setting me up. I'll never work in the pharmaceutical industry again if she's successful. Maybe I'll even wind up in jail. I'm in deep shit financially. I need a job, and pharmaceutical manufacturing is what I know…

The phone rang. Echo answered, "Yeah."

"She left the restaurant for the office ten minutes ago. She has about an hour's worth of work to do. Be careful. Steve may have gone back with her, that brown-nosing bastard."

"I'll be careful."

In the ten minutes it took to drive to the Purity building, Echo thought, *The wackos that go postal get caught, but I'm different. I have the training and intelligence to pull this off. The plan is thoroughly worked out and pretty foolproof. If anything goes wrong, I can deal with it. I have safe access to the building, all the right equipment, and a sound getaway plan. I absolutely will not get caught. If Steve's with Diane, things will be much more complicated… but I hope he's there so I can make it a twofer.*

Echo pulled into the executive parking area and smiled. Diane's 500SEL and Steve's Vet were both parked in the lot. Echo pulled on latex gloves, stretched on a paper hair net, and moved toward the executive entrance, access card in hand. A nylon jacket, new jeans, and new tennis shoes ensured minimum trace evidence. All would be discarded. Echo flashed the card in front of the reader, punched in the code, heard the expected buzz, and pulled the door open. The guardhouse did not receive an alert that someone had entered the building.

The stairs to the third floor were quieter than the noisy elevator. Echo climbed the stairwell with soft footsteps, carefully opened the door to the executive offices, and ensured that no one was around before exiting. With a silenced .32 ACP pistol in hand, Echo took the long way to Steve's office. The only light came from Diane and Steve's offices and a few exit signs. Slowly and carefully navigating around the square of offices in the third-floor center, Echo headed for the staff offices along the outside wall. Steve Gagnon's office, located just three doors down from Diane's, was first on the agenda.

Steve was talking to his wife, and there was no way to tell how long the conversation might last. Echo frowned, thinking, *Shit, I'm a sitting duck. Diane could walk out of her office at any time. Steve's chatting with his Barbie doll wife, asking if their blond and beautiful all-American kids finished their homework. Ain't that the fucking sweetest thing I ever heard? Steve Gagnon, a brown-nosing, backstabbing son-of-a-bitch who'll do anything to anybody to advance his career and who takes out his frustration on his family. I'll bet Heather got a few bruises when Diane got the job instead of him. How could Heather, a beautiful woman with so much in her future, have picked him? How could she stay with him after all the abuse? After tonight, she'll be rid of him and have lots of money to raise her two kids. I'll be her hero, and she'll never know.* Echo slowly slid toward the floor. *At least I'll be partially hidden by the partition. If he doesn't stop talking soon, Diane will get it first.*

A little over a minute later – seemingly a lifetime – Steve hung up. Knowing Steve's back would be to the door, Echo quickly moved into Gagnon's office, closed the door behind, and leveled the gun at Steve's head.

"Working late, are we, Mr. Gagnon?"

"What?" Steve said as he turned. "What the fuck, you're pointing a gun at me. You're wearing a hairnet." Steve sounded calm, but his heart was pounding like bass from a subwoofer in a teenager's car.

"No need to be concerned. I just need to talk to Diane, and since you're here, I hoped you'd help."

"Come on, put that fucking gun away." Steve's eyes opened wide and he involuntarily moved back in his chair.

"Now, get up off your ass and come around to the side of the desk. Then get on your knees and put your hands behind your head. Don't worry. I just need to search you before we go to Diane's office."

"You're not going to get away with this, no way. Just use your head and leave. I won't tell a soul you were here." As he spoke, Steve dropped to his knees.

"It's a real shame Diane got the corner office instead of you." Steve didn't reply. "I'll bet that really pissed you off. I'll bet Heather cried when you hit her – didn't she? And I'll bet you felt good, maybe even powerful, because you could bring that beautiful woman to tears." Steve started to say something, but Echo interrupted. "Don't try to deny it. I know. In fact, we all know. We just never cared. You know, Steve, you're a real prick, and I'll take great pleasure in killing you. Yes, great pleasure."

Steve thought, *Shit, I shouldn't even be here. I just tagged along to show Diane how dedicated I am. Now I'm going to die, and I'll never be CEO. I'll never have the power and the money I needed so everyone would like me...* The gun discharged with a spit, and not an instant later, a hollow point bullet tore through Steve's heart. The bullet's impact drove Steve backward, and he rolled over his calves and landed on his back with minimal noise. Steve died moments later, ending his days on this earth at 14,323.

Jesus, that was good, exulted Echo. I'd almost forgotten how good it felt. The killing machine strikes again. Blood-soaked Steve's shirt and ran into the carpet. *I need to make sure he's dead without stepping in his blood.* After checking for a pulse and finding none, Echo backed away and looked carefully at the carpet for any sign of blood on the new tennis shoes. Outside the office, the hallway was thick with silence. *If Diane heard the shot, and I don't think she did, she'd come looking for Steve to see what made the noise. She'd never suspect there was any danger. After all, this is an absolutely safe environment.*

The hall remained dead quiet when Echo emerged from Gagnon's office. Walking away from Diane's office and around the section of interior offices was the best way to prevent alerting her. Thanks to the high-quality commercial-grade carpeting covering the concrete floor, there was no creaking or groaning of floorboards. Outside of Diane's office door, Echo noticed light shining under the door of her private bathroom. If she emerged at this moment, she would see an intruder. Echo heard the water running and, realizing that she could walk out at any second, hurriedly moved to the other side of the door.

Meanwhile, Diane was standing at the sink, looking at her reflection and pondering her life. *No one back home in North Carolina would believe a black woman could have an office with a private bathroom. Hell, they'd find it hard to believe a black woman could have a private office. Thank God for Bob Cohen. Every other white son-of-a-bitch in this company — shit, in this country — is a racist. They all see me through prejudiced eyes. But Cohen is different… he knows my value to Purity, and he knows I can get things done. The people I have working for me are the incompetent ones. Goddamned Steve Gagnon is still pissed I got this job. He even told Hazlitt I don't know how to run the site. Doesn't he realize he's wasting his time? The real disappointment is Messina. My fellow blacks said he was genuine and didn't have a racist bone in his body. Man, were they wrong! He fights me on everything. He just can't keep his big mouth shut. At least Stanley and Waters don't try to fight me. I just wish they had the brains to help me. After I get rid of Gagnon and Messina, I can replace them with people who support me. I'd better finish this little project and get home to miserable old Gordy.* She turned and walked to the door.

The bathroom door opened, and a second later, Diane's back was to the office door as she walked to her desk. With two long strides, Echo moved in behind her and, in one quick motion, tripped and shoved her simultaneously. She screamed as she fell face first, but fear tightened her vocal cords. Defying all logic, she immediately tried to get up. Echo jammed a foot against her back and pushed her down hard.

Face down on the floor, Diane heard her office door close. A command came from behind her. "Stay right there until I tell you to move, or you'll be dead before you get three inches off the floor." She heard the gun cock for emphasis.

The blinds on the five windows on the outside walls rattled shut. The asshole was taking no chances.

Diane kept her face buried in the carpet. Fear flowed through her body like electricity through a wire. Would she be beaten? Would she die? She needed to get control of herself and somehow gain the upper hand. The asshole's voice seemed familiar, but she could not put a name to it.

Nonetheless, deep inside, she felt that she could intimidate her attacker. If only she could control her thoughts and emotions, she could triumph. She was determined to fight, and she was determined to come out of this alive.

Echo, likely facing prison because of Diane's role in the conspiracy, wanted her to know that she had caused this mess. When the conversation ended, she would die, and the corporate world would lose a second heartless manager.

"Slowly get to your knees, then turn and face me." As Diane complied, Echo spoke. "That's a good girl. Well, well, Diane. It's time we talked about your little plot."

Diane suddenly put a name to the voice. *The bitch worked for me.* As she turned to face her assailant, now was the time to take charge. "Are you out of your mind holding a gun on me? I'll talk to you tomorrow, after eight. Now get out of here so I can get back to work," she commanded.

"You're going to be more difficult than I imagined. I guess all the assertiveness training is working. Or is it you just don't listen? Silly me! I thought the gun would make a difference."

"Get out before you get in too deep. I'll just forget you were here, and we can both get on with our lives." As she spoke, she started to get to her feet, resolute. *I will survive tonight.* She looked dead into the eyes of "the killing machine" and then, with all the force she could muster, said, "You're not going to shoot me, you fucking honky." Then she screamed. "Steve, get to my office now! Right now!"

Because of her little stunt, she would die not knowing why. Echo squeezed the trigger. The bullet hit her a quarter of an inch above the bridge of her nose. On impact, the front third of the hollow point bullet peeled back, creating jagged metal edges that split her skull and literally tore her brain apart. The unnecessary second shot did the same to her heart. She died seconds later, ending her days on this earth at 15,795.

Echo, disappointed, had wanted her to know how the conspiracy she was involved in had caused her death. Instead, she had forced the matter. *She had balls*, Echo thought. *I'll give her that, at least. She took charge as if her assassin would just hand her the gun and leave. Fortunately, the others will know why they're going to die. Their time will come soon enough. For now, I need to focus on ensuring I didn't leave any evidence.* After picking up the two shell casings, examining Diane's desk, and examining the office floor for any footprints left in the fresh blood, Echo was satisfied. After following the same procedure in Steve Gagnon's office, Echo was convinced that the job was done.

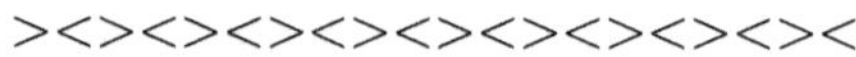

Most of the lights were off in the large brick colonial that occupied the center portion of the three-acre lot, which was taxed by the village of Upper Brookfield, New York. Its large front porch was flanked by two columns adorned with acanthus leaf capitals. The front door opened to a large foyer covered with imported tiles. A spiral staircase ascended to the five bedrooms where two of Armstrong's three children drifted off. The family room was dark except for the flicker of the Sony TV tuned to an inane prime-time sitcom. Gordy, lounging in an oversized chair, stared at the actors without seeing them. He was concerned about his wife.

Diane had called from the office at around 8:00 pm and told Gordy she would be home in an hour and a half. Now it was ten-fifteen with no word. *Just like her to get sidetracked and forget about me*, Gordy thought as he picked up the phone and called her office. No answer. Next, he tried to reach her on her cell phone. *She's probably on her way home and has the phone turned off, the scatterbrain.* Ten minutes later, he decided to call the guard to see at what time she had left.

The lone guard on duty checked the monitor. "She left at about 8:45 pm."

"Are you sure? She only has a thirty-minute commute."

The guard rechecked the monitor and said, "She used her card to get in at 8:06 pm and exit at 8:47 pm. There's no other activity tonight."

Gordy's concern grew. He needed to know if she was on her way home without her cell phone on… or. "Look, could you check her office? She should have been home an hour ago if she left at quarter to nine. Please check and call me back."

Gloria Ruiz carefully locked the door to the guardhouse after putting the 'Be back in five minutes' sign on the door. She headed for the back door to the building, flashlight in one hand, keys in the other. She had never been inside alone before. Ruiz knew that Mrs. Armstrong's office was on the third floor at the opposite end of the building, and she would have to make her way up dimly lit staircases and hallways, most likely for no good reason. *Nothing ever happens here,* she thought. Gloria had taken the security guard job five months ago after struggling to obtain a degree in accounting. A security guard was a long way from an accountant, especially when working the four-to-twelve shift. Yet here she was, flashlight in hand, walking up the back stairwell, stomach churning, hands shaking, and intently listening for any sound.

Gloria noticed the light under Steve Gagnon's office door as she passed and suddenly felt uneasy. She stopped for a moment and listened. She shook off the uneasiness and continued on her trek. As she reached the door to the corner office, Gloria thought, *Nice that a black woman could get a job like this. Maybe there's hope for me.* She gently knocked on the closed door before pushing it open. Gasping, Gloria stared at the blood-drenched body and froze. She noticed the blood surrounding Diane's head first, then her eyes drifted to the thick reddish-brown liquid on her chest. When the scene's reality finally settled into her brain, she clutched at her stomach and vomited uncontrollably.

Jim Hines vigorously brushed his teeth as he listened to Mary Ann rustle across the bed to answer the ringing phone. Jim's thoughts drifted to her and sex. She was unbelievable. He was having better sex than an overweight, fifty-five-year-old man could imagine. After Rita, his wife of thirty-one years, had died three years ago, he struggled to find any real purpose and meaning in life. She had been his soul mate and the only woman he had been intimate with until Mary Ann came into his life. Rita had waged a long, debilitating battle with cancer that she ultimately lost. At age 50, Rita had moved into a nursing home; one year later, she died. The emotional cost had been far more devastating than the financial burden to Jim. Watching her lose all ability to function during the last years of her life could only be tolerated with the aid of a bottle. After she died, Lieutenant James G. Hines, Nassau County Homicide Detective, had poured himself into a bottle and had not emerged for months. Depressed and contemplating suicide, Jim had been staring at his dinner at a local diner. Mary Ann, a waitress, was heading home when she had noticed Jim, a steady customer for the last six months, and had asked if she could join him. They talked for hours that night and soon started dating. After almost a year, Mary Ann had moved in.

Jim replaced the handset and looked longingly at Mary Ann, disappointed that he would not be able to finish the fantasy he had started while brushing his teeth, and said, "There's been a murder at Purity Pharma in Garden City, you know, the castle on Stewart Avenue. And I have to go."

As Jim turned left off Merrick Avenue onto Stewart, the flashing lights of the police vehicles and ambulances bouncing off the concrete building gave the scene a carnival-like ambience. He immediately began worrying about the crime scene's integrity and hoped that the first patrolmen on the scene were experienced. His commander had ensured that he understood that this case could draw as much media attention as the George Floyd and Eric Garner cases combined. Two executives locked in a guarded building had been murdered while they worked. The top executive at the site was one of the victims. The fact that she was black would only amplify the media's interest. Jim's commander had told him that he would be the primary on this case because he was the best detective in his command and had considerable experience with handling the press.

After making his way up to the crime scene, Jim first sought out Karen Parisi. His captain had explained that she was initially assigned as the primary detective. When the brass had gotten word of the victims' stature, they had decided that Jim could better handle the assignment. Karen had been told that she would not be the primary on the case and was told to stay away from the press. She would be Jim's partner instead. Jim guessed that Parisi was in her early thirties. She stood about five-foot-seven, and though not overweight, she was thick through the torso and had a solidly athletic appearance. Karen was a classic beauty. He felt that she would have a good chance of beating him in a fair fight.

Jim hated working with female detectives. He always felt unsure of what to do or say, as if everything he was conditioned to believe about women was wrong. He would try to be friendly and get a look that said 'pig.' Worse, the word in the department portrayed Parisi as a staunch feminist who had ruined her last boss's career. Jim approached her with all his defenses on red alert. *All I have to do is get my black ass fired before I qualify for my pension,* he thought. Tomorrow he would try to get her replaced with a man.

"Look, I didn't ask for this assignment and I really don't want it, but I'm stuck with it. Now tell me what you've learned so far." Jim's tone suggested that he did not truly mean what he said.

Karen decided to stick to facts and only the facts. "The victim in the corner office was a black woman, the Site Director, Mrs. Diane Armstrong. She was shot twice, once in the head and once in the chest." She pointed as she spoke. "Armstrong's husband called building security at ten-fifteen, worried about her because she didn't answer her office phone or cell. The security guard, Ms. Ruiz, immediately left her post at the rear of the building to check. Approximately ten minutes later, she found Armstrong's body. She immediately called the Head of Security, a guy by the name of Russ Cady, who then called us. The vomit on the floor belongs to Ms. Ruiz. Officer Gizzi then found a white male's body three doors down, a Mr. Steve Gagnon, the Director of Manufacturing. He was shot once in the heart. Judging by the damage to the bodies, a hollow point bullet was used."

Jim looked like he wanted to say something, but remained silent. Karen continued. "There are two ways to gain access to the building. One is to enter through the front door from the executive parking lot, called, of all things, the executive entrance. The other is from the employee parking lot at the rear of the building through the guardhouse where Ms. Ruiz is stationed. Getting in through the executive entrance requires an encoded card to be held up to a card reader near the door, then entering a three-digit number on the keypad. The three-digit number must correspond with the card. When someone uses the executive entrance, it automatically records the cardholder's name and the time of entry in the security system. It displays the information on the screen in the guardhouse. The computer beeps to alert the guard. The exec must call the guard to let her know all is well. If there's a problem, the executive won't call or give the guard a code word. The code words are changed weekly. When entering through the guardhouse, the employee must show the guard a company-issued card with a picture."

Jim interrupted, "Do we have any video from the executive entrance?"

"No. I asked why and was told the execs wanted privacy and felt the card system was all the security that was needed," Parisi continued.

"Tonight, Diane Armstrong entered at precisely eight-oh-six and called Ms. Ruiz at eight-ten. She said Steve Gagnon was with her and that all was well. Ms. Ruiz said she sounded fine. We'll have to verify, but it looks like she called her husband just after she arrived. To leave the building by the front door, you have to hold your card up to the reader and push the panic bar on the door. The three-digit number isn't needed. The information is recorded in the system and shows up on the guard's screen. The system shows that Armstrong, and the guard assumed Gagnon, left at 8:47 pm. It was after ten o'clock when Mr. Armstrong called, worried about his wife. We need to find out if Armstrong definitely called her husband and, if she did, at what time. We also need to determine if Gagnon called anyone. Obviously, the killer left at 8:47 pm, but did he come in with Armstrong and Gagnon? If he did, how did he know Armstrong had to call the guard, and when she called, how did he keep her from giving the guard the code word? Or did he come in after they arrived, or was he here in the building already? Also, Armstrong still had her card, so how did our killer get the system to record her name?" Karen stopped and took a look at her notepad before continuing.

"Two drugs containing Class 1 controlled substances are manufactured here. Narcotics are stored in a vault on the first floor, and Mr. Cady is doing physical inventory. The narcotics in the vault are worth about $30 million. Armstrong had the combination, so she may have been part of a theft gone badly. But I think it's unlikely." Karen turned both palms up and tilted her head in a gesture indicating that she was finished.

"Where was she before eight?"

"According to Cady, two bigwigs from corporate headquarters in Delaware are visiting. They had dinner at Ben's with the local execs."

"Why did Armstrong and Gagnon come here after dinner?"

"Cady doesn't know. We need to get the other execs in and ask."

Jim was impressed. Parisi had hardly referred to her notes but gave a clear and concise report. She obviously had something between her ears. *Too bad*, he mused, *that she won't have a chance to work on this case.* Carl Magnotta was Jim's choice to replace Parisi. He and Carl worked well together, and that was important. Perhaps she was brighter than Carl, but Carl was easy to work with. He thanked her and asked if she would show him around and introduce him to Cady and Ruiz.

Jim toured the crime scene, talked to the officers who were first on the scene, and then spent some time with the medical examiner. He interviewed Ruiz and Cady. He learned that the crime scene yielded little, if any, evidence. No shell casings, few fingerprints, and no bloody footprints. Cady told him the narcotics in the vault were all accounted for. He also confirmed everything Parisi had told him. *Young, beautiful, and smart. Parisi really should have become a lawyer*, Jim thought, surprised and thoroughly impressed.

He asked Cady to assemble all the dinner-meeting attendees in a large room where a police officer could monitor and limit the talk about the murders, then close the building until further notice.

Gary Hazlitt was sipping a VO on the rocks and enjoying the luxurious appointments of his room at the Garden City Hotel when Bob Cohen called. Bob was near hysteria but managed to tell Gary that Diane and Steve were dead, murdered at the office. The police had sealed off the building, and he was having a hard time getting more detailed information. Cohen's distorted voice playing through the phone receiver verged on a shrill screech. "Get over to that fucking building, find out what the hell's going on, and report back to me! What'll the press say? Imagine if this damn thing gets on television! Think about that, Gary – think about the hell we'll be in!" Bob Cohen had always amazed Hazlitt, perpetually concerned first and last about himself.

It was after midnight when he roused Pamela and drove the five miles to the building. Immediately upon entering, they were stopped by a police officer. He and Pamela were quickly led to a conference room and told that someone would be with them shortly. Eventually, they learned that Waters, Messina, and Stanley had also been asked to meet. A police officer was stationed in the conference room.

Tuesday 12/2 (Just after midnight)

They waited in the mahogany-paneled, oval-shaped conference room. The door and the paneling had the same finish, giving the effect of a continuous wall when the door was closed. Twenty chairs surrounded a conference table made to compliment the room's shape. The remaining participants from last night's dinner occupied five chairs. Pamela Robinson and Gary Hazlitt huddled together at one end, whispering to each other while occasionally looking up at their guard. Phil Messina, Lorraine Waters, and Paul Stanley sat silently at the other end, obviously shaken by the night's events.

When Jim Hines entered the room, Gary Hazlitt immediately knew that he was in charge of the investigation and responsible for his and Pamela's captivity. It was not that Jim Hines was a large, physically imposing man that led Hazlitt to his conclusion; it was the stern look in his eyes and how the other officers deferred to him. Before Lt. Hines could introduce himself, Hazlitt started speaking. "We are being held captive in our own building, not permitted to use the phone, and our conversations are being monitored. I find this treatment completely unacceptable. I must immediately call our CEO to let him know what's going on."

As Hazlitt spoke, Hines stood at the end of the conference table, both hands in fists, knuckles on the table, leaning slightly forward. He waited, wanting to be sure Hazlitt was done before he spoke. Everyone in the room was a potential suspect, and he wanted to hear everything they had to say.

"I am terribly sorry for any inconvenience I may have caused you, but as you know, we are investigating two murders. And besides, Mr. Hazlitt, you and Ms. Robinson intruded on a crime scene in the middle of our gathering evidence. Letting you walk around could have contaminated valuable evidence. As for your conversations being monitored and not being allowed to use the phone, you must realize that you were the last to see the victims alive. Besides the killer, that is."

The room was silent for what seemed like an hour before Lieutenant Hines spoke again. "I'm Lieutenant James Hines with the Nassau County Police. I've been a homicide detective for well over twenty years, and I intend to solve this case. We need to conduct preliminary interviews with each of you to find out what happened yesterday. After being interviewed you will be free to go about your business, but until then, you will remain in this room."

"We cannot give you any information on the substance of our meeting, as it is extremely confidential," Hazlitt volunteered.

"That's all right for now, but if I determine it's important to the case, I'll let you know," Hines said, looking self-assured. "Mr. Hazlitt, you're first."

Hazlitt's appearance, considering it was well after midnight, surprised Jim and Karen. He wore a golf shirt open at the neck, a pair of dress slacks, and brown loafers. The shirt and slacks looked like they had just jumped off of an ironing board and onto his body, and the loafers as if they had never been worn. On the other hand, Gary did not look as good as his clothes; his coloring could be best described as sickly. His six-foot-two frame carried too little weight, and the sacks under his eyes had a hint of black. Judging by Gary's jowls, Jim guessed that he was in his sixties. The trio walked to an unoccupied office in the Human Resources area.

As soon as all three were seated, Jim began standard interview proceedings. "This is a preliminary interview. You are not a suspect, and your participation is strictly voluntary. I will be asking questions about your involvement with the victims. Your overall knowledge of the victims and any background information you can give us will help our investigation. Okay?"

"Whatever, let's just get on with it. I have a lot to do," Gary said.

"Let's start with your full name and position in the company."

"Garrison K. Hazlitt. I am the President of the Manufacturing Division. Diane Armstrong reported to me, and Steve Gagnon reported to her."

"What was Diane's position?"

"Diane is, ah, was the Site Director. Officially her title was Director of Garden City Operations. She was personally responsible for all site operations. Gagnon, Stanley, Waters, and Messina worked for her."

Hines rubbed his brow and said, "Tell me a little about the Company. I seem to remember there were a couple of different names on this building in the past."

"This business started as Endall Pharmaceuticals in the fifties. A few years later, it developed Thinadin, which is still the best anticoagulant on the market." Gary paused as if waiting for some sort of accolade. When none was provided, he continued, "In the early seventies, McKenzie Chemical bought Endall and made it part of their pharmaceuticals division. It was part of McKenzie until McKenzie and Saga Pharmaceuticals formed a joint venture: the Purity Pharmaceutical Company. McKenzie contributed its products, assets, and people, and Saga contributed money and marketing and development expertise."

"I'm not familiar with all these big business terms, but I think I understand. Tell me what you know about Diane from a work point of view."

"She started working for me a couple of years ago. I was Site Director before the joint venture. When I was promoted to this job, Diane replaced me. Before her promotion, she was the Manager of our Atlanta Distribution Center. She was an outstanding employee and is a great loss to our business." Gary sounded very business-like.

Hines decided to see if Hazlitt would open up. "Did any employees have a problem when she was made Site Director? Being a black woman, you know… not the picture most employees are used to seeing in the top job."

Gary answered immediately. "No, our employees understand our commitment to diversity. Our CEO, Bob Cohen, emphasizes it continually, and they recognize that Diane was the best-qualified person for the position."

"Hmmm. No problem having a black woman in the top job, interesting. Let's talk about the killer. How do you think he got into the building without triggering the computer in the Guardhouse?"

"The only way I could think of is that he entered with Diane and Steve. But coming in with them doesn't explain Diane's call to the guard." Gary's manner remained stoic.

"No other way you could think of?" Hazlitt said no, and then Hines asked, "Of the people at the dinner last night, who are you closest to?"

"I don't get close to people at work, but if I must answer, I would say Pamela Robinson."

As Jim Hines got up to say goodbye to Hazlitt, Karen asked, "Excuse me, Mr. Hazlitt, but do you know why Diane and Steve returned to work tonight?"

Hazlitt flashed a look neither Karen nor Jim understood, then replied, "Pamela thought of some information we needed for tomorrow and asked Diane if she would put it together. Steve just tagged along."

"Why would Steve do that?" Karen asked.

"I'm not sure. Steve might have been trying to get on her good side," Gary replied.

"Thanks again for your help. We'll get back to you if we have more questions," Jim said as Gary left. "Would you ask Pamela to come in?"

Before Pamela entered the room, Jim turned to Karen. "Great question. We'll ask Pamela exactly the same question. What did you think of Mr. Hazlitt?"

"Personally, I don't like him and I think he's holding back some information. But if you ask if I think he's involved, I just don't know. God, the man's rigid, like he has a pole up his ass. What do you think?"

Just as Jim was about to answer, Pamela entered the office. Pamela Robinson looked tired, very tired, just as you would expect someone to look at this time in the morning. Her eyes were puffy, and her shoulder-length hair looked as if she had barely had time to run a comb through it. She wore a loose-fitting blouse over a pair of slacks.

After some preliminaries, Jim went through a gauntlet of opening questions that Pamela answered similarly to Gary. He and Karen learned that Pamela was the President of the Proprietary Pharmaceuticals business and was responsible for all worldwide operations involving the development, sales, and distribution of drugs developed by Purity.

Jim leaned forward and folded his hands on the table. "Ms. Robinson, tell me about Ms. Armstrong. Were you close friends or just co-workers?"

"I can't say we were close friends. We were as close as two women who have routine contact get to each other. We shared some personal things and talked over lunch on occasion, but we didn't see each other outside of work."

"Mr. Hazlitt filled us in on Diane's background, so why don't you just tell us about her at work? Tell us any problems she might have had with others, or maybe someone who might have been concerned about her skin color."

"Diane moved up pretty rapidly and was not prepared to handle the complexities of this operation. She was not the first Site Director to face a steep learning curve, but employees had less patience with her than her predecessors. I believe it was because Diane was black and tended to be very autocratic. She came across as uncaring to the people who worked for her. Her management recognized the problem and was trying to help her deal with it."

"Hold on a second," Jim interrupted. "Do you mean Gary Hazlitt was teaching her how to deal with people?"

Pamela thought for a second before answering, her eyes moving side to side, letting Jim and Karen know she was trying to precisely frame her answer. "No, Gary was not the best person to help Diane. She worked with Bob Cohen. Unfortunately, he doesn't have much time, so progress was slow."

Jim asked, "You said it was partly about race. Tell me what you mean?"

Pamela hesitated again, thinking before responding. "I have never heard anything specific, but there is an undercurrent at Garden City and the Purity Headquarters. Bob Cohen believes in diversity and promotes minorities and women at every opportunity. Needless to say, white males are not happy. But it goes beyond that; old-timers feel the new managers don't know the business, and we are having operational problems as a result."

"Tell us about Steve Gagnon."

Before responding, Pamela took a deep breath and let out what Karen saw as a heavy sigh. "Steve was a completely different story. He joined the pharmaceutical business twelve years ago as a Process Engineer. Like Diane, he moved up the ladder pretty quickly. In addition to being an excellent engineer, Steve had that all-American boy look, a combination that helps a career. When he was given a chance at supervision, he shined. He got things done, his organization routinely finished its tasks ahead of schedule, and Steve made sure everyone knew it." Pamela thought, *The son-of-a-bitch beat schedules by encouraging his people to take shortcuts and not follow procedures, but I'd better keep that to myself.* She said, "Steve was sure he would get the Site Director's job after Gary moved on. He was devastated when Diane was chosen. He lobbied the decision-makers, letting them know he knew the operation better than Diane and had an excellent track record. But in the end, she got the job."

Jim watched Pamela's mannerisms and her eyes; he listened to the sound of her voice. She was being careful, but he thought she was being honest so far. "Gary said Steve may have been trying to get on Diane's good side. Do you agree?"

"Yes, he took brown-nosing to a new high. In fact, when I asked Diane to return here and put together some information, Steve was standing right next to her and immediately volunteered to accompany her. He said he was buried with work and could use a head start for tomorrow."

"We're done for now, thanks; Officer Parisi and I are going to take a break. Would you ask Paul Stanley to join us in about fifteen minutes?"

Again, Karen felt that Jim had missed a question and asked, "When did you realize you needed the additional information?"

Again Pamela hesitated before answering. "After dinner, Gary and I spent a few minutes planning the next session and decided we needed some personnel information on several employees. I suggested we ask Phil Messina since he heads the HR group."

"Why didn't you ask Mr. Messina?" Karen followed up.

Pamela didn't want to answer, but it was a direct question. "For some reason, Gary's not real high on Phil, so we asked Diane."

After Pamela left, Jim said to Karen. "Again with the good questions! The fact that Robinson volunteered she was the one who asked Diane to return to the office either means she was not involved or she's astute. I think Hazlitt or Robinson may be involved if Diane's office was the planned killing ground. Also, I believe it was because the killer was able to defeat the security system. Let's get more detail on the security system from the next three. Any solid suspects yet?"

"No, not really," Karen replied. "Both Hazlitt and Robinson are being real precise with their answers. Also, they were both involved in getting Diane here, but I wouldn't call them suspects yet."

"Maybe corporate types are naturally controlled. Anyway, let's get some coffee." As they walked to the coffee machine, Jim reconsidered his earlier thoughts about Karen. *She asked some pertinent questions, and we got some good information. She's alright.*

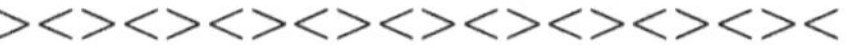

After listening to Paul Stanley's answers to the preliminary questions, Jim concluded that the Director of Research was not a player in this drama and cut the interview short. He asked Stanley to leave and waited for Karen to ask a brilliant question. When she didn't, Jim felt relieved and asked Stanley to send in Waters.

Jim had been overwhelmed by Lorraine Waters' appearance the first time he laid eyes on her. Now, as she entered the room, he took her all in. Lorraine stood about five-foot-nine and had a model's long, lean body. Her skin, the color of coffee with a little milk, was as smooth as fine china. Her brown eyes, narrow nose, and thin lips looked like

Michelangelo had arranged them on her oval face. Except for her brown eyes, Lorraine's features were the exact opposite of Jim's; he was sure that several white people were part of her family tree.

As she took her seat, Jim felt her presence, intelligence, and self-confidence radiating from her. Feeling a little inadequate, he asked, "How are you doing, sister?" He immediately realized how stupid he sounded.

Lorraine took the question in stride and replied. She knew he was flustered; she had that effect on older men, especially black men. "I'm doing fine, thanks."

Jim took a second to gather himself and then said. "Ms. Waters, please tell us what you do here."

"I'm Director of Quality Assurance. I ensure all products are produced following our Standard Operating Procedures. My people do all the testing required to ensure our products meet all specifications. I'm also the primary contact with the FDA. I handle all requests for information and host them for on-site audits."

"Let's talk about the killer for a minute. How do you think he got into the building without triggering the computer in the guardhouse?"

"The only thing I can think of is that he hid in the building after it closed, hid from the cleaning people, and then went up to the office area and – and, well, you know. But how would he know Diane and Steve were coming back?"

Jim had already considered this possibility and had planned to investigate it. He believed that it was best not to question Lorraine about this theory, so he moved on. "I understand that you worked for Ms. Armstrong. Were you friends?" Jim noticed that Lorraine's eyes darted from side to side before she answered.

"We weren't close friends. We mostly had a working relationship."

"I'm surprised that two black female executives, who worked together every day, did not see each other for social reasons. We blacks generally have a lot in common just being black, and tend to relate to each other both on and off the job." Jim wanted to see if Lorraine would confirm Pamela Robinson's view of Armstrong. "Were you jealous of her, or did you think she didn't deserve the job?"

"Being black women was the only thing we had in common. As for being jealous, I'm a realist. I know I don't have the experience to do the Site Director's job, and when it opened, I had no expectation of getting it. I was surprised, though, when Diane got the job because she didn't have the technical background for the job. Still, I have to admit she was much better at handling company politics."

"Do you know why Armstrong and Gagnon returned to work after dinner?"

"As I was walking out of the restaurant, I heard Pamela Robinson ask Diane to put some information together for our meeting tomorrow… I mean, today. I don't know why Steve was here. I would venture to guess he was simply acquiring some brownie points."

To Jim, it seemed a safe bet that Gagnon was a suck-up and was with Armstrong to improve his standing with her, making Armstrong the target. "Do you think race might be a reason for the killings?"

"I guess it's possible. Minorities and women are moving up fast, and there's a lot of animosity throughout the company.

Higher-level management jobs were the exclusive domain of white guys with technical degrees for a long time. They got almost all the promotions. When minorities and women, especially those not technically trained, started getting promoted, the old guard believed it was the beginning of the end of the business. And they were very vocal about it. If the murders were racially motivated, you'll have a lot of suspects."

"Can you give me a few names?"

"Not off the top of my head. I would have to think about it for a little while." Lorraine shifted in her seat, ran her fingers through her hair, and prepared for a follow-up.

Jim decided to take a different approach. He anticipated working closely with someone from the company to solve this case but had not picked his mole yet. "Are you close to anyone at work?"

The question caught her off guard, and she took a moment to answer. "I get along best with Phil Messina." Lorraine noticed Lieutenant Hines roll his eyes and quickly added. "And before your mind rushes headlong into the gutter, it is strictly a working relationship."

"My mind isn't in the gutter. I'm just surprised you're so close to Messina. Isn't he one of those older white guys that have problems with women and minorities?"

"Far from it. Phil is the least biased person I know. He doesn't see me as a woman or as black. He sees me as a human being and treats me as one. In fact, he treats everyone that way. When I first moved into management, Phil took me under his wing and taught me how to do the job." Lorraine decided that she needed to explain. "I was working as a Chemist in McKenzie's Medical Diagnostics Division in Delaware when I was promoted to Production Supervisor. After the initial euphoria of the job wore off, I realized I didn't understand how to deal with all the problems I faced daily. At first I went to my boss, but I soon realized I wasn't getting much help. He'd give quick answers and then a lecture on how I was a 'big girl now' and should know how to do my job. I was in HR making some benefit changes when I voiced my situation and frustration to the Personnel Clerk. By the way, Lieutenant Hines, she's black, and we got along very well." Jim did not seem to react, so Lorraine continued. "Anyway, she suggested I talk to Phil Messina, who was the Human Resource Manager at the time. She said he was pretty easygoing and would take the time to help me. So I called him."

"And he helped?" Jim wondered.

"He did more than help. Beyond just answering my questions, he helped me think things through independently. I'd describe a situation I was facing, and rather than tell me what to do, he'd solicit my thoughts. I'd tell him how I'd handle a problem, and he'd ask questions or talk about company policy. By the time we finished, I knew how to deal with the problem. We've had many similar talks over the years. As a result, I've become very good at working with people and dealing with people-problems. *He* is my brother." Lorraine threw out the last part as a bit of a dig at Jim.

"Sounds like a great guy," Jim said, not taking the bait. "I'm done. Karen, do you have any questions?"

"One or two, if that's okay. Ms. Waters, both you and Mr. Messina were transferred from the Medical Products Division. When was that?"

"I was transferred to Garden City a little over two years ago, and Phil was transferred about a year ago."

"What other management people came from the Medical Division or any other McKenzie Division?"

"None. When I was asked to come here, I was told the culture in Pharmaceuticals was inbred and needed some experienced people from other parts of McKenzie."

Karen hesitated and said, "I think that's it. Let's talk to Mr. Messina."

All three stood and, after shaking hands, Lorraine Waters turned and walked out of the office. Jim and Karen stood and silently looked at each other before Karen spoke. "I think we need to explore her relationship with Messina a little more deeply." Jim agreed, and they waited to conduct the last interview.

A casual onlooker watching Phil Messina and Jim Hines shake hands would find the resemblance between the white man and the black man remarkable. Both stood about six feet tall; both had broad shoulders, large chests, and thick buttocks and legs. A layer of fat covered both heavily muscled frames, indicating athletic men not doing enough push-aways from the dinner table. Only their skin color (Phil's olive, Jim's black), and their general facial features identified one as Italian American and the other as African American.

Jim motioned to a chair and asked Phil to have a seat. "Mr. Messina," Jim began.

Phil interrupted, "Please call me Phil."

"All right – Phil. Tell us about your job. What is it you do here?"

After getting comfortable in the chair, Phil replied, "My title is Director of Business Resources. I'm responsible for several staff functions, including Human Resources, Medical, Safety and Security, Environment, Finance, and Production Planning and Control."

"Sounds like a difficult job."

"Not if you have good people working for you." Phil's response was accurate enough. He wished that all of his employees were good people – not just a few.

"Do you know why Diane and Steve returned here after dinner?"

"In so many words, Diane told me Pamela – that's Pamela Robinson – needed some information from the Personnel files and didn't trust me with the task. And as usual, she'd have to put in the time to bail me out."

"Seems as though Diane was not one of your biggest fans," Jim mused. "Why do you think Mr. Gagnon was with her?"

"I think Steve was making a few points. He had a knack for making points."

"How did you and Ms. Armstrong get along, and do you think she was doing a good job?"

Before responding, Phil wondered if the truth would get him in trouble, but he quickly shook it off as usual. "We barely tolerated each other, let alone got along. I think she did a lousy job. She didn't have the technical skills or the people skills for the Directors' job or any other job in management. She was a condescending, arrogant, patronizing snob who couldn't care less for the people in this plant. She only cared about kissing

Bob Cohen's ass so she could get ahead. She would have ruined this operation given enough time."

The attack on a fellow black frustrated Jim, but he gained some control before responding. "That's a pretty harsh assessment, so I take it you didn't like working for a black woman."

"Hold on! Don't put words in my mouth. I didn't like working for Diane Armstrong, and I didn't like her, period. Is that clear?" Phil was irritated. He did not like being spun.

"Okay, okay, it's just that you obviously got angry when you answered the question. I assumed your anger had something to do with Diane's color. A normal assumption in today's world, I'd think."

"Yeah, I tend to get a little carried away when I talk about Diane, but it's purely focused on her character, not her race."

Jim looked deep into Phil's eyes and felt that he was telling the truth. "Do you think you should've gotten the job instead of Ms. Armstrong?"

"I am not remotely qualified for the Site Director's job. I don't have the education, I don't know pharmaceutical production, and I don't have connections in Purity. So, if you think I killed her to get her job, you're wrong. I have already reached my level of incompetence."

"Do you have any ideas as to how the killer made it past security and managed to enter the building?"

"For the killer to have gotten into the building unnoticed by the guard, he must've had a valid access card and a matching code. And he would've also needed to modify the security program in advance so that when used, the card wouldn't signal the guardhouse or register on the database. I think we need to check the security program code. I can't think of any other way to get in."

"Good thought. Who do I contact to investigate?"

"Russ Cady is the expert on the system. I'll ask him to work with you."

Karen looked at Jim. He gave her a slight nod before she asked, "Usually, murders are motivated by things like money or sex, but in this case, we think the murders may have been motivated by race. That's the reason for the direction of Lieutenant Hines's questions. Do you think race is enough of a problem in this company to motivate someone to kill two people?"

"I find it hard to believe that anyone in this company would commit murder for any reason. But two of my fellow managers are dead, and it looks like an inside job. If someone associated with the company is the killer, race is only one possible motive. You're probably not aware of this, but the company and this site have gone through major changes during the past year: changes that have negatively impacted almost every employee's life. Earlier this year, we reduced our employment by one hundred and forty-five employees. Some of the reductions were voluntary, and others were forced. The impact on the employees we let go is apparent, but it also impacted the remaining employees. Besides the obvious – having to work harder – they also lost the sense of job security they had since coming to work here."

"Tell us more about the reductions. Would I be right to call it downsizing?" Karen asked.

"In this company, as in others, re-engineering, downsizing, and force reductions all blur together. We offered all employees an incentive to resign, an incentive everyone in management knew would attract few volunteers. The employees selected for reduction were told to 'voluntarily' take the incentive or be terminated with no incentive. The employees who were let go weren't prepared. They thought they'd work for this company until retirement. The employees we forced out were the higher-paid employees, between forty and fifty-four years of age for the most part. They're the people who have the most difficult time finding a new job." Phil continued, "It was a major shock to these employees and their families because it was the first time in the history of this pharmaceutical business that employees were forced to leave."

Karen looked at Jim. "You're responsible for Human Resources, so we'll need your assistance." She turned to Messina. "We need a list of employees who had serious problems losing their job or were simply hotheads. And we need it starting with the most likely first."

"I don't know the background of each individual, but I'll work with the folks in HR to come up with a list. I'll have something for you by tomorrow afternoon."

Jim had enough information about the company for now. He wanted to better understand Phil Messina himself. "Thanks, the list will be important to our investigation. We've heard Bob Cohen promoted many women and minorities since becoming CEO. Do you have any thoughts on Mr. Cohen or his policies?"

Phil thought about giving the politically correct answer and painting Cohen as a good man trying to help people, but instead, he spouted, "Bob Cohen is a racist, and his policies are racist."

Jim, visibly angry, responded, "So you believe following Affirmative Action laws and promoting people who have been excluded from the economic mainstream of this country is racist?"

"I think when a person's race is the only basis for making job placement decisions, it's racist by definition. And it is not a law. Affirmative Action is a civil policy. At first it required businesses to affirmatively recruit and hire qualified minorities and women for open jobs with a goal of achieving demographic balance. Now, it's about giving some people opportunities at the expense of others based on race and gender."

Jim looked at Phil as if he had just spit on one of his children. Karen, believing that no good could come of continuing, took charge. "Mr. Messina, I think we have enough for now, and we look forward to receiving the preliminary list. Thanks for your time."

After Phil left, Jim, red-faced with anger, stood up and shouted to the room, "Asshole!!"

The interviews lasted until three in the morning. Lorraine was waiting when Phil emerged. Simultaneously, they said, "We need to talk." They headed to an excellent all-night diner on Old Country Road. They sat quietly in a corner booth, sipping coffee for about fifteen minutes before Lorraine spoke. "I can't believe they're dead. Murdered. We were with them last night talking, laughing. Someone shot them. I can't believe it." The stillness of the diner filled the air before Phil responded.

"This doesn't happen in the business world – in our world – and it doesn't happen to people we know. Our lives are insulated from murder. Murder only happens in the real world. We only have to put up with the constant political bullshit in the corporate world. I feel disconnected from reality. You know I didn't think very much of either of them, and I know you didn't either, but I can't believe someone killed them." Phil went back to his coffee. They talked about the murders and the interviews for a while, knowing it was futile but feeling the need to continue to talk about it.

When Lorraine sensed that they had no more to say about the murders, she changed the subject. "The FDA review is starting Monday, and with the plant in an uproar, I'm worried we'll foul it up. I've spent a lot of time trying to get things ready the last couple of weeks. Now I'm not sure we'll be prepared."

"You'll get it done. By the way, how's your mom doing?"

"Hanging in there for now, but she's pretty sick. I desperately need to get some sleep. I'll see you tomorrow, ah, today for round two."

Tuesday 12/2

The wake formed an ever-widening highway of white on the blue water behind the ship. Diane and Steve's killer looked out over the highway while leaning against the stern rail of the Bridgeport to Port Jefferson Ferry, protected from the cold wind by the protruding passenger compartment. The events of last night were exhilarating. Echo was filled with feelings of power that he had not experienced in 30 years.

Enough self-congratulations. It's time to go over every detail again and make sure I didn't miss anything.

After killing the bitch I carefully checked her office and body for any trace of evidence. I picked up both shell casings and made sure I left no footprints. Next, I looked for any other bits of possible evidence… I even checked her desk to make sure she didn't somehow jot down my name. I know it wasn't possible, but I had to check. Then on to Steve Gagnon's office and the same drill. Echo carefully visualized his movements in both offices before feeling comfortable that he had attended to every detail. *I took the stairs to ground level, flashed the card with her number at the reader, and exited to the executive parking lot. I removed the latex gloves and hair net and put them in a plastic bag. I drove straight from Garden City to the motel in Nyack.*

Echo had chosen a motel with outside access to the rooms to avoid entering the lobby. Once in the room, Echo had stripped bare and put everything in a large garbage bag, then took a long, hot shower. At 2:00 am, everything from the crime scene except the gun had been tossed into a dumpster three miles from the motel.

To establish an alibi, I left home yesterday morning, drove straight to Nyack, and had spent the afternoon shopping at the many antiques stores in town. I purchased a few items and made sure that I received dated receipts. I talked to enough people and passed out enough business cards to be remembered. I checked into the motel around five and left for Garden City around six. The Route 9 Motor Lodge was not the kind of place where the clerks noticed the comings or goings of their guests. Perhaps not an airtight alibi, but it's a pretty good one.

Soon the gun would be tossed into the Long Island Sound. Echo needed to wait for the other passengers to settle in for the trip. The open-top deck was empty because of the chill, but the entire railing was visible from the bridge, it was too risky to toss the gun from the top deck. When the time was right, Echo slowly pulled out the gun and dropped it over the main-deck railing. The killer then casually turned around and walked into the passenger area, the last of the evidence gone.

The salt water of the Sound will destroy the barrel's rifling, making it impossible to get a ballistics match in the unlikely event the gun is found. With the last evidence gone, I can relax over a much-needed coffee.

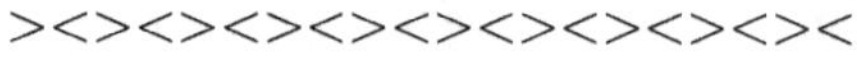

After three hours of disturbed sleep filled with images of blood-spattered bodies, Phil arrived at work. The building was almost empty, aside from the few employees required to work today. They felt compelled to talk about the victims. According to these hallway sleuths, the prime suspect was an unemployed black man from neighboring Hempstead doing drugs in the executive parking lot when Diane and Steve had shown up.

Phil's first order of business was checking Abby's progress on assembling the list for the police. He had called her last night after his interview. He had asked if she would come in early and compile a list of employees that she believed might have grievances with the company and management. He also suggested organizing the list starting with the most likely suspect to commit murder. Abby was explaining why she was uncomfortable with the assignment when Gary Hazlitt's assistant interrupted, "Phil, Mr. Hazlitt wants to see you, now!"

"He was here this morning and asked me what I was doing, and I told him. I hope that was okay," Abby said as Phil was leaving.

"I don't see why not. He probably wants something else," Phil said as he walked out.

Gary Hazlitt had set up shop in an office emptied by last year's downsizing. He was in charge of the site until further notice. He had spent most of the morning on the phone with Bob Cohen, Pamela Robinson, and several corporate lawyers. Other than his brief visit with Abby, the summons of Phil Messina to his office was Hazlitt's first acknowledgment that there was anyone else on the site.

As Phil cooled his heels, Gary was on the phone again, chair turned, back toward Phil. Not sure why he was there, Phil took stock of the man across from him. Hazlitt had that distinguished waspish look: tall and slightly underweight, gray hair peppered with black. His well-tailored suit added to his corporate-executive appearance. Phil had worked in Hazlitt's organization for a year yet did not know him. Hazlitt guarded his inner self the way Purity protected the formulations of its products. Everything with Hazlitt seemed to come down to "image." That was quite unlike, Phil had heard, the man who had first joined the company. Gary Hazlitt was a naturally reserved man, but he had made an extraordinary effort to get to know the people who would work for him when he arrived. Hazlitt was most comfortable in his office looking at reports or putting together a proposal; he loved the detail and tended to overanalyze before coming to a conclusion. He was visibly uncomfortable when dealing with HR problems, but the individuals involved typically viewed him as genuine.

Gary Hazlitt had changed fairly dramatically. Rather than working hard to understand and deal with the problems he faced on a daily basis. He instead, worked to see where the political winds were blowing and how they might benefit him. His dealings with the people working for him became superficial and sometimes nasty. He hardly listened to his subordinates. He always complied with his boss's demands, no matter the impact on employees. He was no longer the constrained boss who was genuine in his dealings and detailed and thoughtful in his business decisions. Who said 'old dogs can't learn new tricks'?

Gary placed the handset in its cradle and rotated slowly to face Phil. "Thanks for coming," he said with little emotion. "I understand you asked Abby to put together a list for the police. I hope you haven't made any commitments to Lieutenant Hines."

"During my interview last night, I volunteered to give him a list of employees that might have reason to kill Diane or Steve. Any problem with that?"

"I've been on the phone constantly with folks in Wilmington – mainly Cohen – trying to decide how we're going to work with the police in this matter." Gary, looking uncomfortable, hesitated for a moment to gather his thoughts. "You need to be involved because you're the one who will put together whatever information we decide to give them and because you're the head of Human Resources. You'll add some credibility to our position. But Wilmington is concerned you'll become a loose cannon, as is your style, and provide information we don't want the police to have. So I'm telling you now: you will do what you're told if you want to continue working here."

Phil shifted in his seat, deciding not to say anything yet. Gary stared at Phil condescendingly, his mouth curved in a slight smile. "Our corporate Legal Department feels we can only give the police limited information or we'll be in violation of the Privacy Act. Anything we give the police automatically becomes available to the public after the case is closed. You've seen how the assholes from the press are circling around this case. We won't do anything to hurt the public image of this company, nor will we open Purity to lawsuits."

Phil sat up in his chair and leaned forward. "You haven't mentioned the part about helping the police solve the case. For Christ's sake, Diane and Steve were brutally murdered. Two people you and I worked with every day were shot in cold blood in this building, and you're worried about the goddamned Privacy Act and lawsuits? And you're telling me if I break ranks, I'll be fired? Where the hell did that come from?"

Gary put his elbows on his desk and intertwined his fingertips, a slight smile on his lips. "I didn't ask for you to be involved, and for your information, I don't want to work with you. But I have my orders. For your own good, you'd better understand that I guarantee I'll fire your ass in a heartbeat if you do anything contrary to what I tell you. You've known the company position for two minutes, and you're already causing me problems. You need to think about how your life will change without this job." Gary waited until Phil nodded. "I'll take that as a sign you understand. The police will be here in a little while, and I want you here when I talk to them. Now get out of here and wait by your phone. I'll call you when they arrive."

When Phil returned to Hazlitt's office, Jim Hines and Karen Parisi were sitting around a small, round table and talking with him. As Phil walked toward the table, Gary looked up at Phil and, as if the earlier conversation had never happened, said, "Good morning Phil. Please have a seat. Lieutenant Hines was updating me on the case. Jim, Karen, I believe you know Phil Messina from last night. He's the head of Human Resources, and he'll be our key contact with you on this case. Jim, please continue."

Jim nodded in acknowledgement of Phil, then returned his attention to Hazlitt. "So far, the autopsies haven't told us much more than we'd already surmised from the crime scene. They died about the same time, probably within fifteen minutes of each other. The forensic evidence indicates they were both on their knees at one time. In fact, it looks like Mrs. Armstrong was knocked to the floor and scraped her knees. Mr. Gagnon was shot once, in the heart, with a hollow-point bullet. The bullet literally vaporized his heart. He died almost instantly. Mrs. Armstrong was shot once in the head and once in the heart. It appears the first shot was to the head and the second shortly after that to the heart. The bullet to the heart was unnecessary. The placement of all three shots was close to perfect. The shooter is very proficient with a pistol and knows exactly where to place the shot for a quick kill." Jim stopped, looked at Phil, then glanced at Karen before returning his gaze to the person he believed was in charge. "Any questions before I move on?"

Gary waved his open hand in front of his body and said, "Continue."

"Both offices were cleaned before the murders, so we hoped to only find prints from the victims and the killers. So far, the only prints we've lifted belong to the victims. There were no shell casings, nor were there any footprints in the blood. Hair and fiber evidence will take a long time to sort through, but I suspect nothing of significance will be found. Before I get to our theory on this case, I'd like Karen to tell you a couple of things we learned during the interviews with the execs, your security people, and the victim's spouses." Jim looked directly at Phil for a second before nodding to Karen.

Karen stood, walked around her chair, put both hands on the chair back, and leaned forward while looking down at the others. She felt more confident from this position. "Each victim called home after arriving at the office. Mr. Gagnon spoke to his wife for about five or ten minutes. He gave no indication anything was wrong. In fact, Mrs. Gagnon said he was in a particularly good mood. Mrs. Armstrong talked only briefly to her husband, saying she had about an hour's work to do, then would come straight home. Mr. Armstrong said she sounded a little agitated, but that was normal for her lately. Mrs. Armstrong checked in with the guard when she first arrived and gave no indication of any problem."

Karen paused for a moment and stared at the two executives. She had their full attention. "The information gathered from the executives is useless for the most part. It looks like Pamela Robinson asked Mrs. Armstrong to return to the site and put together some information for a meeting the next day. She says it was a spur of the moment, unplanned request, and she had discussed it with you, Mr. Hazlitt, before asking. Per your direction, Mr. Hazlitt, no one would divulge the reason for the meeting, only that it was important to Purity and needed to be kept confidential. We were informed Purity laid off many employees, or in your terminology, downsized, earlier this year." She walked around the chair and directly faced Hazlitt. "Mr. Hazlitt, it is important to our investigation that you tell us the reason for the meeting."

Gary Hazlitt smiled briefly. "In a week or so, I'll be able to give you more information, but for now, no one outside of Purity must know. Isn't that right, Phil?"

"Right."

Jim jumped in, visibly angry, but his voice remained calm. "Look, this is a murder investigation. A week could cause the trail to run cold. We need to know why you and Ms. Robinson were in Garden City yesterday."

"Sorry," replied Hazlitt as he turned to Phil. "Please explain to the officers why we are prohibited from saying anything yet."

Phil knew he was being tested, and he was pissed. He believed no harm would come to the company or its employees if they assisted the police, but he needed to remain in Hazlitt's good graces. "I don't believe anything we discussed at the meeting had anything to do with the murders. And giving out that information could seriously jeopardize the company. As

Gary said, we will be better positioned to tell you in a week or so."

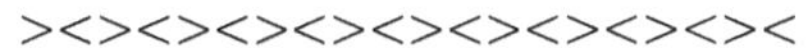

Karen was a little surprised by Phil's comments. After the interviews, her instincts had told her Phil was different from the others – less guarded – but now he seemed scared. "Well, at any rate," Karen continued, "We don't have a lot to go on, but we have come to some preliminary assumptions. The killer definitely knew what he was doing. He's most likely a professional. The killer was either in the building before the victims arrived or gained entry shortly after. In any case, he got past your security system, either through the security guard at the rear entrance or the card reader at the executive entrance." Karen believed that the killer had inside help or information but kept it to herself. "We believe Diane was the target. We don't know how the killer got in, how he knew Diane would be there, or why he did it.

"We need to understand any issues within the company, and we need a list of past or present employees you feel would be most likely to commit this crime. We also need access to your security system."

Gary thought for a few seconds. "I've thought a lot about what happened last night and about the company. Diane may have been a black woman, but I seriously doubt that was the issue. She was a good human being and treated everyone fairly. She was well-liked by all the employees at Purity. You need to understand we – this site, this company – are like a family. We take care of each other. I think you're barking up the wrong tree. This most definitely had to be a random act. No one associated with Purity would ever do such a thing." Gary placed Phil directly between a rock and a hard place. "Phil, how should we respond to their request for a list of suspects?"

As six eyes turned to Phil, he felt anger welling up in his gut. He knew that the correct answer was 'no problem, you'll have it in a couple of days,' but he also knew that it would cost him his job. The answer to Gary's question came hard. "We're not the police and shouldn't make any judgments about our employees. Therefore, we'll provide an alphabetical list of current employees and those who left within the past year. Any interview with a current employee will have to be attended by a corporate lawyer." Gary looked pleased with Phil.

Jim Hines knew that the company didn't have to give anything more than a list, and he knew that the people on the list weren't legally required to talk to him. But this would slow the investigation to a crawl. He appealed to Gary. "We need more. It'll take months to randomly interview people and to try and piece together the information. You know your employees, and you know who may have had issues with Mrs. Armstrong and Mr. Gagnon. Don't tie our hands."

"For now, I have to follow Phil's advice," Gary replied. "But I'll talk it over with our legal people and get back to you in a week or so. In the meantime, Phil will give you the list he described. Now, I have a million things to do." Gary rose, his hand extended to Jim.

After instructing Abby to simply print an alphabetical list of current and inactive employees for the police, Phil stopped in the men's room on the way back to his office. He looked in the mirror and was disappointed in the man who looked back.

The workplace had changed a lot in twenty years, and now he was conforming: something he believed he would never do.

Phil was seething. *That fucking son-of-a-bitch set me up. Now it looks like withholding the possible suspect list is my idea, as if I have something to hide. That son-of-a-bitch. Time for me to use my connections.* He called Greg Iverson the minute he got back to his office.

Marge, Greg's administrative assistant, answered promptly on the first ring. "Purity Pharmaceutical Company, Human Resources Division, Mr. Iverson's office." After a few pleasantries, Phil asked to speak to Greg. When Marge said he was in a meeting, Phil replied in a manner unusual for him: "Listen, Marge, you'd better get him on the phone right now. Nothing is more important than what I need to talk to him about." Startled, Marge put Phil on hold and rushed for the conference room.

Greg, not hiding his anger, spoke into the phone. "This had better be the goddamned most important thing in the world I have to deal with right now, and the only thing I can think of is that the murders have been solved, and you want me to be the first to know."

"The murders haven't been solved, but I needed to get your attention. It seems you've been avoiding me lately. I called to get some advice on how to handle Hazlitt. He just set me up with the detectives investigating the murders. First, he tells me to go along with him when he tells the police we're not going to help them identify any suspects or else I'll be fired.

Then he puts me in a position where I have to tell the police what we won't give them, and he says he'll think about it and that he has to seriously consider my input. I've been set up."

Greg was silent for a few moments before speaking. He and Phil had maintained a close working relationship for a long time. Greg considered how much he could tell Phil without causing himself significant problems. Phil had always honored confidences, but he also had an overdeveloped sense of right and wrong. Greg decided to proceed cautiously, knowing that Phil might overreact. "I'm going to tell you some things you shouldn't know, but I feel you have a right to know. I want you to listen and try not to interrupt." After a short pause, Greg began. "We are in the process of identifying which managers will lose their jobs in the next downsizing. It's being done at the top levels, and we are sworn to secrecy. In a recent meeting, Skip Benson tried to defend Sal Rosaro, who was under attack by the others. He brought up that Sal was only a year and a half from his fiftieth birthday, and if he lost his job now, he wouldn't see any pension money until he was sixty-five. He would also lose his medical insurance. What do you think happened?"

Phil knew both Sal and Skip well. Both had worked in the Human Resources function for years. Both were good men with strong beliefs regarding the ethical responsibilities of large corporations to their long-term employees. They understood that the longer an employee worked for a company, the more his financial future depended on continuing employment. The size of a pension and the associated benefits depended on the number of years of service and the employee's age when he left the company. The company had designed the formulas to reduce turnover and give employees a reason to stay. "I would hope after considering the value of Sal's experience, his accomplishments, his age, and his service, he was removed from the list."

"I'd like to tell you you're right, and you would've been a few years ago, but things have changed far more than you realize. Greg knew that Phil was out of touch with the new 'corporate reality,' a reality that Greg himself, could no longer accept. "After the meeting, I told Skip he would not be needed at the next meeting. Then I added his name to the layoff list right next to Sal's."

Phil's jaw was trembling. He wanted to reach through the phone and pull out his long-time friend and mentor's heart. Greg was normally compassionate in his dealings with people, but now he sounded like an executioner. "Either you're bullshitting me, or you've become someone I don't know anymore."

"I'm not bullshitting you, I'm telling you how fucked up things are… and there's much more, so sit back and try to listen. I'm leaving in March with a deal. I leave quietly in exchange for a lot of money in addition to my pension and benefits. I signed the agreement three weeks ago. Unlike Sal and Skip, I'm over fifty and will get a pension and health care. But I couldn't make it on that alone, so I negotiated a deal, and I'm getting over a million in stock options." Greg paused for a second, and Phil filled the void.

"Why the hell would Cohen agree to give you that much money to resign?" Phil's mind was working overtime. Greg seemed like a different person.

"I'll get to that in a minute. First, you need to understand what's happening in the Human Resource arena. In the old days, we worked from a set of principles: principles shared by senior management, principles that guided our actions and decisions. We created policy, solved problems, and worked with employees and management, always guided by those principles. We worked to balance the conflicting needs of employees, stockholders, and the government. And, even though we weren't unionized, the threat of unions heavily influenced our policies. Well, you know as well as I do: unions lost their power, and the government is less interested in enforcing employment laws." Greg knew that Phil was aware of the changes but wanted to give him an overview of how they affected the corporation and its employees. "As you're thinking about this, don't forget the impact of competition and diversity."

Phil, well aware of the impacts of both, had not considered the totality of the effect of these forces acting on corporations. Nor had he assessed their impact on him.

Greg continued. "CEOs no longer have to worry about anything other than stockholders. When the employees accepted downsizing without seeking help from a union or the government, they became like cattle being led to slaughter. They lost their power. As a result, our treatment of employees continues to worsen. It won't stop until employees take a stand and get the unions, or the government involved. This has also had major impacts on us, the Human Resource professionals. With employees accepting the abuses of management, the old role of Human Resources is no longer of value to the company. Why does Management need our help when deciding how to handle employees when it can pretty much do whatever it chooses? We've become dinosaurs." Greg stopped, giving Phil time to consider what he had just said.

Phil was quiet. He had not taken the time to reflect on how fast the corporate world was changing. He was dumbfounded.

"I have to get back to the meeting. Think about what I said, and for God's sake, don't tell a soul about Sal or Skip or especially my deal. I'll call you in about an hour or so." Greg hung up.

Phil told Mary Margret that he wanted no visitors or phone calls except from Greg Iverson. Then he began to think through what he had heard. His thoughts drifted back to the beginning of his work life.

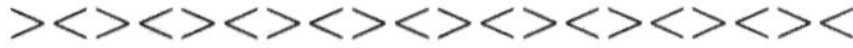

It was a bright June day as Phil and Rose drove south on the Pennsylvania Turnpike, headed to Delaware and a new life. Phil would start work in three days for the McKenzie Chemical Company in their newly formed Medical Diagnostics Division as an Electronic Technician. Phil and Rose looked forward to a great future; the world looked ripe for the picking.

Phil's first year on the job flew by. The pressure to produce and ship instruments was intense, but surprisingly the overall work environment was friendly. He returned home from work each night and told Rose about his day. Phil found it challenging to describe how he felt about the company to Rose. As he was 'the new kid,' his coworkers helped him willingly. They recognized that he had the education but not the hands-on experience to quickly identify and fix malfunctions. Phil attended meetings that reviewed project status and the financial state of the Medical Diagnostics business. He was amazed. He didn't feel like a low-level worker. He believed he was an essential part of the business.

As the years passed and the success of the new instrument out-performed even the most optimistic projections, Phil's delight with his job continued. Despite petty bickering, jealousy, and even some backstabbing, the employees pulled together. He matured quickly. The responsibilities of supporting a family and raising a daughter had changed him.

Phil was soon promoted to Production Supervisor and began his management career with the largest chemical company in the world.

Now, his job, career, and family were in jeopardy.

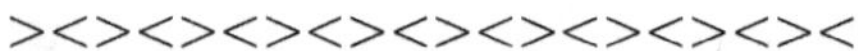

Greg called back as promised. "Have you thought about what I said? Do you have a better feel for reality?"

"I'm getting there, but I still don't understand what's going on with you. You're leaving before you qualify for a full pension. The company is giving you over a million dollars for leaving. I need a little more information before that makes sense."

"The way Sal and Skip are being treated is just one of many such situations. The pressure to produce and reduce staff simultaneously has turned Cohen's staff into a gang of thugs. They'll do or say anything to protect their people and put someone from another organization on the block. Staff groups like HR and Finance are considered dead weight, and the people in those groups are being demonized. I decided I can't be part of it any longer, and I can't change it, so I'm leaving. It's as simple as that."

"Okay, so you're leaving, but why should the company give you any money?"

"A couple of reasons. First, Cohen wants one of his 'yes' men in this job, and I still have enough support in McKenzie that he can't simply move me out. Second – and I'm sure you can relate to this – HR is involved in all things concerning employees: the good, the bad, and the ugly. Mostly, we're involved in management – employee conflicts, sexual harassment complaints, affairs, OSHA complaints, and so on. If you stop to think for a minute, you'll realize you have enough knowledge to cause many problems for many people. Well, I know a lot about Cohen and some others, and I made sure he knows I know."

"I don't think what I know is worth a million dollars, but good for you. I'd much rather you stay, but I'm happy for you if this is what you want."

"You haven't asked me about your situation. Are you afraid of what I might tell you?"

Phil was instantly uncomfortable. "I already have reason to be afraid, but I didn't think you'd tell me."

"Well, you're wrong. I've already told you enough to get me in trouble, so I may as well go all the way. Cohen wants you out, and as a result, his staff wants you out. You still have support in McKenzie, mainly in Roger Hanson, and you're safe for now. But Cohen just needs one screw-up on your part to chisel away at that support. And believe me: Hazlitt is looking for you to screw up. So you're right, you're being set up. You're not on the list now, but it's only a matter of time."

Phil was stunned but not surprised. In fact, for some strange reason, he felt liberated. "So, how much can I get for what I know?"

"Start putting it on paper. We'll talk. Call me in a couple of days. I won't avoid you."

"I've been thinking about the good old days, when we all could be taken at our word and didn't spend our time and energy covering our asses or setting up co-workers."

"It definitely was better, but I'm sure it wasn't as good as you remember." Greg hung up before Phil could respond.

Phil leaned back. His initial feeling of freedom had already disappeared. He was in no position to leave the company after only 22 years. *Tony is still in college*, he considered. *I wouldn't see any of my pension until I'm 65, and I borrowed against my 401K to pay for Tony's tuition. I have a large mortgage, and the housing market is soft. Shit, I need to protect my ass.*

Phil picked up the phone and called Abby. "With Steve, so to speak, 'gone,' I've been trying to decide if I still need to mine information from the batch records or just tell Hazlitt what we were told about the issues in Production."

"If you tell anyone in Production Management what you heard, you'll have to tell them who told you. Just because Steve's not around doesn't mean Frank and Gino won't face reprisals. And you – we – will lose the confidence the employees have in us. I think you have to find it."

"I thought that would be your answer. I'll look at the Batch Records but remember, I'll need your help. Catch you later." Phil hung up.

Phil called Lorraine next. "Hey, how are you doing today?"

"Barely passable and a little busy right now. I assume you want to get together and talk. How about in an hour?"

"Sounds good. I'll come over to your office." Phil thought Lorraine sounded down but attributed it to the past day's events.

Phil looked at the pile of paper on his desk and decided to spend some time getting caught up. He turned to his computer and started with his e-mail.

Lorraine's appearance shocked Phil. She seemed depressed. Phil spoke gently. "Something happen today?"

Lorraine looked up, her eyes red, and said, "I found out my mother is dying. She took a turn for the worse, and I need to be with her. I'm leaving as soon as I get things in order, and you're the last to-do on my list for today."

"I'm sorry. If I can do anything, let me know. Are you sure you want to take the time to teach me how to review Batch Records or do you want Abby to train me?

"Yes, I'm sure, but I'm only going to give you an overview. Abby knows the details, and I trust her. She can teach you the specifics of what to look for, but you're my official stand in.

"Look, I know you also want to talk about last night, but I can't. I hope you understand. Are you ready?"

"Fire away."

"Our job, Quality's job, is to make sure all the important steps and in-process tests described in the Standard Operating Procedures are followed and documented properly. The Batch Record is the record of everything that happens – even if it's not in the SOP – while a production lot of a drug – a batch – is in process. While I'm with my mother and the FDA, you will be doing what I normally do. You'll be the final review to ensure everything was done and documented properly. In a way, it's easy because the people in Quality have looked at the Batch Record closely and usually have solved every problem before you see it. But you have to be careful because everyone involved is human, and humans make mistakes. When you sign off on a batch, the product will be shipped. If there are any problems in the marketplace, everyone, including the FDA, will run straight to the Batch Record. So treat the job with more than your normal amount of attention to detail."

"Thanks for the vote of confidence. Now get out of here and go to your mother. And, hey, let me know what's happening. I might be able to help."

"Good luck, I'll call you. And thanks."

Phil proceeded straight to Abby's office. "Do you have the time to educate me on reviewing Batch Records? Lorraine obviously trusts you."

"I'm ready, so let's do it now. Lorraine talked to me earlier. It's a shame about her mother."

"Yeah, she seems to be taking it pretty hard. By the way, why don't you review the Batch Records instead of me? It'll save the training time."

"I'd probably do a better job, but you know our policy. The final review of the Batch Record and the sign off to release the product for shipping must be done at the director level. Besides, it makes the FDA happy to see a high-level signature. Normally the final review of a Batch Record is a pretty straightforward process, just making sure the i's are dotted and the t's crossed. But since we've been told about the crap going on in Production, we'll look hard at each folder. Production needs accomplices in Quality to cover their trail."

"Lorraine really trusts her people," Phil said. "She believes them when they say the procedures were followed. I don't understand why in the world the people in Quality would take a chance and violate that."

"As far as most people here are concerned, Lorraine is an outsider, as are you, and she's only at Garden City to get her ticket punched. The real power at Garden City resides in the hands of the management that has been here a long time. It doesn't matter that Lorraine is the Director of Quality. The power is in the hands of her middle management because they'll still be here long after she gets promoted."

"Do you think we should tell her about the possible problems in Production?"

"Not yet. We need to honor Frank and Gino's trust in us. Besides, you'll be doing Batch Records for now, and I'll be looking over your shoulder so nothing will slip by. We may even solve the problem before the FDA meeting is done."

"Okay, let's get moving."

"All right. I promised Lorraine I wouldn't turn you loose on a Batch Folder until I was satisfied you knew what to look for. I know you have an overall knowledge of how production works, but bear with me while I fill you in on the details."

Abby took a minute to gather her thoughts. "When a new batch of a drug starts production, Quality gets the latest version of the SOP, puts it in a folder, and delivers it to the Granulation Area. As you know, the SOP details all the steps required to produce a specific drug, equipment used, operator training required, equipment cleaning process, and test specs. When a step is completed, the operator signs and dates the SOP. The results of any tests are entered into the Batch Record, signed, and dated. Preparing the granulation is like mixing the dry ingredients needed to bake a cake. First, the raw materials are prepared, and then they're combined and mixed according to the SOP. The active ingredient, fillers, and binders are required to make a tablet. The binder, usually a wax, holds the granulation together after being compressed into a tablet. Depending on the drug being produced, the active ingredient may need to be run through a sieve to attain the right particle size. It may have to be milled or freeze-dried. Next, the raw materials are poured into a V-blender in the proper ratios. After blending and mixing, the granulation is poured into drums and delivered to the Compression Area."

"I follow you so far, but what do I look for to prove what Frank and Gino told us?"

"Hold your horses. I'll get to it. For now, let me explain what happens in the Compression Area. The basic process of compressing granulation into tablets is easy. An operator has to set up the tablet press, pour the granulation into the hopper, turn on the press and watch the tablets stream into a drum. As the tablets come off the press, the operator randomly tests them for dissolution and hardness. Two things are critical when setting up a tablet press: first is making sure it's properly cleaned. There must be no carry-over from the previous drug run on the press. And second is making sure the correct tooling is installed. If you remember, that's what got those two employees fired. Once the granulation is compressed into tablets, the number of tablets produced must correlate to the expected yield. Then the area Quality rep pulls a random sample and sends it to Quality's chemistry lab for final testing. The drums of tablets are labeled and placed in the Hold Area until the chemistry tests are completed."

She continued, "Packaging is where tablets, bottles, caps, labels, pledgets, inserts, and shipping containers come together to make the finished product."

"Hold on," Phil interrupted, "what the hell is a pledget?"

Abby smiled and replied, "So you've been in the Pharmaceutical Business for a year now, and you don't know what a pledget is. Well, let me educate you. It's the soft fiber wad we put in the bottle to prevent the tablets from breaking during shipping."

"I'll think of you every time I open a bottle of Advil."

Laughing, Abby got back to the task at hand. "The best way to cover the Packaging operation is to see it. I have set up a tour for us tomorrow morning. The critical things in Packaging are that the labels and the inserts are correct, and the right number of tablets is in each bottle. Now I'm ready to talk about how to look for the problems Frank and Gino laid out for us."

"Yeah, but I still think you should do the work, and I'll just sign."

"Exactly what Lorraine was afraid of. Just relax. You won't have to work too hard."

"Good!"

"Now, may I continue?" Phil grinned and nodded. "The Batch Records will have been through so many reviews by the time they get to you, they'll seem perfect. You'll find a signature everywhere one is required. All the test results will be properly documented. You may find a minor problem, but it'll be easy to correct. Remember, your job is to make sure the record is complete. You're the final review, and that's all anyone will think you're doing."

Abby continued, "After reviewing the folder for completeness, start looking for signs that steps may have been skipped or procedures were not followed exactly. First, look for inconsistencies in an individual operator's signature. His name may have been signed by his supervisor or the area inspector."

"Hold on. You're saying a Quality Control Inspector would sign for an operator?"

"Sure, since they work together and know each other. If a signature is missing, the area inspector usually calls the operator and asks if the step was done correctly. The operator says yes, and the inspector signs the procedure. It's not a guarantee the step wasn't done, but it's possible. Next, look at the time it was signed and see if it makes sense. Finally, look at the test results. Do they vary within the allowed tolerance, or are the results mostly the same? For example, the in-process hardness test done in the Compression Area is generally viewed as unimportant. If an operator doesn't get around to running the tests, he'll just fill in the blanks, and most of the time, he'll repeat the same number.

"Seems pretty easy, but it doesn't seem like I'll come up with anything conclusive. Just suspicions."

"You're right. The next step determines if we can prove what Gino and Frank told us. And you'll be happy to know I'll be helping you with this part. We know what equipment is needed when a drug is in Production. We know how long it takes to complete a certain step and what steps must be observed by a supervisor. We also know what critical steps can only be done by an operator specifically trained to perform that step. We have access to the attendance records of all the operators and supervisors. All we have to do is lay it all out, dates and times. Assuming Frank and Gino were straight with us, we should find plenty of inconsistencies: examples of production shortcuts, steps done by untrained operators, and document falsifications. The proverbial smoking gun."

"I've had enough for today. I'm ready to start tomorrow, and I'm glad you're going to help me. I'm going back to my office to clean up a few things, then I'm out of here."

Phil was in the middle of moving some paperwork to his outbox when Gary Hazlitt walked in and sat down. "We'll have our first planning meeting on the upcoming downsizing next Monday night at six. In addition to Pamela Robinson, Kathleen Connolly will attend the meeting. I scheduled to accommodate Lorraine and hope she'll make it. We'll need the complete backgrounds on some employees. Here's the list. I want performance rating, summaries of the performance reviews, education, the employee's last five jobs, family status, and special skills, if any. I want it in my hands Thursday afternoon."

"Is this what Diane was doing last night?"

"Yes, but she was only doing it for Gagnon, Waters, Stanley, and you. You're doing it for the rest of the management team. Remember, on my desk Thursday afternoon." Hazlitt rose, turned, and walked out of Phil's office.

Phil put the list aside. Tomorrow was soon enough to start. He wrapped up the last of the paperwork and checked his e-mail. After replying to several e-mails, Phil headed home to Oyster Bay.

That night, as Phil lay in bed next to a sleeping Rose, he thought about the day's events. He was in trouble. Cohen wanted him out, Greg Iverson was leaving, and his support in McKenzie was one screw-up away from becoming extinct. Phil had no idea how to handle the situation, so he rolled over and drifted off. He'd find an answer. He always did.

Wednesday 12/3

As she and Phil concluded their tour of the Packaging Area, Abby said, "Well, do you have a better feel for Packaging and some of the complexities involved in getting pharmaceuticals to market? Remember, it's critical that only the correct tablet gets into the bottle and that the label and insert are right."

"I know a lot more now than I did this morning. I think I'm ready to start reviewing the Batch Records."

Abby stopped in front of the stairs, "I need to stop by and see the Compression Supervisor. I'll catch you later."

As Phil walked back to his office, he visualized the Packaging Operation Abby had just shown him. Phil remembered videos he had watched on the TV of tablets dropping into plastic bottles and bottles moving between two rails. He concluded that the videos presented an accurate picture of a packaging line.

The machinery and conveyor system of the packaging lines flowed through three rooms. In the first room, bottles and caps were loaded into large hoppers that fed them, properly oriented, onto separate conveyor systems. The bottles, open-end up, lined up in a long queue that ran into the next room. The caps did the same.

The second room, a cleanroom, was the only room where the tablets would be exposed to the environment. A cleanroom was simply a confined area of positive pressure to prevent dirty outside air from entering the room. The positive pressure was created by continuously pumping air into the room, while HEPA filters in the incoming airflow kept it clean.

The drums of tablets received from the Compression Area were transferred to hoppers in the cleanroom. From the hoppers, the tablets flowed to fill tubes. In this case, the machinery filled each of ten fill tubes with one hundred tablets. Ten bottles were indexed under the fill tubes, and the tablets were dropped into the bottles. The filled bottles moved from under the fill-tubes to the next stage where the pledget was inserted, then moved to the capper. Ten more bottles moved under the fill tubes, and the filling process was repeated. After the bottles were capped, they continued traveling along the conveyor to the automatic labeler. After the labeling, each label was optically verified. The bottles, along with an insert sheet, were boxed, then placed, by Production operators, into shipping cartons. They would sit until Phil reviewed the Batch Record and authorized their release for shipment.

Phil stopped at Mary Margaret's desk before going on to his office. "Anything exciting happening?"

"No. Everyone's pretty upset and pretty much just going through the motions. They're barely talking to each other. I still can't believe it happened. Do you know what the funeral arrangements are?"

"Both viewings are Thursday. Fortunately, Gagnon's is in Hicksville, and Armstrong's is in Westbury. So anyone who wants to go to both will have time. The funerals are Friday: Gagnon's at nine in the morning and Armstrong's at two-thirty. Are you going?"

"Just to the viewings. I can't deal with funerals."

"I know what you mean. I'll be working on a project in my office, so only interrupt me if it's important. And tell Abby I'd like to see her around four to talk about Batch Records."

Phil was working on the information for the Monday meeting when Mary Margaret opened his office door. "Lieutenant Hines is on the line. He said it was important."

Phil nodded and picked up the phone. "Lieutenant Hines, what can I do for you?"

"I'd like to talk to you, and it might take some time, so maybe we can do it over dinner. I've always wanted to eat at that Sicilian Restaurant in Oyster Bay: you know, the one that serves all that exotic seafood and the black pasta. They make the black pasta with squid ink, I think."

"You mean Piccolo Sicilia. And you're right, that's how they make it."

"That's the one."

"What do you want to talk about?"

"Just some things about the case, strictly confidential. I want your take on some things, and I want to do it face to face. Just between you and me."

Phil was quiet for a couple of seconds. "What time?"

"Seven, and I'll even pick up the check."

"See you then," Phil said, wondering if he was a suspect.

Phil spent the rest of the morning and part of the afternoon working on the personnel information Hazlitt had requested. He would review it again tomorrow before giving it to Hazlitt. The phone call from Hines was in the back of Phil's mind the entire time. He was getting ready to look at the first Batch Record when the phone rang. He answered, "Messina."

"Phil..." Lorraine's voice was immediately recognizable, despite the crying and sniffling. "My mother has just passed away. I was with her, and we talked. We talked all day. Phil, she's gone, she's really gone. She had such a tough life, and just when it should be getting easier and she should be enjoying life, she dies. She never had a chance to enjoy life. She did everything for my brother and me, and what did we do for her? Nothing!"

"I'm really sorry. I know how much you loved your mother, and I'm sure she was proud of you. You were the joy in her life. Is there anything I can do to help?"

"Just be there for me. You're the only person in the world I can really talk to now. So please be there for me."

"I'm just a phone call away."

"Thanks. I know I can count on you. I have to go now. My brother needs me. Phil … Thanks again." She hung up.

Phil leaned back and thought about Lorraine. She was close to her mother and would be mourning for a while. The FDA audit started the following Monday, and the meetings dealing with the upcoming downsizing would start that evening. Phil vowed to help her any way he could, then turned his attention to the first Batch Record.

"Hello."

"How are you doing on this fine day?" Echo said with a little sarcasm.

"Are you crazy? You know better than to call me here."

"Relax, I'm calling from a payphone up in Connecticut. I called the main number and then a couple of extensions before dialing yours, so it's not traceable. No need to worry. Everything is under control."

"Nothing went wrong Monday night, did it?"

"Smooth as silk. Everything worked out. Even Steve being with her didn't cause a ripple. In fact, it was a bonus: not just killing him, but hearing Diane yell for him just before I pulled the trigger."

"I don't want to know the details. I just want to know that everything is handled. I can't get caught. I can't go to jail."

"Stop worrying. You just take care of your part, getting me access and information. I'll do my part to perfection. You can rest assured of that. I'll leave no evidence behind, and I'll have an alibi just in case the cops somehow stumble onto me. None of us will get caught. The cops aren't smart enough to figure out we're the ones behind this. Now let's talk about the future. I've decided the bitch is next. I have the perfect alibi arranged for Monday night. All I'll need from you is information."

"Why wait until Monday night? Why not take out the other one sooner?"

"Because I don't have the plan for him completely worked out yet. And since you're so afraid of jail, I have to be very careful. You don't want to get caught, do you?"

"Knock off the sarcasm. What do you need?"

"I need her room number, and I need her out of her room for at least an hour. I'll fill you in on the rest later."

"I'll see what I can do. Are you going to the funerals?"

"Why should I attend the funerals of that black bitch and her butt-licking white boy?"

"Because people talk."

"You attend. I'll be right here in Cargill Falls, Connecticut, looking for antiques in the many fine shops in town. I have to make a living."

"Have it your way. But let's get something straight: you may enjoy what we're doing, but I don't. This is something that has to be done, not something I want to do."

"Bullshit, you just want to get even with Cohen. So stop the mightier-than-thou crap. I'm not just some hired gun. I know you, and I know what motivates you. Revenge and power."

"Where can I reach you?"

"I'll call you."

The line went dead.

Phil carefully reviewed every page, checking each step to ensure that it was signed. He looked over signatures for consistency and analyzed data sheets for any indications that test results were forged. He repeated the process three times, taking detailed notes as he went.

When Abby arrived for their four o'clock meeting, she immediately said, "My god! You're actually working! I'm surprised your forehead isn't covered with sweat. God, I wish I had a camera." Abby paused for a moment, put her hand on her chest, and then said, "Okay, I'm over the shock. Let's get down to business. Did you find anything?"

"You'll never make it as a comedian, so you'd better keep your day job. Oh, I just realized that keeping your day job depends on me. Continue the comedy routine, and you'll be on the unemployment line soon." Phil tried but failed to look severe and started laughing. "Pull a chair around. I have a lot to show you."

Phil began when Abby was seated. "First, I want you to look at signatures I think might be forged."

After Phil showed her the questionable signatures and the suspicious test results, Abby said, "I'd say we have good reason to look deeper. What do you think?"

"No question. It's going to get complicated when we try to analyze equipment usage. We have to track usage of the sieves, the mills, the wet granulation oven, the fluid bed dryer, and the 30ft and 40ft V-blenders. That's not to mention factoring in clean-up time, and that's in the tower alone. In Compression, we need to look at four different tablet presses and the coater. Without even considering Packaging, we're facing a major task. I'll design a spreadsheet that will help us get the entire picture of the production operation."

"You've really come a long way with computers. You turned one on the first time about two years ago, right?"

"You have a good memory. I have time tomorrow morning to get started. In the meantime, I think it's all right to release these batches. Do you agree?"

"Based on the final test results and their overall Batch Record, I'd release Thinadin and Relieve. I would hold Trexaline based on the number of potential issues in the Batch Record. I'll do a little investigating for you."

"Thanks. I gotta head out. I have something to do tonight. See you tomorrow."

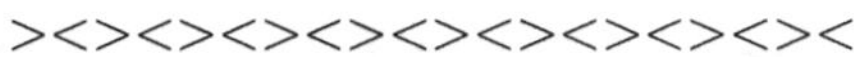

Phil walked the three-tenths of a mile to Piccolo Sicilia. The Messina home was outside Oyster Bay's business district, right across from the Public Library. The business district served the surrounding upscale towns of Laurel Hollow, Muttontown, Center Island, and Upper Brookville, which accounted for the abundance of high-quality restaurants, high-end retail shops, and watering holes.

The chilly night air stimulated Phil's senses. He was on the edge of full alert. He entered the lobby and was greeted by the pungent smell of spices and cooking seafood. He hung his coat, spied Lieutenant Hines, walked over to the table, and sat down.

"Mr. Messina, I'm glad you came. I'm looking forward to a great meal and interesting conversation."

"Phil. We've been through this before. Please just call me Phil."

"Okay, it's Phil, if you call me Jim."

The waiter appeared and took drink orders. Phil ordered Jameson on the rocks, and Jim ordered a 'Godfather,' which was mostly scotch with a bit of amaretto.

"How do you like living in Oyster Bay?"

"I've only lived here about a year now, and I truly like it. I feel so at ease here that I seldom lock my doors when I go out. It's great living so close to downtown. The taxes, however, are a whole other story. Where do you live?"

"Seaford, on the other end of the Seaford-Oyster Bay Expressway. It's about a 20-minute drive here. I work out of the Merrick precinct, so I'm close." Jim stared at Phil, then said, "Would you like me to tell you why I wanted to meet?"

Phil nodded in the affirmative.

Their drinks came, and each took a swallow, then Lieutenant Hines put his elbows on the table and leaned forward. "We started looking into the backgrounds of Purity's employees, beginning with the execs at last Monday's dinner meeting and some of the execs from Headquarters. You're a pretty dull group overall, but we found juvenile records on two of you, much to our surprise. I have a close friend in the department in one of the jurisdictions, so I could get a copy of the file and talk to some retired officers who worked with that juvenile. The other was from Scranton, Pennsylvania, and I don't have any contacts in that department, so I came up empty."

Lieutenant Hines took another swallow. "Since I couldn't get your juvenile record, I wondered if you might fill me in on your troubles with the law?"

Phil had believed that his juvenile record was sealed, and that no one, not even the police, could find out he even had one. Now, twenty-five years later, he sat across from a detective investigating a murder, and his juvenile record was the topic of discussion. "My juvenile run-ins with the law are sealed, and I sure didn't plan on discussing it tonight."

"Come on now, you know I'm investigating a double murder, and I need information. I have no physical evidence, nor do I have any real leads. The alphabetical list you gave me is useless. Now you're telling me you didn't plan on discussing it tonight."

"Am I a suspect?"

"Absolutely, and you will be until you're either cleared or convicted. I don't think you did it, but I can't be sure. I'd like to understand your run-ins with the law, and since I can't get the info any other way, I thought I'd ask you straight out."

They sat and stared at each other in silence, neither wanting to be the first one to break down. The waiter interrupted the contest to take their orders. Jim ordered calamari for an appetizer, then ordered Vitello Melanzana: fried veal topped with prosciutto, eggplant, provolone cheese, and a marinara sauce. Phil also ordered the calamari, but took involtini di Pesce Spada – a grilled, breaded swordfish stuffed with shrimp, fresh tomatoes, breadcrumbs, and Parmesan cheese – for dinner.

The quiet stares resumed until Phil broke the silence: "If I tell you about my run-ins with the police, what's in it for me?"

"Nothing, except my gratitude and the knowledge that you cooperated with a police investigation into two brutal murders."

"Okay. I'll tell you, but I need to tell it my way. That way you'll understand my situation a little better before you make any value judgments."

"Sure."

"I won't bore you with all the details, but I need to give you a few to help paint a picture. My parents are both first-generation Americans, and both were raised in poverty." Phil took another swallow of Jameson. "Both my parents worked for minimum wage, and as a family, we had food on the table, some ratty clothes, and little else."

Phil continued, "From age fourteen, I hung out with the neighborhood guys most nights. It was during those nights that my problems with the police occurred."

He looked Jim, who responded with a nod, in the eyes. "My first encounter with the police happened when I was fourteen. One night I was with some of the guys having fun doing a little vandalizing: things like tipping garbage cans, pissing on shrubs, and the old 'place a burning bag of dog shit on the porch and ring the doorbell' trick. We caused quite a bit of havoc before the police caught two of us. We'd caused enough damage to compel the police to bring us in and make an example of us. They wanted us to rat on the guys that got away, but we didn't."

The appetizers were served, and Jim and Phil focused on the calamari. The two agreed that it was excellent. Phil wolfed down about half of his plate before continuing.

"My father kicked my ass when I got home and promised that he would kill me if I did anything like that again. I stayed out of trouble with the police for about three years."

Jim interrupted. "I assume you did some things and weren't caught."

"If I did, they won't be discussed tonight. My next encounter with the police happened when I was seventeen. It was a stupid stunt, and it was serious enough that if I was eighteen, I would have been in deep shit. It was about two in the morning, and three of us were walking home from a night of drinking and shooting pool when we decided it would be better to ride than walk. We tried hitchhiking, and a drunk picked us up within a few minutes. He swerved all over the road, and we thought he'd get us all killed. My buddy Vito, who was in the front seat, slammed on the brakes and guided the car to the curb. We should have walked the rest of the way home, but instead, we pushed the drunk guy out of the car and drove it to our neighborhood. Before we got there, we were pulled over by a cop and were all arrested for grand theft auto and underage drinking. As I said, it was a stupid thing to do, but we got caught and paid the consequences. Fortunately, we were all under eighteen and the consequences were minimal. That's what's in my sealed record."

Jim knew that Phil had told him the truth. The sergeant he had reached in the Scranton Police Department had faxed him Phil's file. Sealed records or not, a murder investigation engenders cooperation. One of the comments in the file had indicated that Phil was a good kid with some bad friends. "After a start like that," Jim asked, "how did you wind up a director in a large company?"

Both were silent while the waiter cleared the table and served the salads. Phil picked up his fork and asked, "Are you enjoying the food so far?"

"It's excellent. I'm looking forward to the main course. I'll bet you get this kind of cooking all the time."

"A little jealous, are you? I usually have food just as good, if not better — but a little different. My mother's parents came from a small town in central Italy, and since she did all the cooking when I was a kid, she made foods from that region."

"You're lucky. As you can tell from looking at me, I enjoy food." Jim patted his stomach.

"That makes two of us. Let me answer your question before I forget. I had no intention of going to college when I was in high school. After graduation, I landed a job in the cutting room of a clothes factory. There were hundreds around Scranton supplying the garment centers in New York. One hot, humid Friday, I looked at my paycheck and decided I needed to do something different. I applied and was admitted to a two-year technical program at Penn State's Scranton campus. I did well, graduated, and was hired into McKenzie's Medical Diagnostics Division Production Department. The business grew, and I grew with it."

"I think you're being modest. You're in a big job with lots of responsibility. Not bad for a poor street kid from Scranton."

The waiter removed the salad plates and promptly served the main course. The presentation piqued both men's appetites, and their dishes were almost clean before either man remembered the other was nearby.

While enjoying the main course, Jim decided that Phil was the person he wanted on the inside. Now, all he had to do was get Phil to agree. "I need to talk to you about one more thing. To solve this case, I need some help. When interviewing suspects, I have to understand your company and its issues. I can't just be aware of them. I need to know what downsizing is, exactly, and how it affects the employees and their families. Is race an issue in the company, in the murders? Is something else involved? And the big one: who should I look at first? Looking at people in alphabetical order will take too much time and waste too many resources. In short, I want you to teach me about Purity Pharmaceuticals and be my eyes and ears inside the company. I want you to work with me. I want you to help me understand the issues that may have resulted in two people being killed, and I want you to help me find out who killed those two people."

"Do you realize what you're asking? If I help you, I could lose my job. And you just said it's a good job."

"You and I will be the only ones who know. It'll be absolutely confidential."

"Come on, that's not possible. I don't know most downsized employees well enough to give you a suspect list. I'll need to work with Abby. That makes three. And what about your partner? She'll make four, which is more than enough for a leak or a slip. One slip and I'm unemployed."

Hines paused. "You're right. I'll have to let my partner know, and I trust her. Do you trust Abby?"

"Yeah, she's as trustworthy as a human being could be." Phil looked off into space. "I'm both worried and intrigued by your offer. I'll think about it." He pushed the remains of his food around the plate for a while, then asked, "You seemed uncomfortable when the subject of your partner surfaced. Do you have a problem with her?"

Jim decided to play it straight. Phil had been honest with him. "To tell you the truth, I'd prefer working with someone else. Someone I understand and can better relate to, an older guy, someone with the same experience as me."

"Why don't you just ask for a new partner? Handling a case with this much notoriety should give you some leverage."

"I already asked, and my captain gave me an emphatic NO! Told me if I asked again, I'm the one that would be reassigned."

Phil suspected that Hines was holding back but let it drop. "If I decide to work with you, I want to meet in Oyster Bay. I think the chances of us being seen together are less if we meet here. And I expect you to buy dinner."

"You're being a little paranoid, but that sounds fine."

They passed on dessert, and Jim asked for the check. As they were leaving, Jim said, "Don't take too long deciding. I need help, and I need it fast."

Thursday 12/4

Abby stopped by Phil's office to drag him away from his computer and get him to lunch. "I can't believe you aren't done yet. You're only creating a simple spreadsheet?"

Phil oriented the monitor toward Abby. "Sit down for a minute. I want to show you what I've been working on all morning. I started out designing a spreadsheet to handle the data we'll be recording from the Batch Records but quickly realized we wouldn't get the reports we needed to thoroughly analyze the data. Instead, I started designing a relational database. So far, I've completed the tables and most of the forms. Let me show you."

"Amazing. I didn't know you could design a custom database."

"Yeah, this stuff comes pretty easy to me. Now let me puff up my chest and show you what a genius I am. Are you ready?" Abby nodded. "First, I've designed several tables." Phil walked Abby through the design of the database and solicited her input. After they both agreed that they would get the information they needed, Phil asked, "Impressed?"

"Very. I'm impressed: first, that you know how to design a database, and second, that you worked all morning without talking to anyone."

Phil smirked. "Before we head to lunch, I have a couple things on my mind. One has to do with my future at Purity. It seems you were right. Cohen isn't a fan of mine, so I have to watch my step."

"I'm glad you finally appreciate your position. Now you'll be able to make better decisions. Maybe you'll watch your mouth and keep out of trouble."

"Maybe. Let's go to lunch."

It was five-thirty before Phil decided to call it a day. As he cleaned off his desk, the phone rang. He answered as he always did at work. "Messina."

"Phil, it's Lorraine. I wanted to let you know my mother's viewing is this Saturday at noon. The burial will follow immediately, but it's for family only. Can you make the viewing?" Her voice was weak, and it was apparent that she had recently been crying.

"Sure. Where is it?"

"It's in my old neighborhood, East New York. The funeral home is next door to my church. You remember where I took you and Rose to see the eighth-grade graduation?"

"Right off Linden Street."

"Right."

"I'll see you Saturday." Phil placed the handset in the cradle and finished cleaning off his desk.

Friday 12/5

As Phil signed the guest book, he scanned the inside of the funeral home. Steve Gagnon's body lay in a bronze casket surrounded by numerous sprays and bouquets of flowers. His wife and children stood in a line perpendicular to the casket, greeting mourners. Steve Gagnon's wife and children and his parents and sister were in attendance, but few neighbors or friends had come. Gagnon, as with most executives on the rise, had moved every few years. He had also worked over sixty hours a week, which was not a good formula for making friends or meeting neighbors.

Phil waited in the short line, greeted Gagnon's family, and conveyed his condolences, after which he wandered to a backroom. He chatted with several of the Purity people in the room, all the while hoping that he would be able to make a quick exit. Phil had just excused himself and made his way to the door when two men in a small alcove caught his attention. Bob Cohen and Paul Stanley were involved in an animated discussion. To Phil's surprise, Stanley looked as if he was the aggressor. Stanley was obviously upset, his face reddening, the level of his voice increasing. He was leaning into Cohen. Cohen was trying, with little success, to calm Stanley. As Stanley's voice rose, Phil was able to pick up a few words. Suddenly, Cohen grabbed Stanley by his shoulders and held him at arm's length. Cohen said a few sharp words and walked away. Phil heard a few more of Stanley's words before Cohen ended the conversation. They talked about the FDA and "relieve" in the context of the upcoming audit, then something about 'time.'

Bob Cohen spotted Phil, walked directly over to him, and said, "Phil, my man, I haven't seen much of you in the last six months, and this is a lousy reason for us to get together. We've lost two good people – both murdered – and Purity will suffer their loss. Have the police found anything?"

"Not that I know of. It's only been a couple of days. Gagnon's family looks like they're coming apart at the seams," Phil said, trying to change the subject.

"I think it's a racial thing," Cohen said, ignoring Phil's reference to the Gagnon family. "Maybe New Yorkers aren't ready to work for a black woman or see a black woman in a position of authority. I feel it's all my fault. I shouldn't have promoted her. I just try to do the right thing; that's all I ever care about, doing the right thing." Cohen shook his head. "By the way, did you notice how hard Stanley's taking it? Keep an eye on him. I think he may be having a breakdown."

"Okay."

"And Phil, I hope you listened closely to Hazlitt. He has your best interests at heart, and so do I. So stay in line. Be a team player." Cohen turned and walked away.

Phil stared at Cohen's back for a couple of seconds, then made his way to his car. During the twenty-minute drive to Westbury for Diane's funeral, his thoughts focused on the little encounter between Cohen and Stanley. He had known Paul Stanley for a little over a year and had never seen him angry or contentious. Paul rarely raised his voice or challenged anyone, especially someone in a higher-level position. Paul Stanley standing toe-to-toe with the CEO was entirely out of character.

Again, as he signed the guest book, Phil took stock of the room. Most of the mourners worked for Purity Pharmaceuticals. Phil made his way through the line, paid his respects to the family, and headed for the back room. He chatted with some of the employees while planning a quick escape. As Phil was slinking toward the door, he felt a tap on his shoulder and turned to take in all five-foot-one inches of Melissa Vega looking up at him. Phil had met Melissa Vega on his first day at Garden City. In fact, she had presented him with his first problem. Melissa had just returned to work after having a baby. She had desperately wanted her work hours changed from full-time to working mornings from seven to eleven. Her husband's job had required him to be at work at three in the afternoon, and since he worked in the city, he needed to leave their Long Island apartment around one.

Melissa had worked for the Compression Area supervisor, who had claimed that he needed a full-time secretary because of the significant workload. Melissa, however, had believed that she could complete all of her duties in four hours. Phil had worked with the supervisor and with Steve Gagnon to resolve the problem. Gagnon would not cooperate, so Phil found Melissa a part-time job in the Quality organization and then forced the move. Melissa was eternally grateful, and Steve Gagnon was eternally angry.

"Hi, I'm so upset about this. I cry all the time. I can't even look at the casket. I feel so bad for Diane's husband and kids. And to think she and Steve were killed in our building where they should've been safe." Melissa choked the words out through tears and put her head down, sobbing. Her mascara was a muddy smear under her eyelids.

Phil put his arms around her and held her gently, then said, "I'm with you. I've worked over twenty years and never would've believed something like this could ever happen." Phil bent his knees to get to eye level and wiped a tear from her cheek. "How's your little one?"

Melissa smiled, brightening slightly. "Oh, he's great, and he's walking now. You know, I still appreciate all you did for me."

"Are things still going well at work?"

"Yes, it couldn't be better. Lorraine is a good person and makes sure I'm being treated right. Hector is doing well in his job too. He's up for a promotion, and if he gets it, I may be able to stay home full-time. You know, if there's ever anything I could do for you, all you have to do is ask. I owe you."

"You don't owe me a thing. I was just doing my job, but if I need a favor, I'll be sure to ask." Phil looked at his watch, "Can I walk you to your car?" She humbly declined, so he found his way out alone.

Phil navigated through the relatively light traffic on the Northern State Parkway, his mind still wandering in the funeral homes. *Melissa knows most of the employees at Purity. Maybe she'll tell me which employees were angry enough to kill someone, and then I won't have to get Abby involved. I might just call Hines tomorrow. God damned Stanley standing up to Cohen, I can't believe it.* By the time Phil pulled into his driveway, his desire to help Lieutenant Hines was fading.

"Did you enjoy the funerals?" Echo chided.

"Oh yeah, they were great fun." Replied Echo's co-conspirator.

"Good. You'll have more to attend soon."

"Where are you?"

"Still in Northeast Connecticut. You should spend a couple of days up here to unwind. It's pretty nice, with more trees than people. It's like going back in time."

"That's nice. Are you ready for Monday?"

"Everything is planned out. Did you take care of your end?"

"She'll be at a meeting on Monday night from six until nine. That should give you plenty of time."

"That it will. I know you can't give me the room number yet, so here's the number of a payphone." He repeated the number twice. "Call me at exactly six-fifteen."

"Have the cops talked to you?"

"Hell no. Just make sure you do your job. Now get off my back."

The line went dead.

Echo walked into a large antiques store to look for some small pieces to buy. The thirty-thousand square foot shop was crammed with items from the seventeen-hundreds to the nineteen-fifties. You could shop for days and still not see everything. According to a sign above the check-out desk, over two hundred dealers rented space here.

This is what I want to do, Echo thought. *No one to answer to, no one to tell you what to do and when to do it. The dealers look like they don't have a care in the world. That's the life I want. No pressure, no worries. But I can't seem to make it, and hell, I'm smarter than any two of them put together. But it's not to be. After finishing this little project,*

I'll be back in the pharmaceutical business, under high pressure, lots of people telling me what to do… but lots of money. I'll figure out this antiques business someday.

He picked up a plate that was marked forty dollars and marveled at it. *I saw one just like this in New York for twenty, and for the life of me, I don't see any difference. Well, I can't make any money on it.* He put the plate down and walked a few feet to a display of teapots. A couple picked up the plate that he had been studying and smiled at one another. The woman said that they should sell this in their shop for close to one hundred dollars.

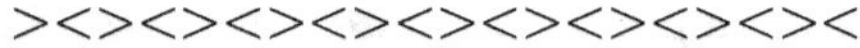

After spending most of the day attending funerals, Phil returned to his office. He wanted to check messages and clean up any last-minute paperwork so that he could devote Monday to reviewing Batch Records. Tonight, Rose was traveling to Delaware to take care of a friend who had just had breast cancer surgery, and Phil planned to drive her to the train station. But first, he wanted to call Lieutenant Hines and tell him that he would have to find someone else to work with him. It was a difficult decision and Phil was still waffling, but he could not risk losing his job and all he had worked for.

He read through his messages, found three from Hines, and dialed his personal number.

"Lieutenant Hines."

"Phil Messina. You called?"

"Phil, I need an answer, and I need it soon. But before you give me one, I want you to consider something. Without your help, we'll be wasting a lot of time checking out people in alphabetical order rather than looking at legitimate suspects. It's been four days since the homicides, and we know as much now, or as little, as we did Tuesday morning. Today I had a scary thought: what if the killing's not over? What if there's a killer out there with a hard-on for Purity who's planning to kill again? All I can envision is the body of Lorraine Waters – a lovely human being – crumpled on the floor, staring up at me. We have to get moving. If you've already decided not to help, don't tell me now. Think about what I said first. If you're going to help, then let's get going."

Phil stared at the top of his desk and squeezed the handset, thinking, *You son-of-a-bitch, playing to my conscience. Sure, make me feel guilty, make me feel like I'm responsible if someone else gets killed.* Phil made a quick decision. "Let's meet at Finnegan's Steak House at seven, and we'll talk. If I decide to work with you, you can buy. If not, I will."

"See you at seven."

Phil loved Finnegan's Steak House. He loved the rugged masculine feel, the polished wood, the leather booths and chairs, the large, heavy steak knives, and the meat-and-potatoes menu. He arrived promptly at seven and found Lieutenant Hines occupying a small booth in the back corner of the dining area.

"Phil, how're you tonight?"

"Doing fine… you?"

"Great. Let's get a drink." Jim motioned for the waiter. Phil ordered a Jameson on the rocks and Jim a Godfather.

Jim wasted no time getting to the reason for dinner. "Have you made a decision?"

"Pretty much, but first, I have a few questions. I don't think you told me everything about your relationship with your partner."

"You're very insightful, and you're right. I didn't tell you everything. Parisi recently moved into our precinct, so I don't know her well, but she definitely comes with some baggage. She filed a sexual harassment suit against a superior officer, claiming he gave the plum assignments to the male detectives and had her do all the clerical work. Parisi claimed she tried to resolve the problems with her boss, but nothing changed. She sued and won, then asked for a transfer. Her boss was forced to retire early on a part pension. I didn't want to work with her because I felt uncomfortable. Initially, I worried about everything I said and did. I wanted her reassigned and was denied. I've only worked with her for a few days, but I'm beginning to think she might be okay."

"Oh, great. She might be a bitch, and I'm supposed to trust her with my future."

"She's trustworthy, and I believe she'll keep everything to herself. We're talking about two entirely different things. You don't have to worry about her unless you plan to harass her."

"Why isn't she here?"

"No need. I can fill her in on what we talk about, and while I'm here, she can keep the investigation moving."

"Are you going to tell your boss about my role?"

"No."

"Are you interested in me because I'm the prime suspect? You know, like in an episode of Law & Order?"

"Come on, Phil, I've already explained that. You're a suspect because you were at the dinner on Monday night. But you're not the prime suspect. Unfortunately, we don't have a prime suspect. My instincts tell me you didn't do it, and I'm usually a pretty good judge of character."

"One final question. Will you share all – and I mean all – the information you develop with me, or will the information flow like traffic on a one-way street?"

The question caught Jim by surprise. "There may be an occasion when something is super confidential, but you'll see most of the information. The more you know, the more effective you'll be inside the company."

The two motioned for the waiter. They both ordered the French Onion soup and a salad, and Jim ordered the sixteen-ounce prime rib with mashed potatoes and green beans. Phil took the twelve-ounce filet mignon with steak fries and corn. They also ordered another round of drinks. Before either said another word, the waiter returned with their drinks and a large, crusty loaf of bread on a cutting board flanked by a tub of butter and one of the large, heavy steak knives Phil liked. They attacked the bread, ignoring the drinks as if they had not eaten in days.

"Well, are you in or not?"

Phil was close to a decision but didn't want to answer yet. "It had to be an inside job. The only way the killer could've gotten in would be to rig the security system at the front door. No other explanation makes sense. So, what do you think? Is the killer someone currently working for Purity?"

"Or involved. The killer could be anyone, but it's more than likely that someone in the company is involved. I'm sure of it."

"Okay, I'm in," Phil said with a slight sigh, which could have been construed as either relief or defeat. "Before we start, I think you need to understand my situation at work, so you'll understand my reluctance to work with you. I was told – no, ordered – not to give you any inside information, especially concerning my judgments on the likelihood of a present or former employee being the killer. The chief corporate attorney thinks that if we give you possible suspects, we could be sued for violating the Privacy Act."

"Do you think he's right?"

"He's a she, and I think there's a possibility she's right. I also think the risk is minimal, though. She's just being overly conservative, and Cohen, who is normally a risk-taker, was quick to agree with her. You should also know that Bob Cohen wants me out – fired. The reason isn't important, but he wants me out. I have some support back at McKenzie, but I'm one screw-up away from losing it. So if anyone in Management finds out I'm helping you, it's the unemployment line for me."

"I'll make sure Parisi knows how important it is to keep your involvement quiet."

"Where do you want to start? I can have some names for you to work on by tomorrow night at the earliest."

"I also need to understand the company's dynamics and, more importantly, the people. Between us, we need to get at what motivated someone to kill two people in cold blood. I think your downsizing or the racial problems in the company were the motives for the killings. You can decide where to start, but I need information. I expect we have a large and tasty meal coming and should have plenty of time to talk."

Phil appeared lost in thought for a moment. He was thinking of his conversation with Greg Iverson and wanted to convey the seriousness of the issues. "I think for you to understand – to truly understand – how employees are affected as companies deal with issues like downsizing and diversity, you need to realize that it's all about jobs. Who gets hired, who gets promoted, who gets fired… they're gut issues for sure. When a company plans to reduce the number of its employees, diversity is a consideration. When a company moves to make its workforce more diverse, race and gender influence who gets hired and promoted. To understand the full impact of diversity and downsizing, you need to understand the culture that existed before diversity and downsizing were part of the corporate lexicon."

Again, Phil was lost in thought for a moment. "When I was first hired by McKenzie, a co-worker told me I had it made. All I had to do was keep my nose clean, do a reasonably good job, and make it to retirement. Most company employees believed their jobs were secure. In the sixties and seventies, most large companies pushed the concept of employment for life. They wanted employees to feel secure, and they wanted loyalty from them. They were loyal in return. Benefit programs were designed to reward longevity. McKenzie's pension formula used an employee's age, years of service, and his best three years of earnings to determine the amount of an employee's pension. In addition, achieving a certain age and amount of company service added medical and dental insurance in retirement and a survivor pension. The number of weeks of paid vacation an employee received per year increased with company service.

"Most importantly, job security increased with company service. McKenzie even had a written policy: 'The longer an employee's company service, the more likely the employee will remain employed.' We referred to these benefits and policies as the Golden Handcuffs."

"Sounds too good to be true, kind of like civil servants."

"Exactly my point. New employees found it hard to believe, but the longer they worked for the company, the more it became an expectation, an entitlement. Now add the promotion policy: 'Always look within first.' Companies generally followed the military model and designed their organizations with many levels of jobs. You know, private through four-star general with lots of levels in between. Companies reduced turnover and improved morale by hiring entry-level jobs and filling higher-level jobs with existing employees. Employees had careers instead of jobs, and every so often, they'd move into a higher-level job and be recognized in an organization announcement."

"Did you announce every promotion, even for the lower-level jobs?"

"Sure. When we announced a promotion, the employee felt good for a few days and became more loyal to the company. Let me tell you how it worked at McKenzie. Production and clerical employees were normally hired into entry-level jobs and promoted to higher-level jobs based on seniority and skills, but mostly seniority. Professional and management employees, usually with technical degrees, were hired into entry-level positions and promoted to higher-level jobs based on their qualifications. But longevity received a lot of consideration. Rarely were people hired into high-level jobs from the outside. Promoting current employees always received priority."

"Wait a minute. You were hired into a production job and wound up in management without a degree?"

"I was promoted to first-line supervisor, and after that, I got lucky."

Phil continued, "Like other large chemical companies, McKenzie enjoyed high margins and could support an oversized bureaucracy. Corporate headquarters housed staff organizations like Marketing, Human Resources, and Finance in upscale offices. Duplicate organizations existed at the division and plant levels. Lots of people employed, lots of redundancy, and lots of promotion opportunities."

He stopped. "You look like you have a question."

"I don't know what you mean by high margins."

"Margin is the money that's left after the cost of production is subtracted from total revenue. For example, if a company's gross margin is 50% and its sales are one million dollars, $500,000 is left to pay administrative expenses and taxes. Any money left after that is referred to as net profit or earnings. Are you with me?"

Before Jim could answer, the waiter arrived with two crocks of French Onion soup, topped with thick, gooey, browned cheese that revealed the outline of a piece of round crusty bread. Before the waiter left, Phil asked for more bread and another round of drinks.

After spending a few minutes enjoying the soup, Jim said, "No more drinks for me after this. Unlike you, I have to drive home. As for your history lesson, I'm with you for now, but do I really need to hear it?"

"As I said, if you want to understand today's corporate culture, you should know how it evolved. Besides, I'm almost done."

"Okay, but you haven't talked about race or diversity."

"I will, but for now, I want you to think about the people living in the corporate world I described. They had good pay for the work they performed. Their benefits were generous and improved every so often. Their jobs became more secure with time, opportunity to advance, and excellent working conditions. And when they retired, they received a pension, medical and dental benefits, and the same security for their spouse. I want you to remember this when I talk about downsizing."

"If working conditions and pay were as good as you describe, every employee must've been thrilled."

"You'd think so, but people have a way of getting used to things. Remember: I said employees started believing they were entitled. Entitled to the pay, the benefits, the opportunities, and the job security. They also expected more: more pay, more benefits, simply… more. After the euphoria of getting hired wore off, most employees in large companies believed they deserved more. Unfortunately, the culture of entitlement would be torn apart in ways no one could have predicted."

"I'm beginning to get a picture of the corporate world, but before you start on diversity, I want to get your take on an interview Parisi and I conducted yesterday. Besides, our meals should be coming soon. Okay?" Phil nodded. "We talked to Cynthia Bernstein to understand how the security system might have been tampered with. She said the program resides on the same server as your intranet. She said a firewall was between the two, but a good hacker could get past the firewall and modify the program. She told us she could easily think of twenty-five or thirty employees who have the computer skills to jump the firewall and modify the security program. What do you think?"

"I know my way around a personal computer, but servers and firewalls are out of my league. There's an employee I can ask, though. She's an employee I trust, so I could check it out for you if that's what you want."

"That's what I want."

Jim turned to his right as he heard the sizzling main course approaching. Within seconds, the waiter placed the largest prime rib Jim had ever seen before him. It was beautiful. The look, the sound, and the smell were perfect. Tonight, Jim got both the sizzle and the steak. He looked at Phil, who was poised over his filet with knife in one hand, fork in the other. Jim said, "Talk to you later."

When each had eaten about half of his meal, Jim and Phil slowed down. "How about I give you my take on the history of minorities and women in the corporate world?" Phil said while still chewing.

"Sure." Jim thought of saying, *I'm really interested in hearing a white man's sanitized version of how my people were treated,* but he decided against it.

Phil heard the sarcasm in Jim's voice. He responded, "I have difficulty talking to you about race. You're thin-skinned. But talking is necessary if you're going to understand the underlying anger in the workplace."

"If you're talking about how I reacted to your comments on Mrs. Armstrong's abilities, I attribute them to the fact that black people have to be twice as good as white people to get any credit. I'll listen to your opinions, but I won't blindly accept them as fact. I'll apply my judgment to the message and to the messenger."

"Do what you want with my opinions. If you pay attention, you might see the world through different eyes."

"Just tell your story, and then I'll help you see the world through the eyes of someone who has experienced discrimination firsthand. Someone who believes Affirmative Action has helped and will continue to help minorities and women overcome the repression they have experienced at the hands of white men."

Phil glared at Jim, then said, "After moving to HR, I looked at McKenzie's history of employment policies and was disturbed by what I found. For the most part, Blacks were only hired into janitorial and low-level maintenance jobs. Black employees were not allowed to bid on and apply for higher-paying jobs in the production or clerical areas. In the southern plants, blacks and whites had separate and unequal toilets and locker facilities, which remained in some plants until the late seventies, well after the Civil Rights Act. They likely existed in most large companies as well. The treatment of blacks was probably worse in smaller companies."

Jim, elbows on the table, looked confused. "You know companies had policies to keep blacks out of high-paying jobs – policies based solely on skin color – and yet you're opposed to Affirmative Action.?"

"Before we get into an argument about Affirmative Action, I want to finish. Okay?"

Jim did not say anything nor move a muscle.

"I'll take that as a yes. Women, white women mostly, were hired into clerical jobs and kept out of the production jobs. Even women with college degrees were hired into clerical jobs.

In the sixties and seventies, the workforce was segregated – black janitors, women in front of typewriters, and white men in production. The professional and management positions were literally ninety-nine percent white men."

"I go back to what I said earlier. Companies blatantly discriminated against blacks and women, and you, based on some convoluted white conservative logic, believe doing something about it is wrong."

"I never said I was against Affirmative Action itself, but I'm against it as it's practiced today. But we can get into that discussion later if you'd like. For now, I'd like to continue." Phil paused. "When the federal government started enforcing the law through compliance reviews and discrimination charges, McKenzie began making policy changes. The new policies allowed blacks to try for higher-level production and clerical jobs. But the seniority rules were changed to favor existing employees. White employees."

"Whoa, you're getting a little too technical for me. Let me see if I understand. Before the government started enforcing the Civil Rights Act, blacks were kept in low-paying janitorial jobs. After the government started enforcing the Civil Rights Act, the company changed the seniority rules so blacks couldn't move up to the higher-paying jobs." Phil nodded in agreement. "Those bastards, fuck. I always knew we were getting screwed."

Phil ignored Jim's anger. "Qualifications suddenly became important. Companies started refining tests and defining the education and skills required to hold a job. In most cases, the new qualifications were designed to keep black employees out of better-paying positions. In many cases, employees in those positions didn't meet the new requirements, but they were grandfathered in. Since very few women or blacks were getting engineering or technical degrees at the time, having an engineering degree became critical for promotion into management. So before the Civil Rights Act, minorities and women were confined to certain jobs and were not permitted to advance into management. Companies resisted complying with the Civil Rights Act. They changed to give the appearance of complying but used seniority rules and qualifications to accomplish the same goals. The results were the same."

"So the law didn't matter to you fucking high and mighty executives. What mattered was keeping my people down. Holding the good jobs for you white guys."

Phil was surprised and a little offended by Jim's remark. "So you see me as a white guy. Not as an Italian, not as a WOP?"

"Face it, you're part of the in-group, the good old boys club. You're a white male of European descent. You're not even recognized as a minority by the Civil Rights Act – are you?"

"That's because we didn't go whining to the government about how the world was against us like your people did. We were stereotyped and discriminated against, but we handled it ourselves."

"You just told me that my people had it a lot worse than you did. How about you stop whining and finish your version of the history of blacks in corporate America?"

"One last thought. When the Great Society and Civil Rights laws were passed, the government declared that poverty and racism would no longer exist in our lifetime. How's that working out? The EEOC still adjudicates discrimination charges and requires companies to document compliance with the regulations. The government is still spending massive amounts of money on social programs. It seems to me that the only thing that never dies is a government program."

Jim stared at his plate and played with the remnants of his meal. "I don't accept your explanation. I'm sure the discrimination you described existed, and I believe it came from the hearts of the people in power. Look, I've heard enough. I know we have more to talk about, but I need time to think through what you've said. I also have to get moving on this case, so can we get together tomorrow sometime? Maybe in the afternoon?"

"No. I forgot to tell you Lorraine Water's mother died, and I'm going to the funeral tomorrow. Tomorrow night is fine."

"Please give her my sympathies. Where's the funeral?"

"If you go, she'll know you and I are talking, and I don't want that. The funeral is in East New York."

"East New York! That's the worst section of Brooklyn, worse than Bed Sty. Aren't you afraid some brother will whack you on general principle?"

"Just as afraid as I am that when I go to Little Italy, some 'paesano' will mistake me for someone with a contract on him. Look, I'm going in the daytime, and I've been there before."

"Tomorrow night then. Pick a restaurant."

"I can't handle another big meal, so how about my house tomorrow night?"

"It's all right with me. What about your wife?"

"She's in Delaware. I'll pick up some Nino's pizza for dinner and we can sit around and talk. How about six?"

"I'll be there. But to be honest with you, I'm really bothered by what you're telling me and by your attitude toward us black folk. I'll think about what you said, but right now, I think it's bullshit."

"Yeah, you do that. Think about it. And while you're thinking, try to remember that I'm not trying to be your friend; I'm trying to help you find a killer. You wanted to understand the issues in Purity, and I'm giving you my view. I don't care if you like it or not, so if you want to call it quits, it's okay with me."

"I'd like to, but I need your help. It's just that I always believed blacks were treated poorly and denied opportunity, but to hear you describe it so matter-of-factly really pisses me off. I'll be okay tomorrow night." Jim paid the bill. "I wanted your take on Robinson and Hazlitt tonight, but it can wait for tomorrow night."

Phil showed him how to get to his house. "Just turn at the corner and head up Main Street. Just over that little rise, you'll see the library on the left. Turn left at the library onto Florence Avenue. I'm the first house on the right, number 22."

Jim walked to his car, and Phil walked home. They grunted 'goodnight' at one another but parted without shaking hands.

Saturday 12/6

Phil listened to the silence of his empty home. He had not spent a night alone at home since he married Rose. Whenever Phil was at home, either Rose or one of the kids was also there. *I guess this is part of life as an empty nester,* he thought, looking at his bowl of Cheerios. Phil had eaten Cheerios for breakfast most days for as long as he could remember. Old habits die hard. Working for McKenzie was an old habit he did not want to change, but it was too late now. Working for Purity was a new reality Phil hated but needed to accept. Last night he had set new events in motion: events that had no predictable endings, events that could have significant financial implications. Last night he had made a decision that was destined to impact his and Rose's lives, and for the first time in their marriage, he had not consulted with her.

Fuck it. I'm in it now, and I'll just have to see where it takes me, Phil thought. He picked up the phone and dialed Alice Chen's number. Alice had been working in Boston as a Purity sales representative when Phil had met her at a national marketing meeting. She had a degree in Computer Science and some experience in production planning. Two weeks later, Alice had called Phil to find out if there were any job openings at the Garden City Site. When Phil had probed her reasons for wanting to move to Long Island, he had learned that she was dating a guy from Queens. Their relationship had become serious. Phil had managed to arrange the transfer. Later, they had worked together on a few projects and became friends.

"Hi Alice, it's Phil. I hope I'm not calling too early?"

"Not at all. Good morning, Phil. How are you this lovely Saturday morning?"

"Pretty good. Look, I'm sorry to bother you, but I need some help, and I need it from someone I can trust."

"You can depend on me. You know I won't say anything to anyone."

"That's why I called you. I need to better understand how someone might access the security program, especially the section that controls the card access to the executive entrance. I need to know if it's possible to get into the security system program from our intranet."

"There's a firewall that would have to be breached, but I think I could do it rather easily."

"Once you breach the firewall, try to get into the security system and look for signs that the code was modified and erased. I'd also like to know who else you think can do it."

"I'll get in and check it out. As for who has the capability, I won't know until after I do it and see how complex the security system code is. Most information stays on the hard drive even after it's deleted, so I might be able to find something."

"Can you get in without alerting anyone?"

"Don't worry, I'll protect myself. And I won't tell a soul what we're doing. Are you in any trouble?"

"No, but I will be if word of what we're doing gets out. Otherwise, I'm fine. Do you think you might have something for me by, say, five-thirty today?"

"I'll call you one way or the other."

"Be very careful. And Alice, thanks, bye."

Phil called Abby next to ask her to gather the information Lieutenant Hines needed. Phil expected resistance because Abby knew that he was on Cohen's shit list. He suspected that she did not want to see him fired. She would probably give him a hard time. Phil let out a little sigh and picked up the phone.

"Good morning, Abby. How're you doing?"

"Phil Messina. This'd better not be work-related. My heart can't handle another shock. You hardly work during the week, and you never, never, work on weekends."

"Always the comedian, and still not funny. Abby, all kidding aside, I have to talk to you about a serious situation. Are you in a position to talk? Is George around?"

"George is out running a few Saturday morning errands. The most important is picking up a dozen bagels. He should be back in about half an hour."

"Good." Phil knew that the best way to work with Abby was to be straight with her. "I've started working behind the scenes with the police to help them solve the murders, and I need your help. Needless to say, no one, and I mean no one, not even George must know."

Abby was silent for a moment and then said, "Are you a fucking lunatic? You can't keep the fact you're working with the police a secret, and if anyone finds out, you'll be fired. Shit, the police will slip or, worse yet, let it out if it suits their purpose. You're self-destructive, trying to drag me down with you. What happens to me if Hazlitt or Cohen finds out? Why the fuck are you doing this?"

"I don't understand why I agreed to help. Hell, the only thing I can think of is that it's the right thing to do. Stupid, huh? We both know I'm in Cohen's crosshairs, and I've been ordered to stay away from the police. But I had dinner with Lieutenant Hines last night, and he asked me to help out. He told me the investigation was going nowhere and checking out people at random will take forever. He also raised the possibility more Purity employees might be killed. Abby, I think Hines is all right. He seems like a straight shooter. He'll protect us. I know it's a huge risk, but we can help catch the killer and maybe save some lives. What do you say?"

"I say you're crazy. I say we're both going to lose our jobs, and I say you have no right to drag me into this. You're not being fair. If you want to risk your job, fine, but don't ask me to risk mine. I have a lot invested in this job, and I'm looking forward to a comfortable old age with plenty of money. I will keep this conversation to myself, but I will not help you. I have to go."

Phil heard the phone click and pictured Abby throwing her phone. It was not the reaction he had expected, but was an understandable one. Abby's response caused him to question his decision. He was putting everything he worked for on the line. Abby was right; it was too large a risk to take. Phil was about to pick up the phone and call Hines when it rang.

"Hello."

"You son-of-a-bitch! You fucking son-of-a-bitch! What do you want me to do?" Abby's voice reverberated in Phil's ear.

"Does this mean you've changed your mind? Abby, if you'd called two minutes later, I would've been on the phone with Hines backing out. I think you're right. It's too risky. I'm still willing to call him and get out of this while I can."

"I overreacted. I was afraid of the consequences, but I thought about it, and it's the right thing to do. So I assume you want me to list the most probable past and present employees who may be capable of committing murder."

"That's exactly what I want you to do. Are you sure you want to do this?"

"Yeah, I'll do it. When do you want it?"

"I'd like the first installment today around five. I should be back from the funeral by then."

"Are you going to Lorraine's mother's funeral? Where is it?"

"It's in East New York."

"You're going to East New York? I won't expect an answer when I call 'cause you'll be lucky to get out alive."

"Very funny. Talk to you later. And Abby, thanks. I really mean it."

Phil looked lovingly at his old, mint-condition BMW before getting in and heading to Brooklyn. The drive was mostly on expressways. He picked up the Northern State in Hicksville and headed west, then took the Meadowbrook South, past the Purity building, to the Southern State and west to the Belt Parkway. The Belt Parkway looped through the southern side of Queens County, and Phil followed it west into King's County, which is better known as Brooklyn. He exited the Belt Parkway onto Linden Street and drove northwest through Brooklyn. He'd traveled between two different worlds in a little over half an hour. Like most of the other villages on Long Island, his home in the village of Oyster Bay in Nassau County consisted of generally well-maintained buildings and homes, little graffiti in public areas. In contrast, the East New York section of Brooklyn consisted of poorly maintained buildings and homes, and most surfaces were covered with graffiti.

As Phil passed the multi-story brick buildings commonly referred to as 'the projects,' he recalled the day he had spent with Heather Dougherty, a Purity sales representative. They had made several calls to private practice physicians in the southern part of Nassau County. Phil had observed while Heather pitched Purity's drugs' new uses to pre-occupied and apathetic physicians. After each pitch, she had restocked their caches of give-away medications, and they had moved on to the next physician. When Phil had been getting bored, Heather had driven to a clinic in an impoverished section of Far Rockaway, Queens. Across the street from the clinic were three 20-story brick buildings surrounded by an eight-foot-high chain-link fence. A bracket secured to the top of the fence protruded outward at a 45-degree angle; coiled razor wire covered the bracket. The courtyard contained by the fence had consisted of cracked and broken concrete walkways, dirt, and a few pieces of rusting junk. There were no trees and no grass in the courtyard. Each apartment had a small balcony, and each balcony below the ninth floor had coiled razor-wire fastened to its railing. Thinking of that day brought a heaviness to his chest. No one should have to live that way.

Phil found his street, turned left, and fortunately found a parking spot just as it was being vacated. The funeral home was laid out the same as the two he had just visited on Long Island. However, the furniture and decorations were shabby by comparison. Lorraine and her brother were standing and greeting a short line of mourners. Lorraine looked worn and tired. She had bags under red, bloodshot eyes, and her hair was unkempt. When her eyes found Phil, Lorraine wrapped her arms around him, squeezed, buried her face in his shoulder, and cried uncontrollably. Her body shook and she pressed harder. Her tears soaked Phil's shirt. Finally, Lorraine pulled back, placed her hands loosely on Phil's hips, and gazed into his eyes. Tears cut through her makeup.

"I'm sorry for your troubles," Phil said, not knowing why he used the tried-and-true line from every Italian funeral he attended.

"I know you are, Phil. Thanks for being here."

"I'll hang around awhile. If you get a chance, maybe we can talk."

"I'd like that."

Phil spoke briefly to her brother and then found a seat. Mostly older black women occupied the seating area, chatting quietly. The men gathered in the two rooms at the rear. Loud chatter and occasional laughter reverberated from the back. By comparison, the seating area was peaceful. The overall atmosphere reminded Phil of the many viewings he had attended in Scranton. In fact, the mourners looked like the mourners at the Italian funerals, only darker. One of the men looked just like Mike Salami, and the woman two seats to his left like Eleanor Gatti. Although, at the moment, Phil was the only white person in the funeral home, he attracted little attention. He was just another mourner paying his respects. Phil had felt the same way when he had attended the eighth-grade graduation in the church next door. He was just one of the audience. People had acknowledged him and chatted with him as if he were part of the community. He wondered whether, if the situation were reversed, would white people react differently? The line of mourners waiting to greet Lorraine and her brother was lengthening, so Phil decided to head home. He gave Lorraine a wave as he walked to the door, and she smiled back.

Two black teenagers were looking at Phil's BMW. They were dressed in clothes six sizes too big that hung wrinkled on their bodies. One wore a colorful ski cap, the other a bandanna. Phil walked over to his car and said, "She's in good condition and runs great." Both boys turned around.

The one with the ski cap asked, "What kinda car is it?"

"It's an old BMW 635csi. I've had it a while, and I take pretty good care of it. I'll show you the inside."

One, then the other, looked into the car, touching the steering wheel and the leather seats, but neither tried to get in.

"What kinda engine?"

"It's only a six-cylinder, but it has 230 horsepower with a 6800 rpm redline. It has a real kick."

"How fast you gone in dis?" asked the teen in the bandana.

"I've had her up to 115 mph a couple of times. She feels solid and handles like she's on rails."

The teen with the bandanna replied, "Thanks man, and good luck with her." They both walked off.

Phil sat in the car for a moment before starting the engine, his heart racing. When he had seen the boys, he had almost turned around and walked back to the funeral home. He could have easily assumed they were car thieves or planning a carjacking. As it turned out, he was glad he did not. He preferred to give people the benefit of the doubt. It worked out this time, but he knew one day it would fail.

Phil turned right onto Linden Street and proceeded southeast toward the Belt. He traveled at a reasonable speed in the right lane, taking in the sights of Brooklyn. He noticed an old Oldsmobile Cutlass pass him on the left, the rear seat passenger's eyes glued on his BMW. The car slowed, the windows rolled down, and both the front and rear-seat passengers looked over at him. Phil could feel both black men glare at him. His senses moved to red alert. Suddenly, the car pulled into the right lane just in front of Phil and slowed down. Phil slowed and then looked in his rearview mirror to see if the car behind him looked suspicious. An older black man, the driver, was the only occupant, so Phil relaxed and stayed in the right lane.

The Cutlass slowed again for no apparent reason. Phil guided the BMW into the left lane but did not pass the Cutlass. The driver-side window rolled down, and the driver looked back at Phil and then sped up and cut into the left lane just in front of the BMW. They were approaching a merge; the Belt Parkway service road would join Linden Street from the right, forming a four-lane highway. A mile after the merge, the left lane would exit only onto the Belt. Phil hoped that this experience would end when he got onto the ramp. When the Cutlass slowed again, Phil cut into the right lane, downshifted into third gear, and began to pass the car. They were entering the merge. The Cutlass started to move right. Phil looked to his right and saw an opening ahead; he accelerated hard and passed two cars in the lane to his right, then cut into the open space. After passing a few more cars, he slid into the far-right lane. He picked up the Cutlass in his side-view mirror pinned in traffic about ten car lengths back. The right lane ahead was open, and Phil continued to pick up speed, knowing his exit was four lanes to his left.

As Phil cut left into an almost nonexistent opening in front of an Audi, he heard horns and screeching tires. The commotion caused the car to the left of the Audi to slow, and Phil took advantage of the opening to move left one more lane. He was one lane right of his goal, fast approaching the ramp, but the cars in the exit-only lane were bumper-to-bumper, moving at forty-five miles an hour. Phil aligned his door with the rear quarter panel of a Mustang to his left, and as it followed the ramp to the left, Phil also turned. As he had hoped, the car behind the Mustang slowed, giving Phil a chance to tuck in on the entrance ramp.

Traffic in all three lanes of the Belt was flowing unusually smoothly, allowing Phil to maneuver the BMW into the far-left lane and accelerate to seventy-five miles an hour. Phil kept looking for the Cutlass, but it was nowhere in sight. He exited onto the Southern State Parkway, and when traffic didn't interfere, he sped up to ninety. Phil pushed his BMW at every opportunity and arrived in Oyster Bay without seeing the Cutlass again.

Phil pulled into his garage and quickly lowered the door. He sat on the couch and looked out of the picture window, waiting for the Cutlass to drive by. Was he being paranoid? Did he completely overreact, or was the threat he perceived from the occupants real? Was he set up by comments from Jim and Abby about the dangers of East New York? Did he assume they were after him because they were young and black, or did he outrun a group of thugs who really were after him? Did it really matter now? He was home safe, and he would never know if he had escaped disaster or if he had risked wrecking his BMW for nothing. After about fifteen minutes and no Cutlass, Phil poured some Jameson over ice and waited for the phone to ring.

"I guess you went to East New York and lived to tell about it. You're a lucky guy," Abby said as soon as Phil picked up the phone.

"No problem. You're making way too much of it."

"Yeah, right. How is Lorraine doing?'

"She's not doing too good right now. It'll take time, but I'm sure she'll get through it."

"I've come up with three possibilities for you. Are you ready to listen?"

Phil clicked his pen, positioned his writing pad, and said, "Fire away."

"Before I give you the names, I want you to know that I can't believe any of our employees, past or present, could kill anyone. I'm not accusing these people. I'm simply saying they have reason to be angry. I'll let the cops determine if they did it."

"I understand."

Abby gave Phil the background information on the three. Phil remembered enough about them to know that Abby had chosen wisely. Abby knew the Purity employees much better than Phil. He had only worked at Purity for a year and had only been there a few months when the downsizing had happened. Phil only interrupted to ask a few questions and took detailed notes while Abby spoke. When she finished, Phil asked, "Do any of them have any friends with access to our Intranet?"

"I don't know for sure, but they might."

"Thanks. Now I need the details."

Abby gave Phil the suspect's addresses and other information, such as family members. They chatted a little, then hung up. Phil called Nino's Pizza and ordered two large pepperoni pizzas for tonight. It was five-twenty.

Phil answered the phone. "Messina here."

"Hi Phil, it's Alice. How are you doing?"

"Great, how about you?"

"I'm fine, thanks. I was able to get into the security program through the intranet, and it was way too easy. The firewall is ancient technology. Almost anyone with good computer skills could penetrate it. I was also able to get in and out undetected."

"That easy, hmm. I wish it were harder. How many employees do you think could breach the firewall?"

"Lots, and it doesn't have to be an employee. Anyone could dial in from anywhere and get onto the server. After that, breaching the firewall would be a piece of cake."

"Wonderful. How about finding some code in the security program that was erased? Could you do it?"

"No, the security system is very complicated, and it would take a long time. I'm afraid I'd be discovered."

"We can't have that." Phil thought for a minute, "Hey, I have an idea. On the outside chance that the killer would try to get into the building again – could you come up with a way to track him?"

"Maybe. I'd have to design a module and attach it to the security program. I could write the code offline. That way, I would only have to be online for testing, and it would be possible to do it without getting caught. I'll give it a try. Now, do you have anything else to ruin what's left of my weekend?"

"No, we'll talk Monday."

"See you then."

Phil was returning home from Nino's with two large pepperoni pizzas. The smell was incredible, and Phil wanted to stop and have a slice. As he approached the corner of Main and Florence, he noticed a car driven by a black man turn left onto his street. The car slowed in front of his house and then moved on. He felt sure that the driver was Lieutenant Hines.

At precisely six o'clock, Phil greeted Lieutenant Hines at the front door. "Hello. Any problem finding the place?"

"No. I was a little early, so I drove around the neighborhood. Nice area. You're only two blocks from the bay. Your house looks newer than the other houses, too. They look to be early 1900s."

"You're right. The other houses in the neighborhood were built between 1900 and 1920. My house was built in 1975. My property was the backyard of the brick Tudor next door. The owner needed money and sub-divided his lot. If the rumor mill is right, it didn't do him any good, and he went bankrupt anyway."

"You have a great spot here."

"Thanks."

"I see you made it out of East New York unharmed. How was the trip?"

"Uneventful."

"Good. How is Ms. Waters holding up?"

"Not too good right now, but she'll get over it. She's strong."

"Not to mention intelligent and quite a looker."

"That she is. Before we chow down, I'd like to ask you a question. I'm not sure how to phrase it, so I'll use a short story. I was the only white person at the funeral today. Last June, my wife and I were the only white people in an African American focused church while attending an eight-grade graduation in East New York. We were treated as if we belonged, as if we were, without question, part of the graduation. My wife told me that she was effortlessly brought into the chitchat when she was in the ladies' room and felt very comfortable. I'm guessing you have been in situations where you were the only black in the room, and I wonder how you felt you were treated."

"I'm the only black in the room most of the time, and if you count the times I'm with a few other minorities in a larger group of white people, it will cover most of my life. I rarely feel comfortable when I'm with a group of whites. I tend to get treated two different ways, and both piss me off. First are the assholes who go out of their way to make me feel inferior, or better yet, make themselves feel superior. They say things like, you people have it tough, all the poverty, the drugs, living in ghettos. If you people don't get your act together, you'll never realize the American dream.' Then there are the 'I have a black friend' people. They're worse than the 'you people' assholes. They gush all over you trying to make you believe they don't have a racist bone in their body, and all the time, they'd rather be somewhere else with someone else."

Phil was unsure of how to respond and simply said, "Thanks. What do you want to drink with your pizza?"

"How about a beer? I need to concentrate while you're talking. First, I'd like to tell you a little story about Bob Cohen as we eat rather than get into your heavy-duty analysis of the corporate world. Remember how Wednesday night I told you there were two of you execs with juvenile records? Besides you, Bob Cohen is the other. I also have a confession to make. I knew what your juvie record was before I asked. I wanted to see if you would tell the truth."

"I guess I passed, you bastard." Phil removed the first pizza from the oven and placed it on the table. He walked over to the refrigerator and pulled out two beers. Then he grabbed some paper plates and napkins and put them on the table before saying, "Sure, I'd like to hear about Cohen's record. Mostly because I don't like the son-of-a-bitch, and I might be able to use it against him someday."

Jim ate a slice and picked up the second before starting.

"That's why I decided to tell you. It might come in handy if our little venture goes wrong, plus I agreed to share everything with you. Cohen was abandoned after birth and spent his early childhood in an orphanage. He spent his later years moving from foster home to foster home, always in bad situations. When he was a teenager in Hackensack, New Jersey, his assigned foster homes provided him little more than a place to sleep. Bob was an A or B student throughout middle school despite paying little attention to schoolwork. Sound familiar? He gave his foster parents little reason to concern themselves with him since the social workers didn't worry about kids with good grades. Bob was the leader of the Hudson Avenue Ravens, a rag-tag collection of inner-city kids. They took money from younger and weaker kids, robbed apartments, shoplifted, and cared for each other. They didn't do drugs, steal from old or disabled people, and tried not to hurt the younger kids. They lived by the Italian code of silence… *Omerta,* I believe you call it. If one was caught, he didn't rat on the others. Most of all, they protected their leader because they'd cease to exist without him. According to a retired cop I talked to, Bob convinced his underlings to take the rap for him on more than one occasion. He talked and charmed his way out of custody on many others. Sounds to me as if he was learning about power at an early age." Jim stopped to munch on his pizza.

"He learned his lessons well. He likes having power, and he won't let it go. How did he get from the Ravens to Colombia University?"

"He got lucky. A rabbi from a local synagogue saw something special in him, recognized his potential, and made Bob his personal project. To show him a different world, he took Bob across the river to Manhattan, particularly the financial district: a world of educated men in suits and ties, driving nice cars and eating in fine restaurants. The Rabbi showed Bob what he could become if he got a good education. Bob left the gang and never looked back, his future beckoning him. He focused on high school, getting A's, and spending time with the Rabbi to learn about the adult world. Bob graduated from Colombia with a degree in Business

Administration and a 3.8 GPA. After he went off to college, the Hackensack police paid less attention to Cohen. After he graduated and moved out of the neighborhood, they didn't worry about him anymore. While we're on Cohen, what can you tell me about him?"

"About three months ago, I was on a business trip with a very chatty guy from Marketing who worked around and near Cohen his entire career. Over dinner and many drinks, he gave me his version of Bob Cohen. Are you ready to hear it?"

Jim took a swig of his beer. "Sure, I have all night."

"Right after graduating from college, Cohen joined Upjohn Pharmaceuticals as a sales rep. When the opportunity presented itself, he joined the Pharmaceutical division of McKenzie. He saw a bright future for himself in the country's eighth-largest company. He told anyone who would listen that he would be McKenzie's first Jewish CEO someday. Unfortunately, despite working hard and coming up with many new ideas, Bob didn't make a good impression on McKenzie's senior management. Then one day, just after his transfer to Garden City, Bob met Pamela Robinson. At the time, Pamela was a Quality Control Chemist just two years out of college, and Cohen was the Product Manager for Thinadin and Relieve. One day while having lunch with some coworkers, Bob enthusiastically told everyone about a proposal to increase Thinadin sales that he was about to present to upper management. After hearing Bob's proposal, Pamela, part of the group at the table, pointed out several problems and gave him several suggestions for improving them. Cohen was furious. She'd made him look bad in front of his buddies, but that night as he worked on the proposal, he realized she was right. He changed the proposal, and when 'his' plan worked and

Thinadin sales increased, Management began to see him differently. Apparently, Pamela reviewed several more proposals and found errors or omissions Bob had made each time. Bob began to understand why his career in McKenzie was on the slow track: he didn't pay enough attention to details. Bob could quickly assimilate information and make decisions. Still, he didn't have the patience to get into the details, and he didn't have the technical knowledge to see some of the potential problems. The instant Bob had a new idea, he simply wanted to charge full speed ahead, damn the torpedoes. He also began to understand that he needed Pamela, or someone with her talents, close by. She could look at a situation or idea, get into the details, think it through, and sort out the positives and the pitfalls. She would keep him out of trouble. Bob moved up the corporate ladder as if he had a rocket up his ass. Since his future depended on Pamela, he always found a way to promote her and keep her close by."

"Man, you have a hell of a memory for details."

Phil smiled. "When someone close to the CEO tells me about the CEO, I listen and I commit it to memory. It might be important someday."

"Is anything going on between Cohen and Robinson outside of work?"

"Oh, there are many rumors, but I don't think so. I believe Pamela likes being close to Cohen for the money and the power, but I'd bet she doesn't like him."

Jim drummed his fingers on the table. "Tell me a little more about Robinson."

"I'll bet you see her and Hazlitt as the prime suspects in this case."

"They're on the list for sure but they're not the prime suspects. I'm not sure I see either as capable of murder."

Phil removed the second pizza from the oven and dropped it on the table. "Pamela is a fundamentally nice person in a job in a company that doesn't usually reward nice people. She doesn't fit in. But from what I've heard, she's changing to fit the job requirements, becoming more cutthroat, more like Cohen's vision of a division President. She's technically smart but politically inept. Pamela tends to defer to someone in a meeting, even in meetings she leads. She came to Garden City after graduating from Hofstra with a B.S. degree in Chemistry. She worked there until last year when she transferred to Delaware. Pamela knows everyone at Garden City, and the vast majority of employees like and respect her. I arrived at Garden City after she was transferred to Delaware, so I never worked with her, but our paths have crossed several times. She's the only one on Cohen's staff I trust to be honest with me."

"Does that mean you don't trust Hazlitt?"

Phil thought about his last meeting with Gary Hazlitt. "Not as far as I could spit. He has his nose so far up Cohen's ass it would take the New York Giants' offensive line to pop it out. But I heard he wasn't always that way. He used to be a pretty good guy."

"Did you work with him when you were at McKenzie?"

"No, he came straight from another pharmaceutical company. Like everyone else in Purity, except Lorraine and me, he's spent his entire work life making drugs."

"Do you think either one is capable of getting involved in a murder?"

"I knew you'd ask me that, and I've given it some thought. Off the top of my head, I would say no way. But I don't know the reason, the motive for the murders. Executives make a lot of money and have excellent perks. I think they might do anything to protect their position, including murder. Hopefully, when we find the motive, it'll lead us to the killer."

"It usually does."

They ate in silence until Phil spoke again. "I talked to Alice Chen this morning. She's the computer expert I told you about last night. She easily penetrated the firewall on the Purity server and got into the security system. She verified what Cynthia Bernstein told you: any employee with reasonable computer skills could have modified the security system's code. She also said a good hacker could have done it, so it didn't have to be an employee."

"Great. Instead of narrowing down the number of suspects, she expanded them. I assume you trust her."

"Absolutely. Abby came up with three possibilities for you. But before I give you their backgrounds, you need to understand she doesn't in any way think they're capable of murder. The operative word is possibilities."

"Point made."

"I'll start with Jimmy DiRollo. Jimmy was an inspector in the Packaging Area for twenty-nine years when we forced him out last year. Jimmy was a skater; he got by because he schmoozed everyone. Jimmy worked as little as possible, disappeared from the area routinely, and was even suspected of taking bets on company time. His supervisor joked he couldn't fire him because Jimmy was a made man, under the protection of someone in upper management. Because of Jimmy, we staffed the day shift with two inspectors when only one was needed. Do you have a picture of the kind of guy he was?"

"I've worked with several cops like him over the years."

"Jimmy quote 'volunteered' for the layoff because we told him if he didn't, we would fire him, and he would lose his severance package. After he left, he couldn't get another job making anywhere near what we paid him and wound up working his forty-eight-year-old ass off unloading trucks for UPS at less than half of what he made here. He had a heart attack five months ago, a pretty serious one. Now he's home bound, tied to an oxygen tank, and can't walk five feet without running out of breath. Abby went to his house a couple of months ago to deal with some benefit issues. She said he looked eighty years old, and she felt his family blamed Purity, in particular Diane Armstrong. They referred to Armstrong as 'that black bitch'." Phil watched Jim recoil at the remark.

"Sounds like Abby has come up with a motive, but he has severe heart problems. He'd have to hire someone."

"Abby doesn't suspect Jimmy, but he has two sons and one is real trouble. Jimmy's oldest son Joe has been in and out of jail since he was a teenager. A couple of his robberies involved a gun. She thinks Joe's a possibility, and I agree. Jimmy schmoozed everyone, so he had a lot of friends, and many of them had computer skills and access to our intranet. Any one of them could've helped Joe out. Are you ready to move on?"

"Sure, but what about addresses and telephone numbers to make my life easier?"

"It's all on paper, including the highlights of each suspect. Next is Scott Williams. Scott was a short-service engineer in the Maintenance organization who got laid off last year. He was a bright engineer and a good worker, but he had a strange personality. Whenever I talked to him, I felt like someone had poured a bucket of ice over my head. In my mind, he was just plain weird, but to women, he was scary. That's the only reason he's on the list. Abby and I think he needs to be looked at."

"Abby has good instincts. She'd have made a good detective."

"Next, and last for now, is Kevin McQuet. Abby is considering a few others but wants to check some things out before giving us their names. Kevin is a skinhead covered with colorful tattoos who works in our granulation area. Kevin was quiet and shy, a real loner with no friends – especially no girlfriends. He changed about two years ago when he became a hardcore racist and a white supremacist."

"Why didn't you fire him?"

"He's never done anything at work to give us a reason to fire him. He never does or says anything wrong. We tried to force him out last year, but it didn't work. He stayed and basically challenged us to fire him, and in New York, that's not easy without some performance issues."

Jim stood. "Man, I'm full. I can't eat another slice or drink another beer. But I feel good about this, since I can finally get my team working on real leads. Where's the bathroom?"

"Down the hall, first door on the right. How 'bout we move out to the living room? I'll bring a bottle of Limoncello and some glasses."

By the time Jim returned, Phil had wrapped the three leftover slices and cleaned up the kitchen. Two small, etched crystal glasses and a beautiful bottle of Limoncello decorated the coffee table. Jim looked skeptical. "Is that lemon stuff any good?"

"It's great stuff. It's served straight from the freezer, and best of all, it'll help you digest and make room for dessert. I first had it in Italy and have been drinking it ever since. Come on, give it a try. If you don't like it, I have some other Italian liquors."

"All right, you pour. So, you've been to Italy?"

"Last year. Rose and I spent three weeks visiting the major cities in northern Italy. Best of all, we spent four days visiting relatives in Gubbio. We were treated like royalty." Phil would have gone on, but something about the look on Jim's face changed his mind. "Anyway, it was a great experience, and I was introduced to Limoncello."

"It's pretty good," Jim said, returning his glass to the coffee table. "How about another glass?"

Phil poured. "Are you ready for me to finish my overview of the corporate world?"

"What you told me last night really bothered me, and I'll admit I got a little testy, but I'm over it now. I need to understand your world, so I'm ready to listen. But try to make it interesting, will you?" Jim held a serious look for a moment, then laughed.

"I actually enjoy talking about it. It's my life. But most people find it boring, so I usually don't get the opportunity. You, however, are a captive audience, and I intend to bore you to death." It was Phil's turn to look serious before laughing. "I'll make it as enjoyable as I can."

"Last night, I talked about how minorities and women were on the bottom of the old corporate-world totem pole, and how white men were at the top. The Civil Rights Act began to change that world. While all this was happening, the competition globally increased, and profit margins were squeezed. Basically, large companies were losing their ability to increase prices to cover their increased costs. So, McKenzie and other large companies were moving into the 80s with pressure to have their workforce 'look more like the population of America' and, at the same time, they faced declining profits." Phil sipped his Limoncello. "Do you really like it?"

"It's great, really."

"Good, you'll be ready for the great dessert I picked up at The Bakery on Route 106." Jim groaned, and Phil continued. "To the advantage of large companies, Reagan destroyed the Air Traffic Controllers Union, which weakened unions in general. Also to their advantage, computers were becoming more sophisticated and made the office more productive. This, along with a decrease in the enforcement of most government regulations, cleared the way for corporations to reduce management and administrative jobs: jobs that had always been considered secure. Before the eighties, Production employees were laid off in tough times, not professionals and management. Before I start talking about how the corporation dealt with these pressures, I think you need to know two stories that affected the way the black community viewed McKenzie."

Jim took advantage of Phil's pause. "I'm getting a better picture of all this. I'm not sure how I'll solve the case, but I guess it'll be important. We're going to solve this case."

"All right, first the riots of 1968. You've probably studied the riots after Doctor King was assassinated, so I don't need to tell you about them. After the riots, what happened in

Wilmington caused the black community to hate McKenzie. The riots ended in two days, but the National Guard occupied Wilmington, Delaware for the next nine months. The black community assumed McKenzie used its power and influence to make Wilmington a police state.

"I heard the next story from an employee, a black Ph.D. biochemist. We were talking about McKenzie's difficulty recruiting black professionals. He told me Wilmington was not viewed as a good place for a black professional to live. A large part of that was the black community's animosity toward all McKenzie employees. The animosity resulted from the National Guard patrols and, in part, the Monday Club."

"Hold on, what the hell is the Monday Club?"

"The Monday Club was a social club whose members were employees of the McKenzie family: chauffeurs, butlers, maids, and nannies. If you haven't figured it out, they were all black. On their day off, Monday, they met to talk about their jobs, their treatment, and the McKenzies. According to the story, they would grouse about the work they had to do or the way a family member talked to them. They'd also share some intimate McKenzie gossip. Overall, their animosity and hatred toward the company and the family were because blacks could not get good jobs. They were only considered qualified for menial jobs."

"For what it's worth, what you're telling me squares with the kind of stories I grew up with. I felt all the anger and hatred my brothers and sisters felt when Dr. King was murdered. Dr. King's death motivated me to make a difference in my life, do good for my people, and be a role model. I went to college to prove I had the brains to do the work and to prove a black man could graduate. You've given me added details, but in general,

I knew how blacks were being treated and, to tell you the truth, I don't much care how white people were treated."

"Maybe I can get you to care. Next, let's talk about downsizing and diversity and the impact on black and white people. I'll use McKenzie as an example because I'm obviously familiar with it. Remember when I'm talking about downsizing and diversity, I'm really talking about jobs and who gets them. But first, are you ready for dessert?"

"Not really, but if you insist, I'll have some. What did you get?" Jim asked, seeming to calm down a little.

"Pecan pie and ice cream."

"I'll pass on the ice cream but go heavy on the pie. Pecan is my favorite."

"Mine too. Coffee?"

"Black."

Phil got up and headed for the kitchen. Jim sat back, stuck his hands in his pant pockets, and thought about the case. *Five days and no progress. My captain is on my ass. On the upside, I now have three suspects and I'm learning about the company and the people, but I have no hot leads. I've learned that McKenzie discriminated against blacks and women and fought Affirmative Action. What a fucking surprise. And Messina is trying to convince me the white guys in charge were justified in their actions. I hope I'm not wasting my time with this guy. I don't think I am. I've even managed to find this conservative Dago likable. The worst part of this experience is I've already gained 5 pounds.*

Phil walked into the living room carrying a tray with two large pieces of Pecan pie and two coffees and said, "Let's enjoy the pie before I start again."

"Fine. When is your wife getting back?"

"I'm picking her up in Syosset tomorrow night. I don't know much about you. Are you married or single?"

"My wife died a while ago. We'd been married a long time. It was a tough time for me. I don't like talking about it."

Phil shoveled in some pie, then asked, "Kids?"

"Two boys."

"You sure are talkative when it comes to your private life."

"I don't like talking about my family or me. I never have."

"Okay, a widower with two boys, enough information."

"Look, I'm not in the mood to talk about myself. What I need is to solve this case. So it's nothing personal. I'm under a lot of pressure."

"I figure you know how often I change my underwear, and I know next to nothing about you... but have it your way."

Phil decided to move on. "The first announced downsizing, a few years ago, came as quite a shock to employees. For many, the belief they were secure in their job was shaken for the first time in their careers. McKenzie offered an improved pension to any employee who wanted to voluntarily leave the company. The pharmaceutical division was excluded because the profit squeeze hadn't affected them. The company allowed a maximum of seven thousand employees to take the offer. If less volunteered, the remainder would be fired. As it turned out, over eleven thousand volunteered, and the company backed off and let them all leave with the incentive."

"Didn't increased pensions for eleven thousand employees cost a lot of money?"

"No, it was essentially free. McKenzie's pension plan was overfunded. At the time, they hadn't put a penny into the fund for twenty years. Even with eleven thousand additional pensioners, the pension fund was still overfunded."

"Slick, but didn't eleven thousand employees leaving cause problems?"

"Some critical employees were held for a year or so on consulting contracts to minimize that impact. But overall, the losses were absorbed. McKenzie's corporate gurus began to educate the individual businesses on becoming more efficient. Terms like downsizing, rightsizing, de-layering, organizational effectiveness, increased span-of-control, re-engineering, and restructuring became part of the new corporate-speak."

"I assume downsizing and rightsizing have to do with reducing the number of employees, and re-engineering and restructuring have to do with changing the organization. But what the hell does de-layering and increased span of control mean?"

"De-layering is eliminating entire levels or layers of management. Think of the police. Lieutenants report to captains, captains report to commanders, and so on. De-layering eliminates a level of management. Maybe the rank of lieutenant would be eliminated, for example. Span-of-control defines the breadth of an individual manager's responsibility. If you increase a manager's span of control, you decrease the number of managers you need. In the not-too-distant past, each of the functions I'm responsible for would have a director. I'm responsible for Human Resources, Accounting, Materials Control, and a few other functions. We eliminated a total of three director positions. Remember, margins were shrinking, and the company needed to reduce cost. The fastest way to reduce cost is to reduce people."

Eliminating the rank of Lieutenant in Phil's example piqued Jim's interest. "What happens to the lieutenants in your little case? Do they lose their jobs?"

"Not necessarily. But likely."

"If the functions you supervise used to have a full-time boss, don't you have to bust your ass to stay on top of things?"

"Actually, upper management's job got easier. I know it's hard to believe, but it's true. By eliminating whole layers of management and consolidating the decision-making in fewer employees, the crap we dealt with in the past disappeared. 'Work always expands to fill the available time' is a cliché, I believe, and the time was filled with whining and complaining. Reducing the number of people in management had a couple of positive results: decisions were made faster, and employees became focused on getting their job done. Petty concerns such as the next promotion and office size vanished."

"Okay, I get it."

"In the ensuing years, the businesses in McKenzie were re-engineered, de-layered, and downsized until the employees were numb. Unlike upper management, employees in other positions had their responsibilities increased so much that they became beleaguered. The corporate world was changing fast, and the pressure on its employees was increasing. And I'm not even mentioning the pressure to continually improve the quality of our products and services. McKenzie offered employees incentives like an improved pension or a lump sum payment every couple of years to encourage employees to leave voluntarily. At the same time, they pressured targeted employees to take the offer or else. Over time, the incentives disappeared, and McKenzie used layoffs to fire the people they felt weren't performing well. Management became emboldened because employees didn't run to unions or the government for protection. They just let it happen, like lambs being led to slaughter. The more brutal McKenzie became, the nastier the work environment became. Employees were scared, and protecting their job became the focus of their lives. The pharmaceutical division was excluded from the downsizing and restructuring. Still, the employees saw the impact on their fellow employees in other divisions."

"So you're telling me the constant emphasis on reducing people changed how secure employees felt. It also changed the way employees did their jobs and treated each other on the job. And Purity employees saw what was happening in the rest of McKenzie."

"I've always believed being fired or laid-off is the corporate equivalent of the death penalty. Benefit plans are designed to make it hard for you to leave, to make you want to stay, and it works. You want to stay. But the new reality is that every day you go to work may be your last, which causes a lot of stress. Then, BANG, last January, it happened to Purity."

"So, it's more than last year's downsizing. It's the fear of the future, fear that it'll happen over and over again."

"Give the man a cigar. Remember, Diane Armstrong was the top dog at Garden City. So, who do you blame? Now consider that last Monday's dinner meeting was to plan for another downsizing, even though last January Bob Cohen assured a very nervous and angry Garden City workforce it would never happen again."

Jim nodded gravely. "Parisi and I figured that's what Hazlitt wouldn't tell us. Do you think the employees suspect?"

"You're a good detective, and so are our employees. Gary Hazlitt and Pamela Robinson visiting the site was enough to start rumors. Despite the murders, we're moving ahead with our plans and we have a planning meeting Monday night. My guess is we'll announce another downsizing in about two weeks. Anyone who believed Cohen and felt secure in his job will feel very anxious."

"You had a major role in all the downsizing in McKenzie, didn't you? I can tell. You get real emotional when you talk about it. It must have had a tremendous impact on you, especially since you kept your job and people you knew and liked were let go."

Phil smiled softly, as if pained. "I couldn't begin to describe the impact it had on me. I was in charge of reducing the number of employees in our business unit from about eighteen hundred to fewer than eleven hundred over the last six years I worked at McKenzie. It was constant stress, affecting my wife, kids, and me. But I understood the need. We were losing money, and if we couldn't turn the business around, we would shut it down. On the other hand, Purity is profitable and always has been. The year before the downsizing, we made about $100 million, and we should duplicate that again this year. Purity employees know we're profitable, just like the Medical Diagnostic employees knew we were losing money. At least it made sense at McKenzie."

"Are you making a case for downsizing as the motive, not race?"

"No. Nothing in society exists in a vacuum, and a company is a small society. In my opinion, Cohen's drive to promote only minorities and women causes serious concerns in the workforce. Remember de-layering?" Jim nodded. "De-layering reduced the promotional opportunities, and white men felt locked in their jobs while minorities and women advanced. And if I include the fact Cohen selects the least qualified people for promotion, the feeling of frustration and resentment gets even worse. I think race and gender are a large part of the motive."

"You told me Management was fighting Affirmative Action. What changed?"

"The government did a great job setting standards for job qualifications and tests. They developed the concept of bona fide occupational requirements. Basically, a company had to prove that job qualifications and tests were directly related to the job duties. Let me give you a simple example. McKenzie had a height requirement on operator jobs in its chemical plants. Proper operation of the production machinery required an operator to be tall enough to reach certain controls. The height requirement screened out most women and some Hispanic males. On the surface, the requirement seems reasonable, but if you ask questions like, 'can a platform or step stool be easily used,' the height requirement may not make sense. Corporations and the government started working together to make sense out of job qualifications, and jobs opened for minorities and women."

"Sounds reasonable to me."

"You're right, but it has evolved way beyond reasonable. Affirmative Action no longer means being proactive in recruiting to increase the number of qualified applicants. Today it means 'don't worry about the white guys. It's time for the minorities and women to get their just rewards.' Add the drive for political correctness and the working relationships between men and women and whites and minorities are strained to say the least."

"When people without power start to take power, there's always conflict, so it still sounds reasonable to me."

"I'm not surprised. You obviously think it's okay to discriminate against white men today because blacks and women were discriminated against in the past. You see all white men as the problem whether or not they or their ancestors had anything to do with slavery or discrimination."

"You're damn right. It's time we got ours, and besides, by definition, white men can't be discriminated against."

"Do me a favor. Think about how it feels to be held responsible for everything you say and do at work because you're a man or a white person. Think about being afraid someone may be offended because you weren't up on the latest politically correct term or phrase. Think about being terrified you might lose your job or worse. Think about working with your partner. You're probably tongue-tied when she's around, afraid to say something wrong and lose your fat government pension." The phone rang, and Phil answered it.

Jim finished his pie, took a drink of coffee, and wondered, *How could the son of immigrants, raised in poverty, turn into a fucking conservative? I'll turn him around. He's right about how I feel when working with Parisi, but it's different.* While Phil was absorbed in the phone conversation, Jim wandered around, looking at the knick-knacks and decorations that adorned the living room. He paid particular attention to the family pictures. He assumed some were Phil's wife and kids, and others were individuals, small groups, and large groups. Jim assumed they were extended family. Phil returned, holding a sheet of paper.

"That was Abby. She gave me two more possibilities. Have we had enough of race and downsizing for one night?"

"Yeah, I'm getting a feel for the issues in Purity, and I'll think about what you've said and see if I can connect it to the case. Right now, I'm more interested in working on Abby's suspects."

"I want you to notice that every suspect Abby has come up with is a white male, and I'll bet you every suspect she comes up with in the future will also be a white male. She knows, without really knowing, white men are angry and frustrated with the current workplace culture. Okay, enough philosophy. The first suspect, Gordon Smat, a current employee, works in Maintenance as a janitor doing odd jobs around the plant. Abby picked him because of rumors he was anti-women, always referring to women as bitches and 'hoes.' Also, he's a loner with a gun collection. The other is Jack Higgins, a fairly high-level manager who worked here a long time before being laid off. Abby is going way back on this one. She remembers him bragging about being an expert marksman, and he said he was an expert with a pistol. He claimed he could put a bullet between someone's eyes at thirty feet."

Phil gave Jim addresses and other relevant data on all the suspects and then said, "I've had a long day and need to pack it in. Anything else you need to do tonight?"

"No. When can we get together again?"

"I can meet Tuesday and Thursday. We're meeting to plan the downsizing on Monday. I have heard Hazlitt is planning to meet every Monday, Wednesday, and Friday night until we're done."

"Why are you meeting at night?"

"Because Lorraine is tied up with the FDA all day."

"Okay. See you Tuesday. I'll call to set up a place, and thanks for dinner. It was great, especially the pie. And thanks for your help."

Sunday 12/7

The cursor blinked relentlessly in the upper corner of the Word document Phil had saved as 'Purity – protect my future.' The page was blank, and Phil, chin in his hands, stared at the monitor. He had made a few attempts to type his thoughts but had backspaced the words away. Phil realized he knew nothing of significance about Purity that would protect his job or increase his bank account if he were fired. He was worried that his decision to help Hines was a blunder that would likely destroy the life he and Rose had built.

Phil's Sunday started out as most others had since he had moved to Oyster Bay, except that he awoke alone in his bed. Phil had showered, dressed, and walked into town for a sesame seed bagel loaded with cream cheese and a large coffee at Oyster Bagel. Next, he had stopped at Andy's Convenience Store and picked up a copy of the Sunday New York Times and a couple of lotto tickets. Winning the New York Lottery would solve his financial concerns if only he could overcome the astronomical odds: definitely not a smart bet. This particular Sunday, Phil concentrated on the employment section of the Times, barely skimming the rest of the paper. There were plenty of jobs available, so he decided to put together his resume as an insurance policy.

Feeling pretty downhearted, he decided to give up on protecting his future and work on his resume. He clicked 'File,' then 'New' and was about to open the Resume Wizard when a thought flashed into his conscious mind. *I'm an idiot. Frank and Gino handed me the perfect insurance policy. All I have to do is gather enough data to prove it. Purity would never want the public to know it had been taking production shortcuts. The quality image Purity developed with Thinadin would be lost, as would its enormous profit margins.* Phil sat back, letting his mind roam until he formulated a plan. It came quickly. Tomorrow he would meet with his Production Control people and set his plan in motion, and with enough time and a little luck, Phil would have his insurance. That done, football, especially the game between his Giants and his Eagles, became much more critical to Phil. He shut down his computer in favor of spending a Sunday afternoon in front of the television. He was feeling good about his life again.

Just as the pre-game show started, the phone rang. It was Rose. "Hi hon, how are you doing?"

"I'm doing okay. How about you?"

"I'm a little tired. You don't sound okay… I'll bet going to all those funerals is getting to you. Have you heard anything more about the murders?"

"Only that the police have made little progress, no suspects so far." Phil decided that he would not tell Rose about Hines until tonight. "How's Judy doing?"

"Not good. I feel bad. Judy's in a lot of pain and wants me to stay until Thursday. I know you need me too, but she's in a lot of pain, and since I'm already here…"

"Don't worry about me. I'll be fine," Phil lied. "We have evening meetings all this week to plan the next downsizing, so I won't be home much anyway. And you know there are plenty of restaurants in town, so I'll be able to keep my weight up."

"I know how going through a downsizing affects you, how much you hurt for the people who will lose their jobs. And please be extra careful. You were involved in the layoffs, and everyone knows it. Stay alert."

"Come on, you know everybody likes me."

They talked for a while about the family and Judy's cancer. Rose gave Phil detailed instructions on surviving until Thursday before saying, "Please be careful. I'll be home Thursday night. I love you."

"I love you too. Now let me get to my football game."

Phil settled into his recliner to watch the game. He had visions of watching football until he went to bed, and then the phone rang again just as the Eagles kicked off.

"Hi, Phil." Lorraine's voice was soft and almost garbled, as if she had lost all confidence in herself.

"You don't sound good. What's wrong?"

Lorraine ignored the question. "Can you come over? I desperately need to talk to you. My mother told me something, and you're the only one I feel comfortable telling. I have to tell you now. I can't keep it to myself any longer."

Phil looked at the TV. The Giants were on the Eagles' 45-yard line and driving. He really wanted to watch the game. "I'll be right over."

Lorraine answered the door dressed in gray sweats and red fluffy slippers. Her hair needed combing, and her eyes were glassy. She looked as if she had been up all night. Phil thought she looked both beautiful and sexy. She grabbed Phil by the arms, pulled him into the house, closed the door, and then wrapped her arms around him and squeezed. Her long, lean shape contoured to his body the way a cat would. Lorraine wasn't crying, though there were tears in her eyes, and her body quivered.

She just pressed her body into Phil's and squeezed. She held him tight for a long time before looking into his eyes. "Let's sit on the couch. I have to tell you a story. If I don't, I'll drive myself crazy."

Phil sat on one end of the couch and turned his body toward the center, his left arm on the back and his bent left leg placed across his right leg. He expected Lorraine to sit on the other end of the couch, but instead, she nestled into the pocket formed by his body and left arm. Phil felt desire surge though his body. She stared at the ceiling and started talking.

"You know I grew up in the projects in East New York and that my father died when I was eight years old. My mother worked two jobs to keep food on the table and a roof over our heads. I described life in the projects to you to some degree, but I never got into the emotional damage it caused. I never told you how easy it is to lose hope when you live in the projects and see a world on television that seems unattainable. My mother was always optimistic and never lost hope for my brother and me. She told us over and over we would make it out. All we had to do was listen to her, and she would give us the road map to a better life. My mother worked in a small convenience store during the day and cleaned a couple offices at night. She left early in the morning and didn't get home until around ten-thirty at night, yet somehow, she found plenty of time to spend with my brother and me. She told me what to expect from life as a black woman, and she told me what to expect if I married a black man. She also made sure I knew how important it was to get a good education to take care of myself. She dedicated her life to my brother and me getting a good education and moving up in life. And she forced us to live by very rigid rules when we were teenagers."

Phil wanted to interrupt Lorraine to make sure he understood what she meant by 'life as a black woman' and 'if I married a black man,' but he decided not to. He and Lorraine had had many discussions about race and gender issues. She had told him that frequently, black mothers taught their daughters not to expect as much from life as white women. She said black women were usually invisible to white society, as were black children. A black woman standing at a store counter waiting for service would be ignored if whites were also waiting. White women generally fuss over a white baby and hardly acknowledge a black baby. While most young white girls received messages from society that they could expect a fairytale life, complete with a Prince Charming, young black girls were told how life takes its toll on black men. They should not expect too much from their men. Black men experienced degradation and disrespect every day in the world. Unless a black woman was self-sufficient, she could not expect to have much of a life.

"My brother and I were not allowed out of the house at night Sunday through Friday," Lorraine continued. "When I was fifteen, I could go out with a girlfriend on Saturday nights but had to be home by ten. Dating was absolutely not allowed. I accepted the rules because my mother had given me good reasons why they existed. At least I accepted them until I met Adrian. Adrian was eighteen, and he was hot. He would talk to me as I walked home from school, was always very complimentary about my looks, and was a gentleman. I knew he was a gangbanger and word on the street was he had killed a couple of kids in a drive-by. But when you're fifteen and a cool, good-looking eighteen-year-old is nice to you, anything can be rationalized. One day as he walked me home from school, he asked if I'd go for a walk with him that night. I knew I shouldn't. My mother would kill me if she found out, not to mention how disappointed in me she'd be. But I said yes."

Phil looked at Lorraine. She had not moved since she started talking and was still looking up as if a movie of her life in East New York was playing on the ceiling. He did not interrupt her.

"I enlisted my brother's assistance with a little money and a promise I would cover for him when he was older. The plan was in place. Adrian would meet me at a pizza place three blocks from my house and we'd get something to eat, then we'd walk around the hood. I'd get home long before my mother. I kissed my brother, and I was on my way to my first date. I remember that night as if it was yesterday. It was late spring, and the weather was unusually warm. It felt even warmer because the winter had been colder than normal. Adrian and I sat in the little pizza shop, and over a Pepsi and a couple of slices, we talked and gazed into each other's eyes. I was in love. I remember some girls from school stopping and staring at us. I thought they were jealous. It wasn't until later I found out they were afraid for me. We finished and started walking. We walked unhurriedly, holding hands and smiling. I was the center of the universe, out on a Thursday night, walking and holding hands with a beautiful boy, the love of my young life. I was actually thinking of marriage. Then, as we passed an alleyway, Adrian stopped and looked in. That's when things changed."

Lorraine sat up and moved away from Phil. She turned to face him and held both of his hands.

"Adrian said he wanted to make out and began to pull me into the alleyway. I said no, not tonight, next time, but he laughed and pulled me into the alley. He said we wouldn't take long. I resisted as hard as possible, but I was no match for his strength. I was scared, and at the same time, I was excited. I had never kissed a boy. Adrian led me to a spot hidden from view. I realized later he had planned the whole evening, including this stop. He began kissing me. I responded and was soon experiencing all sorts of feelings for the first time. I enjoyed his lips on mine, and I enjoyed having his tongue in my mouth. And the feel of his hard-on against my body awakened my sexuality. When he put his hand on my breast, I realized we had gone too far, and I tried to push him away. He reacted violently. He grabbed me by my shoulders and pushed me against the wall. A frightening smile formed on his face, and he held me against the wall and began unbuttoning my blouse. He changed into a different person. His eyes became cold and vacant, and I knew he meant to rape me. He reached inside my blouse, unhooked my bra, and told me to take it off. I managed to get my bra off without removing my blouse. I guess I was trying to be modest. When I was done, he put his hand on my breast, caressing my nipple, and started kissing me violently." Lorraine, tears filling her eyes, found it onerous to continue.

"You don't have to tell me this. It was a long time ago. You're way beyond East New York and Adrian."

"Yes, I do. You'll understand why when I'm finished." Lorraine took a deep breath and slowly exhaled. "My mother prepared me for just this kinda situation. She emphasized the need to stay calm and use my brain. She also taught me some tricks I could use if the opportunity presented itself. So even though my sexual desire was long gone, I decided I would act as if I was aroused. That was partly for self-preservation but, more importantly, to give me time to figure a way out. The more I acted, the hotter Adrian got. He moved his attention from my breasts to between my legs. He began to slide his hand inside my panties. I responded by putting my hand on his penis. I eased him away, unbuckled his belt, and pulled down his zipper. I looked in his eyes, acted as sexy as I knew how, and whispered, 'take your pants off, and I'll slip off my panties.' His pants and underwear were off faster than I thought possible, those cold vacant eyes never leaving me. I slowly removed my panties and set them on top of my bra. There I stood, my blouse open, exposing my breasts and my knee-length skirt, the only thing covering the rest of me. Adrian moved in for the kill. As he did, I grabbed his exposed penis and began stroking it. His eyes rolled, and I could tell he was really enjoying it. I moved him back a little and pretended I would go down on him. As I did, I positioned my right leg so it was between his legs. I held his penis tightly in my hand as I moved my head toward it. Partway down, I faked a sneeze. It was the only way to create a diversion I could think of. In one quick movement, I kicked him squarely in the balls. He cried out in pain but didn't go down. Instead, he curled up a little and grabbed his balls. As he did, I pressed my hands on the side of his head and jammed my thumbs into his eyes with all the strength I could muster. He cried out in pain again and reached for his face, and when he did, I kicked him hard in the balls again. This time he went down, screaming. I picked up my undies and bra and his pants and underwear and ran. I ran for two blocks without looking back before I stopped. When I did look back, Adrian was nowhere to be seen. I don't know if I hurt him so bad, he couldn't move or because he didn't want to run around with his manhood dangling for all the hood to see, and I didn't care. I tossed his pants and underwear into a trash can and ran home, a scared little girl wanting her mommy." Lorraine paused.

Phil looked at her, unsure if she was finished.

"No, Phil, I am not done yet, but I'm getting there." Lorraine forced an awkward smile before continuing. "When my mother came home, I told her the whole story, every horrific detail. When I was done, I expected her to tear into me, to really let me have it. Instead, she got this 'I am very disappointed in you, young lady' look on her face. She didn't comment on what happened or my breaking the rules. She was absolutely non-judgmental. She told my brother and me that we were not to leave the apartment under any circumstances until she said it was okay. She then called both her bosses and told them she was sick and wouldn't be in until Monday. Then she went to bed.

"The next day, my brother and I stayed in all day. Some of my girlfriends called, wondering why the word on the street had Adrian out to kill me. I pleaded ignorance. Before she went out Saturday morning, my mother told us she was concerned for our lives and for us to stay put no matter what. After she left, Adrian pounded on the door, screaming for me to open it. He said I was dead if I ever showed my face, and nobody, especially a dumb bitch, could dis him and get away with it. I had brought serious troubles to our home, to my family. Then Sunday night, Adrian was killed in a drive-by shooting, and our family's troubles disappeared. A couple of days later, we got word that Adrian's gang had stopped looking for the shooter, and I was no longer in trouble. It turned out Adrian's gang didn't like him much and, surprisingly, seemed happy he was dead."

"I don't understand why this is upsetting you now. Everything turned out all right. Were you suppressing this memory, and did your mother's death cause you to remember?" Phil asked.

"No. I didn't suppress the memory. In fact, as the story of Adrian and me spread, I became something of a legend. No one knew the whole story, but that didn't matter. After that, the boys I dated always treated me as if I was a princess." Lorraine grew serious and squeezed Phil's hands. "What I'm about to tell you no one else in the world can know. I won't even tell my brother, but I have to tell someone. I have to get it out." Tears welled up in her eyes.

"Phil, before my mother died, she told me what she did that Saturday. She felt she needed to confess. She believed I would be killed if she didn't do something, and she wasn't about to let that happen. She knew a man, a man who came into the store almost every day. They got along, joked, and talked about how bad the neighborhood was getting or how bad the world had become. She'd heard rumors about this man, rumors he was a hired killer, rumors he worked for the mob. She went to his house, told him the story, asked him for help, and asked him to kill Adrian. She offered him a thousand dollars to do the job, my entire college fund. He told her not to worry anymore: it would be his pleasure to help, no charge.

The next day Adrian was dead, and my mother was responsible. My mother is a fucking murderer."

Phil sensed his response was critical. Lorraine was fragile. She had unloaded her burden and wanted to feel good about her mother again, for everything to be okay. "I could only hope I would have the courage to do the same thing if Ann were in danger. To put everything on the line, risk retaliation, risk prison, to protect my family. I believe I have the fortitude, but I can't be sure. Your mother had the strength. She knew what she had to do and dared to act. She's not a murderer. She's a true hero. That piece of shit, Adrian, got what he deserved. He would have raped and killed again. Your mother not only saved your life but many others."

Lorraine stared at Phil for a long time. She was obviously processing his words, thinking about her mother and what she had done. She was trying to put all the circumstances into perspective, including her own role. If she hadn't violated the rules, her mother wouldn't have had to spend the last twenty years of her life as a murderer. "Thank you."

"You're very welcome, my lady," Phil said, acting out a slight bow.

"Phil Messina, I'm serious… thanks." Lorraine was lost in thought, then said, "Can you stay and have dinner with me? We can have Chinese delivered."

"Sure, but I hate Chinese. I'd rather a big cheesesteak."

"No problem. I'll get a chicken Caesar salad. I'll call later. First, I need a shower."

"Settled. I'll watch the end of the Giants/Eagles game while you try to make yourself look a little presentable."

It was the middle of the fourth quarter, and the Giants were up 24 to 7. The Eagles had the ball and were driving. Phil felt relaxed with Lorraine, as he always had. He thought of Lorraine as the sister he had never had. However, lately, especially when she had hugged him, he thought of her as a sexy, desirable woman. Phil put aside his thoughts of Lorraine and immersed himself in the game.

Clean, pampered, smelling good, and for the first time in days, feeling good, Lorraine stopped on the bottom step. She looked at Phil sitting in her easy chair and watching football. *He's so supportive, and he's non-judgmental,* she thought, smiling. *What would I do without him? He always knows the right thing to say, and I know my secret is safe with him. It would be nice if Phil was with me all the time… if he watched football from our easy chair.*

"Ready for me to call in our order?" Lorraine asked as she picked up the phone.

Phil looked up. "You look much better, and it only took an hour and a half."

"I look great. I know it, and you know it, and it only took a few minutes. If I were having dinner with someone special, I'd have taken more time and would look fabulous. Now, do you still want that fatty cheesesteak?"

"I sure do. Fat looks good on me."

While waiting for dinner to arrive, Phil watched the four o'clock football game. Lorraine busied herself puttering around the kitchen and straightening up.

Over dinner, Lorraine asked, "Have you thought much about tomorrow night?"

"I've thought about it, and I've thought about last year."

"Everything you predicted last year has happened. The quality of our products has suffered, we're missing production schedules, interactions between employees are vicious, and the overall environment in the plant is depressing."

"Lorraine, you could have made the same predictions. You saw what happened at McKenzie, but you kept quiet."

"You know why I didn't say anything. It was out of misguided loyalty to Diane Armstrong. I was loyal for the wrong reason: because she was black. I was afraid the other black employees at Purity would ostracize me. Are you going to speak up tomorrow night?"

"I don't know. Things aren't going too well for me right now. And who the hell would listen anyway?"

"That's never stopped you before. And I have a feeling Pamela might listen."

"Maybe it's time I took care of myself."

"You and I are different from our peers. We come from poverty, and most of them come from middle-class backgrounds, if not from privilege. I don't know about you, but I'm not comfortable working with them."

"I don't think it's a difference in background. I always felt comfortable in McKenzie. I think it's Purity."

"That's where you and I differ. I didn't feel comfortable in McKenzie either. And before you lecture me on the virtues of McKenzie's management, remember I'm a beautiful black woman, and you're a big ugly Italian. You didn't experience the sexual crap I did."

They ate in silence, then talked about the murders and the investigation. Phil felt it best not to tell Lorraine about his role with Lieutenant Hines. They talked about the pressure Lorraine would be under during the FDA audit and about implementing another downsizing. Weighty subjects were discussed effortlessly by friends.

After dinner, Phil helped clean up and readied to leave. "See you tomorrow night after you handle those bureaucrats from the FDA, and then we can do some serious job cutting."

"Sounds like an exciting day, full of fun and adventure. Slay the federal dragon, then fire some of our co-workers." Lorraine stood in front of Phil. "Thanks for being there for me." She put her hands on his face, kissed him gently on the lips, and said, "I love you." Then she kissed him again, this time with passion, her mouth opened, her tongue finding his. Her hands moved to the back of his head, her fingers entwined in his hair.

Phil responded. He wrapped his arms around her and held her tight. Their excitement grew with Phil's hands moving around her back, Lorraine's hands moving around his head. In unison, they moved to the couch, passionately kissing. His hand found her breast and her body shook. Maneuvering her against the back of the couch, Phil slid his hand moved under her blouse. He fondled her breast and Lorraine's hand moved to his erection. Phil helped her remove her top. His hand found her breast again, and he gently caressed it. She started to unbuckle his belt, then stopped. Without a word, they both stopped.

Lorraine pushed him away. "I can't do this, Phil. As much as I want to, I can't. You're married, I know you love Rose, and I can't do anything to ruin it for you. I love you too much."

Phil, overheated and out of control, could not believe what he was hearing. He took a deep breath to gain some control of his emotions. He was with a beautiful woman, and she wanted to stop. When Phil finally stopped thinking with his lower head, he realized she was right. In fact, he realized — in a brief epiphany as the fog of lust cleared — that he loved her because she was a good human being. This proved it. "You're right. We can't do this. It would ruin what we have, and I don't want that either."

They both hoped that their relationship would survive and go back to the way it was. As Phil readied to leave again, he kissed Lorraine on the cheek and said, "I love you too." She smiled, and Phil left.

Phil knew he had been weak, that he had caved to the pressure he was under at work – and that this was not like him and would not happen again. He believed Lorraine was reacting to her mother's actions.

Kathleen Connolly glared at her husband. "I can't believe you're not going. It's your only chance to see my parents for the holidays. Besides, we were going to have a romantic week. All I had to do was show my face at Garden City during the day and attend a couple of meetings at night. We'd have a lot of free time to reinvigorate our marriage."

Kathleen and Michael had moved from Long Island to Chadds Ford, Pennsylvania, when Kathleen was promoted to Vice President of Materials for Purity. Before her promotion, she had worked at the Garden City site. Kathleen had counted on this trip with Michael; she was worried about their twelve-year marriage. Michael had changed after the move to Chadds Ford. He withdrew and became very touchy when she tried to penetrate his defensive shield. She knew the reason. He had moved away from everything he knew and loved: his job, his friends, his routine. The move had stressed their marriage almost to the breaking point.

"I can't go with you. I have an opportunity to close a deal. I know this little business you bought me is insignificant to you, but it's important to me. You'll be fine. Mike Jr. can stay with your parents, and you can get some real work done at Garden City," Michael said.

"We need to work on our relationship. Ever since we moved here, the distance between us has been growing. I can't go on this way. I'm sorry I bought you that goddamned business. It's done nothing but cost money and hurt our relationship."

"That 'goddamned little business' is all I got, and this deal could make it profitable. And don't blame my fucking business for our problems. You're married to Purity and Bob Cohen. You spend most of your life at work, and when you're not working, you're thinking about work. I run the house and take care of Mike Jr., and what little time I have left I spend on the business. Hell of a life for a man! I'm not walking away from this deal. It's important to me."

"You're putting me in a bad spot. Because of the murders, Bob doesn't want me traveling alone. He said if you weren't going, he wouldn't let me go. I assured him you were going. Now I'm between a rock and a hard place. My parents expect me, and if I go, Bob will be pissed."

"Stop worrying about Cohen. Go see your parents. Mike Jr. misses them. We'll go on a nice vacation in January. I promise."

"All right, I'll go, but I'm holding you to January."

Monday 12/8

Aside from the hum of some office equipment, Purity's executive office area was eerily still. His plan was in motion, and with any luck, he would find evidence to corroborate Frank and Gino's allegations. When he did, his and Rose's financial future would be secure. Phil arrived at the office around seven-fifteen, much earlier than usual. He was anxious to implement the plan that he hoped would lift the weight of uncertainty from his shoulders. The transfer completed, Phil tucked his laptop under his arm and walked to the Production Control area. Despite the early hour, Phil whistled as his desktop computer transferred the database from its hard drive to the hard drive of his laptop computer.

Joan McMullen, in early as usual, was at her desk. Although it was well before eight, she was already working on today's production runs, ensuring that the needed materials were in place in the Production Areas. She looked up as Phil approached. "Good morning."

"Hi, Joan. Are we all set for today's production?"

"Best I can tell, everything is in place."

"Good, I know you're pretty busy these days, but I have a special project for you. It's full-time for the next eight to ten days."

The look on Joan's face was one of sheer disbelief. "If I'm not here for that long, the place will fall apart. My work won't go away. How do you plan to get it done?"

"How does the Production Area get by when you're on vacation?"

"Pam and Jill share the critical parts of my job, and we hire a temp to handle the routine work. But I only go on vacation for one week at a time, and I work my ass off for the week before and I get everything ready. When I return, Production is near disaster."

Joan reacted as Phil had assumed. A super conscientious employee with an overinflated perception of her value. He had worked with many employees like her over the years and knew how to handle her. "You're right. We can't have Production get behind schedule because of us. They've been screwing up a lot lately and falling behind production schedules on their own. They'd like nothing better than to blame us. I'll come up with another way to get the project done. It's just that the project is critical, and I need someone I can depend on."

"What do you want done?"

The hook was in place. All Phil had to do now was set it. "You know we're going to start measuring cycle-time and try to find ways to reduce it. I thought we could get a faster start if we took a hard look at historical data. I designed a custom database to store the data and then analyze it. I have it on my laptop, and I was hoping you would go down to QC and start entering the data from the old Batch Records. But don't worry, I'll find someone else to do it." He turned to leave.

"Hold on. You said reducing cycle time was important. I've heard that but don't really know what cycle-time is."

Phil had her hooked. "Cycle-time is the length of time it takes to produce a product. In this case, we'll measure how long it takes to produce our drugs. We'll determine how many days it takes from the time raw materials are delivered to the Granulation Area until the finished product leaves our shipping dock. It's important to shorten cycle time as much as possible because we can be more responsive to the customer and save a lot of money on inventory costs. I want to calculate our historical cycle times to set realistic goals, and I want to look at the cycle time in each area. That way, we can find bottlenecks and fix them."

"Would you mind showing me the program you developed?"

"Sure." Phil unpacked his laptop and booted it up. "Does this mean you're considering helping out?"

"Yes, it does."

As Phil and Joan looked at the laptop screen, Phil said, "This is the main menu. From here, you can navigate to the forms used to enter data for each area. Later I'll design the reports we'll use to analyze the data." Phil pushed the button labeled 'Granulation Area.' "The main part of the form is where you select the drug you'll be working on." Phil clicked in the 'find drug' list box, and a list with every drug produced at the Garden City site dropped down. Phil selected Thinadin. The equipment used to make Thinadin, the time on each piece, and other specifications automatically filled in the form.

"As you can see, all the basic information on each drug we make is already in the system." Next, Phil pointed to the sub form. "What I need you to do is enter the actual data from the Batch Records here, then do the same for each area. There's a separate form for each area."

They quickly looked at each form.

"Well, what do you think?"

"I'll help. I know this is important. But I can't let the people in my group down."

"What if you only worked on this project for four hours a day… say, in the middle of the day? You're busiest in the morning and evening, and Pam and Jill can help out. This is so important I'd be willing to approve any OT you need."

"That should work. When do you want me to start?"

"I'll meet you at ten in the QC area, and we'll do the first one together. How does that sound?"

"Fine. I'll see you there."

Mike Jr. slept peacefully, the rhythmic sounds of the train overcoming his excitement at the prospect of visiting his grandparents. Gary Hazlitt, Pamela Robinson, and Kathleen Connolly talked in hushed tones.

"It's a shame Michael couldn't join you, but I'm glad his business is growing. Don't worry. Pamela and I will keep you company."

"We're all staying at the Garden City Hotel. Gary will be here all week, and I'll go back with you and Mike Jr. on Thursday."

Kathleen smiled. "I'm glad you're going to take care of me, but I'd rather have Michael do it."

Both Pamela and Kathleen chuckled. Gary missed the innuendo.

Kathleen continued, "How long do you think the meeting will last tonight?"

"We'll be done by nine. Three hours will give us a damn good start. We have to get everything in place and be ready to announce the downsizing before the holidays. That includes producing a list of employees we're going to pressure," Gary replied.

"Are we going to pressure Messina to leave?" Kathleen asked.

"Not yet. The murders have changed our plans, we need all three directors for now, and Messina still has support in McKenzie," Gary replied.

"Too bad. I'd like him out. He can cause trouble for us. Don't you agree, Pamela?"

Pamela had purposely stayed out of the conversation. Now Kathleen was dragging her in. "I don't think he's a bad guy. He just has this compulsion to protect employees from Management. It's the old McKenzie style. We need to teach him the Purity way."

"Or find a way to fire him. Old dogs don't learn new tricks," Gary said.

Funny. You did, Pamela thought.

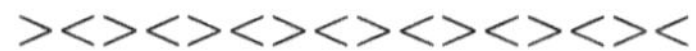

The contents of the open drawer were placed neatly at one end of the dining room table. The false bottom of the drawer was leaning against the wall, and the metal case it usually masked was open at the other end of the table. The foam insert in the metal case had cutouts that perfectly fit ten different pistols. Nine of the cutouts were filled. The missing pistol lay at the bottom of the Long Island Sound.

Decisions, decisions. What instrument should the maestro use tonight? It must be easy to conceal, good for use in tight quarters, and quiet. Ah, the Berretta .22, perfect choice. Echo removed the chosen pistol from its resting place, gripped it in his right hand, and moved it up and down. *Feels good. Nice and light.* He sighted along the barrel, aiming at various objects in the room. *This is the instrument, the instrument of justice, of revenge. It feels good, I feel good, and I'm in charge again, controlling my own destiny.* He put the metal case, missing the Berretta .22 and its silencer, in the drawer, covered it with the false bottom, and replaced the contents.

He found the small case that held his professional burglary tools buried in a suitcase in his bedroom closet. He unzipped the case and made sure it contained all his tools. He then flipped through the twenty-five suits that hung neatly in his closet. He tried on six before settling for a dark gray, wool suit with light pinstripes. It was a little big, sufficient to cloak the Berretta and shoulder holster. He examined his appearance in a full-length mirror from various angles and felt confident the gun he would carry was not easily noticeable.

Joan McMullen, driven by her internal desire to please, had entered data for the last three hours without even breaking for lunch. Taking her time to make sure the entries were accurate, she entered twenty-one Batch Records. As Joan entered data from number twenty-two, Gary Hazlitt entered the QC area. He immediately asked Joan why she was not at her desk. She explained the cycle-time project and showed him the data she was recording.

"And what are you going to do with the data?"

"Mr. Messina is going to calculate the historical cycle-time for each of our products so we can come up with realistic objectives for each product."

"How long will it take you to get the data into the system?"

Joan remembered Phil's original estimate of eight to ten days full time and added a little. "I'm only working on this project four hours a day, so I won't finish for six weeks."

"I'm glad to see Messina and Production Control finally taking some initiative. Keep up the good work," Gary said, a slight scowl on his face.

Pamela Robinson and Kathleen Connolly relaxed over a drink as they listened to piano music in the lounge at the Garden City Hotel. They had settled into their rooms earlier, and Kathleen's parents had picked up Mike Jr. and taken him to their home.

"Bob has done a great job as CEO. When we were part of McKenzie, we added people and spent money as if profits weren't important. Bob's changed all that. Soon we'll have eliminated all unnecessary employees and money will flow to the bottom line. Management at McKenzie and Saga will see what kind of CEO Bob is, and he'll keep moving up. Hopefully, he'll take us with him," Kathleen said.

"Aren't you worried we're moving too fast? The employees are still upset over the last downsizing. We all have major projects in the works. You're in the middle of installing a major computer upgrade to our materials management system and are already a little behind schedule. You'll only fall further behind because of the chaos caused by the job movement and training we'll have to do."

"I'll get the project done on time, and if I don't, Bob will let me push out the completion date. Nothing is more important than increasing profits. We have to show our owners we can run an effective business. Enough about the downsizing. We'll make it work."

They sat in silence. Pamela was frustrated that everyone on Cohen's staff was in a contest to see how many employees they could fire. They were ignoring the long-term impact on the business. At McKenzie, Management had cared about employees. They had taken pride in the fact that turnover was low, and employees had wanted to work for them and build a future. Yet when Bob became Purity's first CEO, that began to change. His efforts to impress the owners and enhance his career would destroy all the company had built. Sure, he continued to promote women and minorities, but only those who would do his bidding: people like Diane and Kathleen, too foolish to see beyond the ends of their noses, too focused on money and power to understand that they were destroying people's lives. *Hell, it's all just a game anyway*, she thought, *and when it comes right down to it, I'm no better than the others*. Did Pamela really care for the employees if, when it was decided they would be fired, she went along and collected her paychecks and her bonuses? She enjoyed the trappings of power, just like the others, and she was afraid to walk away, just like the others. She was just like the people she despised.

"Kathleen, you know the employees at Garden City as well as I do. We even know most of their families. How can you support another round of layoffs? Don't you feel any guilt?"

"None whatsoever. Bob decided it's best for the future of Purity to reduce the number of employees, so that's what I'll do. Fuck the employees. They don't care about me, and I don't care about them. I have a life most people could only dream of, and I won't do anything to screw it up. And don't give me your high and mighty shit. You talk like you care, but you'll do whatever it takes to protect your career, just like me."

"You're right, although it's bothering me more and more lately. I can't sleep or look at myself in the mirror, and I keep thinking about the employees we fired. I always thought of myself as a good person who had principles and would always live by those principles. I know what we're doing is wrong and all I do is talk about it."

Kathleen noticed the tear in Pamela's eye and softened her response. "Try to think about it this way. We're part of a large corporation – in fact, two large corporations – and decisions like this are made at high levels. Our job is to implement those decisions, and if we don't, we'll be replaced by someone who will. Stop letting it bother you. You'll drive yourself crazy."

"I feel like I already have, and I'm tired of it. When I saw this going on in the other divisions of McKenzie, I thanked God we weren't involved. Now we are, thanks to Bob."

After a few minutes, Kathleen asked, "Do you think Diane and Steve were killed because of the last downsizing?"

"Yes, and I think there will be more killings, especially when we announce the next downsizing. You can't do this to people, to families, and just expect they'll accept it and go away. Jobs at Purity are important to people. They make good money and have good benefits. You can't change that and expect anyone to leave happy."

"If you're trying to scare me, it's working. I sure as hell don't want to be the next victim. The only reason I'm here is to visit my parents. Michael and I are going to Disneyland for the holidays, and I couldn't go without seeing them. I really wish he was here."

"Try not to worry. Gary will stay with us tonight until we get to our rooms. He's carrying a gun, and he knows how to use it."

Phil looked over Joan's shoulder at his laptop's screen as she filled him in.

"I entered twenty-six Batch Records today. Now that I have a feel for the program, I'll be faster tomorrow."

"Great. I'll take the laptop with me and meet you here tomorrow at nine. Thanks, Joan. I really appreciate what you're doing."

"By the way, Mr. Hazlitt stopped to see what I was doing in the QC area. He seemed really interested and said he was happy we were taking the initiative. See you tomorrow."

I wonder if he'll have a problem with this. He seems to have a problem with everything I do lately, Phil thought. Back at his office, he copied the data from his laptop to his desktop and backed it up. Just as he finished, Lorraine walked in and closed the door. Phil started to say something, but Lorraine interrupted.

"I want to put yesterday behind us. It should have never happened. I lost control of myself. Maybe it was my mother's death… I don't know, but I should've known better. I respect you too much to let my feelings for you ruin our friendship. I don't want yesterday to affect our relationship. I want to stay close friends."

Phil was tongue-tied. He could handle any other conversation, but one that involved his feelings for a woman, especially a woman other than Rose, left him stammering. "I want to stay close too."

"What the hell does that mean?"

"I don't know. Most of me would like things to be the way they were. But the rest of me would like yesterday to be the norm. I'm confused. I have feelings for you as a close friend, and I have feelings for you as a woman."

"Phil, we have to get over this. I need you in my life, but it'll work only as a friend. I won't… I can't break up your family. I couldn't live with myself."

"Okay, we'll work it out. Let's change the subject. Tell me about the FDA. They left early."

"All we did today was cover the preliminaries. We spent most of the day touring the Production and Quality areas. Then things got a little strange when the FDA advised me what info they wanted ready for the next session. They started with old Batch Records for Relieve from ten years ago. Usually, they only care about current production and only go back a year or so. I have the feeling they were looking for something specific… you know, as if they knew something and wanted to verify it. Strange. Fortunately, I have some time to get the information together. They're not coming back until Wednesday. As with most government agencies, they're in no hurry. They'll get done when they get done."

Phil was pleased that the FDA wouldn't interfere with the Batch Records he needed. "Our tax dollars in action."

"See you tonight."

"I'll be there."

"Friends?"

"Friends."

After Lorraine left, Phil walked down to Abby's office. "Hi, having a good day?"

"Normal, or as normal as a day can get after last week. Two co-workers were murdered, and I'm risking my job by ratting out co-workers to the police for a boss who will get fired. Just a normal day. And you probably want more victims to feed to your lieutenant buddy."

Phil hoped that Abby was kidding. "That's what I want. Have you come up with any others?"

"I have a few more names in mind, but I need to check out a few things first. I need to be sure before I subject them to a police investigation. Any word on the ones I gave you?"

"No. I'll let you know as soon as I hear."

"Are you going to protect me in the meeting tonight?"

"How the hell do you know about the meeting?"

"I have my ways. You didn't think something this big would stay secret for long, did you? You didn't trust me enough to tell me. If I wind up on the block, let me know. I want to start looking for a job. Oh, and so much for Cohen's word."

"Nothing is going to happen to you." Phil now understood why she was antsy. "I didn't think Cohen would go back on his word. I guess you were right."

"Yeah, right. Just let me know if I need to start looking for another job. And try to take care of Russ Cady."

Phil knew it was useless to try and find out where Abby got her information. She would never tell him. He knew it came from a 'friend' in Wilmington, but he didn't know who. In a way, he was glad the rumor was leaking out.

Echo looked closely at item 34, described in the brochure as a Victorian marble-top table with scrolled legs – circa 1900. Echo decided that he would bid a maximum of three hundred and fifty dollars and marked the brochure accordingly. He slowly walked around the large hall, occasionally stopping to carefully observe a piece of furniture or a lamp and jot a note on the flyer. The two hundred or so others in the hall did the same. As they roamed, ostensibly focusing on the items that interested them, they also observed the activities of their competitors. Tonight's auction would commence at around seven.

Echo's reasons for choosing the Amityville auction as his alibi were simple. He wanted to be seen but not observed. Since this was the first time that he had attended the auction, the clerks at the registration desk would likely pay less attention to him than the regulars. He hoped that he would not know any of the other attendees.

Echo finished the preview, identifying over twenty items that he would bid on and hopefully buy. He neatly folded the brochure, slipped it into his jeans' back pocket, and left the building. He walked down the street and stood by the payphone in the convenience store's parking lot. At precisely six-fifteen, the phone rang. He answered instantly.

"Yes?"

"She's in 405," a woman said.

Echo hung up and returned to the auction.

Jumbo shrimps were hooked around the circumference of a large, silver bowl, its center occupied by a smaller bowl of glistening cocktail sauce. A variety of deli sandwich halves were artfully arranged on an equally large tray next to the shrimp. Bowls of potato chips, cheese curls, tortilla chips, and others were scattered on the table. Last but not least, the desserts — cheesecake, black forest cake, pecan pie, cookies, and fudge — decorated a tray near the end of the table. Soft drinks packed in ice sat in a cooler on the floor.

Phil's expression made love to the food in the way a newscaster tries to make love to the camera. "God, I love the pharmaceutical industry. Well, at least I love the food at the meetings."

"You're a goddamned food freak," Lorraine said.

"It's hereditary. Somewhere in the distant past, a 'we like food' gene found its way into the Italian pool, and we've been improving it since. It certainly adds to our enjoyment of life."

"Soon, you'll be perfect. Fat, but perfect."

"You're jealous because we Italians look good whether we're fat or skinny. You black folk are born with two strikes against you. Being fat would be the third."

"Yeah, you're right. You do look good, and you're…"

"Don't say it! We've talked enough about weighty issues, so please lighten up. Let's talk about firing people. It's easy, and nobody gets hurt."

As Lorraine was about to answer, Pamela Robinson motioned her over.

"I'll be back in a minute," Lorraine said as she walked toward Pamela.

Phil piled some food on his plate and sat next to Paul Stanley. They talked about technical problems for much longer than Phil would have liked, but Stanley was on a roll. He quoted test results for Batches in production and theorized technical reasons why the test results were out of specification. Phil wanted to tell him the real reason, but he had to wait until he had proof. When the conversation wound down and Stanley ran out of production problems to talk about, Phil decided to ask about his run-in with Cohen.

"I saw you in Cohen's face at Gagnon's funeral. You were really going at it. I couldn't figure out what would get you so angry."

"What? You're blowing it out of proportion. We talked about the murders, and I got upset. I wasn't angry. I was upset because Diane and Steve were killed in our building. You misread the situation."

"Wow, I was really that wrong? You talked about the murders, and your face was two inches from Cohen's. You were beet-red, and your eyes were wide open. Your finger kept poking his shoulder, and you're telling me you weren't angry? But what I find the most confusing is how I didn't hear anything about Diane and Steve. I did hear the words 'Relieve' and 'time.' Paul, you're bullshitting me."

Paul Stanley's face flushed, and he appeared to collapse into himself. He stared at Phil blankly, as if all the circuits in his brain had shorted at once. Tears began to trickle out of his left eye. "You're wrong. You didn't hear that!" Paul shouted. "I… I have to go." Paul got up and walked out of the conference room, leaving his unfinished meal behind.

Gary Hazlitt, hearing the commotion, made a beeline to Phil and whispered in his ear. "What the fuck did you do to Paul?"

Phil pulled away. "I have no clue. You'll have to ask him."

Phil picked up his and Stanley's leftovers, dropped them into the trash, and left the conference room. As he walked out, he heard Hazlitt announce the meeting would start in five minutes.

Gary Hazlitt looked uncomfortable as he cleared his throat to start the meeting. Pamela Robinson, Kathleen Connolly, Paul Stanley, Lorraine Waters, and Phil Messina were seated around the conference table. Each sat back in a leather chair and looked relatively stress-free considering the subject of the gathering. Phil was sure that the others, with the exception of Lorraine, had worked together earlier to protect their people. Phil and Lorraine were the outcasts in this group.

Hazlitt began. "We'll use a process similar to the one we used earlier this year. As of right now, none of our professional and management employees have a job. We'll re-engineer the job structure at Garden City, reducing the number of positions as much as possible, but at least by a hundred. We must meet our cost objectives. We'll then decide which employees are the best qualified for the remaining positions in the organization and assign them to a position. Those without a position when we're done will be targeted for layoff. Any questions?" Hazlitt looked individually at Stanley, Waters, and Messina as if to say, "You're not dumb enough to ask a question, are you?" When no one did, he spoke. "All right let's begin. We have a lot of time to make up, so I hope you're ready. We'll start with the positions that report directly to the directors. I'll handle the Production organization. Phil, we'll look at the positions that report to you first. Remember, we're not going to discuss who fills what position until we set the organization."

Hazlitt projected a slide that listed the positions in Phil's organization. Phil looked at the list. He had already decided he could eliminate four positions, assuming that he could backfill the openings with the right people. "I could eliminate the Manager of Documentation and the Purchasing Manager," Phil said.

"Hell, anyone could do that. You need to stretch, to look hard at what your people are doing. I think you need to reduce your direct reports by at least four," Hazlitt said.

Kathleen jumped in. "Not to mention that one of the jobs you want to eliminate is critical to Purity's long-term success. We're installing a corporate-wide computer system to manage our materials, from purchase to shipment. You want to take out a key position right in the middle of the project. That's bullshit. You're trying to protect your favorites in HR."

Kathleen Connolly and Joe Jacobs, the Purchasing Manager, were long-time friends. She knew, as did everyone else at the table, that Joe was not qualified to do the Purchasing job, let alone any other position in management. Kathleen also knew that no other director would want him. He would be fired.

"We can combine the duties of the Production Control Manager and the Purchasing Manager positions into one job. One person can handle the job and the project as long as it's someone sharp. Joe can barely do the Purchasing job by itself, and he's been in it ten years," Phil shot back.

Kathleen appealed directly to Hazlitt. "He's not supposed to talk about people. Besides, Joe's a great employee, and everyone here knows it." She turned to Phil. "I'd rather have him in the job than you, Phil. At least he would listen to me and do what I asked."

"As long as you're looking for someone who will only do as he's told, Joe's your man. Why don't you transfer him to your group? Then we'll both be happy," Phil said.

Hazlitt jumped in. "Enough already. We're not going to make progress this way. Phil, I don't think you're prepared to take this seriously. We'll move on to Production, then, since I know I'm prepared. And I'd advise the rest of you to do some serious thinking about your organizations. This isn't easy, but we have to do it."

"The problem is that you're trying to separate people and jobs, and you can't do it. We're not dealing with chairs here. Everybody doesn't fit in every job. We need to consider our employees whenever we talk about how we'll restructure the organization," Phil said.

"Look, I'm running this meeting, and like it or not, we'll do it my way. Now let's get moving."

><><><><><><><

The bidding on the Victorian marble-top table reached three hundred dollars, and three other bidders were still active. Echo raised his number at the auctioneer's call for three-ten. The call immediately changed. "We have three-ten, can I get three-twenty, can I get three-twenty?" After looking around, number 257 raised her card.

Echo got angry. *She's a fucking housewife furnishing her home. I have to get the piece for a good price to resell it and make some money.* The call moved to three-thirty, and Echo raised his number. When the call advanced to three-forty, the housewife placed her number on her lap. After three calls for three-forty, the auctioneer declared the item sold to number 114 for $330 and began describing the next antique. Echo had purchased the table for twenty dollars less than his maximum, but more importantly, he had helped solidify his alibi.

Echo bid on four more items, winning the bid on one by his eight o'clock deadline. He gave up his seat to a woman standing along the wall and moved to the rear of the hall. As attention focused on the auctioneer, Echo slipped out of the hall, just a tired dealer going out for a bite to eat, and made his way to his minivan. The middle and back seats were removed, and two movers' blankets were spread on the floor in anticipation of winning bids on several pieces of furniture. Echo used the space to change into his gray pinstripe suit. After changing, he drove to the Garden City Hotel.

There was a noticeable spring in his step as he crossed the threshold. The lobby of the Garden City hotel was humming. Uniformed bellhops pushed brass-plated luggage carriers followed by obviously well-heeled guests. To his left, guests were two deep at the reception desk. To his right, elevated about two feet above the lobby, the piano bar, where Pamela

Robinson and Kathleen Connolly had relaxed two hours earlier, buzzed with the chatter of the slightly inebriated. All were utterly focused on their activity and failed to notice the slight bulge under the gray, pinstriped suit coat worn by the man with the spring in his step.

There were no people on the fourth floor as he exited the elevator. The hotel's guests were apparently at dinner or in their rooms getting ready. When he reached the door to 405, the professional lock pick was already in his hand. He inserted the choice into the old-fashioned lock and moved it progressively down the tumblers until each was aligned. Then, turning the pick, he opened the door. No one saw him during the few minutes it took to unlock the door. He put on his latex gloves and hairnet and entered the room. He opened the door briefly to wipe around the doorknob with a hand towel and hang the "Do Not Disturb" sign. After a quick look around the room, he took off his suit coat and placed it neatly folded on the back of the desk chair.

Echo checked his watch, thinking. *She should be here at about nine-fifteen.* He pulled his Beretta out of its holster, worked the mechanism, and re-holstered it. *Soon, one of Cohen's girls will check out of the world permanently, and all because she let him run her life… all because she's willing to do anything as long as she moves up the ladder and those big paychecks keep coming. Everyone knows she's dumb, exactly the kind of manager Cohen wants around him: stupid, greedy, and willing to do anything for money and power. She's never had an original thought in her life, so I know it wasn't her idea to set me up, but if any of them is alive when the shit hits the fan, they'll know I'm the killer. For now, they're not sure why Diane and Steve were killed. After tonight, though, I think Cohen will get suspicious, so I need to take care of the others promptly. Cohen believes that only he knows who the players are in his illegal game. But we know. He made a major mistake assuming his communications were secure, but we uncovered his plan. He planned to ruin me, but now his people are dying.* He settled in for the wait.

When Gary Hazlitt finished detailing the cuts that he planned in the Production organization, Phil knew that his people were in big trouble. The plan was less than fair. Despite his concerns, Phil couldn't stop himself. "Production is by far the largest organization at Garden City. It has more layers of management and, therefore, has more redundancy than the other groups. Production management adds little value to the effective operation of Garden City. At best, they pass information to one another. I believe we should make the most staff reductions in Production. You're proposing only minimal cuts, leaving the rest of us to make up the difference."

Before Hazlitt could respond, Lorraine spoke up. "Phil's right. We can easily remove all the Section Supervisors in Production and not miss a beat. They literally do nothing but pass information up and down the organization. If they weren't there, the information would still flow — and it would flow faster."

"We're the ones who make the product. We mix the raw materials, compress them into tablets, and package the product. If we don't do our jobs, we have nothing to sell," Gary responded.

Empowered by Lorraine's support, Phil jumped back in. "Every employee contributes to getting the product to our customers. You can't make a product without raw materials, which have to be purchased, stored, and scheduled. Try making a product without people. People need to be hired and paid, and their problems must be resolved. We need to decide what's best for Purity, not our organizations."

Pamela Robinson tried to end the bickering. "This isn't solving a thing. Gary put the plan for Production on the table. Before we start criticizing it, we'll do the same for every other group. Then we'll see where we are relative to our goal. Paul, you're next. We'll finish up with Lorraine and Phil Wednesday night." Pamela looked at Lorraine first, then Phil. "That way, you'll have plenty of time to get ready. Let's keep moving. I want out of here no later than nine."

Echo set the alarm on the hotel clock for nine. He sat in an upholstered chair with his feet propped up on the bed. Last week Echo had killed someone for the first time in nearly thirty years, and for the first time, he had killed without his government ordering him to. A week ago, he had killed a co-worker: not an enemy of his country, but surely an enemy of his future.

While at Clemson University, Echo had received an ROTC scholarship obligating military service. Two days after completing the mandatory psychological testing, he was sitting outside the captain's office, waiting for his assignment. He had hoped that he could stay stateside. Even though there were no major wars at the moment, the Middle East was hot and a hazardous part of the world. Echo had planned to be an employed biochemist finding the cure for cancer, not an Army Lieutenant, but he needed the scholarship.

When Echo entered the captain's office, he was surprised to find the chair behind the desk occupied by a civilian. The civilian introduced himself as special agent Jerry Benson, CIA. He wanted to talk to him about a unique opportunity to work with CIA special operations, serve his country, and save the lives of Americans. The CIA had been alerted when Echo's psychological test was analyzed. His profile had matched the unique psychology necessary for a CIA assassin. Jerry Benson convinced Echo to go through training before making a final decision. He assured him that the training would be exciting, and that even if he chose not to accept the assignment, the skills he learned would give him a level of confidence that would serve him well in the civilian world.

Echo's affirmative response set in motion six months of specialized, intense training. A great student, he became skilled with firearms, pistols, and rifles. Echo became an expert marksman skilled with a variety of weapons. He learned where to place a bullet or ice pick to maximize the target's chance of dying instantly. Echo was also schooled in the art of disguise and the detailed planning required to avoid capture. He could plan an assassination and get close enough to his targets to use his weapon of choice. He could even change his appearance to protect his identity. Six months after entering the assassin training school, Echo exited a dangerous man.

After graduation, he spent his time at a CIA facility in Virginia waiting for an assignment. He cleaned and oiled his graduation gifts: one a metal carrying case with ten pistols of various makes and calibers, the other a case holding a precision rifle. He also received a case with several ice picks and quick release devices for attaching them to his arm.

When his first assignment came, Echo learned of a conspiracy to kill Mikhail Gorbachev. President Reagan charged the CIA with protecting him, believing that the Cold War would only end if Gorbachev remained head of the Soviet Union. Echo flew to East Germany; his mission was to terminate a high-ranking East German army officer who was involved in the conspiracy. He and two other agents spent two days planning the mission. They had reliable information that the rogue captain was meeting his contact at a small park not far from the zoo. Their plan involved disguising Echo as an old German man, a chore made easy because he, at five-foot-eight, weighed only one hundred and forty-five pounds. With professionally applied make-up he looked weak and sickly. He carried a .38 caliber six-shot revolver in a holster well concealed by his baggy clothing.

Echo arrived at the meeting site at two-thirty. The small, circular park was mainly obscured by the trees planted around the perimeter. A marble fountain surrounded by outward-facing wooden benches occupied the park's center. A small brick walkway circled the benches, while a poorly maintained lawn completed the circle. Echo picked a bench with a view of the entrance and pretended to read a newspaper. He looked like an old man just passing the time.

The captain arrived first and gave Echo a long look over before deciding to stay. About five minutes later, the contact arrived. The two conspirators sat on the same bench and started to talk. Echo slowly folded the paper and stood up shakily, acting as if he had difficulty. The two men bought the disguise and hardly noticed him as he began to walk toward the entrance. Echo dropped his newspaper and slowly bent to retrieve it. When he stood, the .38 was in his hand. His first shot hit the captain in the back of the head, and his second hit the coconspirator in the forehead. Echo hurried to the entrance and into a waiting car. He felt great, powerful, alive, and best of all, as if he controlled the world. Before this mission, he had wondered whether he might throw up or get sick, but he just felt great.

The alarm sounded. Echo quickly got up, turned off the TV, and put on his suit jacket. He removed a plastic bag containing a six-inch strip of duct tape from the inside pocket. Wax paper protected the sticky side of the tape. Echo removed the paper and stuck one end of the tape to the nightstand, then put the paper in the plastic bag and slipped it back into his inside pocket. Finally, he removed the "Do Not Disturb" sign from the door and took up a position in the bathroom, pistol in hand.

When Echo heard the key in the door, he pressed himself tighter against the wall and listened carefully to the voices that drifted in from the hall.

His hand squeezed his Beretta as Gary Hazlitt said, "Do you want me to come in and check out your room?"

"No thanks. I'll see you both for breakfast at seven-thirty. Good night."

As Kathleen passed the bathroom, Echo jumped out from behind her and put his gun to her head. He pulled her into his body with his left hand over her mouth. Through gritted teeth, he whispered, "Don't fight me and don't make a sound or I'll pull the trigger. Now walk with me slowly to the bed and lie face-down." Once she was on the bed, Echo pulled the duct tape from the nightstand. As he turned her head to tape her mouth, his name escaped from her lips.

"Get on the bed on your knees and face into the room. Move back by the headboard." Echo backed toward the TV after she complied, all the while holding his gun on her. He turned the TV on and turned up the volume to silence any outburst she might make when he removed the tape to let her speak. He positioned himself in front of the bed and cocked his Berretta .22. Her eyes, as large as saucers, never left him. She followed his every move.

"Well, Kathleen, are you surprised to see me?"

She slowly nodded.

"Did you have an idea I found out about your scheme?"

She shook her head.

"I'll take your response to mean you didn't know I, or I should say we, found you out?"

She nodded.

"Did you know Diane was involved in the Relieve scheme?"

She shook her head.

Satisfied she was telling the truth, Echo decided to remove the tape and find out all she knew. "I'm going to remove the tape so we can talk, but first, some ground rules. I'll ask the questions, not you. If you lie to me, I'll kill you. If you're honest and don't make any noise, I'll let you live," Echo lied. "If I let you live, I run the risk of your turning me in, but you should know that Mike Jr. will die if you do. Now, do you want me to remove the tape?"

She nodded. Kathleen believed him only because in this horrifying moment, she needed something to hold on to. She would obey him, and she and Mike Jr. would both live.

Echo walked over to her and placed his gun on her temple. "Make a sound and I'll pull the trigger." He grabbed an end of the tape and pulled hard.

Tears filled her eyes and rolled down her cheeks, but she did not make a sound. When she looked at him her eyes were red, her cheeks were wet, and her face was full of fear.

"Let's get started?"

"Okay."

"Do you or Cohen have any idea that I was the one who killed Diane and Steve?"

"No."

"Do you know anyone else involved with Cohen's project?"

"No, I just do what Bob tells me."

"I assume you manipulate schedules to accommodate the problem."

"That's right."

"Did you know I did some testing for the project a few years ago?"

"No."

Kathleen's answer surprised Echo. "Did you know I volunteered to be downsized and then asked for money before leaving?"

"No."

She had to be lying, but why would she? "Are you being straight with me?"

"Yes, I didn't know you were involved in the project," Kathleen said, her fear building as Echo raised his voice.

"That doesn't make sense. When you found out the FDA was getting wise to your scheme, you, Cohen, and the others decided to make me the scapegoat. Now admit it!"

"I don't know what the hell you're talking about."

Echo was confused by her answers. He had to press her for more information. Just then, the phone rang.

Kathleen, convinced that she was about to die, looked at the phone and suddenly lunged toward it.

Echo instantly assessed the situation and squeezed the trigger.

The bullet entered Kathleen's left breast and proceeded on to punch a hole in her heart. The impact of the bullet pushed her back against the headboard. She clutched her chest. Shock and disbelief filled her eyes. Her hands, warm with blood, slowly moved from her chest to in front of her face. They were covered with blood. The color drained from her face. The phone rang again. Kathleen's eyes rolled into her head, and she fell forward onto the bed. Her head dangled partially off the side.

Echo made sure Kathleen was dead with a bullet to the brain. He pulled the trigger. The small-caliber bullet ricocheted inside her cranial cavity, shredding her brain, and she died instantly. She ended her days on this earth at 15,561.

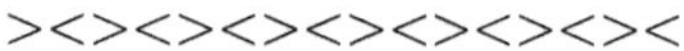

When the phone stopped ringing, Echo stood perfectly still and listened intently. What he heard pleased him. The only audible sound came from the TV. He picked up the remote and pressed the mute button. He again stood perfectly still and listened, and again he heard nothing to cause him to believe the shots were heard. Echo opened the door and looked up and down the corridor. It was empty. He slipped the "Do Not Disturb" sign on the outside knob and closed the door. Echo surveyed the room, looking for any sign of his presence. He picked up the tape he had used to cover Kathleen's mouth. He removed the plastic bag from his pocket, placed the tape in it, and returned it to his pocket.

After checking the room a second time, Echo stood in front of the full-length mirror and examined himself. Before using both hands to smooth his suit, he felt for his gun, his burglar's tools, and his keys to ensure that all were present and accounted for. Pleased with the way he looked, Echo removed the hairnet and put it in his pocket. Still wearing the latex gloves, he left. As soon as he closed the door to room 405, he put the latex gloves in his pocket.

Walking casually through the lobby of the Garden City Hotel, Echo spotted Gary Hazlitt in the lounge. However, Hazlitt faced the piano man and did not see Echo. *He'll find out what I did soon enough,* Echo thought as he exited the hotel.

Echo parked his minivan in a dark corner of the public phone area off the Southern State Parkway and changed clothes. He changed back into the clothing he had worn to the auction. With the exception of the gun and the burglar's tools, everything from Room 405 went into a trash bag. Echo returned to Amityville looking much like an antiques dealer again.

On reentering the hall, Echo stood against the back wall for a few minutes, then gradually moved around to establish his presence. No one seemed to notice. The attendees either talked among themselves or participated in the bidding. When item 549 came up for bid, Echo became involved. He successfully bid on three more pieces before the auction wound down. He paid for his purchases with a credit card, loaded the items in his minivan, wrapped them carefully with movers' blankets, and left.

On the way home, he stopped at a convenience store in Westbury and disposed of the plastic garbage bag in the dumpster before buying a Diet Coke. He would dispose of the gun next. He had the perfect spot in mind.

Echo drove north on Post Road and away from downtown Westbury. When he crossed Route 25, he entered Old Westbury, an exceedingly wealthy residential village of large mansions. Post Road circled around a small pond about a mile from Route 25. The pond, home to ducks and a few swans, was separated from the road by three feet of lawn. A short split-rail fence circled the pond. Echo pulled up and tossed the Berretta .22 into the middle of the pond. Work done, he headed home.

I did good tonight, he thought proudly. *I took care of a pain in the ass and bought some antiques I can make money on. Yes, a good night.*

Tuesday 12/9

Phil snorted as he looked at the clock, picked up the phone, and grumbled, "Christ, it's three-twenty-two in the morning. Hello, who the fuck is this?"

"Phil, wake up. It's me, Jim. Jim Hines. Wake up."

Phil sat up. "Jim, what's wrong?"

"Kathleen Connolly is dead – she was murdered last night in her room at the Garden City Hotel. She was shot in the heart and head with a small-caliber pistol. It's probably the same killer. He knows where to place a bullet. The shot to her head was right out of a mob training manual… a small-caliber bullet ricochets off of the inside of the skull and devastates the brain. Maximum damage, no exit wound, sure death. Again, the killer left very little, if any, evidence. Phil, we need to talk. How about tonight?"

"Okay, I'll call you in the afternoon."

"Call my cell phone. I gotta go."

Phil got up and walked into the kitchen, mumbling as he mulled over the news. *Another murder, just as Hines predicted. Another high-level Purity executive was killed by a pro. Why Connolly, why Armstrong, why Gagnon? Am I in danger? Is Lorraine in danger? Connolly was involved in the downsizing. If I assume Gagnon was killed because he was there, but Armstrong and Connolly may have been killed for some other reason. Lorraine and I are relatively new to this business.*

Maybe we're okay. Phil put some coffee on and was about to call Lorraine when the phone rang.

"Phil, it's Gary. You sound wide awake. I guess I didn't wake you."

"No, I was up taking a leak."

"Sure, please sit down. Kathleen Connolly is dead. Shot twice. She was in her room at the Garden City Hotel. You need to activate your call list and get this message to your people: 'Kathleen Connolly died last night, apparently murdered. We are all enormously saddened and have decided to make attendance at work tomorrow optional. Anyone wishing to stay home can take a vacation day or a day without pay. Otherwise, we will operate as usual.' Any questions?"

"No, I'll get on it."

"One more thing. Cohen wants everyone on the staff to have a bodyguard. Yours will show up at your door at precisely six o'clock this morning. You will be covered twenty-four hours a day. No one else is going to get hurt. We are doing all we can. The police better catch the bastard."

"Does that mean we plan to help them, or are we still going to withhold the information that would help find the killer?"

"Don't start. You know the answer. We will not subject our employees to investigation or ourselves to lawsuits, end of story. The police are responsible for catching the son-of-a-bitch."

"I think it's time to reconsider. What if Kathleen isn't the last?"

"We've hired an expensive topflight bodyguard service. We won't let anyone else get hurt. We're doing all we can to protect our people."

Phil knew arguing was useless. "Okay, I'll call my people."

"And stay away from the police." Hazlitt hung up.

Phil called Abby. She was the only call he made on his call list; she would handle the rest. "Abby, it's Phil. Sorry to wake you, but we have a major problem. Are you awake?" Phil waited a few moments, listening to sheets shifting and groans of complaint before she finally spoke.

"I'm awake."

"Kathleen Connolly was killed last night." Phil filled in the details of the murder and the announcement for today. Abby listened without comment.

"I don't believe it. Kathleen Connolly. I've known her for almost twenty years. Christ, she just made Vice President." Abby stopped for a minute and then continued, "She may have been a bitch, but she didn't deserve to die."

"Abby, I don't know if this has anything to do with the downsizing, but please watch yourself. The company is hiring bodyguards for the staff. I'll try to get you covered, but until then, watch your ass."

"I don't want a bodyguard. I'm not a target — the employees know I'm not calling the shots, so I'm not worried. And you watch my ass enough for both of us."

"That I do, but I might not be around when the killer shows up. For what it's worth, I think you're right, but I'd hate to see your pretty ass shot off."

"Enough about my ass. I have some calls to make."

"Is Joan McMullen on your list?"

"Yes."

"Please tell her I need to talk to her, and I'll call her after six. Give me her number."

"Oh, a little hanky panky?"

"Yeah, I'll see you in a couple of hours. Meanwhile, get that ass of yours in gear and come up with some more possibilities. We have to help the police catch this bastard."

"I've been considering a few more possibilities. I'll give you the details tomorrow… I mean today. Bye."

While struggling to fall asleep again, Phil wrestled with a dilemma: should he tell Rose about Lorraine, or should he let it slide? He had never cheated on Rose, if Sunday even counted as "cheating" at all. Telling Rose might cause long-term problems in the marriage. Phil sighed, stood up from his bed, and paced for a while before lying down on the couch, deep in thought.

Man, I hate this shit. I've never even thought of cheating. Oh, I look, sure, but I never touch. But Lorraine… what a woman. Smart — no, super smart — and sexy. Christ, she's breathtaking. How in the hell could an average man resist her? It's not possible. Who the hell am I kidding? I'm married and married means something. Married means staying away from all women except your wife, even when a smart, sexy woman finds my fat ass attractive. And now Kathleen Connolly has been murdered, lights-out halfway through her life. Three high-level employees of Purity were killed by an assassin the police think is a pro. If he is, who hired him? At least I feel good about helping the police. I didn't stick my head up my ass and let the corporate assholes slow down the investigation.

Phil fell asleep on the couch and dreamt that he was in bed with Lorraine. When he was enjoying himself the most, the doorbell jerked him awake. Startled and disappointed, he looked out of the sidelight to see a six-foot-six, two-hundred-and-fifty-pound giant standing on his porch. The giant's close-cropped hair highlighted his chiseled facial features. By the way his visitor's expensive suit framed his physique, Phil guessed that he did not have an ounce of fat on his body. Phil, dressed in sloppy sweats, opened the door to greet his wrinkle-free guest: his bodyguard, presumably.

"What can I do for you?"

"Mr. Messina, I'm Harold Yasika. I work for the Aldridge Agency," Mr. Yasika extended a huge hand containing a business card. "We've been hired to protect you. Three of us are assigned to you in eight-hour shifts twenty-four-seven."

Before the bodyguard could get another word out, Phil said, "Come in out of the cold. I'll put on some coffee, and we'll talk."

While Phil brewed the coffee, the bodyguard sat rigidly on the sofa. Phil pondered a problem. *How am I going to see Hines tonight? Does this guy have to report my movements to anyone?*

"How do you like your coffee?"

"Black."

Figures. Phil carried two steaming cups into the living room. "Tell me how this works. Are you by my side all the time? Do you sleep in my house? Just how close do we have to become?"

"Before I answer, I will tell you about our firm. We are the best personal protection agency in the world. Our specialists are hand-picked based on intelligence and physical skills from thousands of applicants. We are trained in personal protection techniques and the use of various weapons. Half of those selected for training fail to graduate. The few that graduate are the best. We will not fail to protect you. If it comes to a choice between my death or yours, I will die for you."

Wow. Phil had just heard a canned advertisement live. "You must make a lot of money to be willing to take a bullet for a stranger. I'm impressed. How about my questions?"

Mr. Yasika did not visibly react to Phil's sarcasm. His manner remained slow and deliberate. "We will do our best to be invisible. We will be around when you are at work but not in your office with you. When you are driving, we will follow you. When you are home, we will be outside. Your life must be as normal as possible, but we will be there to protect you."

"Do you report my movements or contacts to anyone?"

"Yes, a complete report of your activities will be sent to our headquarters. Your CEO is the only one in your company allowed to see the report."

Great. Meeting Hines tonight will require some creativity. Phil stood up. "Would you finish your coffee outside? I have to get ready for work."

Mr. Yasika dutifully left.

Phil called Joan McMullen. "Good morning, Joan. It's Phil. I assume Abby called you and told you about Kathleen Connolly. How do you feel about it?"

"I can't believe this is happening. I met Kathleen on my first day at work. We never became close friends, but we chatted every now and then. She was a hard person to get to know."

"I know what you mean. I'd only talked to Kathleen a couple of times, and she was strictly business. I hate to put this on you, but I need you to come in today if it's at all possible. If you planned not to come in, I'd like you to reconsider. If you feel I'm putting pressure on you, you're right."

"Stop worrying. I'm almost dressed and should be at work by seven."

"Thanks. I'll meet you in the QC offices at nine."

Phil called Lorraine.

"Good morning. Are you okay?"

"For now, but I'm scared to death. Phil, this has to do with downsizing. The two most visible people involved in last year's downsizing at Garden City, besides Cohen, were Diane and Kathleen, and now they're dead. Are you and me next? Jesus, people are getting killed, and we're planning another downsizing. It doesn't make sense to continue."

"You're beginning to sound like your old self. Let's invade Hazlitt's office today and try to get the planning sessions stopped."

"I'll set it up. The FDA is not coming in today."

"Okay. Try to set it up for one. I'm busy all day except from one to two."

"Phil, the more I think about this audit, the stranger it seems."

"Because they want to start with old folders?"

"No, it's more than the folders. Their whole approach is different. Instead of auditing records to ensure we're following procedures and good manufacturing practices, it's more like they know something is wrong and are trying to prove it. They ask questions about how long it takes to accomplish steps and how long it takes to move material and paperwork. Normally they only care that procedures are followed."

Phil frowned, digesting the new information. *Why would the FDA care how long it takes us to produce Relieve?* "Have you met your bodyguard yet?"

"Yes, and I have to admit I feel safer, and hotter, having him around. He is one fine specimen of a black man."

Feeling a pang of jealousy, Phil said, "I'm glad for you. I'll see you at work."

Phil waited as Abby shuffled through her notes. He had been seated in her office when she arrived a few minutes ago with a large cup of coffee in her hand. "How many are you going to give me?" Phil asked.

"Two, but understand I had to stretch to come up with them. I don't think either of these two could kill anyone. I've looked at the master list numerous times, and I can't come up with any others."

"Maybe we'll get lucky. We have to do everything we can before more people get killed."

Abby filled him in on the details and then reminded him again of her concerns. "I don't think Tim Anderson or Jack Goloski are capable of killing anyone. In fact, I'm sure they're not. The only reason I'm volunteering their names is because of the circumstances surrounding their terminations. Please make sure Hines understands."

Phil promised to explain her concerns to Lieutenant Hines, then returned to his office, picked up his laptop, and headed for the Production Control offices.

"Joan, thanks for coming in."

"I had a million things to do today. I'm upset about Kathleen, and I'm concerned for all you other big shots. We'll be unemployed if we don't keep the business running. Are the police making any progress?"

"Last I heard they weren't, but that was a couple of days ago. Well, here's the laptop. I hope you can get some inputting done today."

"Actually, with the reduced production schedule today, I'm caught up until Thursday morning. I'd be happy to spend that time inputting. And, if you want, I could work some overtime."

"Work as much OT as you want. Just make sure I know when you're working and that you're not here alone."

"Thanks, I'll get a lot done. Before you go, rumor has it that certain high-level people, like you, have bodyguards?"

"The rumor mill is right as usual, but keep it under your hat. Unless, of course, the whole plant knows already," Phil answered, always amazed by the speed at which information flowed.

"It's pretty much common knowledge, but thanks for sharing. I'll call you by five."

"You're welcome."

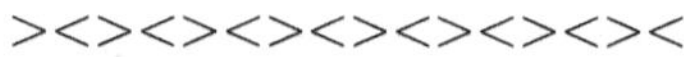

Phil spent the rest of the morning reviewing Batch folders and entering the data into the database. He called Abby several times to get her opinion, but overall, he was getting better at reading them. He grabbed a quick lunch before heading to Gary Hazlitt's office.

Pamela Robinson and Lorraine Waters were waiting with Gary Hazlitt when Phil arrived.

"Now that we are finally all here, let's get started. Lorraine, you asked for this meeting," Hazlitt said.

Phil looked at Lorraine to see if she wanted him to start, but she said, "Three of our peers have been murdered, and I believe it's because of the downsizing earlier this year. We should stop meeting or discussing another downsizing until the police catch the killer. Diane, Kathleen, and Steve were strong advocates of the last downsizing. They talked openly about how important reducing the number of employees was to our business. Our employees thought they only cared about the company and were cold and insensitive when it came to the needs of employees. The four of us in this room are viewed the same way, and I believe we may be the next targets."

Gary responded, "We have no idea why these killings are happening. For all we know it could be completely unrelated to downsizing. The way the police are making progress, they may never solve this case. We have to move ahead. Bob Cohen expects us to have everything in place and be ready to announce right after the holidays. Besides, no one knows why we're meeting."

Lorraine answered, "There are no secrets here. Word is already drifting up from Wilmington that another downsizing is coming. Our evening meetings have stirred up the rumor mill, and our employees aren't stupid."

Before Gary could answer, Pamela did. "You're right, Lorraine. Rumors are floating and employees are beginning to feel insecure… coupled with what they've heard about the murders, they're downright scared. But we have to lead them through these tough times. We have no choice. We absolutely must reduce people next year. Cohen has already made commitments to our owners. Besides, we have the best bodyguards money can buy. We're safe."

Phil started to say something when Lorraine cut him off. "Safe? Three people are dead, and you say we're safe? The police think the killer is a pro, and you say we're safe. I don't feel safe, and what about the other employees, especially those who helped us implement the downsizing? Are they safe?"

"Lorraine, you're overreacting. We can do this. But we have to be a team and all pull together." Gary's comment was obviously a platitude.

Phil started to say something when Lorraine cut him off again. "If we were a team, we'd all have input. We wouldn't only listen to your interpretation of what Bob Cohen wants."

"Lorraine, you're not being fair. I'll tell you what: we'll continue the planning meetings, but I'll let Bob know we want to delay announcing the downsizing as long as we can or until the killer has been caught. That's the best I can do right now." Gary stood up as he finished the sentence, trying to end the meeting.

Lorraine didn't take the hint. "I think you're wrong, and if someone else is killed, I'll rub your nose in it in public." She looked right at Gary. "You and Pamela are playing Russian roulette with our lives, and I don't think you know what you're doing."

Gary looked at Phil. "Will you try to talk some sense into her?"

"I can't. I agree with everything she said. We need to stop right now. Maybe that'll save some lives."

"I understand your concerns, but if Diane, Kathleen, and Steve were killed because of the last downsizing, postponing the next one won't solve anything. I think we need to move ahead." Pamela ended the meeting with civility.

Phil walked Lorraine back to her office. "You're back. The old Lorraine is back. Man, I missed you, but you're back."

"Yeah, and it feels good. You can thank my mother for my return."

Phil looked up. "Thank you, ma. Thank you very much."

"Phil, we have to do something. What about your godfather in McKenzie? Can you talk to him?"

"I'm not sure anymore, but I'll try."

On the way to his office, Phil thought about Lorraine. *Now that she's her old self again, I might be able to talk to her about the Production issues and maybe even my involvement with the police.* Phil turned around and headed back to Lorraine's office.

"Lorraine, I'm involved with something you should know about."

"I'm not sure I want to know."

"Before Thanksgiving and before all this other shit started happening, two Production employees talked to Abby and me about some production problems. They said Production was not following SOPs, falsifying test results and batch records. They said their supervisors were pushing them to do it and threatened to fire them if they didn't go along. I've been entering a lot of production data into a database to see if we can find some patterns that support their story. Look, I didn't tell you because they swore us to secrecy, and to tell you the truth, you haven't been yourself, so I wasn't sure what you might do."

Lorraine was angry, but mostly with herself. "You were probably right not to trust me. I lost my commitment to doing the right thing when Diane was appointed Director of Operations. I crawled into my shell to avoid butting heads with another black woman. It didn't matter that she was incompetent. I might have overreacted if you told me, but I'm back. My mother's in me."

"Good. I have one more thing to tell you. I'm working with Lieutenant Hines, to help find the killer. I gave him some names to check out and insight into Purity's culture. He's now checking out five names, and I have two more to give him tonight."

"Are you crazy? You're risking your career." Lorraine stopped for a moment. "I guess you know that, though. You're just doing what you think is right."

"Actually, I'm scared to death. I can't afford to be fired, but I have to do what I have to do."

"What can I do to help?"

"Nothing right now unless you can think of some suspects, but I might need some help later this week. See you later."

"I'll call if I think of anyone."

Phil spent the rest of the day reviewing Batch Records and entering data. At five Joan McMullen, laptop in hand, stopped by Phil's office.

"I can work until eight tonight. Bill Edwards is working and we'll stay in touch. I don't think either of us is in danger because the killer seems to be after you execs."

"You're probably right but be careful anyway. I assume you brought the laptop so I can download the new data."

"Right, and I got a lot done. I'm getting fast."

Phil transferred the information from the laptop to his desktop and returned it to Joan.

"Joan, be careful. Thanks for all your help."

"You're very welcome."

Phil called his personal bodyguard and told him that he was ready to leave.

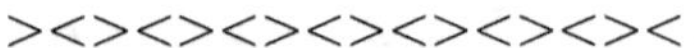

During the day, Phil made arrangements to meet Jim Hines in Oyster Bay at Teddy's Tavern. Teddy's Tavern had received its name because President Theodore Roosevelt had frequented the tavern when he stayed at Sagamore Hill, his summer White House. Sagamore Hill was about three miles from the village of Oyster Bay. In those days Teddy's Tavern did not have a phone, and the President had to walk across the street to the drugstore to conduct the nation's affairs.

Phil's plan to shake his bodyguard so that he could meet with Lieutenant Hines required the cooperation of his neighbor. They were not close friends, but he and Al had talked several times over the four-foot hedgerow that separated their properties.

"Hi Al, it's Phil. Phil Messina."

"Phil! How are you doing? I've been reading about the murders in your company. I'm sure they've had a devastating effect on you. I didn't call you because I figured you had enough on your mind. After the killing last night at the Garden City Hotel, I really got worried. You're not in any danger, are you?"

"I don't think so, but I have a company-paid bodyguard sitting in his car in front of my house. In fact, that's the reason I called you. I need to meet someone at Teddy's tonight, and I don't want my bodyguard to find out. I plan to crawl through the hedgerow in the back and sneak out through your yard. Any problem?"

"I guess not. Are you sure you'll be safe?"

Phil heard the suspicion in Al's voice. "I'll be fine. And Al, it's okay for Rose to know. I just can't have my bodyguard find out."

"Okay, no problem."

Next, Phil called his bodyguard. "This is Phil Messina. I have the house alarm set, and I'm going to plop my ass in a soft chair in front of the TV and probably fall asleep. So, try not to bother me."

"Sleep soundly, Mr. Messina. Rest comfortably knowing that you'll be safe. I'm watching out for you. Good night."

"Thanks."

Phil immediately left the house through the back door. When he got to the hedgerow, he looked for the small opening that the neighborhood kids used to shortcut through his yard. He found it and quickly realized that the opening was tiny, and he was not. *A good argument for losing weight,* he thought, bending down. Sticking his head into the opening, he forced his way through, twisting and turning as he proceeded. After he arrived on the other side, the journey to Teddy's was easy. Phil took a rather long route to ensure that he went unseen by his bodyguard. He arrived at Teddy's ten minutes late.

Phil spotted Hines in a back booth with Detective Parisi. He stopped at the bar and ordered a drink before heading to the booth. "Hello, Lieutenant Hines, Detective Parisi. Sorry I'm late."

Hines answered, "No problem, we haven't ordered yet, but as you can see, we have drinks. Did I see you order a drink at the bar?"

"Yeah, and I could use one. You were right about another murder. We have to catch this bastard. Are you going to fill me in?"

Karen answered, "I will, but I have to leave in about an hour so let's order something to eat. Then I'll get started." She motioned for the waitress, who responded immediately. Business was slow this Tuesday night.

Phil ordered first. "All I want are some appetizers: buffalo tenders, potato skins, and mozzarella sticks."

Karen said, "That sounds good, the same for me."

"Me too," Jim said.

"Since we all want the same thing, why don't we get a couple of samplers? That way, we can try every appetizer on the menu," Phil said, and Jim and Karen nodded in agreement.

After the waitress took the order, Karen studied her notes. When she was done, she looked at Phil. "Connolly was shot first through the heart. Then, the gun was pressed against her head and angled upward. The killer used a .22-caliber pistol. It's an MO used by organized crime: a sure kill with a minimum of mess. The bullet through the heart was well-placed, so the killer knows what he's doing. We believe she was on the bed kneeling when the first bullet hit her in the chest. She fell forward, and then the headshot. We believe he was in the room waiting for her and overpowered her when she returned from the meeting. The maid remembers a 'Do Not Disturb' sign on the door when she went to the room to turn down the bed and leave a chocolate. She also remembers hearing the TV. Gary Hazlitt doesn't remember the sign on the door. He said it would've alerted him to a problem."

"I assume Hazlitt didn't go into the room," Phil said.

"No. He said he asked Connolly if she wanted him to go in, but she said no. Pamela Robinson remembers it the same way. If he went into the room, he'd be just as dead as Connolly. I have a few more things to cover, okay?" Karen waited until Phil nodded. "We've gone over the room with a fine-tooth comb looking for evidence, and despite the fact we have three bags full, I'm predicting we have nothing useful. Lastly, we removed all the hardware from the door to determine if he had a key or picked the lock. The hardware is high quality, so it would take an expert with good equipment to pick it."

Just as Karen finished, the food arrived. Jim and Phil ordered another round of drinks, and Karen passed. They each filled their plates and spent a few minutes eating before Phil said, "I did a little research on Connolly. Would you like to hear what I learned?"

"Sure," Jim replied.

"Kathleen worked at Garden City before being appointed Vice President and transferring to Wilmington. She worked in the Quality Control Labs as a lab tech hired straight out of a local college. She was appointed to her first job in management about seven or eight years ago. Because of her poor people skills, most people on-site were surprised she was moved into supervision. The rumor was that Bob Cohen made it happen.

By all accounts, she did a lousy job. The people working for her always complained to HR or filed grievances, and schedules were routinely missed. Despite her poor performance, she was promoted several more times, ultimately landing as Materials Manager. Again, rumor had it that Bob Cohen was behind the move, and again she did a lousy job. She held the Materials Manager job long enough to cause many problems before being appointed Vice President last year. Just after she was appointed Materials Manager, her home and car were vandalized a couple of times. The police were contacted and investigated. They discovered two Purity employees were to blame. The employees said they hated her because she mistreated people and they couldn't stand seeing her getting promoted. The employees were fired but did not go to jail. Interesting?"

"Very interesting," Jim replied. "Connolly, like Diane Armstrong, is one of Cohen's favorites. And like Ms. Armstrong, she was promoted even though she didn't have the skills to do the job. The two must have been of some value to Cohen, though."

"I think their value to Cohen was that they'd do whatever he asked without asking any questions. Neither one was smart enough to see the big picture, nor would they have gotten the jobs without Cohen's intervention. Plus, they were not a threat to Cohen himself. When I look at the upper management in Purity, it's obvious to me most of Cohen's selections fit the mold."

"But how does that tie to the murders?" Karen asked. "Let's assume the killer's targets were two high-level female managers who would do anything Cohen wanted to be done.

What does that tell us about the motive? It seems to rule out downsizing as a motive."

"Not necessarily," Phil said. "Both Diane and Kathleen were major players in the downsizing."

"So were you," Jim said. "If that's the motive, you'd better watch your ass."

"That's what my bodyguard is for."

"Anything else on Connolly? I want to talk about the leads you gave us," Karen said.

"No."

"We've done preliminary checks on the five suspects, and at the moment, only one holds any promise. Before I get to the suspect we like, let me tell you why we ruled out the other four. Scott Williams was at his mother's house in Riverside. Her neighbors verified he was there. Also, Scott filled his gas tank at around nine o'clock on the outskirts of Riverside, putting him about two hours from Garden City. The detectives who spoke to Mr. Williams think he's a very strange duck and, in their estimation, can commit murder. We'll check his alibi for last night, but I suspect we'll find he's not the murderer. The next guy, Kevin McQuet, is a real piece of work. He's an absolute nut case, but he's not a murderer, in our opinion. We were able to talk to him again today, and he has a solid alibi for both nights. You may have a problem with him because he's already crying foul. He claims we're harassing him and that the company set him up. He said he was going to get a lawyer. I doubt he will, but he threatened."

"Great, just what I need: some whacko suing Purity to find out if someone gave info to the police. Goodbye, pension," Phil whined.

"As I said, I don't think he'll do anything. He's a punk. He has a big mouth and no guts, but stay alert just in case. Okay… Gordon Smat, the womanizer, also had a solid alibi last Monday. He's also a punk and a coward. I think he's a real momma's boy, which may explain why he thinks he's God's gift to women. We'll check out his alibi for last night as a matter of good police work, but again our instincts tell us he's not a murderer. We investigated Jack Higgins's military records before talking to him today. He has a good alibi for last Monday and last night. He was in the military for two years in the eighties, but he didn't see any action. He was ROTC and joined a few months after graduating from college. It was mandatory. After boot camp, he was made a Lieutenant and assigned to the Personnel Office. He was stationed in Europe. We went through his record in detail and found no evidence he had any special skill with firearms. We're checking his alibis, but he's not a suspect."

Jim spoke for the first time in a while. "That leaves us Joe DiRollo, and as of now, he's our prime suspect. Karen and I interviewed the family first, then we both tried to interview the son. As a result, we're convinced the son is the man behind the murders. I'll let Karen fill you in."

"We spoke to Mr. and Mrs. DiRollo on Monday. Their reaction to the murders of Ms. Armstrong and Mr. Gagnon was one of glee. Both DiRollos were happy Armstrong and Gagnon were dead. Mr. DiRollo said, and I quote…" Karen looked at her notebook. "'I hope that black bitch suffered. I hope she had to beg for her life, the good-for-nothing whore. And same goes for Gagnon, that ass-kissing, brown-nosing bastard.'" Then Mrs. DiRollo added, 'That company only promotes spades, so they got what they deserved.' Real nice people."

"And you were standing there?" Phil asked Jim.

"I was there, but they either didn't notice or didn't care."

"We tried to interview the son," Karen continued, "but he wouldn't give us the time of day. He pulled a card out of his wallet with his attorney's name on it, told us to call his lawyer, and walked away. Our investigation uncovered some interesting things about the son. We talked to the FBI agents on the organized crime task force."

Jim interrupted, "Joe DiRollo is a soldier in the Trapani family, working for an underboss named Bartocci. He's not a 'made' man yet but will be soon. He's not a triggerman, but he is the go-between for the triggermen for the family. The task force believes that he's arranged several hits. He could have easily hired someone to avenge his father by taking out the executives at Purity, who he believes caused his father's heart attack. Jimmy's boy is a mean son-of-a-bitch… he'd kill someone who looked at him cross-eyed. He's a real greaseball, he…" Jim realized what he had said and just stopped.

Phil's first reaction was surprise. For Jim Hines, a man who reacted to any slight insult to an African American with complete disdain, to call DiRollo a greaseball was shocking. It was hard to imagine politically correct Jim Hines slipping up like that. The look on Lt. Hines's face, his eyes and mouth wide open, and his posture ramrod straight as he pushed away from the table almost set off Phil's second reaction: laughter. He controlled the urge to let out a belly laugh until he looked at Karen Parisi, who was using all her self-control not to laugh.

Still looking like a scared puppy, Jim Hines apologized. "I'm sorry, I didn't mean anything by it. Really, it was an accident."

Phil put on a severe look. "I can't believe you would insult Karen and me by uttering such a vicious ethnic slur. Especially you, Mister Thin Skin."

Karen joined the fun. "I'm highly insulted. We 'I'talians have suffered insults at the hands of you black people for years. Just when I thought things had changed, I find out they've only gone underground." As she finished, she bust out laughing. When she started, Phil joined in, and they both laughed like hell. Jim stared at them in disbelief, waiting for them to stop.

Still snickering a little, Phil was surprised when he looked at Jim. Jim still looked scared. "What's the matter with you?"

"I don't understand what's so funny. One of the people I insulted works for me. I called an Italian a greaseball – not exactly a term of endearment – and you both laugh. I could be fired, for God's sake, and you two laugh. I don't understand."

"I met Joe DiRollo, and he definitely is a greaseball," Karen responded. "Look, I'm not going to turn you in or do anything else over this. You slipped, you're human, and I don't believe you put all Italians in that category for one minute. You're too uptight around me. You measure every word as if you think I'm just waiting to find a way to get you fired. Well, I'm not, so lighten up. I'll let you know if I'm offended by anything you do. Overall, you're a pretty good guy, so just stop walking on eggshells around me and treat me as if I'm a real live human being."

"But you went after Dawson and sued the department. I don't want the same thing happening to me. I need my pension."

"Dawson treated me differently than the male detectives. He assigned me to desk duty most of the time, and when he did send me on a case, it was always easy. I told him I wanted to do the same job as the men – hell, I was in the same pay grade – and I was absolutely capable of doing the same job. Dawson said something like, 'okay, honey, next big case, you got it.' Besides degrading me by calling me honey, he never assigned me to a good case." Karen was on a roll. "And before you get paranoid about being made primary on this case, I know it wasn't your call, and I think the captain made the right call. You have a lot more experience than me, and you're handling the press better than I ever could."

"She's right, Jim. You didn't call me a greaseball, and you didn't call all Italians greaseballs. You called a mobbed-up asshole a greaseball. And I agree with Karen: DiRollo seems to fit all the stereotypes the term greaseball was intended to mean. I understand there are a few assholes that still fit the bigoted images and stereotypes hung on the early Italian immigrants. From everything I've heard, he is one of the assholes."

"Karen, are you sure I didn't offend you?"

"Jim, you're a good guy. You met a guy, a real jerk, who fit your picture of a greaseball, and it just came out. I don't see myself as a greaseball, or a goombah, or a wop, or as any other derogatory label hung on Italians. And more importantly, I don't believe you see me that way. I laughed because I could tell you were scared to death that Phil or I would be offended."

Phil spoke up before Jim could respond. "Even though you take everything said about blacks personally, don't assume everyone else is the same. When I said Diane Armstrong was incompetent, you took it personally. It's as if you were the almighty leader of the black race and had to absorb any perceived insult visited upon a black human being. Well, I don't see myself as the Almighty Italian Leader, and from what I've heard, Karen doesn't see herself that way either."

"All right, you've made your point, but I'm sorry I used the term and I promise I won't do it again." Jim took a breath. "Back to Joe. He has access to professionals, and a professional has committed all three killings. The bullet to Connolly's head is strictly mob MO. In short, DiRollo has means and motive, and if we keep looking, we'll uncover how he created the opportunity. He's our man. I feel it in my bones."

"I agree," Karen said.

"Does that mean you don't need to look at the other two suspects Abby came up with?"

"No, we'll look at them. I don't want to take a chance and miss the killer. I hope you told Abby how important her efforts are to our investigation. It's a lot easier when looking at suspects that have a motive."

"Ditto," Karen said.

"I'll make sure she knows how you feel. Suggesting people she knows might be possible killers has been hard on her. The only ones she hasn't felt bad about were DiRollo and Higgins, and it looks like one of them may be the killer. The next two are people Abby feels couldn't possibly commit murder, but they need to be checked out. Abby can't see anyone else who could even remotely be the killer.

"The first is Tim Anderson. He's about thirty and had only worked for Purity about a year when we forced him to leave. He's the world's nicest guy, the kind you would think couldn't harm a fly. He didn't take getting laid-off hard. In fact, he seemed to understand that his job was eliminated, and he was laid-off, as simple as that. Anderson's father, Brad, also worked for us and was forced to take the early retirement option we offered. He went kicking and screaming. He'd married a younger woman two years earlier, and they had a one-year-old son. He believed no one would hire a fifty-five-year-old man, and he wouldn't be able to support his new family. It turns out he was right. He couldn't get a job. Then about three months ago, his car hit a bridge abutment at ninety miles an hour."

"I worked that case," Karen said. "It looked to us like suicide, but we couldn't prove it. Actually, we didn't want to prove it because his wife and kid would've lost the insurance. It was a new policy. The skid marks were only twenty feet long. Are you saying you think Tim believes it was suicide and is getting revenge?"

"That's what I'm saying, but neither Abby nor I can believe it's Tim. He's on the list because of the insurance money. Brad's new wife and Tim were the beneficiaries for all the insurance Brad still had through the company, and Brad had the maximum. I also found out Brad had taken out a large insurance policy on his own when he learned his new wife was pregnant. There's enough money available to hire a professional. Since the police believe it's a professional, his name has to go into the hat."

"We'll check him out. Who's next?"

"Next is Bob Frazer and Jack Goloski. They're an older gay couple, and both were asked – forced – to leave, and they haven't been able to find jobs. Last I heard, they'd started some sort of small business. Both Bob and Jack worked at Purity for over twenty years and were looking forward to retiring with nice pensions. The older of the two, Jack, was old enough to get a reduced pension. Bob was a little under fifty and only received severance pay. Both Bob and Jack were irate. They ranted about Bob Cohen promoting and protecting women and minorities and ignoring gays. They accused Cohen of being homophobic and of being a closet homosexual. They filed a discrimination charge and made a lot of noise to the press, but in the end, they lost."

"Which one do you think is the killer?" Jim asked.

"Neither Abby nor I think either one could do it, but you need to look at Jack. Jack was a green beret in the military. He was, and probably still is, a marksman. A good friend of his told Abby Jack was an expert with all types of armament: pistols, rifles, and grenade launchers, to name a few. You and I know the police believe the killer is a marksman who knows where to place a kill shot. Well, green berets are taught how to kill."

Jim nodded. "They have the motive, and Jack has the skills. We'll take a close look at these two."

"Abby's been considering Jack for a while but couldn't see him as a killer and didn't put him on her original list. If he turns out to be the killer, she'll feel responsible for Connolly's death."

Karen said, "Tell Abby she's doing the best she can. She's not responsible for anyone's death. Her efforts will save lives. Anyway, I have to go. I'll start on these two leads first thing in the morning. Jim, will you be in the office tomorrow morning?"

"Yes," he said to Karen, and then he turned to Phil. "Can you stay for another drink?"

"I have all night."

They said goodbye to Karen and stopped to order another round at the bar. Unlike the tables, the bar at Teddy's Tavern was crowded with regulars. The dining area was usually full only on weekends. They returned to their table and Jim started talking immediately.

"I've been thinking about the corporate world and the impact on employees by the changes taking place. Change is difficult. I understand people get angry when the world they know changes suddenly, especially when it harms their financial security. I also know people denied an opportunity because of the color of their skin or their gender can also become angry. I know I get defensive when a black person is criticized, and I know I shouldn't, but I feel personally attacked. Then, like an idiot, I slur Italians in front of two Italians, two friends, and you laugh. No anger, you fucking laugh. The only thing I can figure is it's a black thing."

"If you mean the negative stereotypes of blacks are much harsher and run much deeper than they do for other ethnic groups, you're right. If you mean many blacks wear their color as a chip on their shoulder, you're also right. If you mean being black in America means being degraded every day, you're right again."

"Very philosophical. I'm glad you know those things intellectually, but it's different when you experience them. It becomes emotional."

"You're right. I don't know how it feels. It's not possible. Only a black person can know. But I know you can't change your skin color, and most of the time, you can't change how others think. You can, however, change how you think and how you react."

"It's always bothered me that other ethnic groups come to this country and assimilate while blacks just remain at the bottom socially and economically. Italians started coming to America in the early 1900s, a full century after the first blacks were brought here. I know most Italians were dirt poor when they got here, yet today the sons and daughters of these immigrants have prospered. We needed Affirmative Action to get ahead economically, and we haven't progressed much socially. Why do you think that is? Because we're stupid or because we're destined to be the race that holds up the bottom?"

"I happen to have some strongly held opinions on how people navigate their life and on race. Those opinions have been shaped and sharpened during many conversations on the subject with Lorraine. If you're interested I'll be happy to share them with you, but my guess is you won't like what I have to say."

"I guess I'm willing to listen. I can't guarantee I'll agree with you, but I'll listen. I need to stop feeling angry all the time. I need to feel better about myself and my people."

Phil thought for a moment. "We navigate through life guided by – even controlled by – our beliefs. Early in our lives, we form beliefs about ourselves and our world. Our beliefs on self-esteem, the value of education, our intelligence, on race, and on gender are essential to determining the course of our lives, our success in life."

Jim said, "Most poor black kids attend inner-city schools with lousy outcomes, lousy facilities. If those kids thought education was valuable, you're saying they could overcome those obstacles."

"Yes. That would also happen if, in addition, community leaders stopped talking about black people being victims."

"So, in your mind, black leaders telling the truth is what's wrong?"

"I'm saying when people believe they're oppressed, they want – expect – the oppressor to change, when the only people they can change are themselves."

"So the conservative white people that run America won't change. It's the people they oppress that need to change?"

"I think you have your oppressors wrong. Big cities in this country have been run by liberal politicians for many years. Those liberal politicians are primarily black, yet the schools are failing, crime is rampant, and poverties only grown. Look in the mirror."

Jim was lost in thought.

Phil used the silence to add to his points. "I haven't lived the black experience, but I've watched my family evolve. Those that embraced education or hard work succeeded, and those that waited for the government to take care of them are still waiting."

"You're telling me it's our fault. All we have to do is be like whitey, and everything will be okay. Great."

"No, that's not what I'm saying. If you believe you're a victim, blame racism for all the ills of your community: crime, poverty, illegitimacy, and poor academic performance. Blame racism if you look to the government to solve your problems rather than looking to yourself. And if your leaders promote victimhood and fixate on racism, nothing will change."

"So we're different than other ethnic groups. We follow Democrats like sheep and we see ourselves as victims. We want the government to take care of us and see every white wearing a hood. That's how you see us?"

"That's how you see yourselves. I prefer to see Jim Hines."

"You have a point."

"How about we get back to why we got into this conversation? Your anger. I'm not sure how to say this, so bear with me. You think you're responsible for everybody's happiness and well-being, at least for all blacks, and it's more of a burden than you can handle. You think the government should make everything okay, at least okay by your definition. Your frustration increases when things don't change or change too slowly. You see the world as a terrible place for blacks, and you want it to change now."

Again, Jim was quiet for a few seconds before responding. "I can't just stop caring, and I can't stop trying to change things for my people. I won't be happy sitting on the sidelines doing nothing. I'm just tired of being angry all the time and want it to stop. I'll work on changing." He paused for a moment. "I'm ready to go. How about you?"

"I'm ready."

"I'll drop you off by your house, then distract your bodyguard while you sneak in."

"Deal."

Jim dropped Phil off in front of his neighbor's house and drove around the block to where the bodyguard was parked. He stopped by the driver's window and flashed his badge. "I'm Lieutenant Hines. I'm working the Purity case and thought I'd see how things were going."

"Quiet right now."

"Good. Stay alert," Jim said as he raised his window and drove off.

Wednesday 12/10

For Phil, Wednesday started with an uneventful drive to work. It was reassuring that every time he looked in the rearview mirror, his bodyguard was driving the car behind him. Last night's sleep had come hard. His thoughts ranged from his conversation with Lieutenant Hines to Rose's return tomorrow night and everything in between. He thought about the murdered and the murderer. DiRollo, the prime suspect in this tragedy, was a mob-connected goombah retaliating for his father's treatment at the hands of Purity management. Phil knew that if DiRollo was behind the murders, he or Lorraine could be the next victim. Phil looked in the rearview mirror and smiled when he saw Harold, 'the bodyguard,' behind him.

Phil's first stop was Lorraine's office, as he wanted to talk to her before she became too involved with the FDA. "Hi, how're you doing this morning?"

"Fine. I'm glad you stopped by. I want to talk about tonight's meeting."

"Okay, but first, let me update you on the investigation. Hines and Parisi believe Jimmy DiRollo's kid, Joe, is the killer. He has mob connections and contact with professional hitmen. They feel what happened to his father gives him the motive, and he for sure also has the means. If they're right and downsizing is the motive, you and I are on the hit list. Watch your back and stay close to your bodyguard."

"Jesus Christ, my worst fucking nightmare is coming true. I'm scared to death at night as it is. This'll just make it worse. Goddamn it."

"Do you have a gun?"

"No, and I wouldn't know how to use it if I did. Do you?"

"No."

"What the hell should we do?"

"I don't know. Just listen to our bodyguards? I don't know. This is way out of my league. I can't even conceive of what to do. If I come face to face with the killer, I'll probably piss my pants."

"Goddamn it."

They sat and looked at each other, not speaking until Lorraine broke the silence.

"I can't think about it anymore. Let's talk about tonight's meeting."

"Okay."

"I'm going to raise the issues you tried to raise before the first downsizing." When Phil tried to reply, Lorraine kept talking. "I know I didn't support you then. You don't have to repeat it. I thought Pamela would understand. I thought she was different – I thought she was smarter than Hazlitt – but she's not."

"I planned to raise them again anyway, so you don't have to. I'm in some trouble anyway. No sense you get in trouble, too."

"It's better if I do it. I have the advantage of being a black woman dealing with white management. That's a real advantage in today's culture. Neither Hazlitt nor Robinson will confront me as strongly as they would you. They'll be afraid to get too tough with me."

"So you're playing the race card?"

"I sure am. Pamela really pissed me off yesterday."

"I'll do what I can to support you."

"I knew you would. Now get out of here. I have a lot of work to do. Goddamned FDA."

"I'll see you tonight."

Phil's next stop was Abby's office. He updated her on what he had learned last night and asked, "What do you think?"

"I'm not surprised. I believe the DiRollo kid is dangerous, a real psychopath. If he's behind this, you, Lorraine, and Stanley might be on his list."

"I figured that. I've already talked to Lorraine. What about you?"

"I think I'm okay. The DiRollos seemed to like me when I was helping them with their benefits."

"I hope you're right. What I'm about to tell you is none of your business, but I'll tell you anyway. It's my turn tonight to lay out the reductions in my departments. Hazlitt has already spelled out the reductions in Production, and Stanley did the same for Technical. Proportionally their reductions were less than needed, so we'll take the hit. I tried to fight it at the first meeting, and I'm going to fight it again tonight."

"So you're being set up to take the biggest hit. I'm not surprised. What about Russ in security?"

"It's obvious Hazlitt wants the biggest reductions in the HR, Safety, and Security parts of my organization. I'm going to do everything I can to avoid it, but I don't have a lot of hope."

"Should I get my resume out?"

"Not yet, but if it looks like you might have to, I'll let you know." Phil started to get up.

"Before you go, what did the police find out about Higgins?"

"He was a clerk with very little firearm training. It looks like your info was faulty."

"I'm surprised. I thought the info on his military experience was solid."

"You can't be perfect all the time."

Before returning to his office, Phil's last stop of the morning was Joan McMullen.

"Good morning, Joan. How are things with today's production?"

"All the raw materials are in place for today's batches, but we have some material shortages for Friday. Bill Evers is contacting our suppliers and seems to be having some success. I'm going to start working on the cycle-time project in about half an hour or so. Can I work some OT tonight?"

"Sure. Under the same conditions, make sure someone else will be here while you're working."

"Don't worry. I'll make sure I'm covered."

"Joan, thanks again for all you're doing."

Phil had an hour before he and Alice Chen met to prepare for the weekly scheduling meeting. Each Wednesday, Production, Technical, Quality, and Production Planning representatives met to firm up the Production schedule for the next week and rough out plans for the next three weeks. Production Planning tracked Marketing forecasts, Finished Goods inventories, and Raw Material inventories. The status of technical problems, utilization of production equipment, and staffing were integrated to develop the production schedule. Phil decided to work on Batch Folders and was just about to begin when Alice walked into his office carrying what looked like a five-hundred-page computer report.

"Phil, we have a major problem! Thinadin inventories at our distributors have dropped below the critical level. The scheduled production won't cover the shortfall, even if every batch we make is released. We have to bump up the other products scheduled for tomorrow and Friday, and we have to schedule production this weekend."

"Hold on a second. How the hell did that happen?"

"It's more important that we solve the problem than try to place blame."

"You're right, but politics aren't logical, and I need to know how this happened before I talk to Hazlitt."

"Okay. As best I can determine, several problems ganged up on us. Marketing forecast a small increase in sales for Thinadin after the FDA approved it as a treatment for atrial fibrillation. They then began aggressively informing doctors of the new indication for Thinadin. Sales of Thinadin increased slowly at first, just as Marketing predicted, but recently they took off and drained the pipeline. We just got the inventory numbers today. Adding to the problem, we're rejecting a higher percentage of Thinadin batches than ever before. We have fifty million tablets sitting in the reject area. And obviously, the murders have slowed us down. The first two are by far the biggest problems."

"Why are we just getting the inventory numbers? I thought the Atlanta Distribution Center closely monitored inventories of all our drugs, especially Thinadin. We should've known we were in trouble before it got critical."

"It happened fast. Suddenly, doctors all over the country started prescribing Thinadin to heart patients with atrial fibrillation. With inventories already lower than normal because of production problems, we dropped below critical levels. It just happened. Can we start solving the problem?"

"Sure. Can our plant in Puerto Rico produce more product?"

"They'll do two extra batches by next Tuesday. Remember, we're the primary producer of Thinadin, and as a result, it's our responsibility. They'll help as much as possible, but they won't bail us out."

"Do you think Quality will release any rejected batches? Or can Technical solve any of the problems with the batches?"

"Highly doubtful."

"Assuming the current reject rate, how many batches do we have to produce to get us out of trouble?"

"Seven by next Tuesday and three extra a week starting next week to meet the higher demand Marketing is now forecasting."

"Jesus. Do we have the raw materials to make that much Thinadin?'

"We have plenty to get started, and we're already preparing to order more."

"Good. Let me take a look at our Finished Goods inventory levels."

Phil and Alice spent the next hour going over the inventory levels and Marketing forecasts for all the products made at Garden City and developed a workable Production Plan. The plan called for significant overtime, which would be a problem with the holidays just around the corner and the current turmoil in the company.

"Do you think Production will agree to this?" Alice asked.

"They'll grouse a lot, but what choice do they have? I need some time to prepare, but before you go, I also need to know how you're doing on our little project."

"I'm still working on it. I plan to have a little program to test by this weekend, but I won't know until after the test if I can give you what you want."

"I have faith in you, Alice. You're as good as they get around computers. It'll work."

"Wishful thinking. I don't have the same level of confidence as you. It's a complicated program and it has to be installed without anyone seeing it, which isn't an easy task. I'll call you this weekend."

"It's not wishful thinking. I just think it'll be critical to catching the killer."

"Do you really think he'll try to get in the building again? He got Connolly in her hotel room."

"I think Lorraine and I are probably on his list, and I think he may try to get in the building again."

"Christ, thanks for all the pressure."

"You're welcome. Now get out of here and let me prepare for the meeting."

Echo stared at the drawer containing his weapons. He had a problem: a big problem. *The police are already talking to me, asking where I was when those bastards were killed. How could they zero in so fast? How could they find me out of the hundreds of possible suspects? Someone at Garden City is talking to the police, giving them leads.*

Fortunately, I have good alibis for both nights. Detailed planning and planning for contingencies pays off. The police seemed satisfied with my alibis. They're probably checking them out, but there's nothing for me to worry about. I covered my tracks. The big problem is the bodyguards. Bodyguards, they hired bodyguards! I have to find a way to kill him, and it has to be soon. I should've seen it coming, I should've planned for it. Hiring bodyguards was a logical move I didn't anticipate. Shit.

Echo got up and walked around the dining room. *All right, what do I know about him? What do I know about his habits? First, I have to determine where I'll kill him. Then I'll come up with the how. It should be simple, but the bodyguards, the fucking bodyguards.* Echo walked to the mirror and stared at his image. His hair was combed and neatly trimmed; his face was clean-shaven. His Oxford shirt was clean and well pressed, the collars buttoned down. *I planned this operation to the minutest detail, and so far, everything has gone as planned. Sure, Steve Gagnon following Diane to the office was unexpected but easily handled. The bodyguards — the well-trained — present a real problem. My next two hits have twenty-four-hour a day bodyguards.* Echo looked at his reflection again. *Not bad for a guy over fifty. A good diet and an exercise routine have kept me looking good. Hey, wait a minute... my problem may be solved. If I remember right, he lives in a pretty isolated spot.* Echo looked up the address and got out his map of Suffix County. *I have to drive out and check it out. It may be a great spot. I also have to decide whether or not to tell my co-conspirators about my visit from the police. There's time for that later. Now I have to focus on my next assassination.*

The scheduling meeting was a disaster. Phil carefully explained how the inventory problems with Thinadin came about and the plan he and Alice had worked out to re-build inventory. The attendees from the Production Area blamed Phil and the Production Planning group for the problem. The attendees from Production ignored the fact that Marketing had under forecasted demand and that the Production Area was making lots of defective Thinadin. They said Phil should have seen it coming. They complained that he had not done his job, and that now they would have to work overtime during the holidays to make up for it. Phil had explained the situation to Gary Hazlitt before the meeting and believed Hazlitt understood. However, Gary sat silently, a slight grin on his face when Phil looked to him for support. He let his underlings create the impression that Phil was to blame. When the meeting ended, the attendees, including Hazlitt, ignored Phil as they left.

After the meeting, Phil hid in his office. Usually, he would have talked to Hazlitt to straighten out the impression left by the meeting but he knew it was useless. He also knew his days as a Purity employee were numbered. Once again, the thought of losing his job seemed to make him feel better. All he needed was time to collect the data that might protect his and Rose's financial future.

Toward the end of the day, Phil called Joan McMullen. "With all the commotion in the area, were you able to enter any data today?" Phil hoped for a positive answer.

"Since my raw materials are in good shape, my supervisor left me alone. I got a lot entered, and I'm working OT tonight. Do you want me to come over and download the data to your desktop?"

"Yes. I'll be here for another hour."

"Oh, what about your meeting tonight?"

Even though he shouldn't have been, Phil was surprised she knew about the meeting. "So, you know about the meeting. Do you know the subject?"

"Yes, we all do."

"Great. To answer your question, I'm going to dinner first."

"I'll see you in twenty minutes."

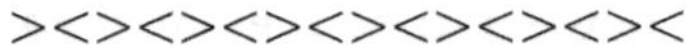

North Point Road was about ten miles long and ran from the Village of Northport to the tip of the Point. Echo knew his next victim lived near the Vanderbilt Mansion close to the Point. When he reached the mansion and still had not found the house, he parked his minivan and looked around. The enormous mansion, surrounded by a fourteen foot high stonewall, sat on the right side of the road. Echo learned from the sign attached to the stone wall that The State of New York, current owners of the Vanderbilt Mansion and grounds, opened both to the public from 9:00 am to 4:00 pm for a small admission fee. The back of the mansion overlooked the Long Island Sound to the east. A large, open parking lot to the left of the road overlooked the Sound to the west. At the moment, the parking lot was almost empty. Echo drove around until he found a small space behind a shed to hide his minivan.

Echo left the parking lot, turned toward the Point, and discovered that North Point Road turned right and dropped about fifty feet before ending at a large cul-de-sac close to the Long Island Sound. Three houses sat on the right side of the cul-de-sac. On the left was a densely wooded area. According to the number on the mailbox, the house farthest from the Point belonged to his next target. No one was around, so, pretending to be taking a casual walk by the Sound, Echo peered into the wooded area until he found a perfect hiding spot.

Phil's stomach burned. Grimacing in pain, he thought, *Is this what an ulcer feels like? Like someone's stuck a knife into your stomach.* He had begun having stomach problems shortly after starting his job at Garden City. At first, it was a slight burning sensation. Later it had progressed to more of a sharp pain, as if his stomach was in a knot and a bodybuilder was pulling it tight. Now it felt like he had a knife in his stomach, and that the bodybuilder was twisting it. Phil needed to be alone, to think. His life was falling apart, and it was happening fast. For the first time in his adult life, he believed the problems he faced were unsolvable. Dealing with his co-workers in an honest, upfront way no longer worked. He decided to drive to Jones Beach and park overlooking the ocean. It was practically deserted at this time of year.

Phil parked in the row closest to the ocean then powered the window down so he could listen to the soothing sounds of the sea. His life had started to turn sour a week ago with Abby's assessment of his uncertain job future. Then the murders had come along, and things had proceeded downhill from there. Others had caused some of the problems he faced, but he was to blame for the rest. He had made decisions that could very well ruin his marriage. On top of that, he might be the target of some madman with an axe to grind.

Phil found the rhythmic sounds of the waves the screeching of the seagulls therapeutic. He let his mind wander.

Rose is coming home tomorrow night, and I have a lot to tell her. I put us in harm's way by agreeing to work with Hines. As a result, my job and my pension are in jeopardy. Not only am I in Cohen's crosshairs, but I'm also probably in the killer's crosshairs. So tomorrow night, Rose, the best wife a man could have, will come home from a week of taking care of Judy and find out I fucked things up good. She's strong and, over the years, has taken most problems in stride. She'll deal with the fact that Cohen wants to fire me and the killer wants to kill me.

Phil watched a seagull peck at the carcass of a dead horseshoe crab. *Working with Hines when Cohen and Hazlitt are looking to fire me can only be described as stupid. Why did I do it? Because Hines said more people might be killed. Well, Connolly was killed, and nothing I did helped. And if the killer decides to kill someone tonight or tomorrow or whenever, will risking my job make any difference? I doubt it. We, the executives, have bodyguards.* Phil looked in the rearview mirror. *Mine is sitting on the hood of his car, looking around like a secret service agent. But I still don't feel safe. Well, I'll just tell Rose what I did. What choice do I have? I can't undo it. She'll accept it. She'll support me no matter the outcome.*

Phil got out of his car and started walking on the boardwalk. His bodyguard followed. As the bodyguard closed the distance between them, Phil turned and said, "I need to be alone to think. Could you hang back?" The bodyguard nodded and Phil continued to walk while rehashing the same questions and arguments without coming up with any answers until it was time for the meeting.

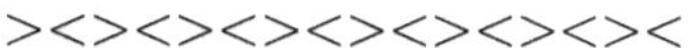

Phil walked over to Lorraine at the food table. "Hazlitt and Robinson outdid themselves. The food is better, and there's more of it." Lorraine nodded in agreement. "Are you going to go through with it?"

"Why not? I'm only doing the same thing you did last time. You got nowhere because nobody, me included, supported you. I expect you'll support me this time, and I'm going to play the race card."

"My support is nothing compared to the fear an intelligent, forceful black woman strikes in the hearts of her white management when she's adamant about an issue. Since you have the power, you might as well use it."

"I intend to. I'll push hard."

"I'll be right behind you. Are you ready?"

"Oh yeah. How come you're not eating? I'm not used to seeing you surrounded by food and not trying to eat it all."

"I'm not hungry." The bodybuilder twisted the knife in Phil's stomach.

Phil and Lorraine talked about the upcoming meeting and the issues she planned to raise. Phil coached her on how to present her case diplomatically, but Lorraine told him that this was not the time for diplomacy. Hazlitt called the meeting to order at six o'clock.

"Let's get started. We have a lot to do and not a lot of time to do it. Last time Paul Stanley and I charted the cuts we planned to make in Production and Technical." Hazlitt started tearing off pages from a chart pad, and Paul Stanley hung them on the wall. "These charts show the cuts we recommend. I'll do the same thing for Quality and Business Resources when we're finished. Then we can start staffing the jobs and see who gets targeted for downsizing. Lorraine, if you're ready, would you go first?"

"I'll be happy to." Lorraine picked up a stack of papers and shuffled through them before looking Hazlitt directly in the eye. "The cuts you and Stanley proposed are bullshit, meaningless. Your organizations are grossly overstaffed for the work you have to do, and the cuts hardly touch the fat, let alone the muscle. You're leaving Quality and Business Resources to make up the difference, and I know Quality is already having difficulty getting our job done. You have layer on top of layer of supervision that do little more than talk to each other."

Hazlitt interrupted. "Pamela and I will decide how many people each organization loses after we see the whole picture. For the first pass, your job is to cut your organization as much as possible to get a realistic picture. And I expect you to do that… NOW!"

"We, Garden City, need to reduce our operating costs by twenty million dollars next year." Lorraine continued as if Gary Hazlitt's words were never spoken. "The cuts you and Stanley propose are insignificant. They only add up to about seven million dollars. Since you have almost seventy percent of the employees, you're sure not trying to cut as much as possible. You're sandbagging."

Again, Hazlitt interrupted. "Lorraine, I just told you, nothing is final. After looking at all the proposals, Pamela and I will decide how much each organization is cut. Please let us see what your proposal is for Quality."

"Okay, I'll propose enough cuts to get the twelve million we need to make your – and I emphasize 'your' – objective, Mr. Hazlitt and Ms. Robinson." Lorraine reshuffled her papers and then looked at the obviously perplexed meeting leaders. "First, we should eliminate company-paid food at all meetings. Only management employees benefit from it, and we can sure as hell afford to pay for our own food if we want it. It's mostly a symbolic act, but employees see their co-workers, their friends, losing their jobs while we dine on company-paid shrimp and plan the reductions."

Pamela Robinson stood up. "Lorraine, you're wasting our time. We're here to talk about reducing our workforce, and you're trying to take us down a different trail."

Lorraine bristled. "We should be here to save twenty million dollars without risking the future of the business. I want to cut unnecessary spending without affecting the business's operation. In fact, if we do away with the perks we managers receive, the morale in the plant will improve and so will our productivity."

"Lorraine, you know that Phil tried to raise these issues last time. He got nowhere. Now let's move on. We don't have all night," Pamela said with a raised voice.

"If we had listened to Phil, three of our peers would be alive. Pamela, I intend to continue unless you or Gary gives me a direct order to stop. And if you do, I am walking out that door."

Pamela and Gary looked at one another, neither wanting to commit. Finally, Pamela spoke. "Go ahead."

"When we travel, and I mean Management, we go first class. We stay in four and five-star hotels, eat at the best restaurants, and fly first class. Again, our employees see this and have difficulty reconciling the money we spend while laying off their peers. When employees are transferred to Garden City, they stay at the Garden City Hotel for over six hundred dollars a night for up to five months. They could stay at the Island Inn for less than a third. In fact, we can stop relocation altogether until we get our financial house in order." Lorraine paused. When no one spoke, she continued. "Rumor has it that a project to upgrade the Management offices in Wilmington has been authorized. The project totals out at three million dollars, with a half-million designated to be spent on the CEO's office. Half a million for one office? We could save seven jobs easily for the cost of one office, and by not spending the three million, we could save forty jobs. Yet we only think about saving money by firing people. We don't consider the impact on our employees and their families."

Pamela took advantage of the pause. "If you're done, I'd like to discuss the issues you raised."

"I'll tell you when I'm done. Lastly, I think we should eliminate the performance bonus due next February. We claim that the bonuses are based on the performance of the business. If the business is performing so poorly that we have to fire people, then no one in Management has earned a bonus." Lorraine picked up a pack of papers and started handing them out. "My proposals are spelled out in detail. The savings total out at over thirteen million dollars. I'm done."

Pamela could tell from the look on Hazlitt's face that he wanted no part of dealing with Lorraine. "I appreciate your effort to try to save jobs, but I doubt we'll be able to implement your suggestions. On the surface your recommendations sound good, but they don't help our financial performance and you know it. Saving money on capital expenditures by canceling the office project does not affect our operating profit since the money comes from our capital budget. As for eliminating bonuses, I think it would severely hurt the business. Our professional and Management employees consider the annual bonus a normal part of their compensation. Eliminating it would cause our good people to leave. The savings from your other recommendations are insignificant and are not worth implementing. Can we move on now?"

"Do you actually think you can dismiss my suggestions with that pap? I'm not stupid. You and the rest of the Wilmington Management talk out of both sides of your mouth. The reasons you give when you support something or challenge something are situational, and you're doing it again. I know the money for the office project comes out of the capital budget. I also know that capital spending affects cash flow when spent and then flows to operating expenses as depreciation. Pamela, six months ago, you used the effect on cash flow to turn down buying new capital equipment for the Technical Department. Now it's not important. As for the bonuses, the party line has always been that bonuses are not guaranteed and are only granted if the business is performing well. Now you're telling us they're considered part of normal compensation, and people might leave. Well, ain't that the point."

Pamela again looked at Hazlitt and knew he wanted to stay out of the conversation. "It's been a long day, and I don't want to waste everyone's time tonight. Lorraine, I'll see you tomorrow after the FDA leaves. We can resolve this then. This meeting is over. Plan on getting back together next Monday. I'm sure Lorraine and I will have this worked out. Good night." Pamela and Gary left without a word to anyone.

Phil and Lorraine walked to their cars. Phil said, "I don't suppose you need my help tomorrow."

"You're right."

Alone in bed for the last night, Phil tried to make sense of the day's events. At first, facing Rose tomorrow night was all he could think about. After considering the pros and cons of telling Rose about his Sunday afternoon with Lorraine, Phil decided not to tell her. That settled, the events of the day drifted into his head.

It was a significant problem for him that Thinadin's Finished Goods inventory had fallen below the critical level for the first time in history. Since Garden City was the primary producer of Thinadin, Phil's Production Control Group were to ensure that Thinadin inventory levels never dropped below critical levels. Production Control was to blame, and the buck had stopped with him. Sure, Marketing had missed the demand forecast, and Production at Garden City had produced fifty million out-of-spec tablets. Unfortunately, facts made little difference in today's corporate culture. Word was already spreading that Phil was responsible, and Production would have to work overtime to bail him out. Surely Hazlitt would use the issue to erode his support and ultimately cost him his job. Phil Messina was about to face termination.

Corporations have many names for the ending of an employee's career. To name a few, employees could be downsized, right-sized, RIFed, ROFed, laid off, re-engineered, or delayered. It had always amazed Phil that a corporate executive would go to such lengths to use words designed to ease his conscience. Recently a particularly creative CEO had said that his company would reduce five thousand jobs through 'involuntary attrition.' 'Involuntary attrition' was a nonsensical term. Attrition was, by definition, voluntary, the employee's decision. Phil's view of corporate life was a little simpler; an employee either left a company voluntarily or involuntarily. Employees told to leave were, to put it simply, involuntarily terminated. Phil had seen many of his co-workers terminated at both McKenzie and Purity. In fact, he had played an essential role in determining who had been terminated. The employees' reactions would forever occupy a part of Phil's mind. The reactions varied, but they were all variations of horrific. The older and higher-paid an employee, the more serious the psychological damage was. To management employees, their job titles were more than descriptions of their job duties. Job titles were their self-esteem. Employees who equated their personal value with their position suffered the most when they were terminated.

Phil puzzled over the same question, putting himself into those employees' shoes. *Phil Messina, Director of Business Resources, Purity Pharmaceutical Company. If I lose my job, will I lose my identity? How will I see myself? Will I even be able to go on to find another job? Will I be able to support Rose, Ann, and Tony? Can I survive as plain old Phil Messina without 'Director of Business Resources' tacked on?* He was only sure that he needed Rose's support to survive… which was another reason for not telling her about Lorraine. He felt better.

On a positive note, Lorraine's performance at the meeting had been nothing short of spectacular. She had played the race card and trumped Robinson and Hazlitt. The advent of Affirmative Action and laws against discrimination had changed the power balance and shifted it more in favor of women and minorities. Lorraine was smart enough to know it and bold enough to use it. Pamela and Gary were afraid that Lorraine might file a discrimination charge or talk to Cohen and accuse them of being racists. Once Pamela and Gary demonized Lorraine and got Cohen's blessing to deal with her, the downsizing would be back on track. She had managed to delay it only temporarily.

Phil got out of bed and looked out of the front window. His bodyguard was walking around the house. He felt safe, physically at least. He smiled halfheartedly and, returning to his bed, closed his eyes and let his thoughts swim around in his mind. *Things will be better tomorrow. Rose will be home, and I'll have my best friend to talk to. Maybe I'll call Greg or Roger tomorrow, and I can start feeling more secure about my job.* Phil drifted off to sleep thinking about his work life in McKenzie and his relationship with Roger Hanson.

Phil's relationship with Greg Iverson and Roger Hanson had been built on a foundation of mutual respect over many years. Phil had worked with Greg on many successful projects, and they had effectively managed a variety of employee problems. Phil considered Greg a good manager and more importantly a good man. Roger Hanson, despite being a much higher level routinely sought Phil's advice on issues he was grappling with. Phil thought highly of both men and believed they felt the same about him.

Thursday 12/11

Thursday was quickly turning into the worst day of Phil's career. No one was clamoring to see him, his phone rarely rang, and his email messages dropped to nearly zero. Was it possible that a general announcement had gone out to all Purity employees? He wondered what it could say. *Hear ye, hear ye! Phil Messina mismanaged the Thinadin inventory, and our customers, who really need the drug, will die. We'll go out of business, too, unless, of course, Production pulls off a miracle and bails us out.' Sounds about right.*

Phil had seen it happen to other high-level managers. They had become invisible when word had leaked out that they were being terminated. Besides a nod or two in passing, all communication by co-workers had ceased, as if guilt by association could also end their careers. Phil needed a friend, and it appeared he had none. Just then, Abby barged into his office.

"You're in deep trouble. The rumor mill is churning, and you're the grist. You know I have a close friend in Wilmington who is in a position to know what's happening, so take what I tell you seriously. The rumor is you dropped the ball on Thinadin, didn't do your job, and as a result, we could stock out of Thinadin. Cohen's going to Roger Hanson to tell him why you need to be fired."

"Am I the only one in Purity who knows that Production Control did nothing wrong in this?"

"Nobody cares. Remember Chuck and Karen? Nobody cared that they weren't trained. Chuck installed the wrong tool in the tablet press, and Karen didn't catch it. They were the scapegoats then, and now it's you."

"Great. Do you have any idea what I can do?"

"There's nothing you can do in Purity. Cohen wants you out, and this is his chance. Even if he had nothing against you, he would never blame Marketing or Production. It's time to talk to your friends in high places."

"Okay. Okay, I'll call Hanson. Anything else you want to talk about?"

"Everything else is irrelevant compared to your problems. Deal with yourself first. I'll talk to you later."

After Abby left, Phil sat in his office staring at the paintings that decorated the walls. He was paralyzed. He couldn't move, couldn't think. He was dead, terminated, a terminated man walking. Phil's throat quivered and a tear formed in his left eye. *Christ, I'm a wimp.* Phil struggled to gain control, and when he did, he called Roger Hanson.

"Phil, I haven't heard from you in a while. How are things in the pharmaceutical business?"

"Have you heard about the problem with Thinadin?"

"Yeah, Cohen called me. We're meeting next Tuesday so he can fill me in. Apparently, the situation is serious enough to put our Thinadin business at risk. He plans to fire someone. That wouldn't be you by any chance, would it?"

"Probably. I seem to be the bad guy, according to the rumor mill. I'd like to tell you my side."

"Cohen has talked to me about firing you before. Each time I've told him, 'That doesn't sound like the Phil Messina I know.' He seems to think you hurt the business more than you help. But this sounds serious. Can you meet with me Tuesday?"

"Sure. You'll protect me until then?"

"Unless you're the killer. Be in my office at nine o'clock in the morning. I'm meeting with Cohen at one, and I'd like your side of the story before meeting with him. And Phil, I know you don't like asking me for help, but I'm glad you called. You're in some trouble, and I'm going to be involved in the decision-making. See you Tuesday."

Hope. Phil had hope. Roger's tone indicated that he was on Phil's side. Roger had let him know, in so many words, that his side of the story would be heard and given as much weight as Cohen's. Phil scheduled a meeting with Alice Chen; he needed to be armed with facts when he met with Roger. Suddenly he felt better. The storm clouds dispersed, and his mind was bright and sunny.

Echo pushed the button that brought the paper target forward. He examined it closely. Although the three bullets made a hole in the target only a little larger in diameter than a single bullet, he was not satisfied. Echo readjusted the laser scope on his Marksman rifle. After adjusting the scope, he hung a new target and sent it out. He stopped the target when it was forty-five yards out, about the distance he would be from his human prey. Echo slowly squeezed off three more shots before bringing the target back. Again, all three bullets went through the same hole. It was dead center. The adjustment was perfect.

Echo mounted a fresh target, sent it out forty-five yards, and fired three times as fast as possible. This time the target had three holes in it. He brought the target forward, carefully looked at the scatter of the bullet holes, and frowned. He was rusty. The holes were within a quarter of an inch of each other. Not good enough. Echo repeated the process until he was satisfied with his speed and accuracy. It took over an hour. He carefully disassembled his rifle and put the parts into their cutouts in the metal case. He would be successful tonight.

Feeling confident, Echo stopped at the first payphone he found. When his accomplice answered, Echo said, "Another perfect job and another bitch dead."

"Did everything go according to plan? No complications?"

"As I said, perfect. I bought some antiques at the auction and established a great alibi if the police ever look at me." Echo decided that telling his accomplices about the interview with the police would panic them, heightening the chance that they would make a mistake.

"Great! I… I mean, we have nothing to worry about. Two to go, and we're done. How's your planning coming for the next one?"

"I'm going to kill him tonight, and don't worry, my plan is perfect. All I need is for our partner to call me on my cell phone and let me know when the target leaves work."

"Your cell! That's easy to trace."

"Stop worrying. We have it worked out. I'll expect a call around five or six. And before you ask, the bodyguard will be no problem."

"Okay. What about your alibi for tonight?"

Echo slowly inhaled. He hated answering to inferior people. "I have the best possible alibi: no alibi. If I'm asked where I was tonight, I'll just say I was alone. It happens. With two great alibis already, I figure that not having one for tonight will confuse the cops."

"Don't screw with me. That's taking too much of a risk. What have you planned?"

"Relax, it's a great idea. With no verifiable alibi, all I have to do is say, 'If I killed anyone, I'd be smart enough to make sure I had an alibi.' Since I have an alibi for the other two nights, they can't pin the murders on me. It's brilliant."

"I don't buy it. You need an alibi. It can wait until you set one up. Let's hold off."

"I'm the one doing the killing. I'm taking all the risks. So, I'll do it my way. When you're the one pulling the trigger, you can do it your way."

"We're all taking a considerable risk, not just you. I'm telling you to postpone tonight until you have a better plan."

"I'll expect a call tonight!" Echo hung up.

Pamela and Lorraine met over lunch, which was the only time Lorraine was free of the FDA. Pamela had the cafeteria deliver sandwiches and drinks to her office before the meeting. She had personally paid for the lunches rather than billing them to the company, conceding to Lorraine. She wished she had gotten to know Lorraine better over the years. In fact, she hoped that they were friends. They mostly agreed on the problems with the downsizing. If Pamela could depend on their friendship, she would tell Lorraine that she had already talked to Cohen about the other ways of saving money. He was only interested in the number of people that he could cut. She could explain that reducing the number of employees had become a contest between the Business Unit leaders in McKenzie and Saga, and that Cohen wanted to win. He wanted to impress his management. He needed to be accepted by his peers. Yet she and Lorraine were not close friends, so Pamela would defend Cohen's position of reducing people rather than cutting expenses.

"Lorraine, thanks for coming. I know you're busy with the FDA and lunch is the only free time you have today, but we need to talk. Before we start, how is the audit going?"

"I don't really know. I'm not sure. The auditors are only reviewing old Relieve Batch Records. I just sit around and wait for them to ask a question. This meeting is a chance for me to do something more constructive. By the way, why are you meeting with me? Hazlitt is the acting Site Director."

"I'm in charge of the downsizing. I've let Gary handle the meetings, but I'm accountable for success or failure at Garden City. You pointed out some areas to save money and maybe minimize the number of people who lose their jobs. You also pointed out some symbolic things we could do to soothe the bad feelings of the employees who will stay with us. I'd like to discuss them with you one at a time, so we don't get confused. Okay?"

"Sure."

"Let's start with company-paid food at meetings." Pamela pulled out a sheet of paper and handed it to Lorraine. "This is an announcement to all professional and management employees stating Purity will no longer pay for food at meetings. I'd like to issue it under your signature since it was your idea."

She's good and as cold as ice, Lorraine thought. *If I don't sign, it weakens my position on other issues. If I sign it, I'm the bad guy with my peers.* Lorraine signed the announcement. "No problem."

"Great. We won't save enough money to save any jobs, but as you said, it'll save us from bad feelings with the workers. Now, on to your suggestions on our travel policy."

She probably has another memo for me to sign, Lorraine figured. "I think there are two issues: the frequency of our travel and the fact that we travel first class, stay at the best hotels, and eat at the best restaurants. We could easily cut our travel budget by seventy-five percent with no negative impact on the business. That would save jobs. If you have a memo for me to sign, I'm ready."

"There's no need for a memo. We're not going to change our travel guidelines. We're in the pharmaceutical industry, and the other companies allow their employees to travel, eat, and sleep first-class. We compete with those companies for employees, so no change in our policy."

"That doesn't make sense. The other pharmaceutical companies aren't downsizing, so there's no comparison. We need to let our employees know that despite the fact that we're making money, we're not making enough money to satisfy our owners and need to cut costs. We'll have changed our travel guidelines to save jobs. If we're honest with our employees, they'll have no problem sacrificing a little. It's win-win, and any employees that quit because we've changed our travel guidelines don't deserve to work here, and besides, they'll save the jobs of people who want to work here."

She's right, and she's taken the high ground. And here I am trying to defend Cohen's decisions that I don't support, Pamela thought. She leaned forward. "All of your arguments have been considered, and the decision has been made. We're not changing our travel guidelines."

"I assume Cohen agrees, or you wouldn't be so decisive."

"You're hearing the decision from me. If you want to talk to Cohen, go ahead. Now let's talk about the Managers' Meetings."

Lorraine interrupted. "If you've decided to turn down all my recommendations, tell me now so I can leave."

"I prefer you receive the benefit of my thinking before I give you my decision, but feel free if you want to leave."

Lorraine got an idea and pulled a writing pad out of her briefcase. "I'll stay. I want to hear your reasoning. Do you mind if I take notes?"

Pamela nodded. "The semi-annual Managers' Meetings are important because they facilitate internal communications between departments. Surely you see how important they are to our future success. You're right about the money we spend. We do go to good hotels and resorts, and we have fun in addition to work. But again, it's important to help us retain our good employees. The cost is justified." Pamela felt self-conscious, and she thought that she was babbling. Lorraine took notes the entire time she talked as if she was recording what Pamela had said word for word. Lorraine's notetaking unnerved her.

"Pamela, I never said it was all or nothing. We can save most of the money we spend and still have productive meetings. Think about how the meetings are run. I've been to two, and I know you've been to a lot more. Each meeting location is better than the last one, and the first one I attended was great. We're there for five days: three days of meetings and two days of fun activities. We fly over five hundred people to the meetings from all over the world, we pay for four nights of lodging at some of the most expensive hotels and resorts in the country, and we wine and dine them. Then there's the little thing of the gifts. Every night a present is on the bed when you return to your room. I'm not talking little trinkets, and the last time it was expensive. Since I've been here, I've received a sterling silver paper weight, an expensive tablet, and a Waterford Crystal in the shape of the Capitol Dome, to name a few. I find the meetings so formal and scripted that they're boring, and I can't wait to go home. And I'm not the only one. Most people think the meetings are a waste of time and money, and the only reason we have them is that top Management likes to throw a party. To spend that kind of money while we're eliminating jobs makes me sick."

"I understand your feelings, but we like the Managers' Meetings as they are, so no change." Lorraine made another note, and Pamela became a little more self-conscious. "You heard my responses to eliminating bonuses and the office project, and I stand by them."

"Your responses are naïve at best. You've argued for spending three million dollars to renovate the corporate offices, including half a million dollars for the CEO's office. You've also said it doesn't affect operating profits, but that doesn't pass the smell test. That money could be spent on salaries only when it hits operating expenses. As for the bonuses, you can't wave a magic wand and make bonuses part of normal pay when you've always said they were based on the performance of the business. Pamela, we're in trouble at current staffing levels, and we can't afford any more reductions. I'm rejecting more batches now than I ever have. You're a good manager, and I can't believe you support this."

"Do you really believe in your recommendations, or are you fronting for Phil?"

"I resent that. Do you think I can't stand up for myself because I'm a woman, or is it because I'm black? Whatever your prejudice, I'm doing this on my own. I'm only angry that I didn't support Phil when he tried to get these ideas considered."

"I only asked because he raised the same issues. And I resent your implication that I'm prejudiced."

"And I resent that you don't believe I can think for myself."

Pamela considered telling Lorraine how she really felt but decided not to. "You know my position, and my position also happens to be the corporate position. I'd like your commitment to publicly support the downsizing."

"I don't think I can do that."

"It's your job to support Management decisions. I'd hate to see you end your career by making a bad choice. We're going to cut jobs whether you support it or not. Your decision will only affect you. Lorraine, you're on the team or you're not."

Lorraine could not believe what she was hearing. She had joined McKenzie right out of college and had never considered changing jobs, nor had she ever been threatened with termination. "Pamela, take a close look at me. I'm a thirty-three-year-old, attractive, well-educated black woman who is the Director of Quality for a large company. How long do you think it will take before I have ten job offers?" Lorraine walked to the door, turned, and said, "I wonder if the press would be interested in this story?"

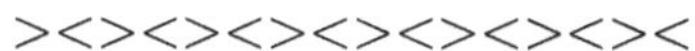

Phil's meeting with Alice Chen went a long way toward easing his concerns. Alice understood the various factors that led to the Thinadin supply crisis, and better yet, she had documentation. By the time the meeting had concluded around one o'clock, Phil was well prepared for his Tuesday meeting with Roger Hanson. Phil suggested that they head to the cafeteria, but Alice reminded him that she did not eat lunch.

When Phil got to the cafeteria, it was empty except for Frank James. The cafeteria workers had everything, except the sandwich fixings, put away. Phil opted for a roast beef and provolone cheese sandwich on Italian bread and a Diet Coke. Frank picked up his lunch to move to another table as Phil started to sit down.

"What the hell? Are you afraid to be seen with me?"

Frank glanced at Phil in frustration. "It's been over two weeks since Gino and I talked to you, and nothing. You forgot about us. You're too busy cutting more jobs to do anything about our problems."

"How about having lunch with me, and I'll fill you in on what I've done so far."

Frank slowly sat down. "Okay, I'll listen, but no bullshit."

"As we speak, Joan McMullen is going through batch records and entering the information into a database. When that's done, I'll be able to look for discrepancies." Phil explained in detail how he would look at equipment usage, employee time off, and test results. "It takes time to get all that information into the computer, but I should have enough to find the smoking gun by this weekend."

"That sounds alright. I guess Gino and I are just getting antsy. I bet you'll find a ton of problems."

"I should have kept you up to date. I just wasn't thinking."

"No problem. By the way, I heard we're running out of Thinadin and will have to work lots of OT, and it's your fault. Is that right?"

Phil filled Frank in on the facts. "It's partly my fault. I should have seen it coming. You guys made a lot of bad Thinadin, though, so you're not blameless."

"I guess not. I have one last question for you. Are you going to fire a bunch more people?"

"I can't answer that question."

"You told us there would be no more downsizing. Did you lie to us?"

"I reminded you that Cohen said there would be no more downsizing. I believed him at the time."

"I hope you look at the people in the offices. There are a lot of people sitting on their asses doing nothing."

"I hear ya. How are things going in Production?"

"Same, except we're careful now that the FDA is here. The big boys don't want to get caught."

"I gotta get back. While you're looking at your computer this weekend, look at Relieve. I heard we're getting short on inventory."

"Thanks for the tip. I'll see you." That's all Phil needed: another product dropping below critical.

When he got back to his office, he found a phone message from Lieutenant Hines. It was unusual for Hines to call him at work, so it had to be important.

"Thanks for calling back. I want to run something by you. Jack Goloski could be our guy. He was a Green Beret, and according to his record, he was a regular killing machine. He drew some tough covert assignments and returned with notches on his gun. Unfortunately, some of his missions are still classified. They must have been beauties. I'm trying to get the files opened, but so far no luck. After reading his file, I interviewed him yesterday morning and came away feeling he's not a killer. He's still mad and says you guys ruined his life after he was loyal to you. We're checking his alibis as we speak. So far, they're holding up. I know Abby thinks he wouldn't hurt a fly. What do you think?"

"I agree with Abby. I really like the guy, and I don't blame him for being mad."

"It might be a waste of time, but I'm trying to get a court order for twenty-four-hour surveillance. I don't think I have enough for a judge, but it's worth the effort."

"What about Anderson?"

"He's clean. He has a rock-solid alibi for both nights."

"At least you have two possibilities. I just hope you catch the killer before he gets to me."

"You're getting paranoid. When can we meet?"

"I'm free tomorrow night, but I need to shake my bodyguard and I don't think I want to do that."

"Let me figure something out. I'll call you."

Gary walked into Pamela's office about thirty seconds after Lorraine left. "How did it go?"

"I played hardball just as Bob advised, and I tried to get her to support the downsizing. She wouldn't. I threatened to fire her, and she told me she could get ten jobs in a week. She also threatened to go to the media."

"She's tougher than we thought. She wouldn't go to the media because no one would hire her if she did. Also, if it looks like she'll turn in her resignation, Cohen will offer to make her Site Director."

"You're kidding? He's already offered the job to Harry Loeb."

"He'll put him in another job. Lorraine's not ready for the Site Director job, but he'll do it anyway."

"If she goes to the media, it could be deadly."

"She won't."

Echo pulled into the Vanderbilt Mansion parking lot at about twenty past five and parked behind the small building. Earlier, he had taped over the switches that activated his minivan's interior lights when the doors were opened. Echo removed his Marksman rifle and a small tripod and walked into the woods. He dressed entirely in black, including a ski mask he pulled over his face as soon as he entered the woods. After a short walk, he settled into a spot that gave him the best line of sight to the front of the house. He set up the tripod, lay down on the cold ground, and sighted the scope. Satisfied, he stood up, shook off the chill, and leaned against a tree.

He set his cell phone to vibrate; she would call as soon as his target left the building. He had purchased the throwaway cell phone a couple of weeks ago and given her the number. When he had scouted the area the other day, he had checked the phone for service. It had plenty of signal strength. Nodding to himself, he mulled over the new alibi he had come up with. *All I have to do is wait. I must have patience. Patience is critical to success in this business. My alibi for tonight is simple yet elegant. If asked, I will simply tell the police I was Christmas shopping up at the Miracle Mile, and no, I didn't buy anything, just shopping. That implies that I didn't need an alibi. Elegant.*

While waiting, Echo reminisced about his time as a military assassin. And how he became known as 'Echo.'

The soldier sitting next to him during training noticed that he repeated every crucial point that came out of the instructor's mouth. He mumbled the words, but it was clear that he was repeating what the instructor said. Soon he became known as 'Echo.'

He became known as Echo, "the killing machine," after his next assignment. His superiors told him that the assignment would be difficult, and they were right. His target was a Russian officer equivalent to a five-star general in the U.S. Army. General Boldyrev was responsible for all military operations in and around Moscow, which provided him detailed knowledge of troop positioning and movement. He could use that information easily to arrange Gorbachev's death. The assassination was complicated because he was always surrounded by Russian soldiers. Echo watched Boldyrev's home every night for a week, trying to find a weakness in his protection. When it seemed there was none, a car finally left Boldyrev's compound at eleven-thirty pm. The car returned at five am. The following Tuesday night, Echo sat in a car with two operatives and waited.

At eleven-thirty the car left the compound, and this time Echo followed. His destination was a bar and whorehouse frequented by both Russians and American businessmen.

For the next two weeks, Echo patronized the bar. He found out that Boldyrev had been a regular for years. He always visited the same whore, in the same room on the same night of the week. A pattern was all he needed. He started seeing the prostitute in the room next door to Boldyrev's whore, paying her for a whole night of pleasure. When he was convinced he was beyond suspicion, Echo reserved her for a Tuesday night.

After several hours at the bar, he and the hooker climbed the stairs to her room. It was eleven o'clock. After one last roll in the hay, he killed her. Then he waited for Boldyrev.

Just after midnight, Echo heard activity in the room next door. He waited until he was sure that the General had only one thing on his mind, then staggered into the hall. On his right wrist Echo had a leather cuff which held an ice pick that would quickly drop into his hand. He also had a forty-five automatic in his shoulder holster. Acting drunk, he staggered over to the bodyguard standing outside the door. The bodyguard smiled as Echo staggered toward him. When Echo got close, he positioned himself so his chest was perpendicular to the bodyguard's left arm. Echo slowly raised his left hand as if to show the bodyguard something.

When he had the bodyguard's full attention, he released the ice pick into his right hand. He thrust it into the bodyguard's neck just below his skull and up into his brain with a smooth, quick motion. His left hand continued upward and covered the bodyguard's mouth. The shock of the ice pick entering his brain caused the bodyguard to black out instantly. He died moments later. Echo then slowly lay the dead man on the hallway floor. He had to act fast. He drew his forty-five and kicked the door open. Boldyrev was on top of his whore when he heard the door burst open. He rose up and turned toward the door, the perfect target. The first bullet hit him in the right temple. His whore sat up, and the second bullet hit her between the eyes. The third bullet tore the back of Boldyrev's head off.

Echo was down the fire escape before anyone in the building had a chance to react. The waiting car whisked him to the U.S. Embassy. He felt a rush, just as he had after his first assassination, but it was not as intense this time. He wanted that feeling again. Maybe next time would be like the first time.

Echo felt confident. He also felt a vibration and answered his phone.

"He just left."

The drive would take about forty minutes: the last forty minutes of Paul Stanley's life.

Echo first heard the cars, then saw the lights coming around the corner at the top of the hill. He was already lying in position on the cold December ground. Paul Stanley parked in the driveway, while his bodyguard parked in the street. Neither car obstructed Echo's shot. Both men walked up the steps, Stanley in front, his bodyguard one step behind. Just before they reached the porch, a small red dot appeared on the back of the bodyguard's head. It was immediately followed by a bullet hole. The bullet's force knocked the bodyguard into Stanley, who fell onto the steps partially under his bodyguard. Stanley tried to move the bodyguard and crawl to the porch, but it was too late. A bullet hit him in the back of the head, and less than a second later, another bullet pierced his heart. Paul Stanley's days on earth ended at 19,965. His bodyguard's days on earth ended at 9,023.

Echo ran through the woods to his minivan. He knew that he did not have much time. He tossed the rifle into the back of his minivan along with his ski mask. Echo knew that the police would use North Point Road to respond to the call and might even set up roadblocks, so he turned onto a side street at the first opportunity. He drove through the residential areas on the west side of North Point Road, never exceeding the speed limit until he reached route 25A and headed home. He had mapped out his escape route in advance and driven it twice in preparation. He arrived home around seven, too early to dispose of the evidence unobserved.

Phil's cell phone rang. "Where the hell are you?" Jim Hines shouted.

"I'm in the Oyster Bay train station waiting for Rose. We're going…"

Jim interrupted. "Paul Stanley's been murdered. Put your bodyguard on!"

Phil handed the phone to his bodyguard. "It's Lieutenant Hines."

After a few minutes on the phone with Hines, the bodyguard handed the phone to Phil, put his hand inside his jacket, and gripped his gun. He was shaken. "What's going on?" Phil asked Hines.

"Paul Stanley and his bodyguard were shot, ambushed. As soon as your wife arrives, I want you to go straight home and send out for dinner. I have two Nassau County Police officers on their way to the train station. This bastard isn't going to kill anyone else."

"Jesus Christ, is Lorraine okay?"

"She's fine. I have cops on the way to her house now. Parisi is talking to her right now. Be careful. I'll call you."

Phil hung up and then looked at his bodyguard. He was on full alert, his hand was still inside his jacket, and his eyes were darting around the train station. He was upset and maybe a little scared. "Did you know Stanley's bodyguard?" Phil asked.

"We were good friends. I can't believe he's dead. Son-of-a-bitch!"

"The train should be here in ten minutes." Phil's cell phone rang.

"Are you okay?" Lorraine asked.

"As of right now. But I'm definitely scared. This guy is good… bodyguards don't stop him. If we're on his list, we're dead unless the police catch him."

"I'm scared too. I don't want to go to work tomorrow, but I have to."

"Lorraine, I understand."

"I know. I'll see you tomorrow."

The train was early, and since Oyster Bay was the end of the line, it was almost empty. When Rose got off, she and Phil hugged and kissed, then Phil pulled back.

"Paul Stanley was just killed, so we need to go straight home. This is my bodyguard. Let's go."

"Phil…."

"Let's go."

The walk home was short, and Phil and Rose walked fast. The bodyguard moved from the front to behind them as they walked. As they approached the house, a Nassau County patrol car pulled up, and two officers got out and walked over to Phil and Rose.

"Please go straight inside and stay there. We'll be here all night. You'll be safe," one of the officers said.

Phil's cell was ringing as they walked into the house. It was Greg Iverson. "I just heard about Stanley, and I can't believe it. He was the least threatening guy on the staff. I would've thought you or Lorraine would have been the target because you were heavily involved in the last downsizing."

"Thanks."

"Sorry. What do we need to do to help the police? You said Hazlitt only wanted you to provide general information, and they wanted suspects. We need to give them suspects. Phil, start working on it, and I'll call Cohen and square it with him."

Phil thought about telling Greg about his involvement with Lieutenant Hines but simply said, "Okay."

"Phil, I'm serious. I'll make it happen."

"I'm serious too. I'll put a list together."

"I'll call you tomorrow."

Phil turned to Rose. "We need to talk about some things. Are you up for it?"

"No, I'm pretty tired and a little shaken, so let's just go to bed."

"Okay."

The phone rang. Rose said, "I'm going to bed. Try not to be too long."

"Phil, Bob Cohen. Have you heard?"

"Yes."

"As soon as I heard, I got on the phone with Gail. I told her I didn't care what her legal opinion was or if we violated the Privacy Act or any other goddamn law. Our people are dying, and we need to help the police. I just finished talking to that Lieutenant Hines and told him you would have some suspects for him tomorrow. Can you deliver?"

"Sure."

"Phil, I'm serious. I want Hines to have that list."

"He'll be interviewing suspects sooner than you would believe possible."

"Good, I hoped you'd see it my way. Get it to Hines tomorrow. I think that guy Jack Goloski, the one that sued us, should be on the list."

"Done."

"Phil, stop fucking around. I'm serious. Call me tomorrow and let me know who's on the list." Cohen hung up.

Five minutes later, the phone rang again. "Phil, it's all over the news about Paul. I had to call to see if you were all right. I guess you are."

"Alice, I'm fine. I appreciate your concern. I haven't watched the news. What are they saying?"

"They're making a big thing out of it, you know, 'the fourth Purity executive murdered in two weeks.' They're talking about the downsizing we did and implying an angry former employee is murdering the people that cost him his job. They're saying all the executives at Purity are in danger and that the company hired bodyguards, but they're not doing any good. Is Lorraine okay?"

"She's fine. I talked to her tonight. The news seems to have the story almost right."

"They claim they've been talking to employees. Phil, I tried to install my program into the security system and it bombed. Do you think I still need to do it?"

"Probably not, but I'd like the insurance."

"Okay, I'll keep working on it. Take care."

"Before you hang up, I got a tip that we're running low on Relieve inventories. Are you aware of a problem?"

"No. I'll check it out."

"Thanks. Bye."

Phil called Abby. "I assume you've heard about Stanley?"

"It's all over the TV. I tried to call you, but your line was busy."

"One of the calls was from Cohen. He told Gail Houseman in Legal that we'd cooperate with the police whether she agreed or not. Then he ordered me to provide a list of suspects to the police tomorrow and let him know who's on the list. Cohen is finally catching up to us."

"Great. I guess we won't be fired if he finds out we're already doing it."

"I wouldn't go that far. Cohen wants Jack Goloski on the list."

"He only wants Jack on the list because he sued us. If anyone asks, I'll pretend I'm working on the list. See you."

As soon as Phil hung up, the phone rang. It was Gary Hazlitt. "I assume you know about Stanley."

"I heard."

"I talked to Cohen tonight, and he wants to give the police a list of suspects. They obviously can't catch this guy without our help. Get on it now and be in my office at ten tomorrow so I can review it."

"Okay. Too bad we weren't smart enough to give the police the list in the beginning."

"If you were a good HR man, you would've fought harder to overrule Legal. But that's history."

"Sounds like a rewrite of history to me."

"Be careful you don't talk yourself out of a job," Gary said as he hung up.

Phil dialed what he hoped would be his last call of the night. He had to wait about ten minutes before Jim Hines made it to the phone. "Hello Phil. Sorry to keep you waiting."

"It's not like you're busy or anything. I just wanted to tell you that Cohen called me and ordered me to give you a list of suspects."

"Yeah, he called me too. I made sure he knew how much I appreciated his help. Phil, call me tomorrow and fill me in on Stanley. I've been ignoring him until now. I really fucked up."

"Okay. Did you have a tail on Goloski tonight?"

"No. I couldn't get a warrant, and I'm convinced he's our man. We found where the killer was hiding. He was about fifty yards from the house and, considering all three shots were exactly on target, we're dealing with an excellent marksman. Mob guys usually like it up close and personal. Jack Goloski is now my prime suspect, and I'm sure we'll have no problem now getting a twenty-four-seven tail. We'll get him."

"Make sure it's before he gets Lorraine and me."

By the time Phil finally got to bed, Rose was sound asleep.

Through sheer force of will, Echo woke up. It was a little after two o'clock on Friday morning. He listened to the rhythmic sounds of snoring emanating from the other side of the bed before getting dressed. He picked up the garbage bag containing the clothes he wore last evening and headed for his minivan.

Echo drove to the all-night convenience store in Westbury and tossed his clothes in the dumpster. He then drove up Post Road into Old Westbury and tossed the barrel of his Marksman's rifle into the duck pond. He envisioned it landing next to the Berretta .22 before driving away.

He had one more target before he would complete this assignment. He smiled. *I saved the best for last.*

Friday 12/12

Rose was still sleeping when Phil left for work; they would talk that night. Phil stopped in Lorraine's office. "When did you get in?"

"About an hour ago. I wanted to mingle with my people and understand how they dealt with Paul's murder. I'm glad I did. It's shaken them. They feel the staff is targeted because of the cruel way we fire people. They're pissed at having to work OT the next three weekends, and they're blaming you. They believe your people in Production Control screwed up, but you're really to blame because you're a lousy manager and don't follow up with your people. They said your head is on the block and you'll be fired next week. Cohen is talking, so he must be pretty confident."

"Yeah, I know."

"I've seen this before, and I'm worried. Your people will pay the price because you won't be able to protect them. You won't get any support from the other managers because you won't be here to repay it in the future."

"Hell, I'm already getting the cold shoulder. I've seen a difference in the number of emails and phone calls I get. It's as if I have a contagious disease. When someone talks to me, it's soft and slow. It's like they think I'm retarded or afraid I might break down and cry. I've seen this happen to others, but it's a lot different when you're the one experiencing it."

"Are you doing anything about it?"

"I'm meeting with Roger on Tuesday morning to give him my side. I'm hopeful. How'd your meeting with Pamela go?"

"Not good. She threatened to fire me, and I threatened to go to the media. I hope she cancels the meetings for now, but I don't think she will."

"Paul's murder got me thinking last night. Maybe downsizing isn't the motive. He wasn't a real advocate of the last downsizing. In fact, he let it be known that he was against it and that upper Management was wrong. He talked to his people as if he had no say in the decisions and positioned himself on the employees' side. The fact he's a white guy kind of eliminates diversity, too. What do you think?"

"It makes sense. But then what the hell is the motive?"

"I don't know, but I think it has something to do with Relieve. I overheard a heated discussion between Cohen and Stanley and heard two words: 'Relieve' and 'time.' Any ideas?"

"No, but is it a coincidence that the FDA is looking at Relieve?"

"I don't know, but it's worth looking into. Could you get some info out of the FDA?"

"I'll try."

"I'm going to do a little digging."

Gary Hazlitt walked into Lorraine's office and announced, "Pamela and I are leaving for Wilmington, and we won't be back until next Thursday. We'll be meeting with the Corporate Staff to reconsider the downsizing. That should make you happy, Lorraine."

"It does."

"You two have responsibility for plant operations. Cohen has prevailed on the FDA to delay the audit, so Lorraine, you're free next week. Phil, I want you to cover this weekend. Lorraine has been busy with the FDA and needs the weekend off. I'll let the supervisors in Production know you're in charge. I'll be in my Wilmington office if you need me. Any questions?" Neither Phil nor Lorraine responded. "Good. Make sure Thinadin gets produced."

After Hazlitt left, Phil said. "Wow, I'm in charge for the weekend before I get fired." Phil feigned excitement. "Lorraine, I need to leave Monday afternoon for my meeting with Roger and won't be back until Wednesday. Okay?"

"No problem, it's important. I'll call the head of the audit team and see if I can get some info."

"Great. Let me know if you come up with anything."

Phil spent the rest of the morning in his office. It was quiet, the phone did not ring once, and no one stopped in to talk or ask for advice. He felt lost, empty inside. The upside was that he entered a good chunk of data into the database. He was having lunch alone in his office with the door closed when Abby knocked once and walked in.

"You're still number one in the rumor mill, with Paul Stanley's murder running a distant second. It's almost as if people are used to the murders, and the thought of a director getting fired is more fun. The supervisors in Production are really putting you down."

"I didn't think I was that bad a guy."

"You're like someone with money who can never be sure if people like you for your money or if they like you as a friend. They only find out after their money is gone. When your power is gone, you find out who your friends are."

"So far, you and Lorraine are it."

"You might be surprised. Your friends are unsure what to say so they aren't saying anything, but you have some friends. You also have enemies, and they're having a lot of fun at your expense."

"You'll be happy to know that Cohen is waffling on the downsizing. I'm betting it doesn't happen this year."

"That's good, but what about you?"

"I'm going to see Roger on Tuesday and fight for my life."

"I hope you succeed." Abby got up. "I'm going to lunch."

Phil finished his lunch and began entering data again, choosing to hide behind his closed door to avoid the employees' gaze and slow, soft talk. He worked on entering Batch Records because, by damn, if he was going to be fired, he wanted a club he could use to extract some money from Purity. Finding intentional wrongdoing in the production process was his only hope, and his family's only hope, of some financial security. Joan, who had entered a ton of Batch Records, had been an enormous help. Phil went into the database and looked at the tables. Each contained a significant amount of data, and he hoped that there was enough to prove falsification. Phil realized that time was running out and decided that today's entries were the last. Tomorrow he would write the queries and reports to help him analyze the information and find anything he could use to protect himself and his family. While he had worked for McKenzie, not once did he hate his work, but he now felt powerless to influence his future. *Well, things change, and I'd better look out for number one,* he thought. The phone rang.

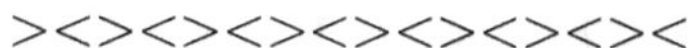

"Phil, do you have time to talk?" Lieutenant Hines said.

"Yeah, go ahead."

"We have tails on Goloski and DiRollo. We're also going to tail any known hitman DiRollo works with. We have a lot of cops on this case and support from the top to get more if we need them. We'll get one of them before he kills anyone else."

"I hate to tell you this, but I think you're wasting your time. Stanley's murder changes everything: he's white and male and a minor player in the downsizing. He aligned himself with the people who worked for him and against upper Management. He told people that he was the only one on Site Staff who fought against the downsizing. He was a closet racist, so neither DiRollo nor Goloski would blame him. They would be after Lorraine or me."

"What? If it's not downsizing or race, what's the motive? You're telling me we don't have a good suspect? That we're at ground zero? Are you jiving me?"

"No, I'm not jiving you. Listen to me. We've been focused on race or downsizing as the motive, and I'm telling you, Stanley doesn't fit. He wasn't a player in the downsizing. Somehow, Stanley could sound off against it and not draw any fire. As the best technical guy in the company, he was allowed to be an oddball. All that mattered was his technical knowledge and ability to solve Production problems. His employees knew he dealt with tough issues by telling them what they wanted to hear, so they looked to other directors to get the straight scoop. Stanley doesn't fit the pattern."

"Great, but I'm not calling off the tails. Do you have any idea what the motive is for four people being killed?"

"Maybe, but it's more like a WAG."

"What the fuck is a WAG?"

"Wild Ass Guess. I think it has something to do with our painkiller, Relieve." Phil told Hines about the incident between Cohen and Stanley. "That and the FDA audit, and now I'm hearing rumors we're stocking out of Relieve when I know we've been making it by the ton. I have no clue how to connect the dots."

"If you come up with anything, let me know. For now, I'm following the best suspects we have. Those are Joe DiRollo and Jack Goloski. What are you doing tomorrow?"

"Working. Call me here if you need me."

"See ya."

The incident between Cohen and Stanley, and Stanley's reaction to Phil's questions, kept replaying in his mind. Phil called Alice Chen to see if she had found anything on the Relieve inventory. Something was there, but what?

"Alice, any luck on the Relieve problem?"

"Lots of information, but no answers."

"Fill me in."

"At the rate inventory is dropping, we'll stock out in a week and a half. We have three weeks of in-process inventory in the form of tablets, but the tablets haven't been tested. Some batches have been sitting in the Hold Cage for weeks, and QC hasn't run test one."

"Why would that much product be sitting in the Hold Cage?"

"I don't know. For some reason, Joe Jacobs has a hold on it."

"Well, let's get Joe to lift the hold and get the product moving."

"Did you forget? He's been on vacation since Ms. Connolly was killed. He's in Wilmington with the family. He'll get home late tomorrow."

"Bring me all the documentation you have and whatever I need to sign to get it to QC for testing. We need to fill up the Distribution Center before we run out."

In a slow, soft voice, Alice asked, "Phil, is everything all right with you? Rumors are floating around that you're going to be fired."

"I think it's possible, but I'm in charge for now."

"If anything happens to you, I'd like you to know how much you've meant to me. You helped me when no one else would even listen. You're one of the few bosses who care about people."

"Alice, I'm not dying. I'll be around to talk to."

"I just wanted to say it."

"Thanks, I appreciate it. When will I see you?"

"In about an hour."

Phil leaned back in his chair and started thinking. *Another connection. Joe Jacobs, Connolly's good buddy, puts a hold on Relieve before testing. But why would Connolly or Jacobs want Relieve tablets piling up in the Hold Cage? What connection did Armstrong and Stanley have to Relieve? It doesn't make sense. I need more information. Abby's been here a long time. Maybe she knows something?"*

"Abby, I need you to test that aging memory of yours. Could you think of a reason we would hold Relieve tablets without testing them?"

The phone was silent for a moment. "No, but I seem to remember a long time ago there was a serious problem with Relieve tablets failing QC testing. It happened to four or five batches in a row, and then it just stopped. I don't remember the details, but George might. He was involved."

"Is he in today?"

"He's working on DR352."

"I think I'll walk over and see him."

Phil and George hadn't talked much lately. When he was a Research Manager, they had attended many of the same meetings. He and Phil had worked on several projects together. Phil had helped George with some personnel issues. Now George was working as a chemist, and he was always buried in the lab. Phil liked George, and he believed that George also liked him. He hoped that George's memory was working today. George's research lab looked like it was lifted straight out of a mad scientist's lab in a Sci-Fi movie. Equipment and instruments, with lights blinking and hoses, wires, and tubing running in all directions, lined three outside walls. George worked at a table in the center of the lab.

"George, do you have a minute? I need to pick your brain."

"I have the time, but my brain is picked over." George twisted two knobs and turned off three pieces of electronic equipment before turning to Phil. "Do you want to go to the cafeteria for a coffee?"

"No, this needs to be private. Can we talk here?"

"No one else is around. Fire away."

"Good. I heard you were involved in a problem with Relieve tablets failing to pass QC. Ring any bells?"

"Yeah, about seven years ago. Why do you ask?"

"I'm not sure. I have this nagging feeling about Relieve. We're running out of inventory at the Distribution Center. We have three weeks' supply sitting in the Hold Cage as untested tablets, and I have no idea why they're on hold. I asked Abby if she knew of any problems with Relieve. She suggested I talk to you."

"We had five batches of Relieve in a row that failed the QC tests. It was very unusual. I was a Research Manager at the time, and it was a Production problem, so I wasn't directly involved. Paul Stanley was given the task of solving the problem. I remember how much pressure he was under. Relieve was a big money maker then, and the big guys in Wilmington were afraid we would lose market share or, worse if word got out, we might lose our entire market. I volunteered to help Paul, to consult. As time went on, I became more and more involved. We couldn't find any reason for the problem. We rechecked raw material, double-checked the production procedures, and verified that all the production equipment was functioning correctly. Then one of the batches that failed passed a retest. I volunteered to work with Paul until we found out what the hell was happening, but he said we weren't going to do anything more with the bad batches. In fact, he told me the tablets were destroyed. I told him it was stupid, and we shouldn't stop until we understood why the batches failed. He told me not to worry, the problem was solved… but that's all he would say to me. I found his attitude very disturbing. I worked hard to help him solve the problem, and all he told me was it's solved, and he wouldn't tell me how."

"He never told you what the problem was. He just let you hang?"

"That's right, and I asked more than once. The only response was, 'we ship no product before its time.' You know, a take-off on that old wine commercial."

"And you have no idea what he meant?"

"No, and since we haven't had any more problems, I've ignored it. I have enough problems developing new drugs without worrying about the existing ones. I never helped Paul with a problem again."

"Was Cohen involved?"

"Oh yeah. Cohen was Product Manager for Relieve and the biggest source of the pressure on Stanley. He pushed hard for a solution and was the happiest guy in town when the batches started passing."

"Thanks for the info. I don't know what it means, but I'll figure it out. I don't want to stock out of Relieve." Phil said as he got up to leave.

"For what it's worth, I think you're getting a raw deal. Marketing is more responsible for the Thinadin problem than you are, but Cohen's always covered up Marketing's issues. You should know you've made friends here even though you're a short timer. My wife is one of them. She's really upset by what's happening to you."

"Thanks. I was starting to believe no one cared." Phil headed for his office.

He puttered around his office until Joan McMullen showed up with the last of the data. "Joan, this'll do it. I don't need you to do anymore. Thanks."

"Because you're going to be fired?"

She was as straightforward as a person could be, a typical New Yorker. "Because I might get fired. That screw-up on Thinadin was pretty serious."

"But it wasn't our fault."

"Some people think it was."

"I hope they don't fire you." She turned and left.

Phil headed home, one Nassau County cop in his car. Two cars followed: one his bodyguard's, the other a Nassau County Police car.

Dinner was great – no, magnifico – and Phil exuberantly devoured his first home-cooked meal in almost a week. Rose had prepared his favorite manicotti and meatballs, then served them with crusty Italian bread and a salad dressed with extra virgin olive oil and balsamic vinegar. They talked about Judy and her cancer. Judy was their age and still had two teenage children at home. She had endured the removal of both breasts before Rose traveled to Delaware to visit and help her get back on her feet. Dinner lasted two hours, and after thoroughly discussing Judy, Rose caught Phil up on their old friends in Delaware. When the dishes were washed and put away, the two sat down in the living room with glasses of Limoncello. Phil filled Rose in. He told her, in detail, about the murders and the investigation. He also told her how and why he had rebelled against a direct order from Hazlitt and joined Lieutenant Hines.

"It's risky, but you're doing the right thing, and if you get fired, we'll work it out. Ann's on her own, after all, and we only have to worry about Tony. I'm not worried. We'll find a way."

"I'm glad you feel that way because I'm in deep trouble for another reason. We're almost stocked out of Thinadin, and I'm being blamed even though it's not my fault. Cohen is going to Roger H. on Tuesday to get his approval to fire me."

"That bastard! He's been out to get you. Do you think Roger will see through Cohen's crap?"

"I'm not taking that chance. I'm meeting with Roger on Tuesday before he meets with Cohen. He'll get my story along with documentation to support it."

"Is he still in a position to help you?"

"Yeah. Roger is on Purity's Board, and he's the guy McKenzie's CEO expects to protect their investment in Purity. I'm also working on something that will protect us financially if I'm fired."

"I can't believe you'd even consider extorting Purity. It's not like you."

"Why not? Hell, I'm being treated like shit."

"Phil, what's wrong with you?"

"What are you talking about? I just told you what's wrong."

"No, it's deeper than that. I can't describe it. I feel you're holding back, not telling me everything. What is it?"

"Nothing! I'm under a lot of pressure at work, people are getting killed, and I may be next. We're running out of Thinadin, and I'm getting the blame and might be fired. I have to go to Wilmington to defend myself. And you ask me what's wrong? Every fucking thing is wrong!"

They sat in silence, sipping Limoncello until Rose got up. "I know when something is wrong, and I know you're not telling me everything. And it upsets me. We've been together for over twenty years, and I know you like a book. Something happened while I was gone, and you're not telling me."

"God damn it! You think you know everything. Stop busting my balls." Phil walked out of the living room, and as he did, he said, "I'm going to bed."

Saturday 12/13

Phil stopped in the Tablet Production Area before going to his office. He wanted to see how the current Thinadin batch was progressing. After all, he was in charge. As he walked into the area, he could see John Cary, the A-Shift Tableting Supervisor, sitting in his office. John sat at his desk reading. Phil assumed that he was reading a magazine or something personal. The Production Department was so overstaffed with supervision that the workload of a Shift Supervisor like John was minimal, providing ample reading time. Shift Supervisors had little to do other than answer an occasional question or sit in on a meeting. When Phil entered the office, Cary quickly folded his reading material and shoved it in the desk drawer. The speed with which he did so showed that it was a well-practiced move. When Cary turned and saw Phil, a smile washed over his face. Phil thought of it as a shit-eating grin.

"I just stopped by to see how things are going with this batch of Thinadin."

Cary stared at Phil awhile, the shit-eating grin still decorating his face. "It's going okay. No need for you to be here. I'm sure I can handle any problem without your help."

Cary usually treated Phil with respect, but the Thinadin shortage and the rumors of Phil's impending termination seemed to have changed him. "So, you're telling me this batch will pass QC testing?"

"I'm telling you things are going okay, and I'm telling you you're not needed here. If I have a problem, I'll call my boss. It's your fault we're working this weekend – yours and that group of numb-nuts in Production Control. So let me get back to work."

"There are fifty million reject tablets sitting in the QC reject cage," Phil growled, pointing his finger at John, "that you made, and you have the balls to tell me it's my fault we're stocking out. You're either stupid or spreading a line of bullshit to protect your ass."

"Those tablets are bad because you decided to get rid of Production operators, thinking you'd get a bigger bonus. Well, it didn't work. Now you're the one who's going to get fired."

"John, you need to get your facts straight before opening your mouth. I haven't been fired. Be careful how you deal with me." Phil opened the door and started to walk out, then did a Columbo. "FYI, I did want to fire most of the Production supervision, including you, instead of the operators. One last thought, Mr. Cary: I hope that every time you signed your name in a Batch Record, you actually observed the operation or did what you signed for." John Cary's face turned bright red. Phil's mouth changed into his own shit-eating grin, and he added, "You'd better pray tonight, John Cary. Pray that I get fired. It may save your job."

Phil kept the grin all the way to his office. The employees he passed along the way said nothing; they just looked at him kind of funny. Phil checked for phone messages and e-mails. He had neither. He then booted up his computer and prepared to analyze the Batch Record data.

Phil started writing queries and designing the reports he needed to determine if the information in the Batch Record matched the availability of people and equipment. Because of his run-in with John Cary this morning, he designed a query to extract supervisors' records. Phil wanted to see if they had signed off on a step indicating that they observed a test or procedure while in a meeting or off-site. Phil reviewed and refined the queries and reports until he was satisfied that the Reports were accurate and detailed enough to analyze the Production operation.

The falsification and shortcutting in Production was far worse, or better, depending on one's perspective, than he thought possible. It was evident from the data that Production was shortening the specified times for blending granulation. On October 10th in the afternoon, for example, the 40-foot V-blender had been used by different products simultaneously. Furthermore, that was not the only time that it had been used simultaneously by different batches of drugs. The same was true for almost every other piece of equipment in Production.

The same pattern held when comparing the dates and times that employees signed the Batch Records with their work schedules. Employees had signed Batch Records when they were on vacation, out sick, or working different shifts. Supervision had allowed employees to perform critical procedures that they were not trained to carry out. The same pattern held when Phil looked at the supervisors. Supervisors observed critical operations when, physically, they were attending meetings or on vacation. According to several Batch Records, John Cary was dutifully performing his supervisory oversight functions while off-site. In fact, he seemed to be in two places at one time more than not. Good-bye, John.

No wonder the failure rate is so high, Phil thought. I got them by the balls. Maybe I'll keep my job, or I'll collect a lot of money. I'll take a few people out with me if I get fired, including Mr. John Cary. Son-of-a-bitch. I feel good. I'm in control.

Although Phil felt good about the results, he also felt a speck of guilt eating away at him. It was hard to understand, but he did not like gathering damaging information on a company that had always been good to him. McKenzie owned half of Purity and would pay half of his ill-gotten gain. *Maybe I can use this info to get back into McKenzie,* he thought. Despite all the conflicting emotions, overall, Phil was relieved. No matter how the future evolved, he had something pretty impressive to take to the bargaining table.

All I have to do now is present this to Roger on Tuesday after showing him the documentation on the Thinadin mess.

Phil looked at his watch for the first time since getting to his office and was surprised that it was three o'clock. He had worked through lunch and realized that he was hungry. Eating could wait; he wanted to look at the Relieve data. Maybe something would give him a clue as to the motive for the killings. As Phil was about to start, his phone rang.

"Phil, Hazlitt. I just talked to John Cary, and he told me you threatened to fire him. What's going on?"

The information Phil now had unearthed gave him a feeling of power. "He wouldn't give me a straight answer."

"Phil, we don't need you causing disruption in Production. They have a lot to do. I think you should apologize to John."

"Gary, you only know half of the conversation, and you've already decided I'm the bad guy. I'm not going to waste my time giving you my side. I'm also sure not going to apologize to a first-line supervisor who won't answer my questions. Now, I have work to do." Phil hung up.

Shit, it felt good hanging up on that prick.

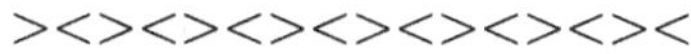

The phone rang again. Phil picked up. "What!"

"Christ, you don't have to bite my head off," Jim Hines said.

"Sorry, what's up?"

"We've gone back to all the suspects and asked them to account for their whereabouts Thursday night, but it hasn't helped much. DiRollo has an airtight alibi, but he wouldn't have been the triggerman anyway. Goloski says he was home with his partner. No one else saw him, so it's weak. He could lie, and his partner would swear to it. Higgins was the only other one without a strong alibi. He was alone. His wife spent Thursday in the city and didn't get home until ten o'clock. If you still think DiRollo and Goloski don't have a motive, do you think Higgins is possible?"

"Other than his being downsized, I don't see any motive for Higgins. We need to find the motive before coming up with any more suspects. Sorry for misleading you."

"We're doing the best we can. Without your input, we wouldn't have made any progress anyway. I'll stay in touch."

"If I have a divine revelation, I'll call immediately."

Phil got back to work looking at detailed information on Relieve batches. The data appeared normal until Phil sorted it by date. He noticed that the time between the completion of tablets and the start of QC testing varied from three to four weeks, an inordinately long time. Six days was the longest any other product sat between the completion of the tablets and the start of QC testing. The average was three days. A world-class Production operation would move tablets into packaging in two hours, not three days, so even three days was long.

Phil scowled and started thinking. *A typical average of three days for our other products versus an average of more than three weeks for Relieve. Why? "We sell no wine before its time." What does that mean? It sure as hell smells, but I can't think of a reason to let tablets sit in a holding cage waiting for testing. Maybe Lorraine knows.*

"Lorraine, it's Phil. Do you have time to talk?" Phil said after Lorraine answered.

"Sure, what's up?"

"I've been looking at some data and discovered something curious with Relieve production. It takes an average of three and a half weeks from the time Relieve tablets are compressed until you test them. Do you know why?"

"No, but a while back, I noticed the same thing. When I checked, I learned Production Control managed the schedule and gave other products priority. I thought nothing of it at the time."

"We have five batches of Relieve waiting for testing, and the inventory of Relieve at the distribution center is running low. Can you get some people in tomorrow to test Relieve?"

"I'll either get someone in or do it myself. I'll be in at about eleven tomorrow morning."

"Great. I'll talk to Jacobs before that to find out why he put them on hold in the first place. See you tomorrow."

Phil, feeling good and feeling powerful, wrapped up work for the day and looking forward to a relaxing evening at home and a good meal.

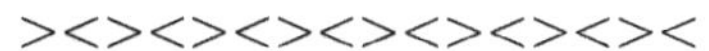

Damn, it's getting cold, Echo thought as he stood at a payphone outside a convenience store in Bayville, Long Island. It was low tide, and the wind off Long Island Sound carried the cold and the smell of decaying seaweed. *Almost done.*

"I thought you'd be at the office," Echo said as soon as the phone was answered.

"And I hoped you'd call."

"Are you hearing anything about the investigation?"

"Not much. Only that the police thought the motive was linked to our diversity efforts, but now that Stanley was a victim, they're confused."

"Typical of a black cop to blame everything that happens on race. Well, that's good. we'll be done by the time they regroup, and they'll never find the real motive. It'll be buried with the conspirators that wanted to ruin me."

"Are you ready for the last one?"

"I have the access card and the code. I assume the security system will be modified, so I should have no problem getting in."

"What about the bodyguard?"

"I have that worked out. I'll get the bodyguard to relax, and then BAM, he'll never know what hit him."

"I hope you'll set up an alibi this time."

The constant questioning would usually aggravate Echo, but he felt good today. He guessed it was because this project was almost over, and he had not heard from the cops again. "There's a large auction on a farm in Compton, Maryland, every Tuesday. The preview is Monday. Monday is crazy:

people coming and going, dealers dropping off items. It's pure chaos. I'll register at about two on Monday, shop around for a while to establish my presence, then leave. I should be ready to take out the last of our enemies by four-thirty. I'll need a heads up on his activities, so get the payphone number at the Sunoco across the street and call sometime after four-thirty."

"I'll get it. Look, be careful. When we finish, no one will be able to figure out the motive, and without a motive, no one will be able to track this to us."

"Then we can run the operation."

"I'll talk to you after it's done. Goodbye."

Sunday 12/14

Phil waited patiently for Joe Jacobs. Last night, Phil had called Joe and asked him why he put a hold on the Relieve tablets. Joe had danced and dodged every attempt he made to pin him down. Finally, his energy waning, Phil had told Joe to be in his office at nine this morning, prepared to discuss Relieve. Phil got in at eight to review the information Alice Chen had given him on Friday. It was nine-ten before Joe Jacobs arrived. Phil was well prepared for the conversation.

"Good morning, Phil."

"Good morning, Joe. I know you and Kathleen were close, so please accept my sympathy."

"Thanks. I've known Kathleen a long time and can't believe she's dead."

"I know what you mean." Phil and Joe sat silently for a few moments before Phil said, "Joe, last night I didn't fully communicate the severity of our problem with Relieve." Phil pulled a report and handed it to Joe. Despite knowing that Joe already understood the problem, Phil gave Joe several minutes to review the information before resuming. "We need to start testing the Relieve tablets, so I need you to remove the hold or tell me why you can't."

Joe Jacobs was a little man with the backbone of a jellyfish. A man who never came to a decision on his own, a man who had followed his bosses' orders his entire career, stared dumbfounded at Phil. "I don't know why I put a hold on the Relieve tablets."

"Well, you should have no problem releasing them to QC."

Joe stared at Phil again. His eyes were darting, his face reddening. Joe looked like someone about to have a heart attack. "I can't."

"You can't. Why not?"

"I can't tell you."

Phil leaned forward, placing his elbows on his desk, and tented his hands. He stared directly into Joe's eyes. "You don't know why you put a hold on five batches of Relieve tablets, you won't take the hold off, and you can't or won't tell me why. Is that correct?"

"That's correct."

"Joe, I'm going to give you a choice, and I'm going to give you ten minutes to make a decision. You will tell me everything you know about Relieve and why the hold is on the tablets. If you refuse to tell me, I will fire you on the spot."

"You can't fire me. I've worked here twenty years and have never been in trouble. What about due process?"

"I knew you were sleeping during Management 101. An employee can be terminated for insubordination. Also, if you refuse to tell me what I asked, you're insubordinate, and I will fire you. Now get out of here and make your decision." Phil got up, walked around the desk, and opened the door. Joe didn't move until Phil shouted, "Get out!"

Ten minutes later, Joe was back. His head was down, and he gazed at the floor as he walked robotically to his chair. Still looking down, he said, "I'm between a rock and a hard place. I know you can fire me for not telling you why I put a hold on those tablets. The person who told me to put a hold on the Relieve Batches never told me why. I was also told not to tell anyone what little I know, or I'd be fired."

Phil interrupted. "Was that person Kathleen?"

Joe nodded.

"She's dead. You need to make this decision on your own."

Joe had tried to call Bob Cohen during the ten minutes Phil had allotted him, but could not reach him. "She told me the orders came straight from Cohen, and if I couldn't get a hold of her, I could talk directly to him. I saw him at Kathleen's funeral and told him we were running low on Relieve. He told me to wait until he said it was okay before releasing any of the batches to QC."

Phil now had a link to Kathleen and the Relieve batches. He knew Joe was worried about losing his job and figured he'd that he would put it to rest. "Thanks for telling me, and rest assured I won't tell Cohen you said anything. I don't expect you to sign PC3543 to remove the hold. Why don't you go home and forget you were here this morning?"

"Thanks."

As Joe was getting up, Phil asked, "I'm curious. how long has Kathleen been asking you to put a hold on Relieve tablets?"

Joe thought for a moment and then replied, "Six or seven years."

"Thanks."

It was beginning to make sense to Phil: Relieve batches failed and sat in the Hold area, then suddenly started passing. Seven years ago, Kathleen, through Joe Jacobs, started delaying the testing of Relieve batches. *We sell no wine before its time*, Phil thought to himself. *Bob Cohen was the Product Manager seven years ago, and he's involved today. I can't articulate a scenario that gets me from the Relieve problems to murder, but I think this is the motive. I feel it. I need to get those batches tested, and I need to see the results. But we must do it in secret.*

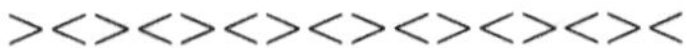

Lorraine unlocked the Hold Cage with her master key. She had arrived in Phil's office about half an hour earlier with a chemist in tow. Phil had told Lorraine and the chemist that the hold on the Relieve tablets would not be lifted. He thanked the chemist, said he could go home, and asked Lorraine to stay. He then told Lorraine everything he knew about Relieve and his conclusions. Lorraine had agreed that they needed to covertly test the Relieve tablets. Lorraine went to the Hold Cage to take tablets from each batch for testing while Phil waited in the QC lab.

"I have forty tablets from each Batch. It should take a couple of hours to complete the testing. I'll print out the results and then delete all records from the computer when I'm done. You can be my go-fer."

"Sure, pick on the dumb kid."

Time passed slowly. The test equipment did most of the work. Lorraine had to make sure that the instruments were calibrated and operating correctly. Phil's job was to make sure that the tablets from the batch record in the computer's memory were the ones being tested. Lorraine printed the results and deleted all the testing from the computer's memory when the tests were complete.

"Every batch failed," Lorraine said, still looking at the printouts.

"Great. Let's go to lunch. We can take a closer look at the results and see if we can figure out our next step."

"It's always about food with you."

"It sure is. Let's go to that little diner on Stewart Avenue."

Phil and Lorraine sat in a booth and studied the test results while waiting for their food. Their bodyguards sat at the counter, eyes roaming over the diner.

"All I see is bad test results, which means we have to make more Relieve in a hurry. Shit. The two products we have primary responsibility for are in deep trouble."

"Stop whining and shut up. I may have found something. Give me your printouts." Lorraine took the printouts from Phil and considered them closely. Phil sat silently. "Phil, look at this." Lorraine jotted some notes on a napkin. "The oldest batch is only slightly out of spec. The next oldest batch is out of spec by a little more, and the newest batch is out the farthest. It's a linear progression based on the date they were compressed."

Phil examined the napkin. "You're right. Okay, genius. What do you make of it?"

"Let me think a minute."

Lunch arrived. Phil looked lovingly at his half-pound cheeseburger and French fries. At the same time, Lorraine ignored her turkey burger and coleslaw and concentrated on the test results. By the time she looked up, Phil had worked his way through half of the cheeseburger and most of his French fries.

"I have a theory."

"Shoot."

"What if seven years ago, when the five batches failed, Stanley found out that over time the results changed, and eventually, after three weeks or so, the tablets would pass the tests?"

"So they just wait three weeks and release the tablets to QC. I don't buy it. What if it took four weeks before the tablets were in specification? We ship no wine before its time."

"Think about it. All that would have to be done is test the tablets until they pass. It would have to be done unofficially, off the record, probably after-hours. Then when they were sure the batch would pass, they would release the tablets to QC."

"If you're right, all we have to figure out is who 'they' are."

"We know Connolly was behind holding the tablets. And we know Cohen was behind Connolly. We don't know if Armstrong, Gagnon, or Stanley were involved. Even if they were involved, why were they killed?"

"I think Gagnon was in the wrong place at the wrong time, but as for Armstrong and Stanley, I'd bet my paycheck they were involved. Armstrong would do anything Cohen asked. Remember the argument I overheard between Stanley and Cohen?"

"Cohen is the key. We need to talk to him, but we don't have any proof that what we think happened actually did happen. We also can't figure out how the murders are connected to the Relieve tablets. Maybe the FDA's audit on Relieve has triggered the killings. I have to get them to be straight with me and tell me why they're auditing Relieve, and I have to talk to some of the long-timers in my department. I can't believe this has been going on for seven years, and no one in QC is aware of it."

"I'll tell Hines our suspicions and see if he has any ideas. Even if the killings and Relieve are related, we can't identify any suspects for Hines. We need to get moving."

"Let's touch base tomorrow morning and see where we stand."

"Okay."

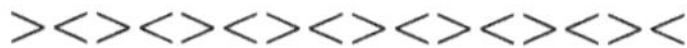

Echo, the killing machine, was packed and ready to go. His suitcase contained enough clothing for two nights, along with his Glock and his ice pick and arm strap. He had one last job to do: one more human to kill, one last obstacle to remove. Then and only then would the conspiracy against him finally be thwarted. He would not go to jail for their wrongdoing. They had met their match. As usual, he was more intelligent and better trained than his adversaries. As usual, he would get away with murder.

Echo told his wife that he was going to Maryland to buy some antiques. She was upset but said nothing. She was worried about finances and was concerned about their future. He had run through two hundred thousand dollars and was now dipping into their savings. He had to admit that the antiques business had gotten the best of him. Echo had bought and sold antiques on a small scale for a few years. He found that most people in the business were free spirits lacking formal education and business knowledge. He assumed that his superior business knowledge, money, and excellent work ethic would give him an edge. He could quickly rise to the top of the business. Unfortunately, the venture did not quite go as planned.

Echo had decided that he would deal exclusively with high-end antique paintings. For years, when he visited antique shops, he would get into lengthy discussions with the owners about antique paintings and period furniture. Echo had not been ready to buy, but he was learning. Then last February, armed with Purity's money, he started buying paintings which he planned to resell at a profit. For the next three months, he built his inventory. He had books that listed the latest prices an artist's works brought at auction. The books also had pictures of the artist's signature and descriptions of his work. Once Echo had a reasonable inventory of paintings, he rented space in a group shop and posted them on the internet. He sat back and waited for the money to roll in.

Despite waiting and waiting, he had very few sales. He was barely covering the rent at the group shop. He took about half of his inventory to a fine arts auction house in Mystic, Connecticut. He hoped to get his money back and maybe make a little profit. With a clean slate, he would do a better job of buying inventory in the future. Echo watched intently as the auction house owner looked closely at his paintings. Echo had placed a sticker on each antique painting with the minimum amount that he would accept for the artwork.

Echo's insides seized when the auctioneer informed him that none of his paintings would sell for his minimum prices. In fact, they would not even bring close to what he wanted. Worse yet, he learned that several of his paintings were forgeries and would not be auctioned at all. Over the next two months, Echo auctioned off all the paintings the auction house would take, and he let the market determine the price. He sold the forgeries openly as forgeries for pennies on the dollar. After every painting was sold, he had less than twenty thousand dollars left in the business. Next, Echo bought furniture and accessories for resale. He called himself an antiques dealer, but he dealt in used furniture and accessories. He could not say that he bought antique furniture because antique furniture was, by definition, well over a hundred years old, and the furniture that Echo bought was made in the early Twentieth century.

Sales came faster, but he had to negotiate the price on every piece he sold. After discounts, he made very little money. After less than one year in the antiques business, Echo was working hard and had to dip into his savings to pay his personal expenses. He needed to get back to what he knew. He had to get a job in the pharmaceutical industry to secure a future. Yet Cohen and his gang were ready to lay all of the blame for Relieve on him. He could go to jail, and even if he did not, he would never work in the pharmaceutical industry again.

Fortunately, he still had friends: friends who warned him, friends who helped him solve the problem. He also had friends who would give him a good job when the killing was over… and the killing would be finished tomorrow.

Monday 12/15

Last night, Phil had given Jim Hines a detailed account of Relieve issues and the covert operation that he and Lorraine suspected. Hines was intrigued but could not see a tie to the murders. They set up a meeting for ten in the morning with Lorraine to determine if she had learned anything new from interviewing her people. Phil had also completed work on the presentation for Roger Hanson. He was ready for their Tuesday meeting.

Mary Margaret informed him that Melissa Vega wanted to see him. When he entered his office, she was sitting in a chair with her back to the door.

"Hi, Melissa. How are you doing this morning?"

When she turned, he could see she that was crying. "Not too good. I have to tell you something. It's very private, so please close the door."

"Okay. Is everything all right with your baby?"

"Yeah. This is about the murders."

"The murders?"

"I have to tell you some things… things I'm ashamed of and things I don't want anyone to know. I really don't want to, but I have to tell you because I might know who the murderer is. I want you to protect me as best you can, but if you can't, it's okay. The most important thing is to stop the killing. It'll end my marriage if Hector finds out, but I can't live with this any longer. Promise to keep me out of this if you can."

"I promise. I'll know better what I can do after you tell me."

"About a year after Hector and I married, I thought I made a big mistake. Things were tight financially, and we fought all the time. Once, he even shoved me. I was immature and later realized I'd pushed him too hard and insulted his manhood because I whined and complained about all the luxuries I wanted. I wanted everything, and I wanted it now. We worked it out. But before I grew up and realized Hector was the right man for me, I had an affair. For years Jack Higgins had been hitting on me, and when I was vulnerable, I agreed to go out with him. That's the part Hector can't know. He's a Latino, he's hot-headed, and he's proud. If he finds out, he'll leave me."

"If you think Higgins is the killer, you're wrong. The police have already checked him out and ruled him out. He has alibis for the nights of the first two murders. He didn't do it."

"That makes me feel better. I thought for sure Jack was the killer, and I thought because I didn't come forward sooner, some of the murders were my fault."

"You have nothing to worry about. But tell me, why did you think it might be Higgins?"

"Because of what he did in the military."

Abby had heard some rumors about Higgins, and now Melissa could validate them. "He was a clerk in the army."

"He told me he was an assassin."

"An assassin. Did you mention that to anyone? Maybe Abby?"

"No, he told me he'd kill me if I ever told anyone, and I believed him."

"Are you sure he was an assassin? What did he tell you?"

"He told me how the military selected him to train as an assassin because of some psychological tests he took. He also explained in gory detail all the different ways to kill people. He told me about the people he killed, all traitors, and how it felt after killing them. He likes killing. He gets high from it. I believed him and started looking for a way out. Right before it ended, which was his idea by the way, he said I wasn't as responsive as I used to be. He showed me the tools of his trade. I know a little about guns, and these were top-of-the-line expensive weapons. One was a marksman rifle with three screw-in barrels and a laser sight he added on his own. But the biggest thing that convinced me he would kill me was when I realized what a cold-hearted bastard he was. I actually believed he could kill anyone without batting an eye. He enjoys it. He enjoys the feeling it gives him, and he enjoys the power."

"And you're absolutely sure you told no one."

"Absolutely."

"I think I should get the police to take another look at him, and I don't think I'll have to get you involved at all. Melissa, I know it was hard for you to tell me. I appreciate your trust, and I won't betray it."

"I know you won't unless you have to. I just hope Jack's not the killer."

"I'll get the ball rolling." Melissa left, and Phil called Lieutenant Hines. "Jim, it's Phil. I just got some information that might be significant. I need you to check it out."

"So important it can't wait an hour?"

"That's right," Phil told him Melissa's story and reminded him of Abby's suspicions. "What do you think?"

"I think I'll re-check Jack Higgins' military record, and I'm going to put his alibis under a microscope. I'm also going to get a warrant to search his house."

"If the military lied to you the first time, why will it be different now?"

"As luck would have it, I just finished a call with the Governor five minutes before you called. He told me I was in charge of the highest priority case in the state and that if I needed anything, I should give him a call. I'll take him up on it and see if he can pressure the Army."

"Highest priority case in the state. If you solve it you'll be a hero, and if you don't, you'll need a job. Talk about pressure. Do you still plan to be here at ten?"

"I'll be there right after I call the Governor and have Parisi recheck Higgins's alibis. She'll hopefully get a search warrant, too. She has lots of manpower to throw at it."

"See you in an hour."

Jim was ten minutes late. Phil and Lorraine were sitting at Phil's conference table waiting for him.

"Phil, Ms. Waters, sorry, it took a little longer than I thought to get everything rolling."

Lorraine replied, "Good morning, Lieutenant Hines."

Phil rolled his eyes. "Christ, I'd swear you two never met. Jim, this is Lorraine, and Lorraine, this is Jim. Now cut the crap."

Lorraine smiled. "And Jim, this is Phil, the asshole."

"Okay," Phil said. "Jim, where do we stand?"

"If it comes back that Higgins was a clerk, then he was a clerk. The Governor said he would personally talk to the head of the Joint Chiefs of Staff, and he said he'd get Randy Jasiak involved if he met resistance. Randy's on the House Armed Services Committee and carries a big stick. Parisi has ten detectives re-checking Higgins's movements on the nights of the first three murders. She's also pushing the DA to get a search warrant. Everything is rolling. Lorraine, how did you make out this morning?"

"The culture in this company is unbelievable. It's so different from McKenzie that it's hard to believe we were part of the same company. I met with six of my people who I felt would be the most open. They've all been here a long time. I asked them if they knew why Relieve tablets were held for a couple of weeks before they were tested. They all said no. I asked again, but instead of asking if they knew, I also asked if they'd heard any rumors. This time they shook their heads. I wasn't convinced, so I told them I believed whatever was happening on Relieve was tied to the murders. If they didn't say anything, any subsequent murders were on them. There was a lot of silence and a lot of looking at one another. Finally, Amy Johnson said she wouldn't keep quiet anymore, and that I had to be trusted. She started to tell me what she knew. The others tried to stop her. They said if they said anything, they'd lose their jobs."

"Sounds like people know what's going on but are scared to talk. Did she open up?" Hines asked.

"She did, and eventually, so did the others. We had it pretty much right. When batches of Relieve started failing a few years back, Cohen set up a covert testing operation which found that the test results changed and moved closer to being in spec over time. He stopped all investigation on the bad batches. When new batches of Relieve were produced, he didn't release the tablets to QC until he knew they would pass the tests. He knew they'd pass because," she looked straight into Jim's eyes, "Jack Higgins would covertly test the tablets until they passed."

Jim's face lit up. "Jack Higgins. Do you know what an employee told Phil this morning about Higgins?"

Phil filled in Lorraine. Lorraine continued, "From then on, every batch of Relieve was covertly tested until it passed, then released to QC. Higgins stopped doing the testing when he left the company, and my people believe Paul Stanley took his place."

"That ties Connolly, Stanley, and Higgins together. What about Armstrong and Gagnon?"

Phil answered. "I think we must assume Gagnon was in the building because he was a brownnoser and was in the wrong place at the wrong time. I think Diane's role was to manipulate inventory numbers. Relieve batches were scheduled for production early to cover the time needed until they passed the covert testing. That was her tie to Relieve."

"I have enough to push the investigation, but I still don't know why they were murdered."

Lorraine responded to Jim. "I don't know either, but what they were doing is illegal, and the FDA being here might've set things off."

"Exactly why is it illegal? The tablets passed the tests." Lieutenant Hines asked.

"It's not that simple. Prior Relieve tablets passed the tests the first time, so something changed. We should've notified the FDA, and I'm sure the FDA would've required us to do a detailed analysis. They might even have asked for new clinical trials. We'd stop selling Relieve while investigating, and if a sound scientific reason wasn't found, we'd have to pull the drug off the market. The FDA requires the production process to be exactly the same as the clinical trials. I'm concerned the tablets continue to change and go out of spec the other way before our customers take them."

Phil added, "Sales of Relieve are seven hundred and fifty million dollars. Quite a loss."

"The FDA must have tight controls on you folks."

"A pharmaceutical tablet is a mixture of chemicals you ingest that causes some alteration in body function, in body chemistry. Personally, I'm glad the FDA has tight standards. What Cohen and his cohorts were doing could have killed people," Lorraine responded.

"Lorraine, if the way Relieve is being handled is illegal, how come your people didn't stop it?"

"Fear. They believed that all Management was involved, and if they said anything, they'd be fired. There was no way for anyone to prove it, and after a while, the whole thing became normal. We ship no wine before its time."

Phil asked Jim, "Any ideas on how to proceed?"

"First, I'm going to get all this information to Parisi, then I'll call Cohen and have a little talk with him. I'll get back to you later. Phil, what time are you leaving for Wilmington?"

"Around two-thirty."

"Phil, Lorraine, thanks and goodbye. I have a lot to do."

"So long, JIM," Lorraine said with a slight laugh.

After Jim Hines left, Lorraine said to Phil, "Can you believe the mentality in this company? I have to start training my people on basic ethics."

"If Cohen had tried to pull that shit in McKenzie, the employees would have been lined up at the FDA office to turn him in. Speaking of the FDA, have you talked to your contact yet?"

"No, she's out until eleven-thirty. I'll let you know as soon as I talk to her."

Jim called Phil a little before two. "Cohen's a son-of-a-bitch. He wouldn't give me a straight answer. I told him we needed his help to catch the killer, and all he did was evade my questions. Finally, I told him I wanted to talk to him face to face, and he gave me twenty minutes of his time provided I show up at six tonight."

"Get packed. We'll drive down together. We can get to Cohen's office before six."

"Cohen has a conference call with the execs from McKenzie and Saga. He claims it'll be over at exactly six, and he has to leave on a business trip before six-thirty. Thanks for the ride. It'll make my life easier. I've only passed through Delaware on I-95. What's the latest we can leave?"

"The fastest I've ever gotten there is two hours and forty minutes. It usually takes closer to three hours, so we'd better leave no later than three o'clock."

"It'll be tight, but I'll make it."

"Park your car in the executive parking area. I'll be waiting for you five minutes before three." Phil almost added 'there are plenty of parking places,' but he thought better of it. "What about my bodyguard?"

"Don't worry, I'll take care of him. I have a lot to do and no time to do it. Now I have to go. I'll see you at three."

"Ten of," Phil said to the dial tone.

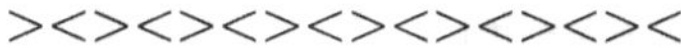

Jack started the engine, and while it heated up, he thought through his plan. *I have the right pistol for the job — a Glock-nine — and I have the ice pick and arm strap so I can take care of the bodyguard. I've checked and double-checked both. I have the access card, and the code is 211. I have enough clothes so I can dispose of these, and I have reservations at a hotel a hundred miles away.* He put the minivan in gear and drove away. *One more conspirator to kill, and I'm done. How disappointing. And I'm off the hook. Their little plan won't be executed because they were.* Jack laughed out loud at his little joke. *Hopefully, I'll have a chance to talk to the prick before killing him. I want him to know why he's dying so he can tell the others when they meet in hell.* Jack guided his minivan onto the westbound lanes of the Northern State Parkway.

"I had to push hard on my FDA contact to find out why they're looking at Relieve. I told her I suspected it might have to do with the killings, but I didn't give her much information. I certainly didn't want to give her information on Relieve she didn't already have. She finally gave in." Lorraine had been sitting on the edge of her chair since walking into Phil's office. Now she sat back. "A while ago, the FDA received an anonymous letter alleging that between eight and ten years ago, Relieve tablets were packaged improperly. Bottles that were labeled wrong and contained tablets of different strengths were knowingly sold. They don't normally check out anonymous tips, especially on a product that was shipped that long ago. Still, the information in this letter was so detailed and described the packaging operation so well they decided to check it out."

"An anonymous tip that had them looking at old Relieve batch records, but not at the time the real problem occurred. The tipster wanted to trigger an audit but didn't want the FDA to discover the problem. That's pretty sneaky."

"I came to the same conclusion. Somebody wanted the people involved killed but didn't want Purity hurt. It worked. The FDA didn't find anything wrong, so they're done. They'll give us their final report in two weeks."

"Good job. I'll fill Hines in on our way to Delaware." Phil looked at his watch. "Christ, I gotta go."

Lieutenant Hines pulled into the executive parking area at ten after three. Phil and his bodyguard were leaning against the trunk of Phil's car. They were cold, but not as cold as they would have been if they were exposed to the wind. Hines got out of his car and walked straight to the bodyguard. "I'm in charge of Mr. Messina as of now. Your day is done. Go home and don't tell anyone Mr. Messina is with me. If you do, I'll have you arrested for obstruction of justice, and obstructing justice, in this case, will land you in jail. Understand?"

The bodyguard faced a choice: not alert HQ and lose his job, call HQ and go to jail. "I understand."

"You'd better." Hines turned to Phil. "Whose car?"

"Mine."

Hines retrieved his suitcase from his trunk and tossed it into Phil's. He turned to the bodyguard and said, "I meant every word. Keep your mouth shut, or I'll make your life miserable." Then he turned and said, "Let's go!"

Phil exited the parking area and turned right onto the entrance ramp for the Meadowbrook Parkway South. He made his way to the left lane and accelerated the BMW to eighty miles per hour. Neither said a word. Phil exited the Meadowbrook for the Southern State Parkway West, maneuvered into the left lane, and again accelerated to eighty. As expected, traffic was heavy, and Phil changed lanes to get around a couple of left-lane bandits and then accelerated to close in on the next car. The BMW responded flawlessly to Phil's touch. The lane changes, acceleration, and deceleration were smooth and effortless. Jim appeared relaxed and confident. He was not being tossed around as Phil maneuvered through traffic, but he was tense. He was not used to traveling at eighty to ninety miles an hour on the Southern State while changing lanes. "Should I expect the same all the way to Delaware?"

"No. I'll make better time when we get on the Jersey Turnpike."

"Better time? I was hoping you'd slow down."

"You're the one who was late. If I slow down, we'll miss Cohen. Is that what you want?"

"No."

"Okay then." Phil moved two lanes to the right and accelerated past several cars before moving back to the left lane.

Jim exhaled loudly and said, "Can we talk?"

"Sure, but you'll have to be patient. I might not respond if I need to concentrate on what I'm doing."

"That's okay with me because, above all else, I want to get there."

Stuck behind traffic moving at sixty, Phil saw an opening two lanes to the right. He downshifted to fourth and moved into the space; in the right lane, he squeezed the throttle and accelerated to eighty-five. Once past the pack of cars, the road was open, and Phil pushed the BMW to ninety as he moved to the left lane. "We should be at the Verrazano in a few minutes. We're making good time."

Jim's heart was pounding. *Ninety miles an hour on the Belt Parkway! Who does Messina think he is, Mario Andretti?* "I heard from the Governor." Phil slowed to eighty, signaling that he wanted to listen. "Jack Higgins was a well-trained assassin in the military. His records were under deep cover. The Federal Government doesn't want the public to know it was in the murder business. Higgins assassinated a total of nine targets. He killed several Russian military officers to protect

Gorbachev, and it was approved by President Reagan. I'd love to hear the details of those assignments.

They were moving at fifty miles an hour in heavy traffic on the Verrazano Narrows Bridge heading to Staten Island. "Jack Higgins assassinates nine people – nine human beings – then gets a job in pharmaceuticals and becomes Joe Exec living in suburbia and raising a family. And no one knew."

"It gets worse. The psychiatrists who talked to him before he was discharged were concerned he would go right on killing. He enjoyed killing and may have even gotten sexual relief from it. The feds were so concerned they watched him for years before they convinced themselves he was okay. When the surveillance stopped, they buried his file so deep the Governor had to prevail on the Secretary of Defense to okay digging it up."

"Have you picked him up or searched his house?"

"The DA turned us down the first time we tried. Wouldn't even go to a judge. He said we didn't have enough for a search warrant. I sent Parisi back to see him with the info from the Governor. We should have enough to get in front of a judge. We'll get the warrant. Parisi is going to call as soon as the judge decides."

"Fucking Higgins, a killer. I always thought of him as a wimp. Goes to show what a good judge of character I am."

Lieutenant Hines's phone sounded off. It was Parisi. "I got the search warrant for Higgins' house, and the DA gave us the okay to take him in for questioning. We're on our way."

"Be careful going in. Higgins is a dangerous prick. Once you get him secured, find those weapons. And Parisi, you're one of the best interrogators I've ever seen, so have at him. We have our man." Jim ended the conversation and turned to Phil.

"We'll get Higgins, and he'll give us his accomplice. Case closed. And Phil, I couldn't have done it without your help. Thanks."

"Don't mention it."

Phil and Jim were heading south on the Jersey Turnpike in traffic moving at eighty miles an hour. They had made good time across Staten Island and over the Goethals Bridge. "We'll be in Cohen's office around six if all goes well," Phil said.

Parisi walked up to the front of Jack Higgins's home. She wore a bulletproof vest under her shirt and a flak jacket over it. In bold yellow letters, 'Nassau County Police' adorned the back of the flak jacket. A helmet protected her head, and she carried a shotgun. Despite all the body armor, she proceeded carefully, checking every window as she approached the house for a sign of movement. Thirty Nassau County police officers surrounded her and the home. She banged on the front door and shouted, "Nassau County Police! Open up, we have a warrant." She waited thirty seconds before ordering the officers to open the door with the ramrod. As she did, the door opened.

Mrs. Jack Higgins, dressed in the same skirt and blouse she wore to work today, said, "What the hell is going on here?"

"Is Mr. Higgins at home?"

"I'm not saying a word until I talk to my lawyer. I know my rights."

Karen Parisi wanted to choke the bitch, but she knew Mrs. Higgins was within her rights. Parisi handed her the warrant and gave her a few seconds to read it. "Is Mr. Higgins here?" she asked as she moved into the house, waving the rest of her team in behind her.

"He's not here, and you don't need those guns. I'm calling my lawyer."

Parisi ignored Mrs. Higgins's comment and proceeded to secure the house.

Traffic on the northern end of the Jersey Turnpike was heavier than Phil had expected, and he was trying to make up time on the southern end. They were running at ninety miles an hour when Phil asked, "Is your badge good in New Jersey?"

"If you keep up this speed, we'll find out."

"Not if my lucky streak holds."

Traffic was light as they drove through mostly rural southern Jersey. Even at ninety, the car felt solid, planted on the asphalt. Jim was thinking about what Phil had said to him after he made that stupid greaseball comment. He had thought about it frequently. "You were right. I take racial issues too seriously and take it too much to heart. I'm not going to stop trying to improve things, but I'm working on accepting life as it is. So, thanks for taking the time to talk to me."

"You're welcome."

"I still have a problem with some of your world views, like black victimhood and the government's role in helping people.

You think people should take care of themselves and that society, the government, should stay out of almost everything. I disagree with you."

"No problem."

Karen Parisi was frustrated. The search had turned up nothing yet, and Mrs. Higgins refused to say a word until her lawyer arrived. Finally, Mrs. Higgins and her lawyer finished their initial conversation and walked toward her.

First, the lawyer spoke. "I'm Russell Bickford, and I represent Mrs. Higgins. How much longer will you people be?"

"Until we're done. Where is Mr. Higgins?"

"Unless you have an arrest warrant for him, that's none of your business. I'll advise Mrs. Higgins to answer after reading the warrant."

"I don't have an arrest warrant, but we must talk to Mr. Higgins."

Attorney Bickford just looked intently at Karen. Karen walked away, and as she did, she mumbled, "Fuck you."

The payphone rang at precisely quarter-to-six. Jack picked up the receiver and listened. "Cohen is alone in his office on a conference call and should be done after six. Everyone else, including our friend, has gone for the day. According to our friend, Cohen should be off the phone by six-fifteen, so once you deal with the bodyguard, you'll have Cohen all to yourself," the woman said.

"I'll have no problem with the bodyguard. Did our friend tell you how late Cohen is planning to stay?"

"A limo is picking him up around seven to take him to the airport."

"I'll be long gone by then."

"This should wrap things up for us. We'll talk after the holidays." Jack listened to the click.

He ran through his mental checklist for the last time. *Everything is in place. Cohen will finally get what he deserves. I'll be free and clear with a lucrative consulting position in Purity, managing the covert testing of Relieve. Ironic.*

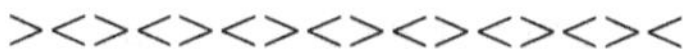

Phil and Jim arrived at Cohen's office door five minutes after six and knocked. "Nice digs," Jim said. "I could get used to working here in a New York minute."

Cohen opened the door before Phil could respond, and he was visibly surprised to see Phil. "I didn't know you were joining Lieutenant Hines. Don't we need you at the plant making sure we make enough Thinadin for our customers?"

"Jim and I have been friends ever since I gave him a suspect list. Lorraine is running the plant."

Cohen looked at his watch, then lied, "I have ten minutes before my limo arrives, so make it quick, Lieutenant."

Jim immediately disliked Bob Cohen. He was obviously a man who cared only about himself. *But when he hears what we know about Relieve, he'll change his tune,* Jim considered. "I think your execs were killed because they were involved in a covert operation. Their objective was to delay the testing of Relieve tablets until they were sure the tablets would pass the Quality tests. Do you know anything about it?"

Bob Cohen looked as if Jim Hines had shoved a sword through him, removed it, and presented the blood covered blade to him on a silver platter. Cohen looked from Phil to Jim as if waiting for one of them to laugh at the joke. "I have no idea what you're talking about. Phil, where did this man get that idea? Where did he learn about our business?"

"From me."

Jim said, "We have a lot of information, and I think you're lying, so re-think your answer."

"Phil, this is all your fault. You did this, you son-of-a-bitch. You're fired, you fucking traitor. Where is your loyalty? I regret the day I brought you into this company. Now get out. I have an appointment."

Phil responded, "You would be better off listening. We have enough information to make your life difficult, and we are willing to give you a break by sharing it with you first. But if you won't listen, we'll share it with Purity's owners."

Just then, the door opened.

Jack Higgins swiped the card in the reader and punched in the code 211. He was dressed in his best business suit. *Too bad it'll be covered in blood when I complete this assignment*, he thought. *But it can't be helped. I have a complete change of clothes in my briefcase.* He walked up the rear stairs to the second floor and into the bullpen. He could see Cohen's bodyguard standing by the closed door to his office. Jack, briefcase in his left hand, looked like the executive he had once been. He walked across the bullpen straight toward the bodyguard.

When Jack got close to the bodyguard, he said in a soft voice, "I'm Jack Higgins from the Garden City Site, and I have a meeting with Jane Downs. Do you know where her office is?"

"No. The name sounds familiar, but I don't know where her office is."

"Let me check… I think I have an office number." Jack set his briefcase on Cohen's secretary's desk, then pulled out a business card from his pocket. Jack positioned himself at the bodyguard's left arm with the business card in his left hand. He simultaneously raised the card and released the ice pick into his right hand. As the bodyguard concentrated on the business card, Jack injected the ice pick into the bodyguard's neck just under the base of his skull and into his brain in one smooth, hard thrust. He brought his left hand up to cover his victim's mouth and gently set the bodyguard down behind the secretary's desk. Bob Cohen's bodyguard, Tim Cavan, died almost instantly, ending his days on this earth at 12,227.

The bodyguard's blood covered the front of Jack's clothes. He drew the Glock-nine and shoved the office door open. He was stunned to see three people in the office.

A disappointed Karen Parisi sat on a dining room chair, waiting for two officers to finish searching the Higgins's basement. Twenty of Nassau County's finest had searched the house and found nothing so far. Mrs. Higgins had spent the time whispering with her lawyer but still refused to talk to Karen. Officer Parisi kept thinking. *There has to be something in the house, some clue to the murders. Mrs. Higgins might not understand her husband was a murderer. He might be killing someone else as she makes tea for that fucking lawyer.*

Mrs. Higgins opened the drawer to the china cabinet and pulled out a spoon. Something about the drawer bothered Karen. Mrs. Higgins' motion didn't seem right; it was somehow out of proportion. The silverware was in a deep drawer, and Mrs. Higgins seemed to pluck the spoon from close to the top. Karen opened the drawer and looked inside, then looked at the front. "Son-of-a-bitch," she said aloud, and she immediately started removing the contents from the drawer.

It was surreal. Standing in the doorway of Purity Pharmaceutical's CEO's office was a man covered in blood and holding a gun. Messina and Cohen stood frozen, but Hines reached for his gun.

Higgins saw the movement and said, "Don't be stupid, Lieutenant. You'll be dead before your body hits the floor. Hands behind your heads, all three of you, now!" Jack closed the door. "Lieutenant Hines, put your hands on that wall and spread 'em. I've always wanted to say that to a cop," he said as he pointed his gun at Hines. "Now, you two follow the good Lieutenant's lead. Good." Jack frisked all three. "Now, everyone on your knees." He watched them intently for a few minutes.

Phil stared at the gun. *Fucking Jack Higgins, a skilled assassin, is standing in front of me, holding a gun on me. I'm dead, I'm a fucking dead man, and I'm not ready to go.* Phil's insides were in an uproar. Stomach acid pressed at his throat. *It's a good thing I just pissed, or my pants would be soaked. Christ, my stomach is quivering, and I feel like I'm going to black out. This isn't fair. I'm too young to die, way too fucking young. Hines will do something. He's trained, and he'll know how to take this prick out.*

"Messina, what are you and the good Lieutenant doing here?"

"We're here to talk about the murders." Phil considered lying, but Jack was going to kill them anyway.

"That explains the Lieutenant. But why you?"

"I'm working with him, helping him out."

"So, you're the reason the police zeroed in on me so fast. What do you know about me?"

Hines answered, "We know more than enough now. We would have arrested you a week ago if you hadn't had good alibis for the first two killings. Obviously a screw up."

"I left myself just enough time to kill Cohen's flunkies. Not too shabby, huh? If you'd looked closely, you might've figured it out. Unfortunately, you're used to dealing with stupid criminals, not smart, well-educated, well-trained killing machines. I thought of everything. Every detail was covered. The perfect crimes."

While Jack talked, Phil surveyed the office, looking for a way out of this predicament. He studied the shelves built into the wall. The built-in shelves were decorated with books, awards, and knickknacks. *If I can get over to the shelves, I might be able to do something.* Phil squirmed as if in pain. He alternately lifted each knee and tried to straighten his legs. He fell forward a little and caught himself.

"Messina, what's wrong with you?"

"I have bad knees, and they hurt. I can't get comfortable. I keep falling forward."

Jack frowned, puzzling over what his next action should be. He had not anticipated three victims, but he would not mind an appetizer or two before killing Cohen. *I should kill him right now, him and that black cop. That would shake up Cohen though, and I want to talk to him. I don't understand why he set me up, and I have to know.* Jack gave Phil the once-over. *He's too fat to be any threat. I'd have a bullet in his head before he moved.* "Messina, you've gotten much too fat for your own good. Your knees can't take all that weight. Okay, you can stand up. But remember: one sudden move, and you're a dead man." Jack smiled. "I always wanted to say that."

Phil stood and casually walked to the built-in shelves and leaned against them. Phil caught Jim's eye and gave him a conspiratorial nod, but Phil did not know why. Maybe he just wanted to feel that Jim was with him. Without nodding, because he was in Jack's line of sight, Jim blinked both eyes. It was enough of a sign for Phil.

"Mr. Cohen, you've been very quiet, and that's not like you. Don't you want to order me around? Diane tried to order me around and look at what happened to her. Kathleen, of course, that witch, misbehaved and the same thing happened to her. Go figure. Did you figure it out after I killed Kathleen?"

Bob Cohen gasped for breath as sweat dripped from his brow. His mind raced in all directions simultaneously, but he could not formulate a coherent thought. "What?"

Jack moved closer and placed the barrel of the Glock against Cohen's forehead. "You'd better pay attention to me. We have a lot to talk about, and I want your full attention."

Cohen did not hear a word Jack said. "Don't kill me. I'll give you money, lots of money. Just don't kill me."

"I just want to talk. Don't worry. If you're straight with me, I'll simply leave."

Neither Phil nor Jim believed Higgins, but Cohen seemed to latch on to it as a lifejacket. "I knew we could work this out. What do you want to talk about?"

"I'm surprised you don't know. Our little arrangement on Relieve seems to have turned sour after I left. That's no reason to set me up for the FDA, is it?"

Cohen's face went blank as if Higgins had spoken in Greek. He looked over at Phil and Jim, hoping for a sign of understanding or support. He received neither. He turned back to Higgins. "I didn't set you up… I don't know what you're talking about."

Clearly angry, Higgins straightened his right arm to line up his gun with Cohen's forehead. "You can't be honest even with your life in the balance. I've read your e-mails. I know that if the FDA uncovers the covert testing, you plan to give them documents proving a couple of chemists and I were the brains behind the illegal operation. I'd probably wind up in jail. Even if I didn't, I'd never work in the pharmaceutical industry again. You and your kiss-ass followers would get away scot-free. Well, they're all dead, and you're the only one left, so you may as well tell me everything about your little plot."

Cohen suddenly realized that Jack Higgins was going to kill him no matter what. When that realization settled into his conscious mind, Bob Cohen, CEO of Purity Pharmaceuticals, pissed his pants.

"Jesus Christ, are you a fucking baby?" Jack said, then started laughing.

While Higgins's attention focused on Cohen, Phil focused his attention on the shelves, trying to find some sort of weapon. The only item that made any sense was a Waterford Crystal replica of the Capitol Dome in Washington DC. The gift had been left on every attendee's bed at the Washington Managers' Meeting a month after the last downsizing. A gold-finished plaque inscribed 'Worldwide Managers' Meeting, Purity Pharmaceuticals, Washington DC' was fastened to the wooden base on which the replica sat. The crystal dome was about two and a half inches in diameter at the bottom and five inches long and pointed at the top. Phil visualized reaching out for the replica, gripping it with his right thumb at the base, and throwing it like a football at Higgins's chest. Higgins would see motion and turn and fire; hopefully, the replica would hit him before firing. Phil, scared out of his mind, decided he would do it.

Cohen, his weasel face red with embarrassment, stared at his crotch. Higgins, still laughing out loud, relaxed his arm. Jim Hines, still kneeling, was expressionless. Higgins, now in control, again asked Cohen, "Tell me why you picked me. I did everything you asked me to do and never told a soul. Was it because I wanted the pay-off?"

Cohen did not move. He just stared at his crotch. The office was silent as they all waited for Cohen to answer. Lieutenant Hines spoke. "Maybe you and your associates got it wrong. Maybe he didn't set you up."

Higgins straightened his right arm again, this time pointing the gun at Hines. "Shut up, I'm talking to him. I don't want to hear your voice again. Understand?" Jim Hines nodded. "Cohen, answer my fucking question!"

Phil decided the time was right. He had visualized throwing the crystal dome over and over again. Phil had a strong arm from years of playing baseball and football. He knew he had the physical skill to hit Higgins, but did he have the mental toughness to risk his life? What the hell? He was dead for sure if he did nothing.

Phil grabbed the crystal dome like a football and threw it as hard as possible. The entire time, Phil's eyes were locked on Higgins's chest. Higgins's peripheral vision picked up the movement, and instinctively he turned slightly toward it, bringing his gun around to fire. The point of the replica struck him in the neck just above his breastbone with tremendous force. Pain seared through his head. The gun fired. Phil threw the replica so hard that the follow-through yanked him forward and bent him at the waist. He charged at Higgins, intending to drive him into the wall. The bullet flew wide, missing Phil by a few feet. Phil charged into Higgins, grabbed his right arm, and slammed him into the wall. He hoped to shake the gun loose or at least be able to control Higgins's arm until Hines could help. Instead, the force of hitting the wall bent Phil's wrist, and he lost control of Higgins' arm. Still in severe pain, Higgins felt

Phil release his arm and raised the gun to Phil's head. Hines was off his knees and moving toward the action. Age had slowed him physically, but he was determined to save Phil. He got to Higgins just as the gun reached Phil's head and reached out to hit Higgins's arm in an attempt to knock the gun away from Phil. The gun fired.

His cell phone chirped, and Jim Hines answered. "Jim, it's Karen. We found his weapons. They were under a false bottom of a drawer in his China cabinet. You won't believe what we found, but we don't know where he is. Mrs. Higgins, on the advice of her lawyer, won't talk to us."

"Hold on, hold on." Jim told Karen about what had transpired in Cohen's office. "Higgins is on his way to the hospital right now. The bullet took off part of his head, but he's alive. Phil's shaken but okay, except his left ear hurts like hell, and he says he can't hear well. I think it'll pass. Tell Higgins's wife and lawyer what happened but play down the extent of his injury. Push as hard as you can. Tell them we know he's the killer, and if they don't co-operate, you'll arrest them for obstruction. Tear the house apart again, too. We have to find Higgins's accomplice. I don't think he'll make it, so we can't count on him telling us. I'll question Cohen again tomorrow. All he wanted to do tonight was go home and change his pants. The man had a little accident."

"How did Higgins get in the building?"

"I found a card on him. It looks like he used a phony card to get into the building, just like he did in Garden City. There's an entrance to the building near the visitor's parking lot. The doors are unlocked from seven in the morning until six o'clock. After six, you have to buzz the security guard. There are also five other entrances on the first floor, and an employee card will unlock the door from seven am to six pm. After six, only the executives can get in with a special card and a three-digit code, much like the way execs entered the Garden City Site. I'll bet he got in one of the five entrances, made his way to Cohen's office, killed the bodyguard, and walked in. We'll know after we analyze the card. By the way, the computer at the guard station didn't register anyone using a card."

"I'll have to get another search warrant, one that's not specific for weapons. I won't leave the house until the warrant arrives."

"Go over all the calls from the house and his cell phone with a fine-tooth comb. I have to go. I'm the only one able to talk to the police. Phil's sitting on a couch in the secretary's area staring at the ceiling. He hasn't said more than three words since Higgins was shot."

Lieutenant Hines completed his account of the events of the evening for the New Castle County police. He obtained their promise to keep him up to date on their investigation. He shook hands with four of the officers and walked over to Phil. "Are you okay?"

"Fine," Phil replied in a voice that said, "No."

"We need to check in to our hotel and get some food. Let's go."

Phil and Jim checked into their hotel, changed their clothes, and made the obligatory calls home. The only place open was an all-night diner on the Kirkwood Highway. Telling Rose about Cohen's office events helped Phil come out of his funk. To put it mildly, Rose was upset and a little irrational. She wanted him home right now and wanted him to part ways with Lieutenant Hines. Phil understood that her reaction came from her love for him, and that she wanted him home alive. He assured her that the killer was in Christiana Hospital, barely hanging on to life, so the danger had passed.

The Elsmere Diner was relatively empty, and they ordered quickly. Phil realized that he did not know much about what happened after the gun was discharged. Phil remembered the warmth of the blood and the blast feeling like a punch. He also remembered Jack Higgins going limp in his arms. Phil's headache had lessened in the four hours since the shooting, but it still hurt like hell. Coming face to face with a cold-blooded killer had shaken him. It made him think about the safe and somewhat dull life he led. Until recently, the corporate world had wrapped a security blanket around its employees and protected them from reality. Good pay, health insurance, retirement plans, and a myriad of other perks relieved them of many of the worries that exist in the real world.

"It seems I checked out after the gun went off. What happened?"

"Well, it's good to have you back. I thought I'd have to eat alone tonight. Do you remember what you did?"

"I remember throwing the crystal dome, slamming into Higgins, and driving him into the wall. I remember a sharp pain in my wrist, causing me to lose my grip on his arm. I remember the gun going off and a severe pain in my left ear that caused me to forget about the pain in my wrist. I remember Higgins going limp. That's it."

"What you did was save my life, and I want you to know I'll never forget it. What you did took balls." Hines filled him in on all the details.

"I was as scared as I'd ever been in my life. I only acted because I knew we were all dead if I didn't. I didn't want to die just yet. It seems to me that you saved my life by deflecting his arm."

"We'd have all been dead if you didn't throw that chunk of crystal. You saved your life and mine and Cohen's as well."

"How is old piss-the-pants Cohen?"

"Old piss-the-pants is fine. He made a beeline out before the cops came, and you zoned out, leaving me to handle the cops. Which I did an excellent job of, by the way. They're going to keep Higgins under guard and let me know when I can talk to him. He's in surgery right now, and odds are less than fifty-fifty he'll survive. We should stop by the hospital before we call it a day."

"Okay. Higgins seemed to think Cohen and his cohorts were setting him up to take the fall for Relieve. There's your motive for the killings. Higgins thought he could go to jail if they succeeded. Cohen denied they planned to set him up, but Higgins was convinced."

"And with good reason. I talked to Parisi just before we left the hotel. She got an all-encompassing search warrant and tore Higgins's house apart. She didn't find much, but she did find a folder with copies of emails between Cohen, Armstrong, Stanley, and Connolly. The emails were from Cohen to one of the other three or one of the other three to Cohen. The gist of most of the e-mails has to do with inventory levels, holding tablets until they're tested, and test results when the tablets pass the tests. They provide proof of the covert conspiracy to violate FDA regulations. Your theories were right. Then, right after the FDA notified Purity of the audit, e-mails flew back and forth dealing with creating documents to frame Higgins. In other words, we have the motive. Seems our man Higgins was connected to Cohen's e-mail account. What we don't have is Higgins's accomplice. Someone in the company helped him: someone who knew computers and had something to gain from the killings. Parisi interrogated Mrs. Higgins and is convinced she had no idea what her husband was doing."

"You've been busy, but we still need to find out who Higgins was working with. So, Mr. Lieutenant James Hines, where do we go from here?"

"Unless you can pull a rabbit out of your hat, the only answer is tedious, boring police work. The first step is for you and me to meet with Cohen. I set up the meeting for eight o'clock tomorrow morning. I can't wait to see his reaction to the e-mails."

"I hope he brings a change of underwear. I have a feeling he's going to need them." Phil snickered.

"Yeah, he strikes me as the kind of guy who needs to be in control of everything and everybody. But having copies of those e-mails gives us the upper hand. Have you talked to anyone in Garden City?"

"No. I'll make some calls tomorrow morning."

Dinner appeared. Both men realized how hungry they were, forgot about the case, and began devouring their meals. Neither spoke until Jim, plate cleaned, sat up straight in his chair and patted his ample stomach. "I was born in Alabama, a direct descendant of slaves on both sides of my family. You can tell from how black my skin is that there are no white people in my family tree."

"What the hell are you talking about?"

Maybe it was because Jim had been close to death tonight or because Phil saved his life – he was not sure why – but Jim said, "You were upset because I never told you about my background. Well, I'm telling you now."

"It's after eleven."

"It won't take long. Do you want to hear it or not?"

"Sure, but I'm going to get a coffee." Phil motioned for the waitress.

"Me too." The waitress took their coffee orders. Jim gathered himself. "We left Alabama when I was seven and moved to Harlem. The 'we' were my mother, grandmother, my younger sister, and I. My father was executed a couple of months before we left." Jim's words were measured. Phil felt Jim's emotion. "He was convicted of raping and murdering a white woman. He was her family's handyman. The day she was killed, she was home alone. Her husband was in Mobile on business, and her son was on a school trip. It was my father's day off, and he was home with my mother. There was only a little circumstantial evidence tying my father to the crime, all of which could be explained since he worked around the house. An eyewitness saw a black man around the house, though, and despite my mother swearing he was with her all day, he was convicted." Jim took a deep breath. "The woman's family was well-liked, and in the eyes of the town we were the family of the man who killed her, so we moved. Life in New York took its toll on my mother. She was sixteen when I was born and twenty-three when we moved to New York. She worked two low-paying menial jobs, and my grandmother took care of my sister and me. My mother was a beautiful woman, and many men were interested in dating her. Unfortunately, one man in the neighborhood became obsessed with her, and when she spurned him, he killed her. Shot her in the face, then stuck the gun in his mouth and pulled the trigger. She was dead at twenty-six." Jim lost himself in memories of his mother.

"You don't have to do this."

"Yes, I do. I have to. A beautiful woman, a good woman who worked hard to take care of her family, was shot in the face by a lunatic. We stayed in Harlem a while and then moved to Hempstead and lived on welfare. My grandmother swore my sister and I would make it in the world, that we'd get good educations and good jobs. She pushed us all the time. She tried to keep us away from the street life, away from drugs, and away from the lazy good-for-nothings that stayed out late at night and skipped school. She made sure we knew that no matter how far we got in life or how much money we made, we should never lose sight of the black community. She drilled into our heads that without help, black people would always be poor and would always be disrespected by others in the world. I listened, graduated with honors, and went to Hofstra. I got a degree in Criminal Science and joined the Nassau County Police Department. Two years ago, I made Lieutenant. I've been on the force for thirty years. Lieutenant isn't a bad rank, but it's not really good either. My sister couldn't resist the street and wound up addicted to drugs. She died from AIDS ten years ago. Before my grandmother died a few years back, she told me I made her proud. She also told me I was strong and had to take care of my weaker brothers and sisters." Tears filled Jim's eyes and trickled down his cheeks. He seemed unaware, or at least he did not care that he was crying. "And I couldn't have done it without affirmative action."

"Jim…"

"Don't say anything. Let's go to the hospital."

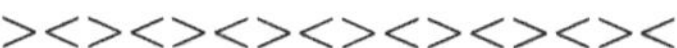

Jack Higgins had been taken to the Christiana Medical Center in New Castle County. As Jim and Phil approached the Medical Center around midnight, it looked like a well-lit spaceship had landed in the middle of dark suburban sprawl. They made their way to the sixth-floor surgical unit. They found a police officer standing guard outside a surgical intensive care room. They learned that Higgins had arrived in the room about twenty minutes ago after a couple of hours in surgery. They had the doctor paged and waited outside of the room. The doctor arrived in about five minutes.

Jim asked, "Is he going to make it?"

"He has less than a fifty-fifty chance. The bullet grazed his brain. He would be in much better shape if it were a normal bullet, but this was a hollow point, and the jagged edges did some real damage to his brain. We did the best we could patching him up. The only thing we can do now is to wait and see."

"When will I be able to talk to him?"

"There's no way to tell. He could wake up tomorrow or in a few days. Then again, he may never wake up."

"I have to talk to him as soon as he wakes up. Doctor, please make sure everyone who has access to his room has my card." Jim handed the doctor a stack of cards and left another at the nurses' station.

Tuesday 12/16

The alarm roused Phil from a sound sleep at six-thirty, and despite only five hours of sleep, he felt great. Charged and looking forward to his meetings with Cohen and Roger Hanson, Phil danced through his morning routine. How would Cohen spin his involvement in the Relieve testing when confronted with e-mails? Would he try to cast blame on his cohorts or plead that he had no choice because he was simply trying to save jobs by keeping Relieve viable? Phil also wondered if last night's events had changed the context of his meeting with Roger. After last night he probably wasn't facing termination, so he did not need to worry about defending himself on the Thinadin inventory problem. All Phil had to do was explain how it had happened. He no longer wanted to work for Purity and would try to use the information he had gleaned from the batch records to force his return to McKenzie. It would likely frustrate Roger Hanson, and Roger was not a man you wanted angry at you. Still, he simply could not continue to work for Purity – certainly not for another sixteen years. Phil Messina, his face covered with shaving cream, believed that the future of the man who looked back at him in the mirror was bright. Just as he finished shaving, the phone rang. It was Lorraine.

"Is this the hero who saved the lives of the Purity CEO and the renowned police Lieutenant? The man who risked his life for the greater good?"

"Good morning, Lorraine. I'm sure you couldn't wait to talk to me and bask in my glory's bright light."

"That and to let you know we're producing more out-of-spec Thinadin. We just finished testing the batches produced this weekend, and we can only release two batches to Packaging."

"Great, give me the bad news."

"We're testing yesterday's production now, and I don't have a good feeling about them either. According to your Production Control Group, we'll stock out by Friday unless we start making good products. That won't happen until we change the way we do things. Fortunately, Abby has an idea: she wants to rehire the experienced Production people we fired last year. I think it's a great idea. What do you think?"

"I wish I'd thought of it. If you rehire the employees who took a pension, they'll lose it, so bring them on through a temp agency and put the rest on our roles. After the inventory is back up, we'll fire the operators who can't make the product and keep the ones that can. I'll square things away here. I hope enough of them want to come back."

"Abby's already calling. We should know where we stand by noon. Good luck with Hanson this morning."

"Thanks. I'll see you tomorrow."

As soon as Phil hung up, the phone rang again.

"Are you okay? I was out late last night, and I just saw on the news what happened last night in Delaware." Alice Chen had more urgency in her voice than Phil had ever heard.

"Ah, a hot date! I'm surprised you're awake this early."

"It was a scorching hot date, but I never let my social life interfere with work."

"Whatever you say. To answer your question, I'm fine. It was a little scary last night, but the good guys won. You sound a little excited this morning. Is everything okay with you?"

Alice ignored the question. "Did Higgins use a card to get in the building?"

"It looks that way. Why?"

"Fantastic! I'm so proud of myself. Wait until you hear this. I finally finished the program and tested it yesterday afternoon on our security program. It worked, and I installed it permanently. I called to tell you, but Mary Margaret said you'd already left for Delaware. That's when I decided to put the program on the security system at headquarters. Since the security systems are basically the same, it should work if Higgins used an executive card to get into the building. In that case, we should have information that will allow us to track the computer used to modify the security program."

It took a minute for the enormity of Alice's message to sink in. If her program worked, they would have a way to track Jack Higgins's accomplice and end this nightmare. "When will you know if it worked?"

"I should know later this morning."

"Alice don't tell a soul what you're doing. Do you hear me? Not a soul. Higgins's accomplice is still on the loose. If he thinks we're closing in – even if he gets wind – that there's a possibility we're tracking him, he could get dangerous. He's obviously very good with a computer, since he modified the security system. The police found copies of Cohen's emails in Higgins's home. He was able to get into Cohen's computer."

Alice interrupted. "If I could get into Cohen's computer, I could track the computer that hacked into his e-mail account. It gives us another option."

"I assume Cohen's computer has to be on the network for you to get in."

"Good assumption."

"Unless the local police took it, it should be in his office. I'll check it out and call you later."

Phil briefed Jim Hines on Alice's call as they drove to their meeting with Cohen. Jim immediately contacted the New Castle County Police and told them not to touch Cohen's computer. He asked the Sergeant to call Cohen and get any passwords for the computer as part of their investigation. That done, Jim thought about the future. *If Alice is successful, we'll arrest the accomplice and close the highest-profile murder case in history. The pols will be falling over themselves to shake my hand in public. I, Lieutenant Jim Hines, might become Captain Jim Hines. Man, that sounds good.* A smile decorated Jim's face for the rest of the ride.

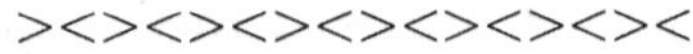

Cohen seemed to have recovered from last night's embarrassment and was prepared for a fight. His first words were designed to put Phil in his place.

Looking only at Jim Hines, Bob Cohen said, "I don't think Phil should be at this meeting. He's not with the police, and he's too far down in the organization to be here while I talk to you."

"Phil's with me, and he has every right to be here. This is not a business meeting. It's an investigation into six murders, and I need and want Phil here with me. If you have a problem, I'll conduct this interview at Nassau County Police Headquarters and compel you to be there. Your choice."

"You can't compel me to be anywhere. I think we're done. Do it through my lawyer if you want to talk to me." Bob Cohen handed Hines a business card.

"You're making a mistake, Mr. Cohen. I have evidence linking you to illegal activities in the production of Relieve, a proprietary pharmaceutical of Purity Pharmaceuticals. Relieve also happens to be the motive in a series of murders I'm investigating. That makes you a material witness, so I'll be able to compel your cooperation. We'll leave now if you want."

"Your evidence is in the Christiana Medical Center in a coma from a bullet to his brain, and I deny every accusation he made. I don't know what he was talking about."

Jim reached into his briefcase, pulled out a stack of papers, and placed them in front of Bob Cohen. "Please read these before you say anymore."

Bob's expression changed from defiance to panic as he read the copies of his e-mails. "Where did you get these?"

"I'll ask the questions. Did you write the e-mails from you, and did you receive the e-mails addressed to you?"

He considered his answer and then spoke to Phil. "If I went to the FDA with the test results on Relieve, they would've stopped production and made us start all over…

Reformulation, new clinical trials. It would've cost us two hundred million dollars and taken at least three years. We sell seven hundred and fifty million dollars of Relieve a year. We would've had to cut hundreds of jobs. I was just trying to protect our employees."

"Don't bullshit me. You were protecting Bob Cohen because no one else means anything to you. You don't mind firing employees. You've demonstrated that by driving downsizing. Bob, you're caught, so just answer the good Lieutenant's questions, and stop trying to play the 'I did it for the greater good' role."

Bob looked at the e-mails again. "I don't know anything about the ones setting up Higgins. They're forgeries. I do recognize the others, though. Yes, I controlled the covert Relieve testing through the people Higgins murdered, but someone else created the other e-mails. They put the gun in Higgins's hand, not me."

"If you didn't plan to set up Higgins, who wrote the e-mails, and why did they want you and the others dead?" Jim asked.

"My guess is someone wanted me out of the way so they could have my job. Whoever it was wanted to take care of any other perceived competition. All those people were killed so someone could climb the corporate ladder. Greed. I thought it was someone we fired. Revenge. But no, it was simple greed."

"Who would be in line for your job?"

"You mean who is in line for my job since I'm dead meat as soon as Hanson and Mooney find out about Relieve? I'm guessing that'll be at your nine o'clock meeting. Right, Phil?"

"Sooner, if you would answer Jim's questions so I can get out of here."

"Do you dislike me that much?"

"It's way beyond dislike."

Cohen spoke to Lieutenant Hines. "Phil isn't in line for my job. He can hardly do his own job. I'd say you should look at Pamela Robinson, John Severen, or Gary Hazlitt."

"Who's your pick?"

"I'd pick Pamela, but she's probably third because she's too close to me."

Jim stood up. "I hope you were honest with me about the emails."

On the twenty-second floor of the McKenzie Building, Roger Hanson's office provided a commanding view of the Delaware River and downtown Wilmington. The well-appointed office suited a man one rung from the top of a fifty-billion-dollar corporation. Phil sat in an oxblood leather armchair across from Roger, who appeared relaxed on a leather couch. A small round table sat between them.

"Hell of a night you had last night, Mr. Messina. Taking out a trained killer with a piece of Waterford Crystal is quite an accomplishment."

"Believe me, I acted out of fear, not bravery. And I'm lucky – we're lucky – that it worked, or Higgins would've had three more notches on his gun butt."

"Still, it was a hell of a daring move. I'm not sure I could've done it. But against all odds, here we sit with the killer in the hospital and you, Cohen, and Lieutenant Hines alive and well. By the way, where is Lieutenant Hines?"

"Using an empty office to make some calls."

"Please give him my regards on a job well done. Anyway, you wanted to talk to me about a couple of things, and I'm sure you'd like to get to them. John Mooney, my counterpart in Saga, will join us at nine-thirty to talk about Cohen's involvement in the underground testing of Relieve tablets. So try to cover your other business before he shows up."

"Is it safe to assume I'm not getting fired for the Thinadin supply problems?"

"Not completely. Cohen has talked to a lot of people, so I need some ammunition to defend you."

Phil pulled a folder from his briefcase, removed four sheets of paper, and handed them to Roger. "You now have all the ammunition you will need. The problem started with Marketing's forecast. After the FDA approved Thinadin to treat atrial fibrillation, Marketing predicted sales would increase by fifteen percent. Sales actually increased by over fifty percent. Their forecast is in the left column, and the actual demand is in the right column. You can see how badly Marketing missed the forecast. Marketing made an all-out effort to acquaint doctors with the new use of Thinadin. When doctors began prescribing it for their atrial fibrillation patients, our inventories began to fall. The Atlanta Distribution Center didn't react and set off alerts when inventories started falling. Based on the way data comes to Production Control from Atlanta, Alice Chen recognized the problem as early as possible. To compound a bad situation, five batches of Thinadin failed QC testing, causing the shortage to be more severe. That's documented on the second page."

Roger studied the documents for a few minutes, then said, "If this is accurate, and I believe it is, you and your people are safe. You did all you could. What's the status now?"

"Production is working all kinds of OT, but they're still making a lot of bad product."

Roger interrupted. "We're not going to stock out, are we?"

"It'll be close. Only two batches produced this weekend passed QC testing. Abby Stall came up with a plan that will probably save us, though. We're bringing back all the experienced Production operators and putting them to work on Thinadin production. Don't worry about how we're dealing with pensioners… just trust us."

"Just tell me we won't stock out."

"I can't guarantee it, but I'm hopeful."

"If we stock out of Thinadin, we'll have generic competition in six months, and we both know what that means."

"It means disaster for the company and the employees."

"Saga got into this joint venture with us primarily on the strength of Thinadin's positioning in the marketplace. They've put a lot of money into Purity they won't get back if we lose the Thinadin market."

"We'll do everything we can to prevent a stockout."

"I know you will. Let's move on."

Fear welled up in Phil's chest. This was probably the worst time to give Roger more bad news, but it would be the best time for Phil to get what he wanted. "A couple of weeks ago, before the killing started, two employees told Abby and me that Manufacturing was taking shortcuts and not following SOPs. They wouldn't talk to their management, so I decided to look into it to see if they were exaggerating. It turned out to be much worse than I expected. When I started hearing my job was in trouble, I decided to use the information to protect my financial interests. What I want now is to be rehired by McKenzie." Phil handed Roger a summary of his findings.

Roger read the summary carefully and then asked, "Have we shipped any bad product?"

"No. I've reviewed all the testing, and I'm sure everything we shipped was good."

"I can't move you back to McKenzie. We signed an airtight agreement with Saga when we formed the joint venture and can never rehire a Purity employee. Saga is looking for a way to break the agreement and moving you back to McKenzie will give it to them. If they pull out, the business will fail. The stakes are too high."

"I can't continue to work for Purity. The culture is poisoned, and it'll never change. I need to protect my future. I'll never be secure as long as I'm working in that organization."

"Your only other alternative may be to resign."

Roger's response both surprised and angered Phil. His knowledge should have given him some power, but Roger had acted as if the information was worthless. "If my only choices are to continue working for Purity or quit, I'll quit. If I thought you'd be around to protect me from the assholes running Purity, I might stay, but you could be fired tomorrow. My first task after I quit will be to give a detailed report to the FDA and the New York Times. I'm not sure what the FDA will do, but I'm sure the Times would love more ammunition in their war with the pharmaceutical industry."

"That sounds like blackmail to me. Are you certain you want to pursue this path?"

"Positive."

Roger thought for a few moments, and when he spoke, he sounded different. He sounded conciliatory. "What I am about to say stays between you and me. The Phil Messina I knew in the Diagnostics business wouldn't consider blackmailing the company, and for good reason: you were confident the company was loyal to you and would treat you fairly, and you, in return, were loyal to the company. Obviously, you don't believe that anymore, and you're right. It's not like that anymore. The corporate world has changed, and the first casualty was loyalty. Old dogs like me don't fit anymore. I'll be fifty-eight in less than a year, and I'm leaving, taking my pension, and running as fast as possible. Everything you've learned about dealing with people and balancing their needs with company profits is considered wrong by the new breed of management. They chew people up and spit them out."

"So why the crap about me being a blackmailer? You wanted me to back off and quit."

"My job is to maximize earnings and protect the companies' assets, and if I didn't try, I wouldn't be doing my job. But you responded the right way. Before Thanksgiving, we asked Cohen to maximize earnings next year because we put Purity on the market. The better the earnings, the better the sale price. He told us he could reduce more people and not affect production or quality. Obviously, he was wrong. Production and quality are already being affected. We'll probably take Purity off the market for as long as it takes to straighten out the problems."

"I assume that means no downsizing."

"It means we'll hire people. Hopefully, some of the experienced people will want to come back. Let's get back to you. We had Purity on the market for seven billion dollars, but the problems with Relieve will surely lessen the value. We'll most likely tell the FDA about Relieve and pull the product from the market. If you expose those procedural problems in production, Purity will be worthless. After you update Mooney on Relieve and the murder investigation, I'll talk to him alone. I'll show him the information you compiled, and we'll work out a deal for you. It won't take long, so I'd like you to hang around."

"Okay."

"It's time to talk to Mooney." As Roger walked toward his office door, he turned back to Phil and said, "You're doing the right thing."

John Mooney, Senior Vice President of Saga Pharmaceuticals, looked every inch a VP of a major company. He fit every stereotype. Phil Knew little about expensive men's suits, but Mooney's had undoubtedly set him back a considerable amount of money. Phil guessed that he was six-foot-two and weighed around one-ninety. He had a full head of jet-black hair, cut long, swept back, and sculpted. Every hair on his head was in its place. Phil looked at his belly and felt inferior for a moment, then reminded himself that the inside, not the outside, counted. He knew that the man under the suit was just a man.

Roger made the introductions and Mooney sat on the couch beside him. "Phil, please update John on the murder investigation and on the testing of Relieve. He knows what happened last night, and he knows Jack Higgins committed the murders. He needs to understand the ties to Relieve and Cohen."

Phil gave the man from Saga a detailed explanation.

Mooney nodded slowly. "So Cohen ran this covert team for seven years. We produced Relieve tablets that tested out of spec right after they were compressed. We waited for them to test in-spec, then shipped them to customers. No one at the Garden City facility raised a red flag."

"That's correct."

"Cohen is one hell of a leader."

"So was Hitler," Phil replied.

"Why did Higgins start killing Cohen's team?"

"Higgins had a file in his home containing email communication between Cohen and his team members. Most of it was normal administration of the team's effort, but a number of the e-mails detailed how the team would set up Jack Higgins as the brains behind the effort if the FDA ever found out. When the FDA told us they'd do an audit of Relieve, the killing started. Cohen admitted most of the emails between him and the others were real, but insisted the ones dealing with setting up Higgins were fakes. I believe him."

"That means Higgins had an accomplice. What is the chance of catching him?"

Phil's first thought was to play the hero and let these two powerful men know about Alice's efforts, but he decided not to. This was not a corporate game. People had been killed, and he had come close to understanding what it feels like to be shot. The fewer people who knew, the better the chance they would have to catch the accomplice without any further damage. "Higgins had to have help, but the police have no leads, so the accomplice will probably get away unless he tries something new."

John Mooney sat back and looked at Roger. He had obviously heard enough.

Roger said to Phil, "John and I need to talk for a while. Please wait outside, and my Administrative Assistant will get you when we're done."

Phil cooled his heels in an empty office for about fifteen minutes before Roger Hanson's assistant summoned him. When he was about to enter Roger's office, John Mooney exited. He nodded to Phil and kept moving. When Phil had stepped inside and closed the door, he said to Roger, "He doesn't look happy."

"And with good reason. Saga has been involved with Purity for less than four years, and we're about to lose a major product and we have serious Production issues. The downsizing last year was ill-advised at best, and we were going to implement another one early next year. That would've destroyed the company. Mooney and his peers at Saga see us as incompetent. I think we can turn things around, but it'll take a few years. He was particularly interested in your summary of the problems in Production and particularly angry at your arm twisting."

"I guess I won't have a long-term supporter in the pharmaceutical industry."

"He'll get over it. He's a big boy. We made a few decisions. Bob Cohen will be fired today, and he'll forfeit his long-term incentive compensation. We're taking Relieve off the market and will notify the FDA of Cohen's covert testing. I'd like to use the detailed data you put together in our discussion with the FDA."

"No problem."

"In the next couple of days, Purity's new CEO, Gary Hazlitt, will offer you a promotion. In the same time frame, I'll offer you a parachute. You'll have a couple of weeks to decide. I'll make sure the parachute is very golden."

"More golden than the handcuffs I have on?"

"Yes."

"Why Hazlitt? Why not Pamela Robinson? I think she'd do a better job."

"She was too close to Cohen. You said Abby helped you put together the data. Is she looking for something?"

"At a minimum, she should replace me. I'll talk to her when I get back and see what she wants."

"I'm going to tell Hazlitt his first act as CEO is to promote Lorraine Waters to Site Director at Garden City. I want you two to focus on producing Thinadin. We can't, cannot, under any circumstances – stock out. We must keep our customers supplied. You can do whatever you think is necessary to produce. Don't worry about the cost."

"We'll get it done."

"You can't openly deal with the ring leaders involved in falsifying Batch Records without exposing that you know, but you need to figure out a way to send a message."

"I'll come up with an idea."

"Good. I'll instruct Hazlitt to get the word out that you and Lorraine are in charge of Garden City and that you have his full support and the full support of John Mooney and myself. The culture at Garden City doesn't welcome outsiders but respects power. With Cohen out, there'll be a major vacuum. You and Lorraine have to fill it."

Phil nodded, got up, and headed for the door. Roger said, "When you're making your decision, remember what I told you about the changes in the corporate world and also remember what Greg Iverson told you."

Captain Larry Oliveri, Jim's liaison with the New Castle County Police, met them at Bob Cohen's office. Yellow crime scene tape still marked the office, but it was empty, as the forensics team had completed its work. The employees in the bullpen stopped working as Phil passed and acknowledged him with a barely perceptible nod and a look that would have been appropriate if a major celebrity had walked by. Captain Oliveri had Cohen's passwords, enabling Phil to boot the computer.

Captain Oliveri said, "Cohen was very cooperative. He didn't even ask why I wanted the passwords. He looked like a beaten man. I'm glad you know how to start that thing. It's a mystery to me."

"And to me," Jim Hines added.

"All I have to do is boot it up, then use the passwords to log on to the network. Alice is doing all the complicated work."

After Phil logged on to the network, the three men had to wait for Alice to call. Captain Oliveri asked about the case in New York, and Lieutenant Hines filled him in. "Nice work, Lieutenant. Closing a big case like this is a real notch on your gun. I bet you have all the pols falling over themselves to give you a commendation."

"I'm just happy to be here to talk about it. I thought I was dead last night. I didn't see any way out of it. Then Phil, the exec, throws a piece of crystal at an armed assassin. I would have been too smart to do that. I kept trying to figure a way to get his gun."

"Our investigation is about wrapped up. We'll be releasing the office today unless you want us to hold it."

"That depends on what we find today."

They talked for quite a while longer before the phone interrupted. "I found the name of the computer used to hack into Mr. Cohen's e-mail. It's 'braveone.' It's not an on-site computer, and it's not on the network now. This guy is good, really good… I had to use every trick in my bag to get the computer's name. I can find out who 'braveone' is from Cynthia Bernstein or wait until he signs into the network."

"Wait for him to sign in. We'll only go to Cynthia if he doesn't get on the network. Alice: you, me, and Lieutenant Hines are the only ones who know about this lead, and it must stay that way."

"Okay, okay. I'll see what I find on the security system."

"Thanks, Alice, and I'll see you tomorrow. If you come up with anything, call."

Wednesday 12/17

Abby said, "Ten Production operators started yesterday and eighteen more today."

"Christ, what did you do? Offer them a million-dollar sign-on bonus?"

"No, I told them they had a chance to get their old jobs back if we could make good Thinadin. That's all."

"With only a possibility of getting their jobs back, five former employees worked the four to twelve shift and five more worked the graveyard. Eighteen more are starting today, some on each shift. You think they'll be able to make Thinadin that passes Quality?"

"I have no doubt."

"So these people are going to bail us out? These people we pressured to take early pensions, and some we pressured to just leave because they were higher-paid and had a lot of vacation time? They'll bail us out and save Purity billions of dollars?"

"That's right. Bitch, ain't it." Abby was updating Phil on her progress. They were in Phil's office having a private lunch. "Our new CEO spread the word yesterday. You and Lorraine have his complete support, and the complete support of Roger Hanson and John Mooney from Saga, to run the Garden City Site."

"It's made a major difference in the way people treat me. Last week most of the employees here would have hardly acknowledged my existence unless, of course, they were on my case for screwing up Thinadin. My phone has been ringing off the hook all morning, and my inbox is jammed with e-mails. I'm suddenly a very popular fellow."

"I'm sure the same is happening to Lorraine. Have you talked to her yet?"

"No, we're meeting at three."

"Rumor has it Hazlitt will name Lorraine Director of Site Operations, and you're in line for a big job in Delaware."

"The rumor mill in Purity is amazing, and the rumor is right on. That's why I wanted to talk to you. I may take the job in Delaware, or I may resign. One way or another, my job will open, and it'll be offered to you."

"I don't particularly want your job. You know I dream of being a secretary again. I don't want more sleepless nights."

"I know. I took the liberty of telling Roger Hanson that you were involved in the effort that uncovered the mess in Production, and you're well aware of the implications to Purity. I asked Roger for a parachute, and I suggested you might also want one."

"A parachute. I like the sound of it, but I wouldn't know how much to ask for."

"Don't ask for a specific amount. Just tell Roger you're interested in an offer. McKenzie and Saga aren't getting along, and they want to sell Purity. They won't have anything to sell if word gets out about both the Relieve scandal and the procedural violations in Production, even though the business is worth billions today. You have a lot of leverage. Because of the problems, we'll be hiring people instead of letting them go."

"So, I'll be able to choose between your job and some money."

"Right. All you have to do is call Roger and tell him you're interested in a buyout, and he'll make you an offer."

"I'll talk it over with George tonight. Thanks. Any idea who Jack's accomplice is?"

"No." Even though Abby was highly trustworthy, Phil decided not to tell her about identifying the computer. "The police will get him, but I think we're safe with Higgins in the hospital."

"Thanks for talking to Roger on my behalf. I really appreciate it. I'd better get my ass in gear. I have a million things to do."

"Okay, get it in gear, and I'll watch it for you as you leave."

"You're still a pig."

"Some things never change."

"How's the testing going with Thinadin?" asked Phil.

"So far, all of yesterday's production has passed and is heading for packaging," said Lorraine.

"Great. I've reserved a truck for making a direct run to Atlanta. We'll avoid a stockout if we can get six batches there by Saturday, and you and I'll be heroes."

"We already are."

"Tell me about your meeting with the supervisors."

"Oh, yeah. First, I fired John Cary for being insubordinate with you last Saturday. Next, I hired Jack Goloski to replace him. Gino and Frank, my new consultants, highly recommended him for the job. Since I wanted another opinion, I asked Abby. She was very supportive. Abby filled me in on his military background, saying his discipline, knowledge, and 'do it right the first time' attitude would improve the operation. Abby also wanted me to make Tim Anderson Lead Operator. I did.

"Then I got the rest of the supervisors together. I told them about Cary and let them know I knew all about the bullshit they were pulling in Production. I made it clear that anyone who made the slightest misstep would be fired. I could almost smell the fear. I told them about Goloski and Anderson and dismissed them.

"Cary stopped by my office and apologized. He asked me to help him get his job back. In my most diplomatic voice, I told him to accept the consequences of his actions like a man. Then I told him to get the fuck out of my office and never show his face again. I think we've sent a strong message." Lorraine added.

Phil nodded. "Before we move on, remember we have a policy against employees involved with each other being in a supervisory relationship. Since Tablet Production is in such a crisis, we should ignore it until it's over."

"I agree. By the way, Hazlitt offered me the Site Director's job today."

"Congratulations."

"I agreed to take it until we get through this Thinadin mess, but I might not want to stay long-term. Gary laughed and said once I was in the job a while, I'd love it. He also said he's been trying to get a hold of you to offer you a job in Delaware."

"I've been dodging him, not returning his phone calls. I don't have the stomach to talk to him today… I'm considering leaving Purity using the info I gathered on Production as leverage. I don't like the new corporate culture."

"I think if you can get a good financial package, you should leave. You'll never be happy in any corporation again. You'll always be trying to change the new reality, becoming a frustrated old man. Then they'll fire you just before you're pension eligible. If you can lock in some money now, I say do it. I don't want the Site Director's job because I'm also thinking of leaving. I want to do something for my people."

"That's noble. And just who are your people?"

"Don't be a smart ass. The poor people that live in the projects in Brooklyn are my people. I want to do something to make their lives a little better."

"As wonderful as that sounds, you'll still need money to live. That is, unless you want to move back into the same projects after your mother worked two jobs to help you get out."

"I know some things. You're not the only one who can get money from Purity."

"I hope you're successful beyond your wildest dreams in extracting money from Purity. They deserve it, and you deserve it. See you tomorrow, boss."

"Grow up."

When Phil returned to his office, he called Alice. Earlier she had confirmed 'braveone' was also the computer that modified the security system. There was no question that 'braveone' was the accomplice. "Has 'braveone' logged on to the network yet?"

"No. I told you I'd call you, and I will. I promise."

"Okay. If you don't know yet, Cynthia is on vacation until Monday. No one knows how to reach her. You're our only hope."

Thursday 12/18

As much as Phil did not want to talk to Hazlitt, he decided to get it over with as soon as possible. "Phil, thanks for returning my calls. I really appreciate it. I hear everything is going well with Thinadin. I guess it takes us old-timers to get to job done. You and Lorraine are doing a marvelous job, and you've saved this company and the jobs of all its people. Let me get straight to the reason I called you yesterday. Phil, I'd like you to move to Delaware and be my Human Resources Vice President. Greg Iverson has decided to leave in February, and I want you to take his place. I won't get into the specifics until you think it over and tell me you're interested. Your salary will be well over six figures, and your bonus could reach seventy-five percent of your salary. It's a very nice package."

Phil choked back a laugh. The sugary sweetness dripping from Gary Hazlitt's words was a far cry from the man who had threatened to fire him. The wind must have started to blow in Phil's direction. "Sounds great. I'll talk it over with Rose and let you know if we want to leave New York."

"I hope you take the job. I need someone with your intensity and willingness to stand up to authority. I'll need an answer in a couple of weeks, but I'd really like you to say yes now."

"I have to talk it over with Rose first. Oh – one of the Production guys is at my door," Phil lied, "and I need to talk to him. I'll call you next week." Hazlitt said his goodbyes and hung up. Phil sat back in his chair for a moment to think. *Not a bad job. If I didn't have to work for Hazlitt, I might take it. But no way I'll work for that unprincipled, go-with-the-flow bastard.*

Phil called Roger Hanson. "I just finished talking to Hazlitt. He made a nice offer and treated me like I was someone special. Didn't once threaten to fire me."

"I'm glad. I think Gary likes you. Since you're on the line, I'll give you your other choice. If you decide to leave Purity, you'll turn over everything you have documenting Production screw-ups and agree to never sue us for any reason. In return, we'll give you stock options in McKenzie and Saga worth one-point-five million dollars. Further, you have to agree to stay with us until the Thinadin crisis is over and until we fully staff the top jobs at Garden City."

Phil had difficulty breathing. "Are you pulling my leg?"

"I'm very serious. One and a half million dollars or VP of Human Resources. It's your choice."

"I'll call you early next week."

"Do the police have any leads on the accomplice?"

"No, nothing yet, but they'll get him. I'm optimistic."

"Call me the minute you get any information."

Friday 12/19

Gino Arnone, Abby Stall, and Phil listened to Frank James in Phil's office. "Thanks. Things have gotten much better in Production. We're following all the procedures, even those that aren't documented, and only trained operators are doing the jobs requiring training. Our bosses are supportive, too. They want everything done right, and we're making good products. The best thing is that the old-timers, the guys who know what they're doing, are back, hopefully for good. We doubted you, but you came through."

"If you and Gino didn't come forward, Purity would've gotten in real trouble," Abby replied. "Because of your heads-up, we discovered the problem before it killed the business."

Phil turned to Gino. "This sounds like some mutual-admiration society. If those two keep talking, I'm going to cry. I already hear violin music in the background. Look, we all did what we knew was right, and this time it worked out. It may not work next time. If the likes of Bob Cohen and Steve Gagnon ever run this company again, it may not survive, and a lot of good, hard-working people will lose their jobs."

"Lighten up. Let's enjoy our success. We'll worry about tomorrow, tomorrow." Gino said.

"Point taken," Phil responded. They sat around for a while longer and commiserated about the bad old days. Abby stayed after Frank and Gino returned to work.

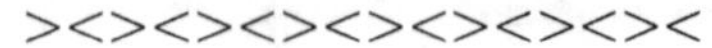

"People in the plant are pretty happy. It's almost like changing the management changed the morale of the entire workforce." Abby started.

"It seems to work that way."

"You seem down today. This is the first time I've seen you this negative. What's up?"

"I'm trying to decide whether to stay or leave. I want to quit, but I'm troubled. Even with the parachute, I'm worried. I've always worked for a big company. What will I do with myself?"

"If it makes you feel any better, I'm wrestling with the same dilemma. George and I are trying to decide what to do. I called Roger, and he made me an outstanding offer. Our attitude is whatever we decide will be right."

"Or as Yogi Berra once said, 'when you come to a fork in the road, take it.' Not bad advice. You're happy with your offer?"

"Very."

After Abby left, Phil went to shipping to check the status of a tractor-trailer being loaded with Thinadin. A trailer had left yesterday for Atlanta with enough Thinadin to solve the immediate crisis. When this trailer-load of Thinadin arrived at the Distribution Center, inventories would be high enough to provide some breathing room. Phil stayed in Shipping until the tractor-trailer left. Feeling good about going home for the weekend, he went to his office to clean up. Blinking on the phone in the middle of his desk was an urgent message from Jim Hines.

"What could possibly be urgent on a Friday afternoon?"

"The governor, that's what. He wants the accomplice found and found now. Is Alice asleep at the switch? Is that son-of-a-bitch getting online, and Alice doesn't know? What's going on? It's been three days and no activity. Does he know we're on to him?"

"Easy, Jim. I just talked to Alice, and he hasn't logged on. She'll know as soon as he gets on the network. We have to go easy and be patient. We'll catch him. If he doesn't sign in, we'll find out who 'braveone' is from Cynthia Bernstein when she gets back on Monday."

"What if 'braveone' is a hacker? She won't be able to help."

"What other choice do we have? We have to wait until Monday. If he hasn't signed in by then, we ask Cynthia Bernstein. We have no other options. Did your people figure out how Higgins had alibis for two of the murders?"

"He was slick. For the night Armstrong and Gagnon were killed, he had proof he was out of town, receipts for hotels and dinner, and purchases of antiques. The night Connolly was killed, he was at an antiques auction and made some purchases. When the facts are closely examined in both cases, there's enough of a time gap for him to commit the murders. We screwed up."

"How's he doing?"

"The doctors say he'll be lucky to make it through the weekend."

"Good thing we have Alice. We won't have much of a chance to catch the accomplice without her."

"We'd better catch the fucking accomplice. I'll call you first thing Monday. I want 'braveone.'"

Sunday 12/21 (Evening)

Fresh from a hot shower, Cynthia Bernstein, wrapped in a heavy terry bathrobe, lounged on her couch. She had a glass of white wine in her hand and Andrea Bocelli sang in the background. Bocelli's beautiful tenor rendition of the Italian lyrics stirred her romantic sensibilities, providing the perfect ending to her trip to Delaware. Her journey had started with a scare, but it had been romantic – even spicy – in the end. When she had arrived home, she had logged into Purity's network and dealt with the emails accumulated over the last five days. There was nothing for her to do now but relax. She would be swamped tomorrow.

A loud knocking on her apartment door frightened her. A woman yelled, "Open the door, it's the police! Open it now, or we'll kick it in!"

Cynthia stood up, ramrod straight, and set her wine glass down on the coffee table. The color drained from her face as she stared at her front door.

Another loud knock reverberated through the room, followed by the woman again. "Open this damned door now! I'm counting to five!"

Cynthia hurried to the door and looked out of the peephole. A woman's face filled the glass. "Who are you, and what do you want?" Cynthia wailed.

"Nassau County Police, Ms. Bernstein!" Karen Parisi shouted. "I have a search warrant, so open the door."

"I'm confused. I have to call my lawyer."

"If you don't open the door right now, we're going to kick it in. Open the door!"

Cynthia tentatively undid the security chain and deadbolt and opened the door a crack. Karen Parisi pushed it open the rest of the way and moved Cynthia back away from the door. Twelve of Nassau County's finest fanned out through the apartment as Parisi shoved the warrant in Cynthia's face. "This warrant allows us to take all computer equipment and all files. Don't touch anything, and don't interfere." The police were already tearing through Cynthia Bernstein's belongings.

"You can't do this! You have no right!"

"This warrant gives us the right."

"I want to call my lawyer."

"Go right ahead," Parisi replied, "but only your lawyer. Tell him we're taking you to the station after we're done here."

By the time Cynthia's lawyer had arrived, all her computer equipment had been removed and most of her files were boxed up and ready to head to the station. He quickly challenged Karen Parisi. "You're destroying her home. I want you to cease and desist right now."

Karen handed him the search warrant and said, "Read it."

Cynthia's lawyer read the warrant and then whispered to her. "They're within the limits of the warrant. You didn't say anything to them, did you?"

"No. You told me not to."

"Good." He then spoke to Parisi. "Ms. Bernstein said you want to question her at the station. Are you prepared to arrest her?"

"No."

"Then contact me tomorrow, and I'll arrange a convenient time for everyone. Ms. Bernstein is tired from traveling and will not be going to the station tonight."

"Have it your way, counselor. We hoped she'd be cooperative, but I guess she wants to do it the hard way." Karen turned and yelled, "Hurry up and get those files into the van! It's getting late."

Monday 12/22

As tears streamed down her cheeks and wet the phone, Cynthia said, "My lawyer just called me and told me they've issued an arrest warrant for me, and if I don't surrender in two hours, they'll come to get me. We're in trouble. They must have some evidence to get a warrant, don't they? I'm scared. I can't go to jail." Cynthia was interrupted when the line went dead.

"Phenomenal, absolutely phenomenal!" Gary Hazlitt, although alone, said out loud as he leaned back in his soft leather chair and looked out of the large window centered in his office wall. There were still several leaves, brown and crinkled, hanging on the trees in the courtyard, and a storm – possibly a snowstorm – was on its way from Cecil County. The approaching storm didn't bother Purity's new CEO. He had other things on his mind.

That's what Cohen would have said. He liked the word… 'phenomenal.' Well, it simply is phenomenal that I'm the CEO of Purity Pharmaceuticals. I've dreamed of becoming a CEO my whole adult life, and that dream all but died when Cohen was picked over me. I couldn't believe they picked Cohen for the job. Didn't they know he was untrustworthy? I guess they didn't because he got the nod. Cohen wasn't deserving of such a high honor. He's a dishonest man who's fucking around with Relieve has cost this company dearly. This time I was picked for CEO… me, Gary Hazlitt! After all these years, I'm a CEO, which is truly phenomenal. They didn't pick Pamela Robinson. That would've given them some brownie points with the Affirmative Action crowd. Instead, they picked me. I haven't had a chance to do much as CEO, but I already regret one thing I've done: offering that prick Messina a job on my staff. I only did it because Roger Hanson forced me to do it. I should have stood up to him. I guess I would've lived with Messina for a while and fired him after Hanson retired. After all, I gave Messina direct orders, and he didn't follow them. He doesn't understand that the chain of command is important, not trying to do the right thing. The right thing is what your boss tells you to do. It's what the CEO wants. Messina really fucked up my life.

Gary R. Hazlitt, CEO of the Purity Pharmaceutical Company. At peace with himself for the first time in his corporate life, Gary Hazlitt reached into his desk drawer, pulled out a thirty-eight-caliber revolver, and put it to the roof of his mouth. He pulled the trigger and sprayed his brains and blood over the freshly painted wall behind his – the CEO's – desk.

Tuesday 1/20 (One Month Later)

Phil smiled at the waiter. "Insalata Mista con Gorgonzola, e Saltimbocca, per farove."

"Selezione magnifico," The waiter responded.

"Grazie."

"Prego. And for you senore?" The waiter addressed Commander Hines.

"I'll have the mixed salad also, with the house dressing and the veal scallops alla Romana."

"Excellent. I shall return shortly with the salads."

As the waiter walked away, Jim said, "Here we are at Piccolo Sicilia, where our alliance was formed. The corporate executive and the police lieutenant were an unlikely duo, initially, but a powerful force in the end."

"I think you'd better cool it on drinks or plan to spend the night in my guest room. I've never heard you wax philosophically before. You must be drunk."

"Mr. Messina, for your information, I'm happy. Cynthia finally told us the whole story, and as a result, the case is tied up in a package with a nice, neat ribbon. Jack Higgins and Gary Hazlitt are dead, and Cynthia Bernstein will spend the rest of her natural life in prison. I'm Commander Hines, and yes, I'm a little drunk."

"What finally made my friend Cynthia see the wisdom in coming clean?"

"The ADA wouldn't back off the death sentence. He kept telling her lawyer that the only way to avoid the injection was to tell all. We had her cold when she logged in to the Purity network as 'braveone.' She had modified the security programs and hacked into Cohen's email account. We found Cohen's emails on her hard drive, including those she and Hazlitt wrote to set up Higgins. Her computer was the source of the e-mails in Higgins's home. The ADA and Bernstein's lawyer believed no jury in New York would sentence a woman who didn't pull the trigger to death. Still, in the end her lawyer wasn't certain, and the threat of death loosened Ms. Bernstein's lips."

"Gary Hazlitt and Cynthia Bernstein… a couple, and a couple of murderers. I'm dying to hear the gory details. Tell me Ms. Bernstein's story."

"She tied everything up nicely for us, except motive. I'm still not sure I understand why they had to kill all those people. Here's how the plan evolved. Cynthia started seeing Hazlitt before his wife died, and it got hot and heavy afterward. One night in bed, Hazlitt mused about how reading Cohen's mind would make his life much easier. Bernstein said she couldn't help him read Cohen's mind, but she could help him read Cohen's email. They laughed about it for a while but took no action. Then one night, Hazlitt asked her to do it. It would be a real kick to know what Cohen was up to."

"Let me guess: it was innocent in the beginning. Hazlitt would know what Cohen was thinking and could get some points by working on it before Cohen asked."

"It was kind of like that until they discovered Relieve. According to Bernstein, something changed in Hazlitt. He became obsessed with the betrayal of Cohen and his gang and began formulating a plan. Hazlitt and Higgins were friends when Hazlitt was Site Director at Garden City. Higgins told him about his military background. Higgins was really talkative about his experiences in Russia."

"Yeah, you're right."

The waiter arrived with their salads and the two dove in, but Jim only had two bites before he felt compelled to continue.

"Hazlitt conceived the idea of the phony e-mails to hook Higgins into his plan to kill Cohen and the others. Cynthia said she wanted to use the information to extort money from Cohen. Gary told her he had plenty of money and wanted something more. Hazlitt immediately started writing anonymous letters to the FDA implying Purity screwed up packaging Relieve years ago. He also suggested that the evidence still existed in the Batch Records. He wanted to motivate an FDA audit tied to Relieve, but didn't provide enough information because he didn't actually want the FDA to uncover the covert testing operation. The letters worked, and the FDA scheduled an audit. After the phony emails were completed, Hazlitt met Higgins and showed both the real ones and the phonies. Since he knew the emails between him and Cohen were real, Higgins assumed they all were. Hazlitt told Higgins about the audit, and together they committed to killing all involved."

"There had to be more incentive for Higgins. He could've simply gone to the FDA and blown the whistle."

"It turns out Higgins was in deep trouble financially. In fact, he had less than ten grand in cash, his house was mortgaged to the hilt, and his antiques business was bleeding money. Hazlitt sent him money twice a month to keep him afloat and promised him a lucrative consulting job with an upfront retainer when Cohen was out of the way."

"Okay, so Higgins had a motive, but I can't figure out what motivated Hazlitt. He had nothing obvious to gain. He could've reported Cohen and the others to the FDA or to Roger Hanson and gotten them all out of the way without having them killed."

"At first, that's what Cynthia thought they'd do, but Hazlitt wasn't happy with that plan. He didn't want the FDA to find out about Relieve because Purity would have to take it off the market, and he was obviously right. He wanted the revenue Relieve generated for Purity to continue. He planned to continue Cohen's covert operation, but by having Cohen and his cohorts killed, he could step right into the lead in a profitable company."

"Man, what a cold bastard."

"Cynthia believed it went deeper. Apparently, Cohen and the others treated him as an outsider. They never let him into the inner circle, no matter how hard he tried to be like them. He was distraught when Cohen was chosen to be CEO over him. He believed Cohen had campaigned against him."

"The part about keeping the revenue stream makes sense, but the other stuff sounds like high school."

"It did to me too."

Their dinners arrived, and both men focused on the present as usual. After a while, Phil said, "Lorraine resigned yesterday."

"Why would she do that? She's the Site Director. I thought she had a lot of problems to solve."

"She gave five months' notice. The problems should be solved by then. She wants to give back to her people by providing quality groceries at reasonable prices. She bought a convenience store in East New York from a Korean family, and she plans to buy more once she gets this one running. Once she has a presence, she'll use her influence to fight against drugs and poverty."

"Christ! Executive to crusader. Do you think she can do it?"

"No problem. Abby also resigned. She and George bought a marina in Florida."

"All your friends are abandoning you."

"I turned in my golden handcuffs for a golden parachute. I've agreed to stay on until the end of this year."

"How in the hell is Purity going to survive with everyone leaving?"

"Large corporations go on and on. Only the employees come and go."

They stood in front of the restaurant, job done and done well. They were two unlikely allies brought together by fate, ready to go their separate ways but not knowing what to say.

"You're not a bad guy for a mean-spirited conservative," Jim said.

"And for an 'I know what's best for everybody' liberal, you're okay," Phil replied.

They looked at each other and then hugged: not a woman's soft hug, but a backslapping, man-type hug. Yet it was a hug nonetheless.

"Let's get together next Saturday night for dinner, this time with the women."

"Phenomenal."

R. F. Mineo

R F. Mineo has had thrilling mysteries on his mind for years. Consistent encouragement from friends and family – and the freedom that retirement affords – catalyzed him to act. To put pen to paper! And so, a new mystery novelist was empowered.

Rich's business career has spanned over three decades, including a prominent role at a large corporation in the Medical Diagnostic and Pharmaceutical business units. What's more, Rich has been the Managing Partner of a small investment banking firm and operated an antiques business. Rich was born in Scranton, Pennsylvania, and graduated from Penn State University.

Rich served as head of the State of Connecticut Fundraiser for the Special Olympics. His other philanthropy includes volunteering at a nearby hospital and the local YMCA. When he's not writing, Rich enjoys biking, bowling, and spending time with his two adult children, three grandchildren, and his wife of 57 years, Wanda.

Rich's work has taken him up and down the Eastern Seaboard, and he has lived in an array of towns, such as Oyster Bay, NY, and Newark, DE. Today, Rich and Wanda Mineo reside in Woodstock, CT.